"Stephen Romano's imagination is so scary-brilliant, you should be required to obtain a controlled dangerous substance license before opening *Resurrection Express*."

—Duane Swierczynski, *New York Times* bestselling author of *Birds of Prey* and the Anthony, Barry, Macavity, and Shamus Award–nominated *Charlie Hardie* series

"Whipsaws along at 100 mph, with so much momentum that the reader feels like if he hits one bump, he'll go straight through the windshield."

—Tom Piccirilli, author of the International Thriller Writers' Award–winning novel *The Cold Spot*

"A high-voltage blast! Stephen Romano's action scenes are light-years ahead of the pack, fueled by muscular prose, terrifying villains, and Elroy Coffin—a protagonist for the ages. *Resurrection Express* is one of the finest examples I've encountered of noir's evolution into the twenty-first century."

—Blake Crouch, acclaimed author of *Run, Snowbound,* and *Abandon*

"A rip-snortin' white-knuckle ride. . . . A page-turner that sinks its teeth into you and won't let go. Stephen Romano has created a meal you will want to swallow whole—it's that hard to put down. A savage and vicious little tale that fans of Don Winslow will lap up. Highly recommended!"

—Don Coscarelli, award-winning director of cult classics *Phantasm, Bubba Ho-Tep,* and *The Beastmaster*

"If I don't get any writing done this week, it's all Stephen Romano's fault. *Resurrection Express* is a great read!"

—Johnny Shaw, acclaimed author of
Dove Season: A Jimmy Veeder Fiasco

"The action is fun and fast-paced in this thriller romp."

—*Library Journal*

"There are some names that all horror, gothic, crime, fantasy and sci-fi genre fans should know . . . but there is a new name that should very shortly be added to that list. . . . My only problem was not being able to get to the next page fast enough."

—*Nerdlocker*

"Romano's ability to write horrific violence and monstrous evil are on display, and the suspense rarely flags. But *Resurrection Express* is not merely horror transposed; it is also a compelling mystery that marks an auspicious crime fiction debut."

—*Crime Fiction Lover*

"The action is fast, furious and unrelenting. . . . Romano's story is brutal and bloody, and reads like an action movie script. But if you enjoy an explosive, suspenseful thriller with science fictional elements and surprises around every corner, you will not go wrong with *Resurrection Express*."

—*BookLoons*

"It comes as no surprise that Romano's debut solo novel, *Resurrection Express*, is a nihilistic piece of entertainment that goes from noir to apocalyptic at the speed of sound. . . . This book is relentless. It has the feel of a grindhouse auteur working with a two-hundred-million-dollar budget."

—*Mystery People*

"A masterpiece of a debut. . . . Relentlessly careens through pages of action, conspiracy, anticipation and outright shock and awe. . . . Romano developed a precise and sophisticated plot of the imminent end of the world as we know it through high-stake games and computer warfare."

—*Feathered Quill Book Reviews*

"Funny, I thought I knew how to spell intense and turns out it is spelled ROMANO! . . . If you are looking for a rush from reading, grab this book."

—*Pick of the Literate*

"Smart and witty . . . a super fast-paced thriller that is guaranteed to pack a powerful punch and mess with your mind!"

—*Booking Mama*

"Filled with no-apology violence, this is a great action thriller. . . . Spellbound readers will appreciate this gory tale."

—*Futures Mystery Anthology Magazine*

"Wow, this book is chock full of adventure. If you like crime novels with a lot of action, this is exactly what you're looking for. Elroy has a fascinating mind as a code breaker, and it was really fun to get into his brain."

—*Appraising Pages*

"Reads like an action movie looks, but this one comes with a heavy dose of internal dialogue."

—**KUT Austin**

"A distinct category of thrillers is emerging from a cadre of writers who also work in comics and/or film. Don Winslow was one of the first; Romano is unmistakably one of them, sharing their commitment to relentless pace, honest emotion, and an insouciance about violence. . . . If you've liked any of the above, you'll certainly like this high-energy first novel as much as I did."

—*Ellenville Shawangunk Journal*

"Shootouts that reduce luxury hotels to near rubble and littered with bodies like a scene out of *The Matrix* . . . more twists and turns than a certain famous street in San Francisco. . . . Buckle up for one hell of a ride."

—*The Mystery Bookshelf*

"Gritty, innovative . . . you won't want to put it down. . . . If this is Romano's debut novel, [we] can't wait to see what he has in store in the future."

—HorrorNews.net

"Action plus pacing plus twists equals . . . one helluva list of ingredients. . . . A novel that is both intensely personal and epic. . . . A sucker punch of a book."

—*Noir Journal*

RESURRECTION
EXPRESS

STEPHEN
ROMANO

POCKET BOOKS

NEW YORK LONDON TORONTO SYDNEY NEW DELHI

Pocket Books
A Division of Simon & Schuster, Inc.
1230 Avenue of the Americas
New York, NY 10020

First Pocket Books paperback edition July 2013

POCKET and colophon are registered trademarks of Simon & Schuster, Inc.

For information about special discounts for bulk purchases, please contact Simon & Schuster Special Sales at 1-866-506-1949 or business@simonandschuster.com.

The Simon & Schuster Speakers Bureau can bring authors to your live event. For more information or to book an event, contact the Simon & Schuster Speakers Bureau at 1-866-248-3049 or visit our website at www.simonspeakers.com.

Manufactured in the United States of America

10 9 8 7 6 5 4 3 2 1

ISBN 978-1-4516-6865-0
ISBN 978-1-4516-6866-7 (ebook)

for
Bryan Geer
my first amigo on this wild escape

for
Rock Romano
my father, who still helps me get there

and, in order of appearance
John Schoenfelder
David Hale Smith
Ed Schlesinger
without whom . . .

Everyone wants to believe they can be saved. Everyone wants a ticket to the promised land. Everyone wants to know that they are the heroes of their own lives, that it all means something in the end, that they are righteous in the face of so many mistakes and sins. Everyone wants to be resurrected. A lot of us die very disappointed.

Toni.

I will resurrect you.

FIVE PERCENT

My fist connects with the soft spot in Coolie's right cheek, just above his lower jaw, and I hear teeth shatter under my knuckles. I hit him just the way you're supposed to, arm straight out, wrist stiff like steel, all forward thrust anchored from the shoulder and popped like a coiled spring at my elbow. You turn your whole arm into a concrete piston when you do that. This guy, he's big and all—but big doesn't mean anything when you go straight for the face. A monster can't grow muscles on his teeth. Giant guys who are used to victory by intimidation never expect it to come right at them like this, not ever. Coolie stumbles back all dazed, the knockout reflex working overtime. I hit him next in the throat, a jujitsu-style straight jab with my fingers. His windpipe closes with a sick crack and he loses all his air. When he drops the shank and reaches up to grab his throat, I kick him dead center, just below the belt. That cancels the fight. But just to be sure, and to make it nice and showy for the boys, I swing around again with the heel of my foot and something that looks like a big red tomato bomb explodes in the center of his face. He goes down on the dirty asphalt, dreaming about whatever.

The crowd goes crazy, like it's a football game.

The smell of blood crawls up my nose, sharp and wet and stinging, like salt water dripping from a rusty razor. I never get used to that. I always avoid it.

But some things are inevitable.

Like the sweaty smiles of two hundred drooling, backstabbing criminal jerks, cheering your name because you know how to kick the ass of a guy twice your size. It's surreal. Like something out of a movie. My name, over and over. And the hand claps, in time with the chant:

"*Coffin! Coffin! Coffin!*"

They clap like this when you go in, when you first walk down the cell block. Some of them spit on you. But they only yell your name out loud when you've earned respect. That's when nobody messes with you. They've seen me jack up six guys in broad daylight, right on the yard, just like this. The tougher guys, the big mean black dudes, they don't chant or clap. But they give you the high nod without a smile. That means you're protected. That means this idiot at my feet will be servicing the gangbangers for six months in the showers. I'll get a carton of cigarettes when I'm out of solitary. T-Jay is my sponsor here, a gnarled ebony giant with a cold fifty-yard stare and a mouth filled with jagged glass. I broke the arm of a dirty white boy who called himself Mentor, just after I got here. He was bigger than Coolie, all full of muscle, but it never matters. Boom. They're down. Then they're someone else's bitch.

The hacks are already sounding the lockup bell, surrounding me on all sides, telling me we can go hard or easy. When a full-view fight like this breaks out on the yard, everybody goes back in the can for two hours. The guys are going quietly this time. A month ago, I had to take on three at once and there was almost a riot. Nobody's in the mood for billy clubs and mace this morning. I give it up with my hands against the concrete, near the basketball stop. They grab my arms and hustle me off. Nothing too rough. They all know I have the cash to pay my way. I'll get a week in the hole, but it'll be easy. It'll give me time to think. One of the hacks kicks Coolie in the guts to see if he's still alive. I made sure he would be. I could have killed him, but I didn't. This won't even go down in the books as self-defense. A few extra bills will make sure nobody saw a thing. I can get word to the Fixer from solitary that I need the money. Second parole hearing in just three weeks. The record has to be clean. I'll be denied early release, right on schedule. But six rejections later, by the letter of this place, I'll be out. That's what the Fixer tells me. So long as the record is clean.

And then . . .

When I'm back on the street, I'll find Hartman and make him pay. I'll look right into his eyes and I'll tell him he should have killed me when he could have. He'll look me in the eyes and beg me not to kill him. I've never killed a man before in my life.

I'll kill him for you.

Toni.

This place is all concrete and corroded metal, almost a hundred years old, renovated once in the seventies. The kind of dungeon that still stands because someone got paid off. My cell is damp and stale. They always stick me in this one when I have to do solitary, because it's close to the main block causeway, and I'm favored by the management. The walls reek of piss and semen and bad mojo. People get sick a lot because the plumbing is for shit and the water is brown. I never drink it. You can buy the bottled stuff for a buck in the commissary. Six bucks gets it delivered to the hole. Been living off Ozarka and Diet Coke for way too long.

Two years down.

I shouldn't even be here.

Not down in the hole with monsters like Coolie and T-Jay.

The good news is that it's a system set up like grade school compared to what I know how to navigate in the real world. They gave me thirty years. I'll only be in for five. I've worked it like a pro, which is exactly what I am. They transfer you to the east side of the top tier with no cellmate when you have a clean record for a while, when you do good in trade classes and group therapy and play nice with others. I've been on the top tier since day one, even though my case file has Organized Crime stamped on it in large red letters. That only cost me six hundred bucks to set up. Little trips like this to the shock corridor are just vacations. Time to get things straight, to plan your next move. You always have to plot everything. It all works if you let it. Once the design is laid out carefully, all the leads running end to end, it's a puzzle that fits together, and the solutions are pure logic. Like a computer program. Like a time lock.

Like everything I know how to do.

They send a guy to get me, three days into my vacation. Strange. They never do anything ahead of schedule here.

The hack's name is Merrick. He's a skinny little weasel with a big red nose. I've known him for six months. He splits my money with four other guys his size. Merrick's voice crackles through the tiny speaker, telling me to step away from the door and put my hands against the opposite wall. The noise is for show because of the TV camera in here.

His key tumbles the lock. I know exactly what the gears and metal rods look like as they move from place to place inside that big steel door.

I could open it using a wire coat hanger and some spit.

That's why they have two hacks with SPAS-12 riot shotguns on the outer corridor. Not to mention that nasty PC-based access grid wired to the main causeway entrance with laser sensors spiderwebbed across the entire cell block. The grid relays to an orbiting satellite. It's not the most sophisticated security system I've ever sussed out, but it's enough to keep me in here. Even if I got through the shock corridor to the main causeway, the 30-cal machine guns on the wall would turn me into deep-fried grits faster than you could call me a dumbass. The guards all have iPhones now, like little pocket video games with custom applications that tell you exactly where to look when a con runs for the wire. It's mostly muscle technology here. Big guns that keep people in line. Targeting systems. Maximum security. Like rigging a rusty old beaver trap with computerized heat sensors. I figured the escape odds once, and five years on the inside working the rehabilitation system was a far better bet. Fifty-seven men have been cut down trying to run from this place, and six of them were wireheads like me. One of them even had a plan all worked out.

Merrick enters the cell, cuffs my hands behind my head and tells me I have a visitor. I don't say a word to him. I never say much to anybody in this place, not even in the classes, and especially not in group therapy. When you're silent and dangerous, they always assume the worst. Merrick and the other hacks just know I'm smart.

I go quietly, even though I don't want to, even though I don't like surprises. Sometimes the hacks will deliver you right to the bull queers. That doesn't happen when you pay the right guys. It doesn't happen today.

Merrick marches me through the shock corridor and off the main causeway. A steel door with a lock older than I am clatters open and sunlight hits me in both eyes like a searing sucker punch. It's seven thirty in the morning. The cons are all doing chow shifts in the mess hall. We're moving across the yard now, towards the main administration building. Only trustees get to walk around in there, and I'm no trustee, not yet. I still don't say a word.

A few more doors, a few more locks.

A long gray corridor that leads to a small white room. In the center of the room is a woman smoking a

cigarette at a brown table behind a wall of six-inch bul-
letproof glass.

She looks about mid-forties, green eyes, a shock of
blonde hair shot through with elegant gray, brand-new
suit jacket pressed like sharp black armor over a white
shirt with a rigid collar, buttoned almost to her neck.
An air of mystery looming in a halo around her face.
Something familiar, something alien. Some papers
spread on the table. An open briefcase at her elbow.
Hard glints of metal in the briefcase, maybe a handgun.

On my side of the glass, there is a thick steel chair
bolted to the floor that Merrick tells me to have a seat
in. He cuffs my feet to the chair, through a loop that
runs to a chain attached to the steel on my wrists. I
could get free of the bracelets easy in two minutes.
The leg irons would be a bigger challenge. By then, I'd
probably be dead. So I settle in. Merrick leaves us alone
together in the room.

The woman behind the glass doesn't smile at me.

"I thought you'd look younger," she says.

Her voice is focused like a laser beam, all precision
syllables and cold logic through the cheap tin speakers
that separate us.

I don't say a word. She drags on her cigarette.

"It says in your file that you're thirty-three years old. Is
that true?"

I just look at her.

The lady smiles a little now, sensing my game.
"Okay . . . you don't have to talk to me. Not yet. But
you'll want to talk to me soon. I promise."

She ruffles through the papers.

"You had a pretty clean record before you went in here. One arrest for drunk and disorderly in Dallas. Your case was dismissed on Deferred Adjudication, but you never had the charge expunged from your record, even after your time as a soldier. I wonder why a pro like you would allow that to stay on there."

Never thought it mattered.

I was a kid when that happened.

It wasn't real.

She sees me answer the question without saying a word and gives me a long, serious glare.

"Look, Mister Coffin, I know what's going on here, and I respect it. Your very survival for the past two years has depended on the cultivation of a certain *image*. But there's no camera in this little room today, no cons. I've gone to great personal expense to arrange a private audience with you and I need to know if I'm speaking to the right man."

I sort of nod to her.

Yes, you're talking to Elroy Coffin.

Yes, I'm the guy who went in for seventeen counts of armed robbery.

Yes, I only went in because I tried to kill a man.

Yes, everything in your silly little file is true.

More or less.

"Okay," she says. Then stubs out her cigarette on the table in front of her. I notice the No Smoking sign behind her for the first time, and I almost smile.

She doesn't smile at all.

"Let's talk about *family*, Mister Coffin. Let's talk about why you're here. I understand what made you want to kill someone. It's the same reason I've used my own personal fortunes to lobby against gun control and death penalty reforms in Texas. I believe in punishment, when the punishment fits the crime. I don't believe in second chances when it comes to the loss of someone you love. Do you know who I am?"

No. But you're going to tell me.

She smirks at the other end of her cigarette. "I'm what you might call a . . . *concerned citizen*."

That's really nice.

"My fortunes were made in the building industry, private sector. My assets are recession-proof. I could buy the lives of a thousand talented young men like yourself. And I have. But one thing money can never buy is *family*. The pain. You know the pain. You live in it here, in this place. You can never be free once that pain takes hold. No prison can compare to it."

This lady has obviously never been in prison.

She's also not a criminal psychologist—she's a rich woman, a powerful woman. I would have known that before the first word left her mouth. The real question is: What the hell is a smart, tough cookie like her doing in a place like this? She could have sent an expert. A lawyer or a lackey, trained to deal with assholes like me. She either made those fortunes of hers by being really hands-on, or she's not who she says she is.

But I don't buy that. Not really.

See, the thing is . . . she's right. About the pain. Nobody knows what the pain is like. Not until you lose it all.

Lose everything.

"I'm not just talking about the horror of lost family,

Mister Coffin—I think you know what I mean. I'm also talking about very real *pain*. The bullet that went in your head. To be honest, I'm not only amazed you lived through all that . . . I'm also a little bit astonished that your faculties remain intact. You *can* still talk, right?"

I nod to her, almost shrugging.

"That's miraculous. A nine-millimeter shot at such close range is usually lethal."

Yes.

Yes it is.

"I've read your case files, studied your hospital psych reports. You made the wrong move because you were obsessed. When we become *obsessed*, Mister Coffin . . . all the best laid plans of mice and men go straight to hell. We see the prize just beyond our reach and it drives us mad."

Yes.

Yes it does.

"The assault charges were nothing—they could have been bought. You had the money. Actually, I suspect you still have the money. They had you cold on the robberies. Why was that?"

You know already. You tell me.

"You were put here by the man you threatened. A man who was your own employer. The Travis County District Attorney's Office knew you were set up. They even waved a deal in front of your face and you told them to go screw themselves. Those were your exact words. They wanted your father also and you wouldn't roll over on him. I admire that. Family is very important to a person like myself."

She pauses. A sly little smile crosses her lips.

"As a matter of fact . . . I've just come from a *meeting* with your father, Mister Coffin. He told me to say hello."

Her words hit me like a wave, my eyes fill with shock.

And it just comes right out:

"Like *hell* you did."

She's one of those people who know everything. Every damn detail of my life, because she has the money to buy men like me. She reads the bullet points off like it's the weekly plot synopsis for some soap opera, reprinted in boring English right out of the *TV Guide*. She knows about the five-man team my father put together more than ten years ago and the reputation we built, cracking safes and security systems. She knows how every generation does it a little better than the one before it.

Ringo Coffin, the old-school machine-gun bandit.

His boy Elroy, the high-tech future of criminal enterprise.

She also knows about everything before that—my bust when I was seventeen, my two years in the army, the *muay-kwon* martial-arts training in Nacogdoches, my honorable discharge, my four-year apprenticeship in Dallas with Axl Gange, the smartest goddamn thief that ever lived, just before he was killed by David Hartman. Big-time shit kicking. Major blood and guts.

Hartman, the Monster.

God damn him.

The woman on the other side of the glass knows about the seventeen jobs I did for that bastard—me on the laptop, my father on the stick. Vaults filled with folding cash.

And, of course, she knows about Toni.

Who could get any man to believe she loved him.

Toni, our one-woman intelligence squad.

Who went with Hartman finally because men like him get what they want, one way or another.

Because Hartman told her I was dead if she didn't.

I didn't care, though—she was still my woman and I wouldn't sign the papers. In Texas, you can't get a divorce unless both parties come to terms in front of a judge. She begged me to do it, told me they would kill me. Said she was saving my life. I didn't care. I would have saved her from him, just like she thought she was saving me, by being his woman.

Hartman, the pig.

God damn him.

I was circling his assets like a shark. His bank accounts and his foreign trust fronts and his contracts with government defense. If you see the leads, all laid out carefully, it all comes together. If you follow the rules and don't get stupid, revenge can be yours. The rules are what kept my father alive for so many years, even after his fall. You go through channels. You plot it all with precision. You don't get caught.

But then . . .

Two hundred pounds of meatball muscle stuffed into jogging sweats tried to kill me in my own house— a very ugly man with a red neck and a big gun, one of Hartman's semi-pro gorillas. The kind of thug you only hire when you're crazy and cheap. The guy's name was

Fred Rogers—*Mister Rogers*, no kidding. I broke both of Fred's legs and dumped him in a parking lot while he cried like a little boy. I told him I was sorry about this. Actually *apologized* to the son of a bitch. He just kept crying. He smelled like beer and mud and gutter trash. Disgusting.

In Mister Rogers's wallet, I found a picture of my wife with her throat cut.

That was the end of best laid plans.

That was when the rage took me.

I started by kicking Mister Rogers all over that parking lot, the whole world falling from under my feet in one blazing moment of absolute despair and hopelessness, all good things blown away and replaced with unreason and straight solutions—the kind that fill your eyes with water and your face with blood, your entire life boiled down to one primal scream as you pound and pound and pound. Mister Rogers was almost dead when I left him. He swore to me that Hartman was the one who did Toni and I believed it. Dumb grunts like that never lie well when their bones have all gone south.

So I walked right up to David's house empty-handed.

Broad daylight, no alibi.

I was going to kill Hartman with my bare hands.

To hell with the plan.

To hell with the rules.

To hell with it all.

A gang of his gorillas were watching a game in the living room when I kicked in the door. I could have taken all five of them easy, but one got the drop on me from behind, a lucky shot. My head still hurts when it's cold outside. I smell gunmetal and roses when I think too hard about it. When I try to remember Toni's face.

Toni was the last thing I was thinking about when they got me, the smell of her and the cold slash of the bullet overloading my sense memory channels like awful white noise on a psychotic feedback loop, as the gorillas dragged me out of Hartman's house, half-conscious and screaming.

They kept me under guard in the hospital, held me with no bail. I didn't know anything about it at first. My heart stopped twice on the operating table. The bad mixture of drugs they gave me cooked what was left of my brain, almost turned me into a vegetable. It took me weeks just to uncross my eyes. As soon as I knew who I was again, I tried to escape from the ward, but that only made things worse. They cuffed me to the bed, gave me more drugs. I sat there for days, hallucinating my life and my talents and everything I ever cared about into some endless black hole. I almost never came back from that.

I can still smell the gunmetal.

Still smell the roses.

The scent of my ruined memories, like faint traces of ammonia and flowers, in the place where Toni used to be.

Her face, lost forever.

God damn them all.

The trial came and went quickly. I couldn't buy my way out, they made sure. Hartman smiled across the courtroom and gave a little shrug, looking like some kind of fat demon in an expensive white suit. That crooked, greasy smile mocking everyone beneath his weight. His mean eyes, full of perverted genius. Even then, I hated looking into his eyes, because of the secrets he kept there, the things I'd seen him do. You only ever meet a few people in an average lifetime who are capable of anything.

And *anything* is a pretty scary word.

So I was up the creek. A washed-up thief with a steel plate in his head, a permanent reminder of that copper-jacketed 9-millimeter buddy that came and went—a magic bullet, they called it. They said I was lucky. I could have lost half my vision and my motor reflexes and everything that went along with it—my life, my profession. Everything. They showed me pictures of what happened to Gabby Giffords—that congresswoman who almost got killed when some random maniac took a shot at her in a parking lot—and the doctors said her bullet was magic, too, but not like mine.

Magic bullets.

Real cute, assholes.

Dad set things up with the Fixer when I went inside, kept what was left of my own money safe. By then, I was back to near 80 percent with my hands and my mind, but so many things were still lost. I still couldn't see Toni's face. The most important face of my whole life, shot to hell in one terrible moment, my mind blown away and patched back together, the sickness that robbed me of damn near everything, leaving me with nothing.

And then it got worse.

Dad stopped coming to visit me in the joint.

That was six months before one of the hacks delivered a package to me in solitary. A bright pink box wrapped up in ribbons with three of my father's fingers in it. There was a note in the package that said this:

You're all alone now, buddy-boy. How does it feel?

They were more right than they could have known.

The downward spiral took me again. My last lifeline to family, cut off forever.

In the dojo, they teach you guided meditation, how to find peace with what you lose and can never have again. That fighting with your hands is a last resort, that the mind is the most powerful weapon. You find that the rage is your best ally. You go down lower and lower, reconstructing the traces, finding what you've lost. It was enough in the beginning to save me from the gangbangers and the skinheads. It was enough to bring back my skill set. I'm almost 100 percent now. I've been able to have anything I want on the inside, just by taking myself there.

But Toni.

That last 5 percent.

I can't resurrect her memory.

I will, though.

In three more years.

That's when David Hartman will die. That's when I'll silence the failure that mocks me. My last, most terrible mistake.

The woman on the other side of the glass sees the hidden rage.

Sees everything.

Anything.

And she says:

"Your wife is alive. My daughter is with her. I can

get you out of this place within two weeks if you agree to help me find them."

This is bullshit.

Just can't be true.

She sees that I don't believe her. Goes into the briefcase and comes up with a photo printed on a slick sheet of letter-sized paper. Holds it to the glass so I can see it. In the picture is the man who destroyed my life, sitting in a nightclub with a pretty blonde on his left arm, bodyguard on his back, a blizzard of beautiful ladies all around them. One of the ladies is a tall brunette, standing closer to them, outlined in disco strobes. My wife was a brunette, under her disguises. I remember that much.

Toni?

Is that her, right there in the picture?

It *seems like her* . . . but hurts my head to concentrate on the image. The sharp stabbing smell of razor blades bathed in ammonia hits me, freezing the tiny plate in my head like ice.

There are no photographs of my wife anywhere, just like there used to be no photographs of me or my father. We never allowed them. Part of the rules. You stay invisible, walk in shadows. Forget about owning a driver's license or a photo ID. Before I went into prison, I even managed to hack my army records and doctor the mug shots. It's harder to remain a ghost in the machine when you go up the creek for armed robbery and attempted murder, but Toni stayed hidden. I'd made sure of that for years.

But *this* . . .

The photograph is grainy and fuzzy. She's got her arm hooked around the blonde's. There's an expression on her face I can't read. I could never read Toni, even when things were good. She was my teacher before she was my one true love.

Would I even know her now, if I saw her?

"That's my daughter, Mister Coffin. And your wife next to her. The picture was taken in a private club, by an undercover police officer who was working for me. He was killed a week later, most likely by the man in the photograph."

"Hartman."

"Men like him disgust me, Mister Coffin. Texas-sized rhinestone cowboys who make a lot of noise and think they can get away with anything. Ignorant mob operators disguised as oil millionaires. They're always fat and foul and doused in cheap cologne."

"David never wore cologne."

"That's even worse."

I look at Hartman's face: the triple chin and gap in his front teeth, buzzed hair and sleepy eyes mashed back into pale red rolls of sweaty dough, all stuffed into that pinstriped suit jacket. The lady is right, of course. He's the kind of maniac who wears what's left of his soul right there in front of you while he rattles on and on about the power and the glory, the rules of being a pervert, all that other stale macho crap that gets far less powerful criminals killed in the street. The kind of maniac who invents new reasons to exist moment-to-moment, crazy and deluded and bloodthirsty. Some people are scared of men like David, and they are right to be, but usually for all the wrong reasons. You have to stand there and take it. You have to listen to them rant and pretend it's profound wisdom, trying to keep your sanity in a room filled with blood. All those men and women who got in his way, all battered and smashed. While I learned the facts of life.

While I learned that love cannot stay.

The concerned citizen sees my eyes, and tries to read what I'm thinking. It probably isn't hard. I've always worn my soul on my face, just like Hartman did. It almost makes her smile, but she only speaks softly:

"Your old friend has been involved with some very serious people in the past year. Lately he's been on the payroll of Texas Data Concepts in Houston as a consultant. Are you up on what that company is all about?"

"That's a silly question to ask a guy like me."

Every good hacker knows TDC, especially the ones who operate in the Lone Star State. They're into everything. Computers, applied sciences, rocket technology. Hell, N.A.S.A. is right up the block.

"Fair enough," she says.

"Hartman is no rocket scientist, that's for goddamn sure."

"That's true also."

"So what's he been up to with smart guys like that?"

"That's a really *good* question, Mister Coffin."

She makes a grin set in steel, withholding the information. Guess that's what I get for calling her silly. I've never been all that tactful in situations like this.

I stare her down for a long second. Then, very slowly:

"Why do you need *me*?"

"You're one of the best. Seventeen robberies under major electronic security, and not a shot fired."

"Those are the ones you know about."

"We know about a few of the other ones, too."

"I was learning then."

"We all make mistakes."

"So you need me to steal something."

She shifts her weight. Considers her next answer carefully.

"Your father says there's no one else on earth who can pull off what we have in mind, Mister Coffin."

"My father's dead."

"No. He's with my people. Has been for a long time. I can't be any more specific than that, not in this room. I need an answer and I need it right now. Are you in?"

Is that really my wife?

Could I see her face again?

Am I in?

I nod to her quietly and she buzzes Merrick to take me back to my cell.

A PISTOL FOR RINGO

There's a ritual when you get out that involves a lot of people in uniforms asking you questions, putting your name on papers, an orientation about seeing your parole officer. They strip you down, shine a flashlight up your privates, grab your sack and tell you to cough. You've seen those movies where they hand you back all your personal effects, too, right? That part is bullshit, at least in a joint like this one. If you're not in city jail or county, they confiscate everything when you go in except the clothes on your back, and if you were wearing a belt, they take that, too. You'll never see that stuff again, so don't even ask. They also take your shoes and let you keep the cheap lace-ups you lived in while you were inside, throw in a pair of fresh socks. They don't let you take anything out, either. Pity, that. But I planned ahead.

The gate rolls open at exactly nine in the morning and I smell free Texas air for the first time in twenty-four months. The cold sharp wind blows through my hair. I wear it longer than I did back in the day, to cover up the nasty scars where they sewed my head back together.

T-Jay told me when I first met him that long hair in the joint was a cardinal sin—it gives you that vaguely feminine look that the functionally homosexual want to know better and it's easy to get ahold of in a scrape. They call it your "love locks." T-Jay gave me that bit of wisdom ten minutes before I kicked Mentor's ass. Nobody ever tried to grab my locks after that.

I pull it back and feel the scum of two years.

You never really get clean inside.

October sure smells damn fine when you're not in prison anymore.

Two giant men in gray suits and black shades are standing just outside the gate, waiting for me. One of them has bleach-blond hair like a surfer, a thick moustache that makes him look old and weird. The other guy is black and young like a football player, balding on top. The football player extends a hand and introduces himself as my bodyguard. Says his name is Washington. The surfer's name is Franklin.

Franklin and Washington.

"Sounds like a law office," I tell them. "Or a California roll."

They don't laugh.

The surfer looks confused.

Washington tells me to step this way.

A black GS Lexus hybrid with tinted windows waits on the curb, just a stone's throw away in the visitors lot.

Franklin the Surfer opens the passenger's door and I see a man sitting inside. His long hair is white, pulled back in a ponytail. He's thinner than I've ever seen him, like a skeleton. Too much drinking. I always gave him grief about his whiskey, even when I was a kid. I sit next to him and the door shuts behind me.

I can't believe I'm really looking at him.

"Son," he says.

"Dad," I say.

We embrace, at the end of a lifetime.

The car is brand new and makes no sound.

It's three hundred miles from the Grandview Correctional Facility near Laredo to the city of Austin. Not exactly a long drive, but we have lots to talk about. Neither of us says anything for a while. I'm staring out the window when I break the silence, watching the highway streak by, not seeing the highway at all.

"You look good for a dead man."

Then I look at him—for the first time, really *look* at him.

He holds up his right hand.

A permanent thumb and forefinger pistol, aimed right to heaven.

"Bang," he says silently. "It's a little joke David Hartman played on me. Said I'd never work again when they were done. He was half right."

The joke is terrifying.

Goddamn.

"I'm sorry, Dad. It's my fault."

"The funny thing is . . . you're probably right, kiddo. But I owe *you* first. And I'll never be able to pay you back, not really."

"*Hartman* did that to you. It wasn't karma points for my bad childhood."

"I know."

"I'm still sorry, Dad."

"You did what you thought you had to do. I would have had your back no matter how crazy you got. You're my son."

"You think what I did was crazy?"

He takes a deep breath. Then speaks, even softer now:

"Elroy . . . you have something inside you I've never understood. It's always frightened me. I've been afraid of it since you were a child. But it's my responsibility because *I gave it to you*."

"That's not true. It just happened."

"It happened because you're the son of a man who . . ."

"You can say it. It's not like we're on trial anymore."

"Maybe we still are. Maybe we always will be."

He might be right. He's a professional killer, after all, and I'm my father's son. But I'm not like him—I've never been like him. All I have is the rage.

"Can you still handle a gun, Dad?"

"I'm learning. But I'll never be the way I was, not like the old days. The big bastard had me in the dark for three weeks, on a ranch just outside La Grange. Our new friend had me pulled out of there."

"The concerned citizen?"

"Yeah. She's been watching us for years, apparently.

Well connected, well funded. She claims she's just a rich lady but I'm not sure I believe that. Her people are real pros. Swooped in hard."

"The suits?" I point at the law partners in the front seat.

"No. Those guys have been watching me in a safe house for a few weeks. Before that it was six months with some other guys. One of the last bodyguards said he was ex-CIA. It only took our new friend four months to buy you out of that hellhole you were in. Wanna know how she did it?"

"Does it matter?"

"She bought the prison board. A million across. That's what she told me."

"Jesus. She could have hired anyone for that kind of cash. What's so special about us?"

"We're the best, remember?" He says that like it's not really true, makes that funny little snort and shakes his head, just like he used to when I did something bad as a nine-year-old. I let it roll off, looking back at the road.

"Dad . . . they told me you were dead. Why didn't you let me know you were okay? You could have at least sent word."

"Had to play this one close to the vest. It's important for our family, son. This is how we finally retire."

"What about Toni?"

"If we're lucky, she'll still be alive when we get to her."

"So what's the plan now?"

"You go through the motions. As far as the law is concerned, you're out on good behavior and it's all been taken care of. Just play nice, like everything's on the up-and-up. They'll be looking out for us. Our new friend, I mean. Her people. We have our first meeting in three days."

"What do they want us to do?"

"Something special."

"A money job?"

"Sort of. It's *important*."

"And the less I know, the better, apparently."

"Something like that."

Doesn't matter. Let them think they own my ass until I find her. Toni was with Hartman in the picture—which means she's still *with Hartman*. But not dead. The photo I saw years ago with her throat cut had to be a fake.

Maybe.

I've got to find out for sure, and I won't have much time to do it.

Just three days.

"It *is* good to see you, Dad. I went a little crazy when I thought you were gone. We still have a lot to pay back with those guys."

"Payback hasn't been good to us. Maybe we should just live."

"How am I supposed to do that?"

"One day at a time."

He looks straight ahead at the road blankly, gripping the air with seven fingers.

"I tried not to involve you in any of this, son. I told them about Mollie Baker first. Even went and saw him in Houston, asked him to come on the team. He's running a bar these days. Told me I could go to hell."

"Still, huh? That's kinda sad."

"Some people never get over things."

Yeah.

He's got that damn right.

"Sometimes I think Toni was all I ever had that defined me. That I'm not even a whole person anymore. It's kind of terrifying, really. To think you're not even the hero of your own life."

"Don't think that way, son. Just don't. We need to live in the moment now. *One day at a time.*"

That was always his way. Zen in the face of pure horror. He was like this when Mom died, too. My masters at the dojo would have called him a pussy. They wouldn't have known the killer inside him, just to look in his face. He was around in the sixties to see the world when it almost changed, all that free love and flower-power stuff. He could have been a seeker, like Mom was. But Mom is dead, and the revolution died with her.

All that's left now is a pistol for Ringo.

We hit town by one thirty. A plate of real food sounds like paradise right about now, so Dad says he'll treat me to a rare steak and peach cobbler at Threadgill's. That was always my favorite. Franklin the Surfer calls in a take-out order from the road and we wait in the car with Washington while he picks it up. Nobody can see us in public together. Our edge is invisibility, for now.

We don't speak to each other while I eat out of Styrofoam.

Not because the food is good.

He's ashamed and so am I.

Austin is a big city, the capital of Texas, but it's a small kind of big city. Hollywood heavies like Robert Rodriguez and Michael Bay make their flicks down the street, but somehow you never hear about it much. Downtown is pretty, there's a tiny cluster of skyscrapers, and you have the south side hipster hives and campus drags over by the university, but it's all very quaint and livable. South Congress Avenue runs like a tacky stream of grimy lights through the heart of everything, spackled with costume shops and vintage clothing stores, breakfast dives and taco stands, and it all detonates in the center of the city, the capitol building looming above the business epicenters and the legendary nightclubs, where guys like Stevie Ray Vaughan became famous. It hasn't changed much in two years. It never really does. There's a sort of funky backwoods alchemy that floats in the air downtown, where the street vendors and the business suits walk side by side, music and merriment and the smell of hot dogs smothered in brisket smothered in four-alarm chili wafts from joint to joint.

Not a lot of Southern accents in this town, either. It's a real melting pot. Most of the artist types sound like they could be from anywhere but here. That's how I sound. When you're down on Sixth Street, the lights and the foot traffic and the multi-symphonic madness is almost enough to make you forget that you're only a few blocks away from where the worst Southern accent on earth used to do his dirty business, just before he became Supreme Dictator for Life.

Governor W wasn't the only criminal to hide in plain view downtown, either.

This quaint and livable city full of starving artists and struggling filmmakers and college students and sweet young hotties, all even hotter to be the Next Big Thing . . . it's a place of earthy illusion and honky-tonk shadow that hides some of the ugliest secrets in the entire world of organized crime. Nobody knows about it because nobody talks, not even the gangbangers. See, the Mafia is everywhere—even in Kansas. We've worked for damn near every one of them. But mostly for David Hartman.

It's always been like that.

Since my professional career began.

Hiding in plain sight, without a driver's license.

Since the day I met him, Hartman had me in his pocket. On that day, I saw him at his worst. And while he did his business, he pulled those insane words out of the air, sounding like a comic-book version of an evil genius, run through the dirty mill of some backwoods Quentin Tarantino sound-bite machine. That part never changed, like the air in Texas never changes, like the streets of Austin never change. While Hartman's insanity just got worse and worse, the more he was able to get away with. His schemes and hustles, backed up by the smartest operators and mechanics on two legs. The streets of Austin stained dark red under their feet, the air hot and ancient.

David Hartman has the thickest Southern accent I've ever heard.

He sounds like chicken-fried steak smothered in cream gravy.

Thick and awful.

If someone thinks you're crazier than they are, they

usually don't know what the hell to do with you, but Hartman was crazier than everyone.

Crazy enough to send us after dangerous people, and not just the mob.

There were politicians, too—guys who greased the wheel, de facto bosses Hartman wanted leverage over. Defense contractors. Lobbyists. He eventually had dirt on all of them. We pulled a file less than an inch thick from a bank vault in Upstate New York that contained the names and locations of thirteen men in the federal Witness Protection Program. Nearly all of them turned up dead a few weeks later. Toni asked me if I felt responsible, and I told her no. I've been surrounded by death all my life. I was trained to be a killer—by the army, by my masters in the dojo.

And yet I've never killed a man with my own hands.

That would make me like my father. I'm not sure I want to be like him at all. It might prove that he's right, about what he passed on to me, just by being a professional shooter. I don't want to believe that. I want to believe in what Toni taught me.

I want to see her again, more than anything.

I report to the Travis County Correctional Office at 3 P.M. sharp, just like they told me to at orientation. Washington escorts me upstairs to see my parole officer while Dad waits for me in the car. The PO is frumpy but nice, a young girl fresh to the business. I can tell she's not on the payroll, but the people above her are. I was pardoned by the prison board for good behavior on a thirty-year sentence and this just tickles the hell out of her. There's nothing in my case file about the six men I nearly paralyzed with my bare hands while I was inside. There's plenty in there about the bullet that nearly killed me and the botched operation that almost vegged my brain permanently. Lots of reports from the docs and psychologists about my selective memory loss. She asks if I still get the dizzy spells and I lay down a happy series of very safe lies. She asks how my motor reflexes are and I give her the fifty-watt okey-dokey. My smile makes her blush. She tells me in that cheerful voice that she likes my long hair—it's very Austin, she says. Then she chuckles that I remind her of James LeGros, the movie actor, and I have no idea who that is, but I pretend to be flattered.

James LeGros is a handsome guy, apparently.

She says that I have a good skill set and that I should do well over the next year. She's assigned me a work program that consists of three phases: first I do six months in an entry-level position at a retail store near campus called Toy Jam, one of those locally owned knickknack businesses where twentysomethings pull down eight bucks an hour. Phase two is a professional job, if I can find one—probably in a computer firm. It has to be approved by the board. Phase three is community service, two hundred hours. She says they let me off lightly.

Christ. Eight bucks an hour.

Good thing this is just a dog-and-pony show.

I play the part and tell her that I won't even be able to afford a cheap room on that kind of money. She says it's no problem because I'll be boarding at a halfway house on the north side for the whole six months. No curfew, but I'm not allowed to have a cell phone. After six months in the toy store, I'm free to design websites and get my own apartment. Random visits from my parole officer, which will be someone else by then. Counseling three times a week. Five years later, I'll be free.

I'm back on the inside, only it looks like the real world now.

I walk out of the office and my football player bodyguard stands up and puts down his magazine. "How did it go?"

"Still a prisoner."

"Yeah, well, not for long."

They cut me loose at the halfway house and I'm on my own. At least that's what it will look like. Washington tells me there will be eyes on me at all times. My new employer wants to look after her investment, but it also has to look legit. Go through the motions. Obey the rules. If anyone messes with me, I'm covered.

Three days. This will be tricky.

At the car, my father kisses my cheek and tells me to hang in there. He finally looks me right in the eye. I can tell he's almost crying.

"You are the hero, son. You're the hero of *my* life. You're a better man than I'll ever be. Always remember that."

The night comes and I have a hard time sleeping.

I'm sharing a room with three other people in a

house that looks like an old daycare center and smells like one, too. No television, no Internet. They served a pretty good dinner, meat loaf and mashed potatoes, better than anything on the inside, but not as good as Threadgill's. I still can't sleep. Not because of all the snoring and mumbling going on in the bunks next to me. In prison you learn to pass out through any kind of noise, with one eye open.

Toni's keeping me awake.

She always did.

She was twelve when I met her. That was when Dad was in prison for the second time, his longest stretch. I met her in the institution where they sent me to live as a ward in the care of the state. She was like me, her parents criminals, her childhood gone, her mother less than a fragment, like mine. In a toilet full of perverts and hateful scumbags masquerading as human beings, she was the only ray of light. She was the one who taught me the importance of language and communication. She taught me that cursing and swearing was for the ignorant and the angry. She taught me how to read. I was thirteen then. The first book I understood was a book she read to me. I can't remember what it was about now.

Is that funny? Probably not.

I was a late bloomer, but I caught up fast. The hardest part was learning not to swear. You can become less ignorant, I told her, but the anger never leaves you—not when you're like I was back then. Not when your world is filled with dirt and disappointment from day one. She said that was no excuse. She said anyone can beat their programming—it's what makes us different from animals. I was able to purge the word "fuck" pretty much from my vocabulary. Toni had a zero-tolerance policy for that one. But the rest of it . . .

. . . well, shit, man.

Pretty soon, my mind was filled to bursting. Toni insisted on the classics first. Hawthorne and Poe. Descartes and Mark Twain. She said to memorize what these men wrote *about* and never mind the exact words. Told me to retain the images, the feelings, the *philosophies*—the worldviews that would shape my adult perspective. These were the geniuses who knew everything there was to know about the unredeemed soul of man, in any century, and the way that technology is constantly perceived and re-embraced time and again by the human animal.

Perception is unreliable.

Language is the glue of civilization.

People are no damn good.

The next year, we ran off together. Walked right out of that place, right under their noses. Slept under freeways, learned the street. Discovered what real love was. Four years running scams, until I was busted. They told me I could spend eight months in a juvenile detention center for being drunk and violent, or I could become a soldier and work off some of that aggression. When I went in the army, Toni told me I needed to learn a trade. We couldn't be common hustlers for the rest of our lives. Hustlers die, she told me. So do soldiers. We must cheat those evil men who want to steal our birthright. We must know the names of our killers in the moment before they make us run for our lives. We must live, and our children must live after us. Otherwise, we're not immortal creatures. Just dead creatures, lost on the face of time.

I loved her best when she spoke to me that way. She was wise beyond anything I'd known before. As if something higher was speaking to me through her words. You think that way when you're in love, I guess.

Though love cannot stay.

I knew that, even as a child.

Knew that so many things were temporary—the most important things.

But I loved her then, loved her so much . . . and so I did it. Trained my body and my mind. We became the best. Traveled from one end of the world to the other. Ten years of ripping off banks. Ten years before the trouble started again. That's what beautiful girls get for being beautiful girls in a world of sharks. Sometimes I wish she hadn't been so beautiful. Maybe Hartman would have kept his hands off her.

Who am I kidding?

I get out of bed and sit on the floor, trying to focus myself. Trying to see her face. Trying to resurrect her. It never worked on the inside. It's still not working. I lost her before I even went in that terrible place of concrete and steel . . . and now . . . now that I know she might still be alive . . . that she's still *his* woman after all this time . . . *that I might still hold her in my arms again . . .*

The smell of gunmetal and roses is more overwhelming than ever.

Down and down, I go.

Lost forever without her.

I remember that her hair was long and black, but I can't bring back the color of her eyes.

They were like firecrackers, but I can't bring them back.

The smell of roses haunts me in the dark.

Agent Washington arrives in the black Lexus with the tinted windows and drives me to my first day at the toy store. I ask him where the surfer is and he says he's with my father. Twenty-four-hour guard on the safe house and they're understaffed today. No one gets to him until we make our move.

Toy Jam is in one of the busiest areas of the downtown campus drag, Twenty-sixth and Guadalupe. The intersection is just inches from the front door of the place, flowing with kids and teenagers and mothers with babies and lots of traffic. Sidewalk musicians play for quarters and scrawl chalk art. Hip cafés on the drag teem with the breakfast rush. A guy wearing a paisley kilt sells mural rugs in a pizza-parlor parking lot across the street. A pay phone near a bus stop, where a bunch of homeless people jabber in some weird language that isn't exactly English. I make note of the pay phone.

Inside, the place is like the toy closet of the nerdiest man-child on earth, with racks of action figures, plastic figurines and wind-ups that look like Luke Skywalker, Speed Racer and evil nuns that breathe fire. Smells like hippies in here.

And speaking of hippies.

The manager is a perky young granola girl with long braided ponytails and striped stockings, and she's only as nice as she has to be. Her name is Sunshine. How adorable. She explains that they've become part of the work release program in Austin because the store has been here for twenty years, time to show some interest in the community, things that matter, world without end, and blah, blah, blah. I don't hear any of it because it doesn't matter.

They make me stock little Hello Kitty trinkets and action figures on creaky shelves for eight hours with only a thirty-minute break for lunch.

I spend that time on the pay phone outside, talking to the Fixer.

I don't know his name, he's a go-between. Talks to my lawyer for me. He's been my buffer between the real world and the world of thieves for almost ten years. My father trusted him with his life and so do I, because it's not just bad business for guys like this to sell out the people they protect—it's suicide. That's why you never know their real names. That's why it's always business and no small talk. There are friends and there are enemies and there are phantoms who walk in your place, selling the illusion that you actually exist. They buy your houses. They pay your taxes. They make sure there are no photographs of you on the Internet. The phantoms know the score, and they walk real soft, but they don't do it for free. Good thing I happen to be a little rich.

I tell him I need a few things arranged by tomorrow morning. Money things. Cash in hand and the key to my safe deposit box. The gear I asked for last week. I'm about to take one hell of a risk and here's the plan. He tells me sure, man, just call up anytime and make my life a living hell. We talk price and he calms down. We work it all out. All the leads are laid carefully from end to end.

Tomorrow morning, my gear. My money. On the grid again.

Back to the store and it's all a blur. Everyone ignores me. No one makes eye contact. I'm invisible. I'm just going through the motions with my hands, pretending to be something I am not. They have no idea who I really am.

Perky little Sunshine tells me what a great job I've done when my shift is over at five. I should expect a raise soon. Awesome. I'll be able to buy a car with the extra fifty cents.

She shakes my hand and sends me out with a big grin, feeling good about her contribution to the community. I leave the store through a glass doorway with silly bell-chimes on it that look like Mickey Mouse, and the black Lexus is on the curb, waiting to take me back to the halfway house.

We ride in silence.

Inside, I'm screaming.

And slowly . . . the rage solidifies into a stream of thought.

Focuses like a laser.

The plot begins to become visible again.

Two days to do it.

The prize, just beyond my reach.

THE GETAWAY

The sun sneaks up and blinds me through the open window of the bunk room. I pull on jeans and a plain black T-shirt my father bought for me, and I wash my face and look at myself in the bathroom mirror. I ask myself if I know what I'm doing.

A voice comes back and tells me full ahead, no fear.

They serve us a breakfast of greasy bacon, eggs and home fries, and then we sit in a little room for a few minutes and "open up" to an underpaid social worker in a clean pink shirt who looks like he has a lot more problems than we do. He gives us a "worksheet" that has neat rows of way-too-general yes and no questions printed on it, which we have to fill out while we eat. Do I feel I can be of use to society? Am I feeling productive today? Is there something I would like to talk about with a friend or a relative? It's a circle jerk that makes my stomach hurt. Maybe it's just the bad food.

The rage, under control now, just enough.

So I can navigate.

Time to run like hell.

• • •

The law partners drop me off at Toy Jam and Franklin tells me to play nice at school. Guess he's trying to be funny. Washington just grunts. Gives me a look of tired contempt I've seen many times before. Franklin just looks bored. I can tell they both had a long drive from the safe house, wherever the hell it is.

Perky Sunshine is happy I'm early. They got a new shipment of Godzilla toys this morning and I'll be pricing them all day because they don't have a point-of-purchase system in this ancient place. You have to tack little stickers on each toy card with a pricing gun that jams every fifth click. I'm carrying a kit bag over my shoulder which is weighed down with a Bible from the halfway house. Nobody notices that I wear it all morning. Nobody even makes eye contact with me in this place, not even Sunshine. Why should any of them care?

Everyone's the hero of their own life.

An hour into my shift, I make an announcement that I need to use the bathroom, head right out the back door and into a narrow alley I cased yesterday that runs along the side of the place. I find my package in an empty garbage can next to the Dumpster.

The garbage can that wasn't here a half hour ago.

I fill the kit bag, leave the Bible. Don't have time to count the cash—it's all in hundreds, should be twenty thousand, walking-around money. A small bundle. The key to my safe deposit box is in a little purple stationery envelope. I tear it open. The key has the number 344 stamped on it. Good, all good. I shove the key in my pocket, along with my new cell phone. It's unregistered, hotter than the sun. The laptop is state-of-the-art. The Fixer had my man Jett Williams put together the kit for me. Me and Jett used to rip off ATMs together, back when you could still get away with cowboy moves like that. His handle in the hacker groups is Remo now—some guys even call him the Destroyer. He threw in a manual lockpick set, for old times' sake. Never can tell when you'll need to get past a real hunk of steel and plastic in our line of work.

I'm set.

At lunch break, I hit a trendy café next door that has wireless. It's a free connection, wide open, but I have custom blackware that makes me invisible. The Destroyer is one of the best there is—way better than I am.

But I do okay.

Shields up, full-ahead maximum warp.

Over a secure IM, the Fixer tells me the rest of the money is safe. He's good, too. That's why he makes the big bucks. His house is one of twenty-three I sneak into through a wire in the next fifteen minutes.

My fingers move fast.

It was always this easy.

I find some of what I need, talk to a few of the right people. David Hartman's lower on the radar than ever these days. My plot to circle his money and take him out where he lives and breathes is outdated. But I don't make any inquiries about Hartman—not directly. I peck around the edges. I ask about Toni. Don't have time to look for very long, either.

But I will.

Soon.

I'm back clicking the price gun on Godzilla one minute late from break. I see perky Sunshine write something on her clipboard.

She gives me a funny look I can't read.

My shift is over quickly and it's time for her to shake my hand again. She's not so perky anymore. Damn.

I notice the Lexus waiting outside through the open glass door. Franklin isn't in the car—he was before. Washington steps out and grins. Sunshine asks me if he's a friend of mine and I tell her he's a state employee, my ride back to the halfway house, no big deal.

She gives me the look again.

Writes on the clipboard again.

She steps outside with me and says hello to Washington, smiling, feeling important. She asks him what his name is. Writes it down. Damn.

And that's when the world fills with thunder.

I see the two unmarked cars almost before they screech up to us, fast steel blurs ripping up the pavement and stopping hard. Doors fly open, Uzis spit rapid fire, one from each car, 9-millimeter semi-auto, aiming carefully at their first targets, which are me and the big guy. He goes for his gun as the shots chew his face off and I hit the pavement behind him with bullets bouncing all over hell and back, shattering the front windows

of the toy store. I don't think I get shot, but who can tell
at times like these? A light spray of red salt water sprin-
kles me from somewhere. The windows in the Lexus
pop like fireworks. I'm behind the door of the car and
9-mils won't get through to me, but that won't last long.
The glass entrance to Toy Jam explodes behind me. I
hear screams, then more screams. Sunshine is dead on
the pavement, still holding her clipboard. The bullets
went through her and killed the glass. Agent Washington has his gun out, dead on his feet, firing as he
wobbles sideways, then lands right in front of me. I push
him halfway up on his side, using his body as a shield
as I pry the pistol from his grip. The intersection in
front of the store is crazy now, campus kids and moms
shrieking in the crosswalk like it's the end of the world,
al-Qaeda style. A big black truck runs the red light and
slams into someone, then skids straight into the two cars
opening up on me, then smashes into the Lexus. I roll
on the sidewalk just as it all comes thundering over the
curb. A sound like metal monsters killing each other in
broad daylight. The Lexus is persuaded to destroy the
entire front of the store, with the two other cars and
the truck right behind it. I think they run over Sunshine, too. That's what it seems like, but I can't tell for
sure because I'm on my feet and running like hell away
from the whole mess, clutching the kit bag for dear life.
My gear rattles at my side, my lungs blowing bombs.
Turns out I'm not shot. I'd be coughing up blood on the
pavement if one of those guys had tagged me. And the
gunfire has stopped. They're all getting mashed back
there instead—an epic pile-up exploding everybody's

ordinary world in a terrible series of deep-bass thunder hits. Another skidding metal blur zings out around the street corner ahead of me just as I duck for the narrow alley alongside the store. My lungs do double duty, my feet slapping pavement hard. More screeching tires, right behind me.

Shit god*damn* . . .

A bullet eats concrete and bounces past my head. Car number three blasts down the alley, straight at me, the gunman at the wheel, the shotgun seat next to him empty. No room to roll out of the way. It's shoot or die and I still have Washington's 9-mil. I sight down in an instant, focusing my next breath into the first shot, just like my father taught me to, and I open up on the windshield. Not aiming at anything special, just trying to scare the son of a bitch. The driver ducks fast under the dash and I miss him with all three shots, punching a spiderweb in the glass instead.

The car keeps coming right at me, filling the entire alley.

I see it in slow motion.

I find my center.

The ground leaves my feet.

I land on the hood and keep on running just before impact, the soles of my shoes scrunching in the glass spiderweb, the roof of the car buckling like a little kid's lunch box . . . and then I'm back on the ground as I clear the tailpipe, but it's a bad landing.

Too bad this isn't a James Cameron movie.

My ankle does the twist all by itself and my legs fly out from under me.

My ass hits the ground, still in slo-mo.

The car keeps on moving behind me.

The crash back there brings me to real time again with a jolt. My center is gone. I'm doomed instead. I can hear shooting and screaming inside the store now.

How did I bring this on these poor people?

What the hell is happening?

The car is smashed into the Dumpster near the back entrance to the store and wedged badly in the alley. I can see the gunman inside as he sits up in the wreck and starts screaming in my direction. Think he's pinned in there. Good.

A thick black man wearing a sports jacket with tweed patches on the elbows and a turtleneck sweater half stumbles through the back door, slapping a new clip in the handle of his Uzi. I want to ask him how many people he just shot inside the store, but I aim the gun at him instead. I put my finger on the trigger, ready to kill a man.

It doesn't happen.

This close, looking at him like this . . . my finger won't move.

I can't do it.

I can't kill him.

He smiles at me, understanding, sensing my paralysis. Three of his teeth are missing, his face covered in razor slashes from broken glass. He spits blood and staggers over, until just ten feet separate us. Knows better than to get any closer. Sights down, grinning toothlessly, like a pissed-off jack-o'-lantern. And he says this:

"David Hartman says hello . . . and *good-bye*."

His gun has a hair trigger.

When his finger hits it, I hear an explosion and the guy falls down dead.

Franklin steps through the back door and nudges the turtleneck guy with his foot, making sure he's not a zombie. He sees the screaming gunman in the car thirty feet away and puts one round through the back windshield. A red paint bomb goes off inside there, and the screaming stops. Franklin doesn't flinch.

"Sorry I'm late, kid."

The shot echoes into forever, smoke rising from the business hole of his weapon, which is bad business indeed: a .375 Korth revolver, 38 caliber, the kind of gun that giants with big hands use when they wanna blow holes in nouns.

That's people, places and things.

He covers the alley, putting his other hand under my shoulder to help me up.

"We gotta move. Now."

It's been a long time since I was in a war zone like this—since I ran with people who killed other people so casually. Thank God for small favors. He starts to run and I follow him. The ankle throbs, but it's not broken. A genuine miracle, that. We move fast, climb the wreck of the car, get to the other end of the alley. I shove the 9-mil in my waistband. No more shots back there, but I can hear the first sirens in the distance.

"We need a car," he tells me, the two of us scoping the next street over, which is almost empty. We cross to the alley behind Tom's Tabooley. There's a 1995

Honda Accord parked near the dishwashers' entrance. It's unlocked, no alarm. I use my kit bag and we're on wheels in less than twenty seconds. The older the ignition switch, the easier it is. You can start a car like this with a screwdriver. Someone screams at us, running out of the back of the restaurant. I gun the motor and leave him quick, turning left onto the next street, snaking through a series of neighborhood back roads towards South Lamar, away from the whole circus.

Feels strange driving a car. Haven't done it in years.

"I have to bring you in," Franklin says, putting his pistol away, scanning the road, his Deep South voice amazingly calm. "We have to get back to our people. There's gonna be cops all over that block inside of five minutes."

"I'm working on it, man. Let's get some distance, then we'll talk about destination."

"You're going the wrong way."

"Look, we're alive, right? Anyway, where *were you* when those assholes started using me for target practice?"

"Getting coffee across the street. I didn't see what happened but I heard the shooting. The guy who survived the truck crash started wasting people inside the store."

"Yeah, I heard."

"I went after him, thought you might be in there. That guy was an animal. Shooting women and children."

"Christ . . ."

I take the MoPac Expressway and we cruise north, ten miles across the city, past civilization and into the lake area. The radio's already talking about the hit. Panic and confusion. Some of them think it really is a terrorist attack. Choppers are hovering downtown. I pull over in the gravel near an old filling station, leave the motor running. The sun is starting to go down. I have no idea what to do.

"We need to ditch this car," I tell him.

"You need to let me drive. I have to get us back to—"

I remember Washington's 9-mil in my waistband, pull it out and thumb the hammer right between Franklin's eyes. "I don't think I trust you."

"Take that gun out of my face right now, kid."

"Then start talking. I wanna know what the hell's going on here."

"I think it's pretty obvious what's going on. Someone just tried to make you dead and I saved your life. Now, if you want to stay alive, I suggest you let me drive."

I keep the gun aimed at him while he stares me down. We stay that way for a few seconds. I try to calm myself. In a long moment of stupid incredulity I flash on the automatic nature of the actions I've been taking, and realize I don't even know who manufactured the gun I'm holding in my hand. It's heavy and compact, black and warm in my grip. Looks like it could be a Taurus or a Springfield. The serial numbers are sanded off and so is the brand name. I shake my head, checking reality, and Franklin scowls down the barrel.

The cell phone in my pocket rings.

I fish it out, not lowering the pistol.

UNKNOWN CALLER.

It could only be the Fixer on this line.

It isn't.

It's only the man who destroyed my life.

"Hey, buddy-boy, are we having fun yet?"

I don't say anything. He laughs at me.

His voice is like a southern-fried pig who eats human flesh.

"I heard you got an early release. I also heard you got a new phone number. Unlisted. Well done. I'll be sure to tell our mutual friend Mister Remo Williams that you're all kinds of grateful. And nice job, running from my boys, by the way. One hell of a professional getaway."

I can't believe this. Jett sold me up the river. Or maybe they just beat my name out of him. Either way, I'm dead in the water.

About a million weird emotions trainwreck inside me, all those plunging wet feelings you get when the business comes down bad, when the whole world turns against you. But all I can think to say to him is this:

"You sick maniac."

He laughs again. *"Now let's not get nasty, old boy. I don't think you want me really-and-truly angry with you right about now."*

"Those people back there . . . they were nothing to you."

"Fuck those people. This is just a warning, boy. I knew those morons would miss and I didn't really care. Not this time. But from now on, anywhere you go, I'll know where that is. And every day you're on the street, someone is going to die. Maybe someone close to you. But mark my words: we're covering all the bases this time and the sky is falling. Think about that while you're running from me. Think about that really, really hard."

"What do you want?"

"Well, hell now. That's the sixty-four-thousand-dollar question, ain't it?"

Click.

I ditch everything. Smash the laptop, the cell, throw it all in the lake. Franklin also tosses his phone. Any chance they can track us where we're going, we can't take it. I just pray to God they didn't get to the Fixer. If Hartman got to Remo through the Fixer, I'm completely hosed. They wouldn't play nice with a guy like that, either. They'll have made him talk about everything. I remember the key to my safe deposit box, still in my pocket, maybe useless by now, maybe not.

We change rides at the magic hour in a used-car lot five miles up the road, covered by the dull copper twilight. Nobody sees us—the place is closed for the night. I get us a shiny almost-new Impala that won't be reported stolen for at least ten hours.

I let Franklin drive.

The safe house isn't even in Austin.

It's near Houston, two hundred and fifty miles.

He gets us there in just under three hours.

No cops anywhere. No choppers looking for us. We're just some other stolen car on the back roads to nowhere. A little damp outside. Fall and winter are never really cold in Texas, not like in other states. Just a ghostly chill to remind you, mostly at night. Franklin does a lot of weird turns down highway stretches I've never even seen, until we finally emerge on 59 North, and I can finally see a few familiar landmarks. He's taking us into Splendora. It's a pissant little settlement a few miles off the edge of Houston—not like a real city or town, just houses hidden by trees. There's a lot of rural communities like this sitting at the outskirts of H-Town, and they're all godforsaken as hell.

A stretch of gravel snakes into a fenced area in the woods. It's hidden real well. A hardened redneck shotgun party with a squad of bloodhounds couldn't find this place. Two guys on the gate, wearing city clothes and combat boots.

A short driveway cuts through a thick cluster of evergreens and opens into a compound. It has a few buildings that look like they belong on a farm, lots of open space, target ranges. More hired hands around, big muscle guys. I can see two of them carrying machine guns near a concrete slab about fifty feet wide with yellow markings like a basketball court. There's an innocent little two-story house nestled near the rear of the compound, also dotted with big guys, four of them, surrounding the perimeter.

When we pull up to the farmhouse, I can tell by the bulges in their cheap sports jackets that they're all carrying backup weapons in shoulder holsters. The one who opens the door and asks me to please step this way has a Ruger SR9 Centerfire pistol visible just under his armpit—high-end hitman gear, very reliable. Nine-millimeter stopping power, with a stainless steel slide and a black glass-nylon alloy frame. You see ex-marines selling those things at gun shows. The guy has a face like the surface of the planet Mars, looks about thirty. All these guys look young, except Franklin. I see the wrinkles on his face for the first time. Why didn't I notice them before?

I follow Mars-Face up the creaky wooden stairs to the porch, where another guy with black hair and a white T-shirt pats me down, looking apologetic. He's strapped with an SR9 also. These guys must shop at the same gun show.

Franklin is right behind me. "We've got a code thirteen, Larry. I gotta get the boss on a secure line now."

Mars-Face squeezes his lips together and shakes his head. "The boss is already here. Get the kid inside."

The house has an old-fashioned screen door that sounds like a mouse getting pissed-off about something when Franklin opens it for me. My father stands up from the couch just inside the living room. He looks like he hasn't slept in two days, since I last saw him. The TV in here is tuned to MSNBC and an image of the toy store I used to work at fills the screen on shaky video with urgent red letters rolling across the bottom:

Attack On Texas Capital

"Son . . . what the hell just happened?"

I shrug at him and say the first thing that pops into my mind:

"You got any beer in this place?"

I drink two Lone Star tallboys and it's like water floating in my guts. I don't even get a half a buzz. Dad tells me they have some whiskey but that's never a good idea. The hard stuff makes me fuzzy and stupid. So do cigarettes. He's still asking me questions and I still don't know exactly what to tell him. I've screwed up here, but how much of this is really my fault? What the hell did Hartman mean? People I care about are going to die. Everywhere I go, he can find me. The sky is falling.

That maniac.

He never did anything this crazy before.

Not in broad daylight.

The TV says ten are dead that they know about, including a mother and her child who were gunned down inside the store while I was running for my life. Identities being withheld until notification of the victims' families. I'm impressed with how fast the word got out. It's been just over four hours since we ran like hell. I shouldn't be surprised. They had the World Trade Center on every goddamn channel before any of us in Texas even knew what was happening. That gives me the wet, slimy feeling again.

I cut off the feeling.

Have to focus on the here and now.

I keep the kit bag on my shoulder this whole time. It still has twenty grand in it, the money the Fixer got me. My getaway insurance. It might be the last money I ever earn, if the key in my pocket is worthless.

Shitfire, Elroy. What the hell do you do now?

Heavy boots clock hard outside on the porch, and I hear the screen door squeak again. A big thick fella with a hard, sculpted face stands in front of me now, brown and mean-looking like an Italian, out of breath. He's decked head to toe in military olive, like a drill sergeant with no decorations. Looks like a crazy man.

He points at me. "Is this the guy?"

He's a good old boy, every syllable dripping with redneck fury.

Franklin stands up from the couch next to me as my father confirms my identity. The good old boy shakes his head at me.

"Mister, you've got a lotta explaining to do."

FULL DISCLOSURE

We leave the farmhouse—me, my father and the guy who looks like a drill sergeant—and cross the open compound to one of the other buildings, near the concrete slab. It looks like a barn. On the inside, too. Even has horses in the stalls and smells like rotten hay. It strikes me as a little odd that I grew up in Texas and I've never been in a barn once or even seen a farm animal this close up. I once saw a movie where Sean Penn played a guy on death row in New Orleans, and for his last meal he had shrimp, and when they brought it to him, he told Susan Sarandon he'd never eaten shrimp before. You never stop to smell the roses when you live the lives we live. But I was never on death row. And I never killed anyone.

Sure as hell tried today, though.

The gun felt cold and unforgiving in my hand when I aimed it—like the revenge I've lusted after for years.

But I couldn't pull the trigger.

The man would have shot me dead.

And I just stood there.

A wooden stairwell in a dark corner that smells raw and unfinished drops below the floor, taking us into a short basement corridor with miners' lights strung along the ceiling and another guy with a Ruger on the next door. He salutes the good old boy in olive green, turns a key in the lock, punches in a code. The security is a joke, I can tell just by glancing. The digital keypad has a SERIO-SYSTEMS trademark on the outer plastic. You blow past those things easy, just by pressing in a row of sixes and holding down the pound key for six seconds.

Through the door, a conference room with a long table and a flat-screen monitor taking up one entire wall. Two flunkies in the room wearing guns in shoulder holsters. Three men and two women sitting at the table, most of them in army green.

At the head of the table, the concerned citizen.

Just some rich lady who spent a million bucks to get me out of jail.

She doesn't look happy, doesn't look upset, doesn't look like anything. She's dressed in black, with a dark jacket and matching blouse. I notice for the first time that she's very thin, her face suspended in mystery by those deep green eyes. She's got a laptop open next to a stack of papers and photos, a pen in her hand. The army guys stand and salute our guide when we walk in.

"As you were," he tells them, and they sit down again. Getting a better look at them, they seem like mercenaries. I've seen their type before, seen a few get killed.

One of them is a young woman, probably twenty.

She's pretty but not gorgeous, has freckles and long red hair in a ponytail. Not muscular, like the others. Her uniform is dark olive, no camouflage patterns, eyes full of smarts, decorations on her shoulder. Gotta be an air force hacker.

She sizes me up, and I see her eyes shift from mode to mode.

Our guide plants his feet on the ground right next to me, and I notice for the first time that he has a mean serrated army knife clipped to his waist—it's long enough to be a sword, the kind you see in movies starring Sylvester Stallone. Wasn't sure those things really existed.

The lady in the dark suit motions to the empty chairs across from her. "Have a seat, gentlemen. We have a lot to discuss in a very short time."

"No shit," our guide tells her, sounding pissed. He doesn't sit when we do. Stands almost at attention near the table, his hands clasped professionally behind his back.

The lady clicks her pen shut. "Mister Coffin, I'd like to introduce Sergeant Maxwell Rainone, U.S. Army, retired."

I raise my hand, like I'm in school asking for my turn to talk. "Excuse me, which one of us were you talking to?"

"What?"

"You said 'Mister Coffin.' That's both of us."

I point at Dad and then at myself.

The Sarge lets out a huff. "Can you believe this little shit? Doesn't even have any *idea* what kind of fuckin' deep shit he's in."

"Please don't be crude," says the lady. "We're here to sort things out, not make more problems." She looks right at me. "It was a valid enough question, Mister Coffin, and so I suggest in the interest of cutting through the confusion that we refer to the two of you by your *first names* from now on, yes?"

"Yes," I say. "I'm not trying to make trouble. It was a little joke."

"The men in this room are trained specialists and weapons experts," she says. "I would expect a man like you to know the difference between trigger-happy morons and real professionals. So let's act professional. Elroy."

So much for stalling these guys with my quick wit.

She takes a breath, and:

"Your actions have caused a major breach in the security of our operation. This meeting was scheduled to take place tomorrow."

"I don't know what happened. They came out of nowhere while I was walking out of the store."

"Who?"

"David Hartman's people."

"That's not good. Does he know about your involvement with myself or this operation?"

"Man, I don't even know your *name*. And *what* operation? You guys just cut me loose without a word and told me to go work in a toy store. Next thing I know, people are shooting the place up."

"I told you what you were being hired for," she says sharply. "My daughter has been kidnapped. This is *serious business*, Mister Coffin."

"None of that business has anything to do with stocking action figures."

The Sarge growls at me. "Don't try to put this off on us. We involved you double-blind because we knew how hot you were gonna be. But there's no way Hartman's people could have moved on you so fast without inside information. No fuckin' way."

"Then you guys don't know David Hartman very well."

The lady shifts her weight, doing that thing where you settle back in your chair with a long dramatic pause to own the room during a meeting. I already called her on the trick of using your name a lot on a business deal—executives in big companies are trained to do that. Makes you feel important while they're calling the shots. Yes, Mister Coffin, we understand your problems. No, Mister Coffin, you don't get to choose the color of the big rubber dick we'll be bending you over with.

I see it in her eyes when she speaks again:

"Actually, we know Hartman quite well. We have our *own* inside information, and we're using it to correct the problem. It may be expensive, but we can deal with it. What we really need to know is what *Hartman* knows. If he's figured out why you were released from prison."

"It didn't seem that way."

"Are you saying you *talked to him?*"

"He had my cell phone tagged."

"You're not supposed to own a cell phone."

"Call me cautious."

"I'd call you a fuckin' *dumbass*." The Sarge's voice is

like crazy dragon breath on the back of my neck. I don't pay attention to it.

The air force redhead keeps her eyes focused on mine.

Still sizing me up.

"I apologize for the cloak-and-dagger routine," says the lady in black, ignoring the girl. "You were released into the care of the state because that was part of the deal I made. There had to be a real body answering questions in front of the parole people for a week before we pulled you out of the halfway house. I got it down to three days after serious negotiations. Everything was arranged. You should have trusted us to take care of you. When did you contact Hartman?"

"I didn't. He contacted me. I made a call from the toy store yesterday. Had to get some personal business worked out, get my gear. That's probably how they knew where I was working. The guy who squealed was an old hacker buddy."

The lady rubs her eyes. "They could know anything by now."

"I didn't talk about *anything*. I don't *know* anything."

"It could have been enough for Hartman to start digging. We should abort the operation."

"I've got a better idea," the Sarge says. "We *accelerate* the operation. Hit him two weeks sooner. Within three days, max. He won't have enough time to figure out exactly what we're after, and by then it'll be too late. My boys are ready to go." He throws a mean glance at my father. "Ringo, you think you can get this dumbass little man of yours up to speed in a few days?"

"Right after you stop calling my son a dumbass."

"I'll think it over." The crazy guy actually backs off a little. He must know my dad's reputation. Wonder if he knows about mine?

The air force redhead's expression never changes through all this.

"I'm not convinced acceleration is the right answer," says the lady in black. "I need to contact my people in the police department again, see how this whole business at the toy store shakes out. Need to put some feelers on the street. This compound is secure. What I need to know now, Elroy, is exactly what you said to this hacker friend of yours, *when* it was said, and what Hartman said to *you*."

Gotta tell her everything.

Don't have anything to lose now.

My life is in the hands of these people, one way or another.

When I finish my story, the Sarge looks impressed, but he doesn't say anything. Must've been the part about dancing over a moving car doing fifty down a narrow alley.

The redhead in olive drab takes a deep breath, folds her arms. Keeps quiet.

"Hartman told you that *people would die*," says the lady in black. "That means we may have even less time than I thought. If he killed all those people just to send a message . . . then we're dealing with a psychopath."

Wow. So you figured that out all by yourself, huh?

"He was always a psychopath," I say. "I told you that before. He's an ape who thinks he's a gangster."

"That much is obvious now."

"It should have been obvious to you from the very start."

"So this is *our fault* somehow?"

"I didn't say that. But Hartman is a redneck. Not some master scoundrel with a grand design. He's got one philosophy that sits on top of everything and that's do unto others and make it permanent."

The lady sighs, leaning back. "Hartman is also a *businessman*. He stands to lose too much if he starts shooting random people on a crowded corner in broad daylight. It doesn't make any sense."

"He's insulated himself," I tell her. "That kind of power makes a crude man less than humble."

"We both know that's true."

"If you wanna know about gangsters, I can tell you plenty. Me and my dad, we've worked for all shapes and sizes, and most of them have the same problem. They all eventually go crazy listening to their own voices."

She narrows her eyes at me. "And what does that mean exactly?"

"It means I've never been in the living room of a gangbanger that didn't have the poster for *Scarface* hanging on the wall."

"I see."

"You know what poster David Hartman had tacked up in his office?"

"I can't imagine."

"Anna Nicole Smith."

She almost laughs. Catches herself, putting a hand casually over her mouth.

"This is turning into a clusterfuck," the Sarge says

suddenly, starting to pace around. "I still say acceleration is the only way to go. The guy's a mad dog. We've gotta hit him before he snaps his leash. Even if he doesn't get to us first, he could make a lot of noise, draw a lot of attention if he fucks up too bad. Another massacre like the one today might totally compromise our objective."

"Duly noted," says the concerned citizen. "I have a question for you, Elroy."

"Yes?"

"Why did you *really* make that call to your fixer? We were taking care of everything."

"I have no idea who you are or what you really want."

"Your father has vouched for us—you're saying you don't trust him?"

"Let's just say it's hard to trust the ground under your feet sometimes, especially when you're sitting in a room full of retired army guys with guns."

"So you don't trust *me*."

"I don't think I have any choice right now *but* to trust you."

Dad leans close to me, almost whispering. "Son, you have to believe me. These guys are on the level. They can help us get our lives back."

"It'll be more complicated now that this has happened," says the lady in black. "I'll have to do a deal with someone to pull you both off the grid in a more permanent way. Once you're officially dead on the books, we can set you up somewhere. Of course, that's after you fulfill our original agreement."

I look her right in the eye. "Of course."

She looks me right back. "I'm dead serious."

And, finally, I see it.

The thing she never gave me time to notice before, back in the joint.

The killer behind her eyes.

She speaks at a low, hypnotizing lull:

"Elroy, I understand your need for revenge. Your need to take matters into your own hands. You had a window of opportunity and you took it. Under the circumstances, I might have done the same thing. But you must understand that's the kind of rash thinking that put you in prison to begin with. You might never have seen your wife again."

"I was never completely convinced she was still alive. I'm still not."

"I showed you the picture. I thought it was clear to you."

"Pictures can be faked."

"Yes, that's correct."

"And if she was alive, I was going to find her myself. My way. I wasn't going to wait around to find out why I was working in a goddamn toy store."

"That's dangerous thinking," says the Sarge. "Kinda makes me feel like you're not much of a team player there, son."

"Think what you want. I did some sniffing around. Nobody I was able to talk to online has seen or heard from Toni Coffin inside of three years. Not since she went with Hartman, and that was *before* I went inside."

"And I say she's still alive," says the lady in black. "That's why you're here. To help me find her, and my daughter. This is our primary objective, Elroy. But as you can no doubt surmise, full disclosure of everything *we* know about Hartman's operation is something I have had to seriously reevaluate in the past several hours."

She's still doing it. Using my name to make it seem like the universe revolves around me. But can I really trust them?

More importantly . . . can they trust me?

"Okay," I finally say. "So I messed up."

She looks me right in the eye again. "We'll put it down to a few simple questions."

"Okay. Shoot."

"Elroy, if you'd had the opportunity, if Hartman had threatened you personally and not been just a voice on the phone . . . would you have killed him?"

"Yes."

"You realize that killing Hartman would have jeopardized our operation, maybe destroyed it?"

"Yes."

"You realize that you would have been a liability at that point and no longer of any use to me?"

"Yes."

"And I might have killed you, just to watch you die?"

My father looks at the lady real seriously when she says that.

I give her a little grin and say: "Hey, you can't win 'em all."

The lady doesn't grin back.

I stop smiling. Then say, very evenly, with as much respect as I can come up with: "Yes. I understand."

Sometimes you just have to play it cool.

Even when they're calling you by name.

Another long silence in the room. The air force redhead across from me downshifts her gaze again, not saying a word, but I can see something that might be vague contempt and puzzlement flash in her eyes. She turns her look inward. Keeping it to herself. For now.

The boss lady stands from her chair. Offers me her hand.

"Mister Coffin, I think we finally *do* understand each other. My name is Jayne Jenison. It's good to make your acquaintance."

I shake her hand.

Her flesh is cold, like the devil's.

The killer inside her glows just beneath the surface.

That night, I stash my getaway money under the bed in my room upstairs in the farmhouse. I don't tell my father about it. I sit on the bed staring at the key to my safe deposit box. It might be useless now. I put it back in my pocket.

I can't sleep. Toni's keeping me awake, as usual. She's pissed off at me. She's screaming that I'm her only hope, that she's still alive, that I've messed everything up. That my plots have failed me, failed us. That I'm too smart for my own good. Too good at too many things. Tricking computers, stealing cars, breaking people's legs with my bare hands, it all has a price, and I've been paying it for years . . . but now my smart self has painted me into a very dark corner. I want to cry. The tears almost come.

No.

Keep it under control, kid.

Keep your game face on.

Keep it under control . . .

My wife screams at me that I'm a diaper-wagging baby. The same cruel way she used to when my back was against the wall, when I had something to prove, those white-hot moments when I knew she was right and I was wrong and I was fighting just to hear the sound of my own arrogant pride.

But her voice is not *her* voice in my memory.

Not at all.

I know it's her, I can *hear the words* . . . but it sounds like someone else.

Something abstract.

Like in a dream I can't bring back.

My head burns white-hot and ice-cold when I strain to hear her. I rub the plate under my thick hair and all the scar tissue. My whole skull itches. The smell of rose petals, canceling out the dampness of the room, overriding everything. Ammonia and a razor blade, the sharp smell of blood, somewhere way back among the important things that are washed out.

The doctors could never give me a straight answer on what it was, the way she was blocked from me, her face and her voice gone, but the memories still there, the details scrawled in abstract. Some kind of regression, self-punishment. A couple of guys told me it was a no-brainer. They actually said that to me. Someone shot you in the head, Mister Coffin. What's the big mystery?

It never mattered to give my condition a name, but they threw around a lot of highbrow terms in the hospital. Cognitive dissonance. Prosopagnosia, face blindness. My favorite was *transregressional selective doorway amnesia*.

I don't even think "transregressional" is a real word.

I started realizing they make this shit up as they go in some hospitals.

My wife would have laughed at those doctors.

I see my father telling me Toni's no good, that I settled for something because I had nothing better, that she finally left me because she was a survivor, not because she was trying to save my life.

Love cannot stay, kid. She was just an illusion.

I know that can't be true. I don't want to believe that's true.

But I see her in Hartman's arms. The sweat dripping off his fat face, into her mouth, which is the mouth of a china doll—a smooth, blank face like porcelain, shattered into pieces. Not her at all. Her face shattered and lost to me forever. Until I can make forever go away. Until I can find her.

I get out of the bed and sit in the center of the floor.

Concentrate hard and take myself out.

Out of the room.

Yes . . .

I see the leads laid from end to end, but I don't trust them now. My so-called plot got ten innocent people murdered by a psychopath who thinks he can play with everyone's life and get away with it. And he's right, isn't he?

I don't trust my own plans.

I have to trust these people.

Toni, I just might have killed you again.

Please forgive me.
Please be alive when I find you.
Please.

The next morning, we all meet again in the war room under the barn.

Jenison tells me I'm now officially dead.

She works fast.

There were two unidentified Caucasian males blown away in front of the toy store during the drive-by, probably homeless guys. One of them roughly fit my description. They pulled prints off the body and guess what. Matched with mine, spot on. Really tragic, a kid that young, out on good behavior, looking to make his life right again, cut down in a senseless random eruption of wholesale violence that's still shocking the nation. My father will die soon, too, but not like this. They have to wait for another opportunity. Dad suggests at the table that he kill himself the next time an old man washes up somewhere in Texas with a shotgun in his mouth. Suicide makes sense. A lot of remorseful fathers do that after their kids check out.

They've decided on the Sarge's acceleration plan. The run is in just three days. It's an old-school sweep-and-clear, just like the kind me and Dad used to pull when we were the kings of the world. A seven-man team, led by him and the Sarge.

I was right about the quiet redhead—she turns out to be a hotshot air force computer specialist. She'll be my right arm during the job.

Her name is Alex Bennett.

She's an airman first class, just three years younger than me.

The flyboys press buttons, the marines blow shit up.

I only know all that because Jenison hands me a folder with some highlights from the lady's service record in it. It's an impressive résumé, but Bennett still never says a word to me. Now that I realize she's so much older than I thought she was, I notice she's a lot more beautiful. But the hard lines that encase her amber eyes tell tales of bad business, all confirmed by the papers in front of me: a fairly recent rotation in Baghdad, during the last years of the war, a couple of black ops before that, all classified. Her job was to deactivate bombs—the high-tech kind. Not pipe explosives rigged to primitive detonators and car batteries in the street. No, we're talking about major works of art, crafted by well-paid professionals. Labyrinthine deadfall canyons ruled by computers and time locks—the kind I bust in my sleep. She has twenty-seven commendations for shutting down that kind of death trap. She's an expensive commodity on a job like this.

Her cold expression steels the air, as Jenison makes some pictures come up on the flat-screen. Photographs of young women.

"Elroy, how much do you know about the business of human trafficking in the United States?" She stops on a photo of the blonde I saw before with Toni. The blonde is standing in front of a church in a schoolgirl uniform, shot from a block away with a telescopic lens, digital camera, probably an XL Canon. Toni had one of those. She was in my dad's face with it all the time, even though she never took pictures of any of us. It was an oddball family joke because they never got along. *Can I shoot you with my Canon, Dad?*

"Not much," I tell Jenison as she folds her hands, finding some Zen. "I know in some other countries child prostitution is legal."

"It's practically legal here, too," the Sarge says. "You just ain't allowed to advertise."

Jenison lets out a grim breath. "What Sergeant Rainone means to say is that this sort of trafficking has reached epidemic proportions just below the radar in the past two decades. Texas has one of the worst concentrations, mostly because of the senators and high-ranking businessmen who grease the wheel. Not to mention well-placed criminal types who are in it up to their eyeballs. Most of these men have stock in major corporations and use their leverage in very bad ways."

"You're talking about David Hartman?"

"Of course I am."

"So you figure your daughter was abducted into some kind of trafficking network for sick richies?"

"It's a little more complicated . . . but, yes, that's the essential truth."

The Sarge chimes in again. "These photos were stolen by our man from a high-security database out of Houston. An encrypted series of sub-files hidden real well in the records of a corporate branch of Texas Data Concepts."

Jenison goes into her briefcase and removes a cigarette from somewhere in there. She doesn't light it. "The IRS was conducting an investigation of David Hartman's assets about a year and a half ago, in collaboration with the FBI. What they came up with was an elaborate money-laundering scam that involved Hartman using his stock in Texas Data Concepts as leverage over some of the CEOs. That was what they *knew* . . . but they could never prove it officially, because people started disappearing, along with certain documentation."

"Doesn't surprise me."

"It shouldn't. What should surprise you is that the FBI backed off and never came at Hartman or TDC ever again."

"The Feds never do that," says the Sarge. "They're like fuckin' bulldogs most of the time. They hold on to a dream or a nightmare."

Jenison makes a disgusted noise. "Sad, isn't it? A fat gangster waves his hand and it all goes away. The case was never even handed off to the Agency. They buried it. Meaning something very big was happening."

"You're saying to me that Texas Data Concepts has been fronting for a goddamn white slavery ring?"

"Not the company itself," Jenison says. "Just some of the executives. We're pretty sure Hartman's still in bed with them. He's been kidnapping people, sending them underground, probably selling them to the highest bidder. Mostly young women. Top-dollar merchandise, so to speak. My people got very close to him, delivered some specific details about the operation. Our last solid connection was these photographs."

"Who stole them for you?"

"The same man who photographed Hartman four months ago with your wife. He got in pretty deep. Undercover as an assassin for Hartman's crew. But he was dangerous, unstable. Had a drug problem."

"So your man leaked some tidbits and got himself killed."

"For starters."

"What's that supposed to mean?"

"After Hartman plugged the leak, they burned everything that could lead anyone back to their trafficking ring. We knew a lot by then. I was following up on the investigation privately. I had all the files from the FBI, but we never found anything new that gave locations where people were being held. We just found little crumbs. Photos mostly. Disgusting stuff. Most of it was pulled off private databases. Laptops and PCs owned by key executive officers of the company. You'd be amazed at how indiscreet some of those people were in their own offices."

"No, actually, I wouldn't."

"My undercover man was good, in spite of his personal problems. He found files that had been deleted. Things we were able to reconstruct. There were a few e-mails that implicated Hartman directly. But it all dried up after my man went away. They locked everything up tight. That was four months ago."

"So what we have here is a bunch of well-connected pervs with stashes of young female flesh all over the state—maybe even the country. You've lost the trail and they torched the leads. You need me to come back at them."

"You're still batting a thousand, Elroy."

"What makes you think I can find something they missed?"

"That's just it—they didn't miss *anything*. My men have investigated Hartman with a microscope. He's virtually sterilized himself. There's one database at a certain TDC facility we haven't been able to crack. It's on a private circuit, completely separated from the network inside the building. A vault. Protected by the most advanced multi-layered security profile any of my people have ever seen."

"You think he's keeping his women in there?"

"Your attempts at humor are wearing thin, Mister Coffin."

"We know he's keeping *something* in there," the Sarge barks. "The objective of this operation is to get inside that vault and remove everything in it."

I rub my chin. "That's a long shot you're talking about. Hartman was into all sorts of nasty business before I went in the can. I had his whole network circled. A lot of that was above-the-radar government contracting. Things like dirty bombs and smart missiles."

"I know all about that," Jenison says. "But missiles do not concern me."

"Well, maybe they should."

"That's not what I'm focused on right now. We do know for *sure* that Hartman is using the Texas Data Concepts facility as his own private fortress. That's how much leverage he has over these people. If he's keeping something sensitive—*anything* sensitive—inside that vault, then we gain leverage over *him* and that puts me one step closer to getting my daughter back. If she's gone underground with the others, we may be able to obtain her location from any encrypted data we recover. You'll help us with that, also."

"The photo you showed me back in the joint wasn't taken that long ago," I say. "Your girl could be in his bed right now."

"And my grandma could be doing his dishes and your wife could be washing his car," the Sarge hisses in my ear. "You startin' to get the *picture*, boy?"

"Please calm down," Jenison says softly. "Hartman hasn't exactly been quiet about his own private harem. He supplies himself and his friends with a revolving inventory of fresh stock. But Hartman mostly sticks to his own stomping grounds. Nightclubs he owns, things like that. He had a rash of bad publicity about a year ago over a Senate hearing he helped to buy, and that's made him gun-shy of public places. The word was that Toni Coffin was looking out for my daughter, making sure she didn't get hurt too badly. Hartman likes to hurt his women."

"I know."

"My daughter is very young, Mister Coffin. Just twelve this month."

Jesus.

She looked twenty in the picture.

I level a serious gaze at Jenison. "Can I ask a favor?"

She scowls back, as if to say my favors are all used up. But then nods slightly, as if to say, *Within reason, kid.*

I look at the giant screen.

The girl smiles back at me.

"The photo when we first met. Could I see it again?"

She curls her lip, reaching for the stack next to her laptop. Pulls out the picture. Slides it across the table. I pick it up and see what could be the face of my one true love, her arm hooked around the blonde's, Hartman leading them through the crowded nightclub. That's what the picture tells me, anyway. I can't be sure at all if it's really her. It's full of fuzz and grain, out of focus, like a notion hardly remembered. And my eyes tell lies now, my heart stonewalled and my head transregressed.

I look at the picture. Look hard for the truth there.

I can't see it.

"Can I hang on to this?"

Jenison nods. "Of course. I can give you a digital file, also, if you like."

"I'd like."

I stare at the photo, trying to picture the scene.

Trying to imagine what was on Toni's mind when the shutter snapped.

"Why was she protecting your daughter? What was in it for her?"

"I don't know, Elroy. Isn't it possible that she saw a child in need of help and decided to provide it?"

The same way she helped me when we were kids, reaching out to educate someone weaker than her. To make us both immortal.

What did you get yourself into, baby?

If that's really you.

"You could have filled me in on all this sooner," I say to Jenison, still staring at the photo. "I could have been using the last few days to look in the right places."

"The fact that you didn't know anything is probably what saved your life," she tells me. "If Hartman had really suspected what you were on the street for . . . if you'd dropped *any* hints to your little hacker buddies online . . . our friend might have made a bigger move, sent more shooters. You'd be very dead right now."

I fold the photo in half, set it on the table in front of me. Tap the table with my fingers. My gears working now, all cycles engaged.

"I still say he's got something bigger to protect than human trafficking. Ten shooters or ten million shooters, Hartman has never been this broad-daylight about killing anyone. I've seen him go pretty crazy, but he's mostly a dirty player who does things in a dark alley— or he just cuts your throat while you're sleeping."

"You also said Hartman was a redneck, not a master scoundrel."

"Yeah."

"People *do* change, Mister Coffin."

"Not David. Not like this. He's a sneaky bastard and he's not complicated at all. What he just did stirred up a major public shitstorm. It's all over the news right now. That's bad business, like you said."

"I did say that. I'm impressed that you were listening. Most people like yourself simply wait for their turn to talk in situations like these."

"That's why most people like myself die young."

When I say that, Alex Bennett finally shakes her head, giving me a look, like, *Oh really?*

Jenison smiles thinly. "Regardless of what you may think or suspect about Hartman, our dilemma remains . . . and our objective is the vault. That is not open for discussion. That's why you're on this team."

"So let's talk about the vault."

"We have specs, but we have no way in," Jenison says. "It's a very dangerous job. *Physically* dangerous, I mean. And for your participation . . . you will be paid two million dollars."

I almost don't hear that last part.

I'm not thinking about the money.

I force myself to.

"Two million is more than I've ever made before. You sure do like to throw your cash around, don't you?"

"I can think of a thousand other ways I'd rather be spending my fortune, Elroy."

"How much do we get up front?"

"Nothing. I'm not a fool. You've already tried to cut and run once, I'll not have it again. Under normal circumstances, I would have written you off. Sergeant Rainone would have enjoyed that, I'm sure."

The Sarge doesn't say anything. Just simmers.

"But you're a unique breed," Jenison says to me. "And this job is important. I'll equip you and keep you alive long enough to do the job. Then my people will cut you loose in Mexico with your money. That is, of course, *if* you survive."

I look at my father. "It's really that bad?"

He looks at me. "Oh yeah, kiddo. It is."

"Then it's just like old times."

Alex Bennett finally uncrosses her legs and leans forward, her searing amber eyes catching the dim light in the room, her voice tough and Southern, like some typical Texas caricature made really damn serious:

"No, Mister Coffin. It ain't."

COFFIN RUN

There are three ways you approach a job like this—three plots of attack. The first is the simplest. You sneak in and steal everything over a wire. Hartman's made that impossible. The second is the cowboy method. You run in making a lot of noise with ski masks on, waving guns and knives and sharp sticks—scare the hell out of them, make them give you everything, then run out. You still need at least one wirehead when you do that. And you have to be ready to kill a few people. That won't work either in this case.

So the third method is the one we're using in three days.

Guns and laptops.

The best of both worlds.

The Texas Data Concepts building isn't located among Houston's downtown business high-rises. It's not even a high-rise at all. It's a tech/administration annex located in a rural area off the main road, just on the outside of the city, one of those small five-stories where the execs mingle with the rank-and-file computer geeks, and certain percentages of the important work and research get done. It figures a vault like this would be located dead center. David must've bought the place right out from under them. They probably don't even do real TDC work there anymore. A perfect cover for his trafficking hub. And whatever else he's got going on. He's been a real busy guy since I went away—and a lot smarter about covering his ass. That's so crazy, the more I turn it over. David Hartman getting smarter seems like the dumbest idea anyone ever came up with in three years' worth of dumb ideas.

Jenison was right—people do change.

But we're always that same dumb bastard, deep down.

I keep that in the back of my mind, as Dad talks to the men on the practice range. They're lined up like a proper army platoon, all at attention. He walks casually up and down the line, like some kind of lieutenant. The first thing he tells them is that a building like this TDC place is a little easier than a high-rise because everything's flat, spread out. They don't have as much muscle on the perimeter itself because they never expect anyone to come at them hard from the outside. Usually, it doesn't make any sense to hit a place this well-fortified electronically. Unless you happen to be us. We've gone into skyscrapers in Chicago and LA before and it was always a bitch. You need a helicopter. At least two men on each floor with heavy weapons, sometimes artillery, depending on the location of the building. On grounds like this, you go in using stealth. Ninja tactics. Nobody even knows we're there. We tie up security guards and stick them in closets. If we're lucky, we won't have to kill anyone. That's what Dad always says before we go in. He's killed twenty-nine men in his life. All on jobs. You do what you have to do.

He's working with the Sarge, who has direct command over his men during the run. We go in armed for bear, all of us. Dad is not just intel—he's on the team, using his left hand. No way he's sitting this one out. He says he owes me.

I watch him on the range as he instructs the men, tells them how to shoot.

He never uses a gun, and that fills me with sadness.

They run through maneuvers for the rest of the day. I don't work the drills with them, but I watch their movements carefully, going over specs on the Texas Data Concepts facility inside my head. I've memorized most of them already.

The outer security on the building itself is cheese. Laser sensors, silent alarm, the usual bells and whistles. There's nothing much on the grounds surrounding the place, either. A wire fence, electrified, and a guard post at the main gate. They'll be armed with handguns, no automatic weapons. We'll be through the fence and inside the building in under five minutes, no casualties. When they run it on a stopwatch, full gear, the Sarge is impressed with how fast his boys move. He huffs the word "outstanding" a lot. Says we might have a chance if the tech kids don't fuck it up. Every now and then he pulls out that evil-looking Rambo knife and slices the air with it to underscore a point. Tough guy or something.

This complex of theirs where they've been prepping the job is the most fortified and expensive I've ever seen, all privately owned by Jayne Jenison. There's an armory in an underground bunker that looks like something out of Operation Desert Storm. Turns out the concrete slab that looks like a basketball court is really a helipad. Guess I get to ride in a chopper, after all. We go in at midnight by truck, just when the night watch starts. We have to hit the safe at exactly 2 A.M.—it's all about the time-lock sensors. Once we're inside, I'll have three hours to break the system.

Exactly three hours.

If it starts looking like I can't break the last level— the most important level—they clear the building and call in the escape helicopter. They'll pull me out along with whatever's in the vault, if I crack it. If I don't, it doesn't matter. That's the deal.

The second, smaller building next to the barn houses the operations ready room and a workshop that has all of our tech gear for the job. It's like a shopping mall for wireheads. Literally millions of dollars' worth of raw stock. Racks of printed circuit boards, memory cards, laptop chassis, processors, custom devices, all up to date and ready to rock. A station full of tools and mechanized equipment for making rigs. The right man could build a supercomputer in this room and fill it with enough blackware to launch rockets at the national deficit.

I walk in, and I'm the right man.

Alex Bennett comes with me. She is professional and polite, not guarded like she was before. She knows everything there is to know in this day and age.

But she never really smiles, either.

We start by opening a laptop with a screwdriver, souping up the memory card and using it to download detailed specs on the vault from a series of discs, while the muscle guys continue to work drills outside. We have just under two days to build a rig capable of cracking the tightest, most dangerous equation ever designed.

The gear is easy. The blackware is, too.

What people don't realize—what Jenison and her people know damn well—is that it's not really about the technology so much. It's about the human being clicking the numbers on the other end. Improvisation. Skill. Experience, too. This vault at Texas Data Concepts will be my Moby Dick.

If Moby Dick was a monster with many arms.

We see the monster in three dimensions, outlined in green neon against the endless black of a computer screen: a steel door almost six feet thick, five coded security levels, three mean interconnected time locks and a series of steel gears up front which we have to break manually. That part is easy. You bring a big drill.

It's the self-destruct protocol that's gonna be the bitch.

A virtual tripwire rigged to nearly ten kilotons of TNT and plastic explosives.

There's no way around it.

One wrong move and we're all dead.

It's a fail-safe that sits on top of everything and triggers automatically, even when you unlock the system with the proper code keys—it has to be shut down from inside the vault, once the door comes open, so it's on a time delay. Three hours, to make sure nobody important gets killed. There are only a few hackers on earth who could get through their security in under three hours. They know damn well it would have to be one serious operator—and they want him taken out, along with everything he was trying to steal. It's that important to them.

A monster job.

An impossible job.

I'm still going to do it.

I know the risk and I don't care.

My wife is waiting for me on the other side, and so is Hartman. Whatever he's up to, whatever his network is really all about—guns, bombs, girls, cold cash—this is where the most important piece of it lives. He's given that away by guarding his secret so mercilessly.

I will show you no mercy, David.

Count on it.

As I run down the vault specs for a second time, Alex Bennett finally cracks something that looks a little bit like a smile. She tilts her head towards the ceiling, staring off into space.

I smile back at her, just a little. "Something's funny?"

"I keep thinking how I ended up here."

Her voice, country-as-hell, but full of smarts. Like some semi-hot farm girl who knows how to fly jets. I don't have a Southern accent like she does, even though I've spent most of my life in the Lone Star State. I've always blamed it on TV.

I lean back in my chair and size her up. "How *did* you end up here?"

"Weird luck, I guess."

"Don't worry. We'll make it out fine."

"It's gonna be close."

"Maybe. I think I can break the firewalls fast. Time locks are always harder. That could slow us down."

"I saw a layered profile a little like this once during my first tour in Iraq. That was a couple of years back. It was a nightmare."

"What happened?"

"The United States Army was keeping bales of money shipped over from America inside a concrete bunker nearly the size of a football field. They said it was twenty billion in cash."

"Jesus."

"A series of computerized minefields were built up around the main entranceway, which was a twenty-foot steel door carved off a totaled anti-aircraft tank—an M1 Abrams. Ever see one of those?"

"No."

"They're big. You see 'em in movies a lot."

"I haven't been to a movie in over three years."

"The ones about the wars over there are really terrible."

"So they built a bunker rigged to blow and then what?"

"The vault was improvised by an infantry wirehead who was killed six weeks later, along with his laptop. They brought me in to figure it out, gave me three days before they dynamited the whole front entrance."

"They blew a few billion back to God, just to open the piggybank?"

"Collateral damage, they called it."

"Only people who think with their guns pull stupid stunts like that. Or people who want to rub out thieves."

I look back at the specs on the laptop screen.

The monster.

"If you had been there, it would have been different," she says. "They could have saved the money. I've never seen anybody who works like you do."

"You've never seen me work."

"Not up close, but I know a lot about you."

"I guess everybody knows everybody in our line."

"If you're looking in the right places."

As she speaks to me, I realize it wasn't contempt in her eyes before. It was simply admiration, locked up tight behind a wall. Her youth is now obvious to me—just a few years, but hard years—and she has respect for my experience as a thief, my reputation in the hacker circles . . . but the whole thing makes me feel a little awkward. I sense her ability to turn her face and her heart to stone, under fire. They try real hard to teach you that in the military. Only a few of us can actually do it.

In bright light, she is a little bit stunning in her red beauty, the top half of her olive drab flight suit tied off at her waist, a galaxy of freckles against dark shoulders, exposed by a gray military tank top. Her form is cut in conservative feminine lines, her assets modest but very appealing. I try not to look for very long.

I can sense that's been a career problem for her, more than once.

We work for hours, way into the night, and then into the morning, building the rig. We talk about her time as a soldier. We talk about her training. She says she knows who taught me. Axl Gange. She says the name with great reverence.

"That wasn't what his mother called him," I say, bent over a series of memory cards with a soldering iron, checking my work with a giant magnifying glass on a jointed steel arm. "He was a Guns N' Roses fan. Always played that crap loud when we were working. His folks named him Norman. He never liked that."

She bows her head, like she knows already. Looks at her feet, then looks me in the eye. "Do you know why I signed up for this?"

"You were gonna tell me a while ago."

"Was I?"

"You said it was weird luck."

"I guess that's part of an answer."

"You don't like giving straight answers, do you?"

"There ain't that many."

She's right about that. Nothing's simple, not ever. I take my best guess:

"Someone in Jenison's crew knew about you through the army grapevine, right? Probably that Rainone guy. And she offered you a truckload of money to come on the team?"

"The job does pay well. But that ain't why I'm really here."

"Yeah?"

"It's Axl Gange. He was . . . close to me."

"Are you related to him?"

She doesn't answer me for a long, long moment.

I know Axl had three daughters and a son. I never met any of them. He never talked about them. I didn't really know who Axl was outside of work.

"No," she says, and it sounds like a lie. "But we were . . . *close*. When I was a lot younger. Before I went in the military. He taught me a few things, but not everything. I wanted to know more."

"It's none of my business."

"It is a little. We have something in common. David Hartman killed our teacher."

"Not many people know that."

"I met a guy from the Army Corps of Engineers who worked for Hartman. He told me they tortured Axl to death."

"Yes. That's exactly what happened."

I shut off the memory quickly, reducing it to dissonant information molecules. It's the only way to deal with that.

"Axl was a good teacher," I tell her. "When he died, I had to work for Hartman. For years. I had to shut up and do as I was told. That made me sick."

"Yeah. Me too."

"He never said anything about you."

"That don't surprise me." She gives a halfhearted wave-it-off with one hand, almost rolling her eyes.

"So you were gonna be a tech thief and you bailed to be a flyboy?"

"The air force was the only place I could complete my training for free."

"Like I said . . . it's none of my business."

"I knew we would be going after David Hartman. And I knew you would be on the job. And I knew Axl trained you. It's my way of getting even, I guess."

"He was the best, no doubt about it."

"I think it's such a goddamned waste that he's dead."

"Most of the things they *don't* teach you about in thief school were things Axl invented. Those are the things you only know if you meet a guy who was under his wing."

"Like what?"

"Like you have to be a *mechanic*, for starters. A *real* mechanic. You know what the first thing he taught me was?"

She shakes her dark red head, smiling.

I solder a lead in place. Perfect connection. "He locked me in a room and told me to find my way out. Took me two days, but I finally figured how the hinges on the door were put together. He said I was a natural."

"He never said that to me."

"You didn't know him long enough then. A woman with your skill set would have dazzled the hell out of Axl on a bad day."

"That's probably true."

"I had to bust my ass before he was happy. He took me through locks first. Old school. You have to learn your ABCs before you get high-tech. Did anyone ever teach you how to escape from police-issue handcuffs without a lockpick?"

"No."

It's impossible. You at least need a bobby pin—or a talent for dislocating your thumbs.

"That was a trick question," I tell her.

She almost smiles again. "Axl was full of tricks, wasn't he?"

"Yes he was."

"Can I ask you something?"

"You're going to anyway."

She folds her arms. "Hackers have to keep up with everything. It's all mercurial, changes every few months. Everybody exchanges information. How did you keep up when you were in prison?"

"I had a laptop in there."

"In maximum security?"

"Like I said, you have to know the old school."

I don't tell her about wiping the memory card and smashing the deck before I handed it back to the same weasel who smuggled it in for me. That was on the day Jenison showed up with Toni's picture. I don't tell her about keeping my data encrypted behind a wall of virus-infection security in an offsite location, or the Destroyer looking out for me, getting things set up with him in the two weeks before my release. I don't tell her about the three hundred grand I may or may not still have in a safe deposit box at the Austin Bergstrom Airport, a few hundred miles from where we stand. Only the Fixer knew about that. He might be the last person ever to know.

She offers her hand seriously, all business now. "It's an honor to be working with you, sir. I won't let you down."

I give her a small smile, but I don't take her hand. "This isn't the army and you don't report to me. It's Elroy."

"Okay. Elroy."

"Can I call you Alex?"

"I don't like my first name. Bennett is fine."

She looks right in my eyes now, and I can see the question lingering in her. She wants to know what I know about Axl. The details about how he died. It's why she's really here. Why she's so serious about all this.

I could give her that. I could tell her all about the

blood and the mayhem and Hartman's sick, twisted grin, beaming across a room tangled in smoke and sweat and screaming. I could explain the horror of watching your elders die slowly. The shame and the guilt, the endless spiral of rage.

I can't give her that.

It would give her nightmares for the rest of her life.

So I shake her hand instead.

When I do it, I wonder if she's Axl's daughter.

That night, I sit on the edge of my bed and stare at the photo. Toni and the girl, and Hartman with them. Jenison gave me a thumb drive with a digital file, containing all the pictures her undercover man snapped, but none of them are important to me like this one is. Because I can tell that's her. Even though I can't see her at all.

What are you thinking about in this moment, Toni? Are you thinking of me?

That poor little girl in the picture with her. I don't even know her name. Jenison's daughter.

I close my eyes and imagine that I am in the room with them: the smell of cigarettes and high-dollar weed, booze and sweat, the thump-boom-crackle of the rave club beat, good guys and bad guys and people who mean nothing to no one, all dancing and yelling and scamming and loving . . . and in the center of it all . . .

David Hartman.

The monster who stole everything.

Right there, barking orders to my one true love, and a little girl caught up in a karaoke disco-ball nightmare.

The music is noise that distracts me. I open my eyes and I look harder. Until my eyes can't look anymore. Until the line between the photo and my dreaming world blurs. And I am lost. Restlessly lost. Down and down . . . *and* . . .

I'm back to that night.

The night of our last job together—me and Toni, and my father.

This all happened so long ago.

The good old days, about to end badly.

That's where you always sat, right at the edge of everything. The risk always sniping at you, the sick thrill of losing it all. The abyss, yawning deep below. We used to call it a Coffin Run—those shotgun-crazy suicide assaults that nobody goes near, not unless they're like us. Unless they're really good at sensing the chinks in thick armor, sniffing out weaknesses, knowing where to hit hard and how to fade away when the smoke clears. It always helps when you're protected by the syndicate going in, but even that doesn't mean a damn thing if you're hitting especially dangerous people. So you work it real careful. You plot things to the letter. You take a cowboy job and you lace it with military precision. That makes you damn near invincible.

And that always started with Toni.

Secret Agent Toni—Bond Girl Toni.

The guy we were going after was one of those fat old-timers with a thing for young flesh—a lot of them are. It's kind of a cliché, really. But the old methods work best, even in the high-tech future.

And why?

Because those old-timers never keep their cash in banks.

Money laundering gets you caught—history proves it, the feds count on it. Coming back on mob assholes in court with tax-evasion charges is the one way to make damn sure every one of them do hard time in the end. As far as the IRS is concerned, you're guilty until proven innocent when there's a river of dirty money flowing through traceable channels. All that goes away if you dig a big hole and bury all your cash there.

We were standing right over the big hole.

And she was casting her line and reeling the old man in like a prize fish, gaffed and helpless.

I was sitting in the truck, twenty miles away from the nightclub, watching him on my screens. His face, a pockmarked artery of age and secrets and murder, carved in thick ugly gashes, his eyes wide and drunk and crisscrossed with jagged red lightning bolts, all brought into my tiny flip-up console with digital perfection from the six invisible eyes placed in her hair and her jewelry. My fingers racing across the keys, commanding software programs that mapped patterns in his irises, cracking the code hidden there. It took only six minutes. Then I had the key to the vault's first lock, built easy from the high-definition scan. Those retina identification panels are easy to fool, even when you don't have direct digital access to the guy's bloodshot baby blues. I used to call it eyeballing your way in. Toni's hidden cameras made it a walk in the park.

She kept the old man on a real short leash all night long, brought him in close so his breath fogged my cameras, his hands crawling all over her. The magnetic scanner in her locket found the three Black Visas and the iPhone in his jacket within seconds but it took a little longer to break the pin numbers. Well-off people carry Platinum cards, but dirty rich depravos pack the Black, baby—and they're always hard. The cell number was easier. Pay dirt number two. Smartphones and credit card accounts are clear windows into every mobster's life. You ride the signal like a rainbow, straight to his pot of gold. You use forged passwords and code clones to break through back doors and private e-mail accounts, all that cyber-jazz interlaced and moving faster than the speed of light—all easy to manipulate and bring under a series of simple commands, when you know how it works. What I needed then was the charm bracelet that governed the outer-security array of his fifty-acre estate in the Bellaire Green subdivision of Dallas. Cluster upon cluster of laser beams and motion detectors, wrapped up in a state-of-the-art Gordian knot of electronic deadfalls and hardwire booby traps, not to mention about twenty guys with guns. The smartphone was my key to the kingdom. I had the knot untangled within ten minutes. Toni fixed him with her smile and worked it easy, as the music in the nightclub pounded hard in my headset.

I hate music.

It's like jagged shockwaves in a sea of logic. Like the ringing in my head, since I was shot there. People in Austin talk endlessly about how Beethoven is hard and rough, how Mozart is light and frothy. They talk about jazz and trip-hop and how white people shouldn't play the blues, unless you're Stevie Ray. Me, I want it all to shut up so I can do my work. I hear the patterns in dead silence. And when a sound happens, I know it really means something.

Like the signal from my father, that his men were in position. Ready for my all-clear. Twelve guys in ninja black waiting in the dark just outside the reach of motion detectors, twenty miles away from the club where Toni worked her magic, the old man inviting her for a spin in his new car. A false pulse, just for three seconds, from my console to the main security booth, telling their computer to open the gate.

Three seconds is an eternity to a guy like me.

In just half that time, I had the perimeter scoped and re-routed, using custom blackware rigged to an infiltrator program. Easy cheesy. Outer security stripped in two more seconds. The bad guys dead in the water, waiting for the big thrust. Toni wasn't even out of the old man's car by the time we moved. They were still on their way to the next club, an old man with brand-new candy on his arm tripping the light fantastic, while my father led A-Team in precise formation through the front ranks of bodyguards scattered across the main estate, taking them out quiet, no casualties. Duct tape and razor wire. A couple of tough guys in the bunch. It's always easy to shut them up fast. Big guys go down harder. B-Team was mine, and we were already at the rear servants' entrance, five guys waiting for the signal to move.

That's how it works. You advance with military precision. You need that kind of training. The timing is crucial. One team forward, then the next, each waiting for the other's word to move again, like fists climbing a ladder.

Twenty seconds and the whole perimeter was covered. Guns on every exit. Bodyguards and estate security brought down hard. The main windows rigged to blow. We used to call it getaway insurance. My eyes blinked sweat away as I glanced at Toni's feed on the six tiny video windows across the top of my handheld: My wife running her nose along thick lines of cocaine in the back of a limo, not batting an eye while the old man talked his trash, pouring drinks, spouting the usual greasy gangster crap about all the things he could do for a woman like her. His voice, loud and clear over the wire, as my fingers worked the locks. No music. Just the silence of logic.

We were inside the house within three more seconds. Moving toward the main corridor. The vault six feet below us, just off the main service elevator. My father waiting with his team to cover our escape. Toni in the old man's lap now, seducing him with one arm behind her back, the drugs hardly even affecting her steel-trap mind. My team down the elevator, into the giant steel-walled strong room. The vault, like a silver monolith, glinting off the miners' lights strapped to our heads. My mind and my fingers, working the numbers, forcing myself to be somewhere else, somewhere far away among walls of pure logic, so I couldn't see his hands all over Toni. His hands, filling the tiny video windows now, touching her . . . and . . .

. . . *and* . . .

The wire exploded in my ear—glass and gunfire and screeching tires, twenty miles away, the limo punched into Swiss cheese from the outside by shooters. We were right on the vault when the shit came down. All that rapid-fire chaos, as Hartman's guys stepped in. He'd warned us not to use Toni on this one, and my father told him to go fuck himself. He laughed and said he would get personally involved if we stuck to our guns, and my father told him to go fuck himself again. Hartman's laughter was ringing in my memory and I was cursing our own stubbornness. I never thought he would really do it. When I look back, the whole thing seems so absurd.

Everything went straight down the toilet at our end. The bodyguard in the limo Hartman ambushed must have signaled a backup unit near the estate grounds—one of those X-factors you always try to anticipate, but you're never quite ready for when that ice shock of adrenaline kicks in and the panic oozes up your throat, my father's voice screaming that the world is ending and we fall back to Plan S.

S for *shotgun*.

At the vault, I was done with the retina scanner and halfway through the time lock when I started to hear the dull thump of explosions inside the house. Three of our own men blown down quick, cluster bombs and return fire hacking the bad guys to hell. The magnificent thunder-blitz of cracking artillery, screams and crashes and hard shells clattering on marble floor. Flesh and bone pounded by solid lead slugs—the kind that tear through a car door with muscle to spare. The hard metal-on-metal pump of pistol-grip assault weapons, like deep pistons chunking in unison with the explosions. I held myself in the silent spaces between the muffled blasts and concentrated on getting the goddamn vault open.

While the good old days ended, just out of sight.

Across town, Toni was pulled from the back of the shredded limousine by David Hartman. Her shoulder, bleeding from a 9-millimeter slug scrape, her face betraying nothing. The old man, forced out right alongside her, shot twice in the stomach, stumbling in the cruel grip of dumb animals. Sliver views of Hartman glowering over the big guy on my six video screens, as I finally cracked open the vault door and sent in the team with their duffel bags and hand trucks.

Rule number one when things go south on a job:

Always go for the money first.

If things get real bad you'll need every penny, depending on what side of the world you're on when the fighting starts. And if you make it out clean, you'd better damn well have something to show your employers, especially when they're already pissed off at you.

I leaned against the wall of the corridor just outside the thick steel door that gave so easy, listening to my father shoot it out with guys in plain black suits on the floor above us, knocking off human lives like they didn't matter at all. Ringo Coffin, the gunslinger, the madman. My father, the shining example and our white knight at the wrong end of a suicide tear, screaming orders to his commandos in a war zone.

David Hartman, hovering on the high-definition video windows, towering over the old mob asshole, playing his song and dance.

Telling him who the boss really was.

The old man, cowering in crunches of broken glass, surrounded by dead bodyguards, his limo shot to shit in the alley just behind him. My wife, held fast, her face still cold as steel, forcing back the pain. David's voice, street Southern and smug as all hell:

"*I guess we got us a situation, don't we, old man? But*

every situation has a solution. Just gotta be a creative thinker. I'm a reasonable guy most of the time."

The last shots fired in the living room, just above us. My father's voice on the wire, telling me all clear, but to watch our asses. Like I needed that.

"But what I can't abide is the improper use of a beautiful lady. I told my people they had to handle this situation a certain way and they fucked it up. I guess you can hear me talking, right, Elroy? I told you not to use the lady. You're way too smart a kid to fall back on sleazy tricks. Now, you're on my shit list. You can take that to the bank."

I shook my head. Too absurd for words. David screws up the whole job, then calls me out for it while he gloats in the street like a cowboy, his thick gravy boiling in my ear like everything bad you think of when the word "Texas" springs into your head:

"I mean, hell . . . I can understand it, of course. I know it's such a gosh darn temptation to use the charms of a lady like this. But I'm a traditional guy. Ladies should know their place, after all. You follow me, right?"

My team, just out of the vault now, hauling almost a hundred million in parcels. That kind of money fits in a much smaller space than you might imagine, even when it's in laundered twenties and fifties. I remember rubbing my head, listening to Hartman's voice, waiting for the next all-clear from my father. Then, the sound of a shotgun from the floor above me, blowing a muffled spasm in my throat, just on the edge of hearing, as I looked at the screen, watching Hartman perform:

"But enough about the ladies. Let's talk about this situation we're in."

He stood over the fat old man, who was begging for

his life. I couldn't hear it. Just Hartman's voice, right in the guy's face:

"It's a king-hell shit pickle, ain't it? But it also ain't what you think. See, I could be real obvious about all this—just put some bullets in your head and be done with it. A lot of people like you think I'm a simple man. I'm here to tell you it just ain't so. Men like me demand respect . . . but our needs are also very specific."

The video windows tilted and swayed just a bit, but when the static cleared, I could see three of Hartman's shooters holding the old man down in the alley, forcing his arm onto the concrete, fingers scraping along bits of broken glass. I could hear his old bones creak and break as they manhandled him, and his screams cut through the wire like needles. I winced away from the monitors for just one second.

And when I looked again . . .

The meat cleaver was flashing in Hartman's right hand.

"This is what I need from you, old-timer. A little show of respect. A few fingers and we'll call it even. Whatdaya say?"

David's signature. Stainless steel, stained by blood. The old man, still begging in a broken garble I couldn't quite hear. My father's voice, sounding the all-clear again. Just about time.

Didn't feel like watching what happened next.

I snapped the handheld closed, threw the rig over my shoulder by the leather strap and followed my boys out, trying not to think about what was going on in that alley on the other side of town: Hartman's sick game, all twisted up and dumbed down in the most inhuman gutter. His cruel laughter and his evil redneck drawl, endless and numbing.

Toni told me about it a month later.

She was just a voice on the phone by then.

It was the last time I ever spoke to her.

She said they took all ten fingers right there in the alley, then shot the old man in the head while he begged them not to. Said she was in the hospital with a cracked collarbone for three weeks. And the whole time, Hartman was there, telling her the way things had to be from now on.

Telling her that if she went back to me, I was dead.

That was when she said I had to give her the divorce—or it would be my hands next on the carving block, and then my life. I knew Hartman would do it. He was crazy enough, foul enough. But I wasn't going to let her go.

I'll never let you go, Toni.

Never.

INTO THE FUTURE

When I wake up, I'm slumped on the bed, and the photo is on the floor. I pick it up and fold it again. Stash it under the bed, with my getaway money. Steel myself for the workday ahead. Have to finish the rig. Have to go in hard and strong.

Back to work, boy.

Back to goddamn work.

Before that happens, I open up the laptop on my bedside table. It's a small deck, compact but powerful. I spend a few minutes running the electronic version of the photo through a series of image manipulation programs, searching for digital anomalies—things that might tip off a forgery. You can always tell when someone messes with something in Photoshop because the pixels will be corrupted in specific ways that only happen when a digital brush or a cloning stamp is used. There's nothing like that in this file. But that probably doesn't mean much. Forgers are also experts at covering their tracks. I use a few other programs to enhance the image. I look for details in the room. Other faces.

Things that might look familiar. I can't see anything. I close the laptop and stare off into nowhere.

Back to goddamn work.

The rig is finished a day and a half later. The main deck is a series of X58 military-spec motherboards, with six core CPUs, each with 18 gigs of memory, all hotwired together in a foldout custom chassis that's packed with more software and hardware. Two additional flat-screens, three for the blackware, two for the main run itself. Two keyboards, six removable hard drives, one terabyte each. Wacom pad, virtual mouse, plenty of external power—a Thanksgiving turkey with all the trimmings. Bennett reads off the specs with robot precision. She's fresh from a war, knows her business. A state-of-the-art material girl.

When we're done with the rig, she breaks out a big black briefcase. Spins it and thumbs the latches.

"This is *my* specialty," she says. "Are you familiar with current deep protocol?"

"Some of it."

Deep protocol. Haven't heard that term used in a while. A little dated, kind of like calling the hackers "cyberpunks." It means specialized gear not yet on the professional market. Military-issue. Stuff you're not allowed to talk about, even if you happen to be in the club. *Especially* if you happen to be in the club. She opens the case and it's Christmas morning. Gadgets straight from Q-Branch, nestled in black foam.

She reaches in and holds up a thick slab of black metal and plastic with a two-inch touch screen on it. It's about the size of a smartphone, but has a molded rubber grip, like the handle of a high-end pistol. She clicks on the power and smiles at the technology in her hand.

"This is a Breaker 248 handheld. Cuts through silent alarms. I didn't get to use them on my last tour, but they would have come in damn handy."

"It's a Swiss army knife," I say, plucking it out of her hand. "You wire straight into an onsite power box and it finds channels off the main power grids. It's even got a cell uplink that talks to any satellites that might be watching the area. Shuts it all down. You can also wire remote sensors to kill certain circuit boards on command. This one is last year's model. They replaced it six months ago with the 300."

"I'm impressed. How did you know all that?"

"Friends in low places."

She almost laughs. "I guess you really *were* keeping up on the inside."

"If I'd had one of these bad boys, I could have escaped from that shithole easy. Their whole security grid was PC based."

She takes another slab from the case and holds it up for me. "How about one of these?"

It looks like a modern radiation counter with an LED window, square with a Velcro harness so you can wear it on your arm.

"Kimble .5 Infiltrator," I say. "Scans for anomalies in air density. Little micro-changes that give away a laser beam or a heat sensor."

"They added the strap-on," she says, peeling the Velcro.

If she was making a joke, I let it bounce off my head.

I reach for the nightvision goggles, whistling as I turn the array over in my hands. "Now this is something I haven't seen yet. I had a pair like this, but there's more bells and whistles here."

She aims her finger at the switches and toggles on the side. "It has infrared in three spectrums. So those lasers don't surprise you as much."

"There's easier ways to check for lasers."

"I know. But it never hurts to be fully loaded. The nightvision is Tech Noir."

Wow.

The marines don't even have this yet.

I slip the goggle array quickly over my eyes as she turns off the lights, and I hit the switch that bathes the whole room in neon blue. She reappears instantly out of pitch blackness, the UV spectrum redefining her in shocking detail. It's not like a white ghost in a sea of Day-Glo green, the way most military X-ray specs are. This is high definition. I can see the pores in her skin.

"Mission goddamn Impossible," I say.

"These are new also," she says, and her Tech Noir outline reaches for the case again. I pull the goggle array off my head and fumble blindly for the light switch. She gets to it first. When the room looks normal again, she's opening a metal box, which is full of white plastic strips, about a foot and a half long. Holds one up for me to inspect.

"Look like wrist cuffs," I say. "Your standard Hefty-bag cinchers."

"Not these," she smiles. "They're lined with a chemically treated titanium alloy compound. Impossible to escape from."

"How do you get them off? Usually you cut the plastic with a knife."

"You *don't* cut them. These little buddies are time-release."

"What?"

"You break the seal when they go on, and the compound begins to mix inside the lining. It's on a six-hour reaction delay. So when your time is up, the lining gives and the alloy dissolves."

"Pretty slick, Slick."

She curls one part of her mouth into something halfway smiley. "That's an old one, Elroy. Haven't heard anyone say that since the eighties."

"Wisdom of the ages, young Alex."

She lowers her head, placing the cuffs back in the box. "Just don't call me Alex, okay?"

"Sorry."

Something bad there, something in her childhood. A woman never tells you twice unless it's serious business. I find myself wanting to ask her why she hates her name, thinking about Axl again. But I think better of it.

"Okay," I tell her. "You keep the MI6 gadgets handy for the run inside. You're up on all the latest wrinkles, so it'll go smoother that way. But once we're in the vault, you follow my lead, understand? You jump when I tell you to jump."

"I won't let you down."

"I know you won't."

We run a few final drills. We've plotted the attack run carefully, but I make her go over it again, and then one more time after that. You have to know it by feel. Play it on instinct. Like fists on a ladder. She is tense and quick and efficient. She is a haunted creature, like all the rest.

I decide that I like her.

The truck and the chopper show up the night before we go in—the big flying machine buzzing like a loud metal beast, hovering over the concrete landing platform that looks like a basketball court. The truck just parks.

I watch the beast, thinking about the monster.

I sit in the living room by myself and keep an eye on the cable and local news channels that night. No more murders in the street. Nothing public anyway. If Hartman's killed anyone, he's not gloating about it.

I use the satellite Internet uplink in my rig and try the Fixer through secure channels. Silence. He's either dead or underground. One way or another, my life's savings from being a crook could be long gone. Have to rely on the moment for now. Concerned citizen Jenison and her crazy plan. That scares the holy shit out of me.

Two million for a job that could kill us all.

Tomorrow morning we'll do the final escape drills in the chopper. Then, at midnight, the monster. And after that . . .

I look at the photo of my wife again, the digital version on the machine.

I run it through some pretty sophisticated programs, but come up with nothing new. This ain't no *Blade Runner* future yet, where you can see anything in a blurry picture of not much. I try hard and all I get is an enhanced blur. I turn off the machine and force myself not to think about it. Head to the kitchen for something to drink.

Agent Franklin is standing at the foot of the porch stairs, guarding the perimeter. It's just now dark, eight thirty. Chilly. I push through the squeaky screen door, walk down and offer him a beer. He politely says no thanks and I just stand there for a few minutes. Crack open the Lone Star I was gonna give him and sip absently at the foam.

"I'm sorry I aimed a gun at you," I finally say.

He almost smiles, looking off into the distance. "No worries. It was kind of a tense moment."

"I like to be square with people. Just wanted you to know."

"I appreciate that."

"You're welcome."

Another long silence before I speak again. I pull a slug off the beer through a mouthful of suds. "So . . . was Washington a friend of yours? Or just another grunt?"

"Little of both, I guess. I'm not exactly broken up about him getting killed, if that's what you're getting at."

"Why not?"

"I was in Special Forces. Gulf War."

That explains a lot. Those guys get so jaded. They pull a trigger and nine hundred human beings disintegrate. You don't get friendly on the front lines like that, it's the death of you. Just ask Alex Bennett.

"Well," I say. "I'm sorry he got killed. Seemed like a nice guy."

"Not really." And he laughs. Softly.

I can see this guy's life now. Really damn clearly. Boot camp as a teenager, a couple of tours, discharged into the Texas underworld as a freelancer. Probably in the early nineties. Bennett had it a lot easier. Her hands are softer.

It's just like I figured: Jenison got all her hired guns out of *Soldier of Fortune*, or something like that. Has them on constant rotation like mall security. I ask Franklin about it, and he senses my agenda right off, knows I'm trying to figure out who these people really are. Then he surprises me. Pulls out a cigarette and tells me he lives in a house downtown with a few other ex-grunts. One of them is a woman. They pool their money, live however they can. Franklin is leaving the compound when we go in tomorrow. They're cutting half the people here loose, and he's got another job lined up that he's late for. He says it like a guy getting ready to go wash dishes.

"What kind of job?" I let the question hang in the air a few seconds before I realize how pointless it is. Why should he answer? What does he care?

He surprises me again with a jerk of his shoulder, lighting the smoke. "You know Jenny Rose's Body Shop downtown?"

"Yeah, but I never went there. Don't like strip clubs."

"I'm supposed to be the doorman for the next six months."

"Get out. Seriously?"

"Yep."

"Doorman at a club can't pay as well as this."

"You'd be surprised. I've hired out on a lot of private

security gigs, and one of them didn't even pick up my hospital tab when I got shot."

I have no idea what to say now. The guy who saved my life with a gun the other day is gonna be tossing drunks out the front gate of a titty bar with his bare hands tomorrow. That just seems wrong.

"Well, good luck, man."

I kill the rest of the beer and turn to leave him, but he stops me with a strange smile. "Hang on a second. I got a question for you."

"Yeah?"

He drags on the smoke. I notice for the first time that's it's a Lucky Strike, unfiltered. Didn't know they still made unfiltered cigarettes.

"You said something when we first met that I never understood," he says. "You said our names reminded you of a law office, then you said something about a California roll. What was that all about?"

"You know, Washington and Franklin. Like when you put a hundred dollar bill over a roll of ones so you look rich."

"They call that a nigger roll, man."

Ouch.

I give him a weak grin. "My wife called it a California roll. Then again, she was kind of big on sushi. She was probably hungry that day and short on cash."

That happened a lot back then.

When we were younger.

He almost laughs again. "That's good. For you, I mean. Washington wouldn't have liked the other version at all."

He goes into his jacket pocket and pulls out a card, hands it to me.

The card has his name and a number on it.

He gives me a high nod and says: "Get in touch if you need any legal advice."

I know that nod. It's the one they give you in prison, when you earn respect. I memorize the number and forget about it quickly.

That was another trick Axl Gange taught me.

Memorizing and forgetting.

I go upstairs to my bedroom. Dad is sitting on the tiny single mattress, staring straight into darkness. He has a flask in one hand. I ask him if he's okay and he doesn't say a word. So I ask him again.

"Son," he whispers. "This is an important thing, what we are doing tomorrow. Important for our family."

"I know."

"No, you don't. This is *important*."

I smell the whiskey on his breath. He always scared me when I was a kid, when he did this. That half-wasted fifty-yard zombie stare, the night before a job.

Before I grew up.

"You need to get some sleep, Dad. And don't drink so much."

"The medicine is cheap. I'm an old man at the end of his life. You're still young."

"I'm into my thirties, Dad."

He laughs. "*Forty* is just when you start to live. Try pushing seventy, son. Try waking up every morning with aches you have no idea what to do with. Or not being able to eat a slice of bread because your guts are on strike and it hurts to take a shit."

"I'm sorry, Dad. I guess I just feel old sometimes. Even now."

"This business *makes* us feel old. But there's a lot more living to do."

I flash on a memory of my mother for a long second.

She has black hair and gray eyes, a lazy chin that droops to her skinny neck, a face filled with resignation to the inevitable—she is beautiful in the way plain women are beautiful. In the way hard women are beautiful. I usually don't like to think about her for long. It makes me angry.

I stare at my father, my upper lip trembling. "Do you still think about Louise?"

"I think about her every day. If she were still alive, we'd never be in this mess. I might not have gone to prison, and you might have gone to school like a normal kid. But she's gone and that's that. We just have to roll with the weirdness."

I remember looking right into the eyes of the man who killed my mother, in a courthouse, when I was just five years old. He was driving a car drunk. She was crossing the road with a sack of groceries. The guy was let out of prison after serving three years of a life sentence.

Yeah, man.

Roll with the weirdness.

"When this is over, I'm done," I tell him. "I'm taking my money and if we find Toni, we're gonna live happily ever after. Like normal kids."

"You can't. It's in our blood, Elroy. It's all we know how to do."

"I'll learn to do something else."

"Like what? What would you do with a normal life? Would you even know *how* to live it? That's my fault. For putting you here, in this world. We can retire, but it'll always be in our blood, forever."

"That's not just your cross to bear."

Dad takes a hit off the flask. Then:

"I never trusted Toni, you know that. I thought she was bad for you. The way she would take over the show. But I was wrong. She was bad for *me*. I think I might've even hated her a little, because she was a reminder of what I did that was wrong. Toni was your *lifeline* when I went away, when I failed you as a father. She taught you things I never even bothered with."

"I taught her, too."

"I know." He almost laughs. "You turned out to be a real smart kid. She was behind you all the way. I never was."

"Sure you were. Nothing was normal, but I always knew you were behind me."

"Thanks." He hangs his head and says it like he's ashamed, like it's something I have to give him, just to make him feel better. He looks off into space again.

Then, almost like he's speaking in a dream:

"You'll see Toni again. I promise. What we are doing is *important*."

"I know."

He gives me an absent stare, looking into the past. "Mollie Baker knows, too. That's why he's not with us."

"Mollie Baker's not with us because he can't get over the past, Dad. That's nobody's fault. Just the way things worked out."

He smiles again, and this time it's really enigmatic. Like he knows a secret and won't tell me what it is. Instead, he gets up and puts his arms around me. Says he loves me.

He doesn't say good-bye.

That night, I only sleep four hours, and they come hard. The worst part is a dream about Toni, of course. She still has no face. She mocks me without a voice. A ghost with black glass for hair, a demon in a red dress. Roses and rusty metal. The sting in my head, punishing me. The little blonde girl in the photograph holds her hand and tells me I am a sinner. I tell her I am coming to save her. She doesn't care. I am a fool to wish her back.

Let me see your face.

Please.

I wake up in a room I almost don't recognize. I get up and sit on the floor, looking at the photograph.

Trying to bring her back.

Trying to resurrect her.

So I don't have to do this important thing.

You can't hear much when you're riding in a helicopter. And there's no such thing as silent running in one of these machines. You can feel them in your chest from a mile away and then they sound like a thunderstorm landing on your front lawn—that's why we're not using it for the approach. It's a military model painted black, designed for troop transport. Old and clunky, retrofitted slightly, but it gets the job done. The pilot looks like a scarecrow wearing a flannel shirt and camouflage pants, and he keeps complaining about how there's no LED readout on the panel, no GPS, and the stick is for shit. He wears aviator shades and has a necklace made out of turquoise. I guide myself out of the noise while we're in the air, ignoring the chatter over my headset. The Sarge barks instructions as we run through the final escape drill, keeping the men pumped with dumb machismo. I'm worried about this guy. We've never had a drill sergeant counting off numbers on a job before. Once, we had an ex-military officer with a bunch of maps helping out when we were planning. It was his job, his intel, so we said what the hell? He smelled like cigars, even when he didn't have one in his mouth. He was an idiot, too. I had to get through one of those tricky security corridors in a bank building on that job. You have to use infrared to check for laser beams along the floor. Banks love their laser beams.

The Sarge barks in my ear.

I don't hear it, or the thunder of the chopper.

I take myself out of it.

Into the future.

I see everything but her.

We set back down on the concrete helipad that looks like a basketball court, and I have to check my watch to see how much time has passed. A little under an hour to circle an area the size of a small city. We were hauling ass.

I take note of the date and time, like I always do just before any job.

October 22.

Eleven thirty in the morning.

Sixteen hours to showtime.

The Sarge lines us up just beyond the dull *frapping* of the dying chopper rotors, tells us we all look like badasses, even me. I give him the finger when he's not looking.

I haul my gear into the ready room, followed by Bennett.

She is wide-eyed, poised to strike.

She tells me again that it's gonna be close. I tell her again that we're gonna make it just fine. We go over a checklist while the men load their weapons. The rig is compact enough to carry in a pack on my back, along with all the power sources, screens and external drives. Check, check, and check. I carry the main laptop processor in a medium-sized Gold's Gym bag. It never leaves my sight. Check again, by God.

The boys are all carrying Mossberg 500 pistol-grip assault shotguns, still the most compact and efficient sweep-and-clear hardware you can buy, twenty years after they hit the consumer market. SPAS-12s are bulkier, harder to run with—the Sarah Connor gun. Meaning they look real good when you're sweaty and snarling in an action movie, but in the real world they can be a bitch. Mossberg fits right in the palm of your hand and cleans the area nice. Just in case, our guys have MP-5 Heckler and Koch machine guns on their backs, all notched up to full auto with home conversion kits. You see those in action movies a lot, too, but they're the real deal. Dangerous hardware designed by the Germans and built on an innovative auto-feed mechanism called rollerlocking, which holds each bullet in place and protects the round in a tiny steel brace for the split second it takes to fire—which means you can theoretically unload on somebody underwater, at below-zero temperatures and in high desert heat, where other guns jam and explode. It's kind of fashionable these days for weekend warriors to argue about rollerlocking on the Internet, now that there's a lot of other innovative ways to shred target ranges with automatic weapons, but guys who really kill people still go old school with HK every time. Dad says there's no other machine gun in the world as reliable—unless you wanna do the AK thing, of course, but those are a lot more expensive. He also insists on grenades, tear gas, plastic explosives, the works. We all wear night colors, not camouflage. I'm carrying a Ruger on my hip and that's it, except for my walking-around money. The getaway insurance, taped to my leg.

Inside the tiny package with the cash is the photo of Toni, folded in half.

For luck, I guess.

The Sarge isn't carrying a Mossberg or an HK. He's got a monster hunting weapon, the invincible Remington Supermag Predator shotgun with a laser scope, modified with a fold-out stock. He's literally armed for bear.

My father doesn't speak to me. Part of the SOP in the final hours just before. Talking to each other has always been bad luck, like seeing the bride before the wedding, I guess. He amazes everyone by field stripping his Smith and Wesson automatic .357 down to the last coiled spring and reassembling it on a table in less than four minutes—with less than ten fingers. He used to do that in under sixty seconds. The younger guys on the team back away from him slowly like he's some far-out old freak.

Bennett nods her head reverently at him.

She respects his years, not like these other jerks.

I come over to her, as the other men file out of the ready room, one at a time, most of them muttering weird half curses, the kind dumb muscleheads come up with when they just don't understand something. She shakes her head after them.

"Punks," she says. "I served with assholes like that."

"There's just two kinds of people in the world," I say. "Us and them."

She looks back at my dad at the worktable, as he starts taking apart his gun again. "He's intense just before a run, ain't he?"

"Yeah. He's old school."

"Those kids today all think *classic* is another word for dumb."

"They've never seen my dad work. He's the best."

"I don't doubt it." She shifts her gaze to me, lowering her voice to something more intimate, confidential. "Can I ask you a question?"

"You're going to anyway."

She tilts her head thoughtfully. "Has it always been like this? You and him, I mean?"

"You mean the family business."

"Yes."

Dad hears the question and looks up from his work, eyebrows raised, almost forcing a killer's smile at us.

I take a deep breath. "Before it was him and me, it was him and someone else, and before that it was some other guy with a big gun. Tech thieves didn't really exist before the seventies. Not in the way they do now."

"Seems crazy," she says softly. "We're only on this

earth a few minutes. And so much has changed in our own lifetime."

She's damn right. We define ourselves through technology, we live on the Internet—the most old-fashioned among us do it every day. But the muscle to control the machines wears out eventually. When we get old and it all catches up to us.

Dad shrugs again.

I know exactly how he would answer her right now, so I say out loud for him:

"The gadgets get smaller, but the guns never do."

She throws me a look. "And dead is dead, no matter what, right?"

I suddenly get a flash from an old Peter O'Toole movie, and I find myself overwhelmed with absurdity.

"Dying is easy," I tell her. "Comedy is hard."

She laughs for the first time since I met her, really loud, as if I've just said something funny.

"Pretty slick, Slick," she says.

A few hours left till showtime.

My stomach is doing outside loops.

I go into the farmhouse when no one is paying attention and I visit the restroom. I sit on the closed lid of the toilet and take the key to my safe deposit box out of my pocket. Stare at it. The tiny little thing could be worth three hundred large. Or nothing at all.

So I swallow it, just to be on the safe side.

It goes down like a metal-flavored sleeping pill.

When I was a kid, just out of the army and running with Jett Williams, we came at banks and ATMs empty-handed, like kung-fu fighters in the street. Nowadays, the money is locked up tight. You have to know every security grid on every corner in every damn neighborhood to get away with wahooing an ATM. You have to be able to trick every eye in the sky into seeing something else. They have digital tattletales and silent-alarm sucker punches rigged to every plastic terminal chassis and keypad. Pry one open with a screwdriver and watch your life go up in flames instantly. It's enough to make you long for the good old days, when easy money was printed on the street.

At least enough to make you really damn afraid of the future.

I have one last bit of business while I'm in the bathroom. Something that Axl taught me, of course, and that something is this:

Always go in with confidence, but prepare yourself for the worst.

I slip my ace into my shoe.

Just like he said.

When I finally flush the toilet and come out, my father is watching. He doesn't say a word, just smiles at me. Time to go, son. Our biggest score yet. Our life's work.

I put my hand in my father's.

We nod, like this is all we have left, this last Coffin Run.

Maybe it is.

THE FACE OF GOD

11:50

October 22 is almost over as we bail from the truck a half mile from the site, split into three teams. I'm on A-Team, with Dad and Bennett. B-Team circles the fence, two men, one from either side. The idea is that they take out any security walking the perimeter and close on the roof, where the main power boxes are located. Then they'll stand by and wait for my signal. C-Team is the Sarge, who'll go in through the front gate with one other man, which is where the two security guards posted there will run into their guns. They're hauling the drill rig on a custom gurney—six hundred pounds of heavy metal on mechanized, all-terrain wheels. My team gets to the primary transformer in three minutes, which is just beyond the fence. I pry the lid and Bennett wires up the 248 handheld, deactivating the alarm systems between the gate and the front glass entranceway to the building. She deep-sixes the power in the fence, too. It's Saturday-morning cartoons, man. Nice and easy. They didn't even have a silent alarm out here. Inside the building, it's a different story. There are five places you can call in the cops, silent toggle switches that are manually controlled by the security guards. Motion sensors on the vault floor. It's all controlled by one little circuit board inside the transformer box, and she gets to it real fast. Attaches a wire on a clip to a mini-processor/transmitter so she can kill the circuit with a remote command on our final approach. Our boys on the roof will shut down the power in the building right after that, and the outside lights. The two guys watching the front desk are the only security the place has on the inside. They'll be in the dark until we get to them. B-Team leader crackles over the headset, reporting in. They've just finished their sweep. Nobody's home. I tell him we're all clear at this end. They roger out and move for the roof of the building now, over the fence. The Sarge whispers in my ear next, says the guard post is terminated. That's our signal from C-Team. I hope he didn't kill them. The plan was to drag the security guys into the woods and tie them to trees. During the dry run, he used the words "guard post secured." I'm worried about this guy.

12:05

October 23 just started, and we're three minutes behind schedule as we get to the front gate. The Sarge and his man are waiting in the little yellow booth. The gate clatters open as they come out to meet us. We use nightvision on our approach. Tech Noir. Bennett hits the 248 remote switch and the silent alarm system inside the building goes. That's right when the two guys on the roof use bolt cutters grounded to a custom circuit sensor to kill everything else. The whole joint gets real dark, real fast.

12:11

Still behind schedule, we get to the main glass entrance doors. The two guards are literally stumbling around inside. They can't see a damn thing and have no idea what's going on. Through my goggles, they look like blind neon video warriors in a blue room. The five of us walk right in, single file through the front door, which isn't even locked. The guard on the left hears the door open and the sound of our footfalls but he doesn't draw his sidearm. Neither does the other one. These guys were trained at Walmart. The Sarge uses the butt of his Predator gun to knock both of them cold with one clean sweep. Two of our men get the rent-a-cops on the floor, secure them with those titanium-plastic wrist-cuff things. The Sarge tells his men to check the perimeter twice before we move again.

12:30

Vault floor. Basement level. We take the stairs. The Sarge and his boys grunt with the heavy equipment. Bennett is a sleek red blur at my elbow, fast and efficient. The room has red emergency lights burning in it, and those lights remind me of her hair. That worries me because the motion sensors are supposed to be deactivated. I tell everybody to hang in the stairwell while I scope it out. I try infrared, then adjust the Tech Noir. Normally, I would light a cigarette and blow smoke into the room—it's the low-tech approach that usually works best when you're looking for grids and heat sensors.

But we have the MI6 Corps of Gadgeteers on our side tonight. So I give the signal to Bennett and she checks the perimeter with a sweep from the Kimble Infiltrator on her arm. No lasers. No motion readers. Nothing. Looks like we already cleaned house. As we step into the room, I tell her to check the 248 remote, make sure the circuit is still closed down at the transformer outside. Everything's cool. The front of the vault is typical, just like in the photos and digital simulations I saw. Dual spinning combination lock system, all solid steel. Easy to cut through. But guarded by a very treacherous mistress. Time to set up shop.

12:40

We pry up the floor, hunting for the main power cables. The vault is on an indie source, probably a generator way offsite. We have to kill that last, after I do the time locks. I unpack the drill rig myself, inspect it carefully. The array has a powerful suction system that keeps it on the floor right where we need to bore the holes. I use a grease pencil to draw a map for everybody. Three key points with the 10-millimeter titanium alloy, and then a final one with the 20-millimeter diamondback, dead center. Bennett unpacks her tools and starts taking apart the main terminal that controls the entrance to the vault. What happens here during normal business hours is that an employee sits down in the comfy little swivel chair and slides his code card through a reader, then two other guys turn their keys simultaneously in the slots on either side of the console—that unlocks the system and allows the guy sitting in the chair to punch in the entry codes. The men who designed this amusing little terminal have no idea how simple it is to use a set of screwdrivers and power tools to replace their screen with yours. But that's the easy part. I use a handheld diamond drill to cut through the two locks while Bennett starts setting up the rig. Once we're past the main panel on the vault terminal, though, it's all about being experienced enough to know what wires to look for, and which circuits to intercept, how to trick the meaty parts into thinking it has a new interface. There's no security at all on the lock system itself. All it does is turn on the computer. Child's play. Bennett checks the 248, just to be on the safe side. Still no silent alarm. Dad says someone needs to walk the perimeter again while I work, secure the whole building. The Sarge tells my father congratulations, he's been elected, and sends one of his men with Dad, up the stairs, tells him to keep in touch—he talks to his boys on the roof and tells them to meet the old man in the main lobby. He puts Dad in charge of the recon unit. I hear two men give a quick *yessir* over the headset. They sound like robots.

1:15

Took us way longer than I thought, even with three grunts working, to find the main power cables under the floor. There's a secondary power backup, too. Didn't see that coming. Wasn't in any of the diagrams. It's encased in a lead pipe with a bunch of warning stickers on it. Shit. I scan the pipe and it's hot. Some kind of synch pulse along the lead casing, separate from the power source inside. Could be an independent alarm, maybe something nastier. We'll have to rig it all to blow, but that's our last resort. Kill the power too early and the big door stays shut. The Sarge tells his men to break out the C-4, five pounds of it. When we set the stuff off, we can take cover in the stairwell or on the floor above us. That much plastic explosive will shred anything living in this room, along with all the primary and secondary circuitry. Bennett has the rig set up. I've almost got it wired in right. Almost, but not yet.

1:35

Sweat in my face. My heartbeat in my ears. The hum in my skull that was never there before. The plate in my head, cold and vibrating. This is taking way too long. Every time I look, there's another circuit I need to kill, or another cluster of wires I need to clip and redirect. Dad comes over the headset and tells us the perimeter is secure. The Sarge says he's going up to check the grounds personally and instructs the men from the roof to relieve his team down here and for Ringo to cover the stairwell. Everyone says they copy that. I solder a lead in place, and the iron slips in my grip. It burns me. I hear Axl in my ear: *Goddammit, kid. Bum-rush the show here. Just twenty minutes . . .*

2:00

I make it in under the gun and as soon as the clock hits two, I click the mouse and my screen flashes all clear. I'm in the system by the skin of my ass. A pre-recorded female voice comes over a speaker in the room, telling us that the code key has been activated and there is now danger and she repeats the word *danger* five times. Three hours now. No room for error, can't lag behind. One wrong move and we all die. My fingers move fast over the keys. It was always this easy. It was never this hard.

2:10

The first firewall is mean. I use one of the Destroyer's old blackware tricks—you run the program, then copy it once you're inside, so there's a ghost in the machine gumming up the works. The security profile gets confused and lets down its guard for just about a half-second, then it starts to get infected while I go for its throat. The first algorithm is a series of zeroes and ones I have to count manually. I read it off to Bennett, who records my voice on a handheld digital unit. I have her play it back to me a few minutes later when I break the second wall and the machine asks me for the entry code. My fingers move as fast as my voice from the recorder narrates the pattern. I see Bennett shake her head, incredulous. I don't think she's ever seen a hacker talk that fast in the real world before.

2:25

Two down. Next wall is a lot tougher. It wants an entry code, then a PIN and then the social security numbers of the two men with the keys. I get through that part easily. I designed the infiltrator program myself while I was in prison, based on something the Destroyer once came up with about random number generators. I run through a billion combinations in one minute while another program stalls the time limiter. You would normally only have twenty seconds to enter the code. The SS numbers are also easy. We had those ready to go, all five hundred employees on rotation in this building. I enter all of them in one fast data spike, like a doctor giving a shot of Thorazine. Then I'm inside the security protocol and its numbers are coming at me so fast I almost get dizzy for a second. Something burns in my head, the smell of rose petals haunting me, just a little. Just enough. My heartbeat speeds up. Faster now. *Faster* . . .

2:36

Next level. Whoever built this thing is a goddamn genius and I want to kill him. I tell Bennett to heat up the Miracle Machine, which she ports in to the rig through a custom adapter that talks to the whole system in a real sweet voice. An angel's voice. Come on, baby, let me have it. I have big tits and a nice ass and I owe you three wishes. Nine different viruses come straight at me. I see them like toxic gas clouds on the second monitor. I send a tapeworm program after them while I crunch the numbers. It's all math at this level. I read some equations off to Bennett. She solves them on her machine, reads them back to me. I get the last number in too late. All my work goes to hell, and the numbers change. It's a smart little bastard. I start again, and almost get it again. Shit goddamn . . .

2:45

I feel like someone just kicked my ass, but after three tries the fourth firewall finally goes. A stinging in my heart. The ringing in my head. I tell the men in the room to heat up the drill rig and they get to work on the first three spots I drew with greasepaint. I tell them to go slow, I'm behind by about five minutes. The drill bit makes a really loud noise as it eats into the steel, but I don't hear it much. I'm in the system deep now. Fifth level. The hardest one yet. The numbers come at me and I fight them with blood in my eyes.

3:12

The drill stops. I tell them to change to the 20-millimeter diamond bit and wait for my command before they turn it on again. I'm past the five security protocols, and I even made up for a few lost minutes on the last one. It's the time locks now. They're always a living hell, and these are the worst I've ever seen—treacherous, time-sensitive deadfalls, all interconnected by a series of complicated algorithms that have to be shut down at specific, automated moments on the clock, all in sequence, before they give way at another specific, automated moment. You can only get into this vault three times a day. It's all worked out to the last microsecond. I have to trick the datastreams into thinking they're moving forward in time, and I'm running every program I've got to do it. Blackware screaming on top of blackware. A virus gets past my firewall, and Bennett has to kill it. I'm getting shredded. Nothing I try works.

4:00

The Sarge comes over the headset and says I have less than one hour left. I tell him everything's fine. My father comes back into the room through the stairwell. He doesn't say a word. He's seen me sweat before. He's never seen me with blood in my eyes—virtual blood, I mean. This is the worst one ever. The guys on the drill ask him if they should be running away. I tell them that might be a good idea. The Sarge crackles over the headset, says nobody moves. A data spike comes at me and almost gets through when he says that and I yell at everybody to shut the hell up.

4:15

I hit a wall hard, and a row of numbers comes at me that look important. I see them and they burn in my memory, as I count off to Bennett. She records my voice and I use the numbers again, feed them back into the system. It's not a code, as it doesn't kill the time locks. I try a variation, start using my number scrambler to search for algorithms in the pattern. The wall keeps coming back. The row of numbers. Bennett tells me it's a decoy, says we have to try another way in. I tell her I know what I'm doing. I've beaten a thousand time locks, just like this one, and the numbers never lie. She yells at me that I'm wrong. I yell back at her to shut the hell up. My head starts screaming. The smell of roses almost overwhelms me in a quick sweet stab. I hardly fight it back.

4:20

Forty minutes on the clock and the time lock's still kicking my ass. It's a steel wall. Still the same row of numbers, taunting me with a quick death. I try another combination to unscramble it, using the stacked number crunchers on disc drive Z. It would kill any normal protocol dead in the water. Doesn't even make a dent in this one. I stack another attack and it brushes me aside. Bennett tells me we need to abort. There's no way past the time locks and there's no time to look for anything else. The numbers are some kind of decoy code. I almost scream at her, but she sees the look on my face as the machine beats me again, and it hits her hard.

4:45

The Sarge's voice starts barking orders to his men over the headset. Five minutes and we run. I get my ass handed to me one more time. It's solid state, but there has to be a way. Axl always said there's a way into anywhere, past any wall, through any lock. And when all else fails? Go for the obvious. What's the obvious here? What am I missing? Goddammit, *what the hell am I missing*? What do those numbers mean? Why isn't this working? Why can't I get past them? Ammonia and raw metal slithers in my throat. The buzzing in my head turns the plate to ice and tries to bore a hole in my brain. The smell of roses replaces everything in the world. I fight it hard. Can't lose it now. Goddammit . . . Toni . . . *I won't fail you* . . .

4:46

I try one more run, right at the wall, and it bounces me back like a hardball. The row of numbers are the key to this whole thing, but every second I spend on it is costing me my life. I'm swimming in lakes of rose petals and the buzzing of a Skilsaw. Bennett tells me it's a decoy again and I still don't believe her. It can't be that simple. The guy who built this thing wouldn't hide it in plain view like that. Would he? Roses. Gunmetal. Buzzing . . . *dammit shit FUCK* . . .

4:47

The Sarge tells us to get the hell out of there. It's useless. Mission scrubbed. This whole place is coming down. The men move for the stairwell. I stay at my console. I steel myself against the agonizing pain that shoots through my head. Bennett says we should move, but I won't move. I'm not even *in* this room. I'm inside myself. Moving through the pain. Ignoring the smells. Seeing and feeling only the numbers. The code. The numbers don't lie. But what is it trying to say? I can't beat this machine. *Yes, I can.* I still have almost ten minutes. Focus up. NOW.

4:48

The Sarge says if I don't move it, he'll order his men to drag me out of there. *You will all die if you don't run now.* The chopper is landing outside. I can hear it over the headset. *Get the fuck out of there now.* No, I tell him. The solution is so simple, I'm just not seeing it. We still have time, just enough time. My fingers land on the keys and I break the numbers, then they reorganize and come back at me again in the original pattern, like a demon that transforms and then finds its true face, snarling the same old snarl, taunting the same old taunt, again and again, until you're crazy and dead . . .

4:49

The Sarge comes over the headset again and orders Bennett to shut down the console, orders his men to take command and escort me and my father to the chopper. Bennett says that's the whole shooting match—we have to run, and we have to do it now. I see her hand drift toward her sidearm. The other men in the room go for their weapons, too, but my father quickdraws his Smith and Wesson real fast, drops both of them into his sights like he's using his right hand. He smiles. Nobody's going anywhere.

4:50

The air freezes. Mexican standoff. Bennett's hand stops, halfway to the pistol on her hip. She tells me to abort. The code is a decoy. We are all gonna die if I don't give it up now. I can't hear her voice. The solution is right there. My fingers move fast. I ignore the buzz. It was never this hard . . . *never this hard . . .*

4:51

The two grunts try to reason with my father, one of them going for his shotgun. My father hisses as he cracks off a warning shot. Thunder fills my ears. The bullet smashes a hole in the metal wall, just over their shoulders. He holds them unflinchingly in the firing line, tells the Sarge over his headset that he will kill the first man who comes down after us through the stairwell. If my son says he can break this thing, he can damn well break this thing. We're going through with it to the bitter end, so fuck you. Nobody draws on him.

4:52

Still no answer from the console. I start clicking keys again and get my ass kicked again. The soft female voice says there is *danger, danger, danger.*

4:53

The Sarge screams at us over the headset. Get the hell out of there. At least send my men out. *Do it now. You are all going to die.*

4:54

My father nods and sends the two grunts through the stairwell. He's not a monster—not like me. Bennett doesn't move. She stays with us. Her face is filled with red determination. My eyes are filled with the future, not this room, not the roses, not the ice-cold metal lodged in my head . . . I'm going to see your face again, Toni . . . one way or another . . .

4:55

My screen shows a red flag. A circuit just tripped inside the system. A really bad one. I talk to the machine, tell it not to kill us. It doesn't listen. This is the final countdown. In five minutes, the second circuit will tell the vault to explode. I won't give up. I tell Bennett and my father to hit the stairwell.

4:56

The machine beeps at me. It knows I'm doomed. Bennett still stays with me. I tell the girl there's no need for her to get killed, too. Run. Get out while you can. My father motions her to the door. Bennett won't move. She says there's no way to beat the machine, not the way I'm doing it now . . . and finally . . . the buzzing in my head begins to recede . . . the smell of roses backs off, just a little . . . and I start to hear her. But it's already too late.

4:57

Three minutes. The most obvious solution has eluded me. It's been right in front of me the whole time. The code *is* a decoy, just like Bennett said. There's simply no way on earth to trick this time lock. I would have found it by now. It's not even on the computer. It has nothing to do with numbers and algorithms. It has to be old school. I tell my father we have to blow the C-4 on the lead pipe. He tells me if we blow it while the time locks are still up, the door won't open, and I tell him that's exactly what we're supposed to think. *Because they knew I was coming.* Do it now or we're all dead. He doesn't hesitate when he hears me say that. Nods and moves like a robot. Hits the switch on the thirty-second timer and it doesn't work.

4:58

Jammed out. The detonator, screwed up by the hot pulse inside the lead casing. We can't blow the pipe. I see my father's face drain white. He starts reworking the sequence on the keypad but it's useless. Hartman, you poisonous snake. Your people designed this death trap just for us, didn't they? The female voice slices the air like a laser—*danger, danger, danger*—and I half expect to hear that awful fat bastard laughing at us over the speaker system. My father backs away, quickly loading an incendiary round into his Smith and Wesson, aiming right at the big clump of plastic explosive, yelling at us to get in the stairwell. Bennett runs for it. I'm right behind her, pulling my father with me. He stands fast, telling me to run . . .

4:59

. . . telling me he's sorry.
For everything.
He tells me to kiss Toni for him when I see her.

No.

No, goddammit.

You're not gonna die for me.

Not here, not like this.

I won't let you die because of my mistake.

I grab him again and it's desperate, as I scream the words—but he spins with the butt of his gun, and something like a rock in a fast wheeze of wind smashes me in the forehead.

Bam.

The world goes almost black as the pain thunders above everything.

I drop to the floor in slow motion.

Seconds pound like hours.

Someone is pulling me back across the floor.

Toward the stairwell.

My breath leaves my body all at once.

I hear his voice shout back at me as I begin to lose consciousness . . . but it's clear as day in my head . . . the last words of my father . . . the man who made me . . . the man who failed me . . . the man who brought us all to this final moment . . .

"I'm sorry, son . . ."

. . . and the whole room behind us explodes.

5:01

I hear the C-4 go off just at the edge of being awake. It's still ringing in my ears as I struggle up from blackness. My forehead swells where he hit me, to save my life. It was me or him.

Dad . . .

I'm in the stairwell with Bennett and we're still alive. The vault didn't blow. Only the power to the vault, and the time lock with it. The door of the stairwell is ripped halfway off its hinges from the concussion of the explosion, jammed into the wall at a weird angle. Bennett has to use her shotgun to clear the way. I don't even hear the blast of the 12-gauge round, my ears are ringing so bad. The door falls into the room and lands with a ten-ton crunch. I struggle to my feet and follow her back in.

Dad . . .

Nearly the whole inside of the room has been obliterated, scorched. Peeled back in layers that expose the circuitry and wire and cables. There's no body.

Not even a corpse for a casket.

Never a coffin for a Coffin, you always said.

I always knew it would be this way, too.

I thought the same thing back in jail, when they told me you were gone and I would never see you again. Now, it's for real.

Forever.

Dad . . .

Goddamn.

And it's my fault. If I had listened to the girl. If I had run when they told us to. If I had never let them talk me into this crazy shit. If our lives had been normal, the way you always said they should be. But everything always goes away. It's all temporary. Family is disposable . . . *love cannot stay* . . .

The rage thunders in me.

I want to kill everyone. I want revenge.

No.

Calm down.

Let it go . . .

But I can't.

I killed my father.

She sees me about to blow, sees the redness in my face and eyes, my teeth grinding in the awful burn of the moment, everything bad surrounding me in a sizzle. And she puts her hands on my shoulders, her voice eerily serene:

"Take it easy. We're okay."

Teeth gritted harder. Reeling it in.

Just barely.

The vault is blackened from the explosion, but it's open. I was right about the indie power source—didn't realize it was controlling the sequence on the time locks until too late. That's what the secondary pulse inside the lead casing of the power line was. I went through all that punishment for nothing. My dad died for nothing.

I killed him.

No. Don't think that way.

He died for us.

For you and me, Toni.

Just don't think about it at all.

We open the thick vault door the rest of the way. It's like pushing your stuck car into a filling station. It would have been easier with more men. They're probably miles away by now. Radio silence. We'll find a way back somehow. Once they figure out the building didn't blow, they'll be looking for us anyway.

This is so bad.

Inside, the vault has smooth walls, no shelves. I run my hands across the shiny steel, looking for hidden switches, depressions, anything. Nothing at all.

Except.

In the center of the room is a black metal suitcase. I kneel down in front of it and flip the latches. It's not even locked. It might explode in my face if I open it.

I don't care. I have to look.

I'm still alive two seconds later.

Inside the suitcase are seventeen flat plastic casings, about three inches square, with USMB ports. Portable hard drives. Latest technology, a terabyte each. The drives are all nestled in custom foam slots inside the case. There's a couple of flash drives, too. I run my fingers along the rows of shiny black.

Click, click, click.

I snap the case shut and say out loud:

"So this is it?"

Click.

Hammer down hard, right behind me.

And the voice of the Sarge, not on the headset:

"I'm afraid it is, kid."

I put my hands up and turn around slowly. I'm looking right down the barrel of his Ruger SR9. At this range it'll remove my heart and feed it to him. His Predator is slung on his back. He wants accuracy, not a two-for-one sale. A couple of his men are just on the other side of the door, Hecklers ready to sling hash.

"You dumb son of a bitch," the Sarge hisses at me. "What were you trying to pull? You could have gotten us all killed."

"You didn't have to hang around. I told you to run."

"Yeah, you did, didn't you?" He sneers when he says that, as if I'm making some kind of smartass remark. Spits on the floor. "Where's Daddy? He buy the farm or what?"

"Something like that."

"I'll be sure to send flowers. Now step away from the merchandise."

Bennett puts up one hand. "Hey, man, calm down."

"Shut the fuck up. *You're* on my shitlist, too."

I don't move.

The Sarge bores into me with his eyes burning white. "I said, step *away* from the suitcase. Come over here next to the girl. You two get real cozy. And get your hands where I can see them. Do it *now*, both of you."

He re-aims his gun right at my head.

I don't move.

"I'm giving you to the count of three, you little fuck."

I don't move.

Dad . . .

This is what you died for?

This was the important thing?

"One . . . *two* . . ."

"Okay, okay, whatever," I finally say.

And I take two steps to the left, next to Bennett.

"Get in here," the Sarge calls to the two men with machine guns. "You guys are in charge of the package.

Keep an eye on our friends, too. These kids are *dangerous*. Ain't ya?"

I don't answer him.

Keep my hands in the air, keep my eyes on the guns aimed at us.

The two grunts beat their feet inside the vault, one of them sliding his machine gun onto his shoulder by the strap, the other keeping a bead on me. The smaller of the two has brown hair and a big scar on his nose, looks twenty or so. The one with his gun still up doesn't look like anything. A ghost in ninja black. He holds his position near the vault entrance. That means one still left, probably covering the stairwell. I'm in a spiderweb.

Scarface grabs the suitcase, steps back behind the Sarge.

The one aiming his Heckler near the door makes a scared noise. "We should get out of here, sir. We're six minutes behind—"

"Not just yet," the Sarge says, taking two steps closer to us with the gun.

"This is *insane*!" Bennett spits. "You can't shoot us!"

"Maybe you're right and maybe you ain't . . ."

He holsters the gun. Pulls that big Rambo knife off his hip.

". . . and maybe there's just not enough room on the express."

Takes two more steps. One more. Almost to us.

Right in Bennett's face now:

"You wanna see the face of *God*, little lady?"

The knife, two inches from her right eye. Closer.

"She did her job," I say. "This isn't the army."

"You're right, boy, it ain't. *This is resurrection.*"
The knife stabs toward her.

The hard scent of erased memories hits me again, and something short-circuits in my brain, slowing every-thing in the world down . . . as the knife glimmers in one white-hot instant . . . a million thoughts super-colliding and pinwheeling back like bullets on a high wind . . . and I feel all of those thoughts and none of them *as they hover at the edge of the Sarge's blade* . . .

And time freezes.

The razor-sharp point one micromillimeter from Bennett's unflinching eyeball.

My fist stabs out.

Catches his wrist in midair.

And then . . .

He almost howls when the crack of bone hits him, senses my training too late, his fingers going dead and letting loose the blade just as I swing up with my right fist, into his jaw. He bites hard through his lower lip. Chokes on a piece of it, blubbing on bloody backwash. Bennett stumbles back into the wall, still damn near paralyzed by the shock of the moment, as I put my palms in the Sarge's midsection, knocking him back into the two guys on the vault door. It's a pushing-hands technique they taught me when I was nineteen, sends your target flying backwards on his own feet with a lot of momentum. When he hits his men, they stumble through the door like ten pins, their heads knocking together. One of them bounces and slides along the floor, dazed. Someone's finger hits the trigger, can't tell who, and a single bullet plays the lottery with us, zanging back and forth all over the steel walls. I hear it buzz past my face like an insect in the half second before I go for the blasted floor of the vault room outside in a roll. There's a meaty slap behind me as the bullet strikes home and Bennett makes a noise like she just swallowed a bug.

I hear her hit the floor as I come up in a fighting crouch, the ghost in black stumbling on his feet, swinging around with his weapon, firing blind from his tumble on the floor. His next shots cut into the Sarge and nearly tear him in half—a quick burst of thunder and a sharp spray of blood and human debris blowing across the room like a slash of black-and-pink and red all over.

Sergeant Maxwell Rainone stumbles and falls, deader than hell.

I roll again and another insect buzzes at me, missing my head by inches.

Just out the corner of one eye, I see Bennett waffling on the blasted floor, blood oozing from her arm. She's struggling to get to the shotgun hanging off Rainone's back.

Scarface swims in semi-consciousness on his feet, trying to put himself in the game again, with the knockout reflex screaming at him that he's defeated. Before he can figure out what happens next, I shoot up from the floor, grab his left leg in a scissor clamp and hit the lower fibula just right so that it blows the bone in half through his skin and clothing. The crack is like a gunshot. No blood jets out, just jagged ivory teeth. I'm shoving him in front of me like a shield as I do that, the Black Ghost firing and firing, the bullets tearing at Scarface, not getting through his Kevlar. I duck behind his body and jerk my eyes shut as he takes all six shots, the sheer raw concussion hitting him like anvils, crushing everything inside his rib cage to jelly. I hear the gun fire three more times, bombs that make me deaf. Scarface doesn't scream, his lungs collapsing. Then, suddenly, there's another roar of thunder and the shooting stops. I hear a body drop to the floor. I don't see what happens to the Black Ghost because I'm still hiding behind my human shield—which is dead meat on two feet now.

I let the body fall and it slops into the scorched floor of the big room.

I see that the Black Ghost is dead on the floor, too, swimming in a lake of his own blood, half his head erased. Someone shot him and it wasn't me. Maybe it was God.

Maybe—

Clack.

Heavy metal on heavy metal.

I look up to see a long black tunnel to nowhere aimed in my face. The guy from the stairwell, his pal Heckler locked and loaded.

"Wait," I tell him, and then I try to say something else, but the sound chokes at the back of my throat as he pulls the trigger.

Too late. I'm already dead, point-blank.

Then something goes *click* and does a sickening crunch inside the gun—and I can't even believe it happens. It's a million to one, the sound of steel snapping in one millisecond as I stare my death right in the eye.

The sound of the rollerlock jamming.

The bullet tries to fire and explodes in the chamber, blowing his hand off.

It's like a white hot *zang* that erases time for a half second, then expands into a high-pitched shriek of tearing flesh and metal, a piece of bloody shrapnel whizzing by my face as I duck the spray.

And then his forehead bursts apart.

He plunges backwards in a meaty thunder and everything he ever had on his mind rains down after him, his blown-to-hell machine gun falling uselessly at his side. He joins his buddies on the floor, all three of them stiff and bloody—wreckage among the wreckage.

Bennett slumps against the open door of the vault, the shotgun smoking.

I almost smile at her.

She lets the gun fall to the floor and clutches her shoulder, which is perforated and soaked through with arterial red now. Starts pulling a field pack off her back, racing to stop the bleeding.

"Fuck," she says, huffing through the pain, her voice fast and desperate. "God *damn fuck* . . ."

I can't think of a thing to say. She looks at the two men she just shot in a sort of detached shock, unwrapping bandages from the kit.

She's never killed anyone.

She's never caught a bullet before.

I can feel it, like electricity in the blasted room.

Three tours on the front lines, death surrounding her from all sides, and she's never had to pull the trigger herself. The horror of it is scrawled on her face, red disbelief glowing bad in a galaxy of freckles. Like a jaded kid who finally just grew up, real fast. I don't envy her that. I'm forcing myself not to think about it. We have bigger fish to fry.

I switch my headset to an outside frequency and start yelling at our ride:

"Mission scrubbed. We're coming out."

The pilot crackles back and he sounds really nervous.

We come out of the building exactly twenty minutes late. Bennett's right arm is useless, trussed up in a sling. The chopper is still waiting. I'm hauling the package from the suitcase in the Gold's Gym bag and part of my rig is on my back, the most important part. The part we'll need later. The pilot looks worried behind the stick. He turns to us as we board the big machine, his words all slurring together in a panic: "You okay? Where's the rest of the guys?"

I pull the pistol off my right hip just as Bennett closes on him from behind, shoving steel against the side of his head.

"Don't get any ideas," she whispers in his ear. "I know how to fly one of these, too."

He freezes. "What the hell are you doing?"

I get closer to him. "Hedging my bets."

GO TO ZERO

Ten miles from the Texas Data Concepts building, we force the pilot to set us down in an open field just off a winding country back road. The sun still isn't up. I tell the man flying the ship to bail and Bennett holds him in her sights while I lash his right arm to a thick tree limb with the titanium plasti-cuffs and pat him down. I take two LG Rumor Touch smartphones and a pistol. He was loaded. I pull the batteries out of the phones and shove them in my bag. It'll be hours before the cuffs dissolve, and hours on top of that before this guy reaches anything that looks like civilization. By then we're long gone, me and Bennett. I've already phoned in our ride to the underground.

It takes us thirty minutes to get to it.

Bennett flies the machine like a one-armed bandit.

I know a few crooks in Houston. Some of them still owe me favors. I have all their phone numbers memorized.

Kim Hammer is a gangbanger who used to be a man—she was a weird piece of work before the operation, but now she's an even stranger lady who still gets respect from the homies and the white-collar mob guys in this town. That's mostly because of her connections inside the Treasury Department that allow her to get unregistered machine guns and other army goodies—plus drugs, fake papers, all the usual gangster business. When I text her that I have a slightly used helicopter for sale, she tells me where to land that bitch and I name my price. She only haggles a few minutes.

After I use the pilot's cell, I pull the batteries again, smash it and toss what's left out the window. Do the same with his backup phone. Even destroyed, those things can lead the bad guys right to you, if they know what to look for and where. I once pulled a trace from an Apple satellite off a ghost signal hovering above the remains of a gutted iPhone that had been snapped in half and tossed in a gutter. It's hard to kill one of those. Better to leave them behind and stay off the grid. LG technology isn't as advanced as the Mac people, but you never can tell. Wireheads get smarter every day. Anyway, I can get new phones at Walmart. They'll be a lot less dangerous to use, too.

As the first rays of morning begin to haunt the horizon, we hover over a concrete landing strip at a compound near the woods just outside of Sharpstown.

I look at my watch and note the date and time:

7:30 A.M.

October 23.

Damn.

Bennett's shoulder is killing her—literally—but she

lands us smooth and easy. There's a Cyclone fence hanging in gnarled tatters on all sides of the tarmac, an abandoned building that looks like the remains of an old factory in the center of everything. Kim's people will meet us here soon. She said it would be an hour. She said this place was secure.

But first things first.

I get out of the chopper and start screaming.

The rage rises to the surface and consumes me under the terrible blowback of the whirling helicopter blades, so loud and raw and primal that my heart threatens to blow and my throat skins itself, like paper peeling from the walls. I fall to my knees and pound the cement with my fists. Red heat rises from my body in the maelstrom. And then everything else explodes, too . . . all the years I worked for Dad, all the years he tried to pay me back however he could, for rolling with the weirdness, the jobs where I watched dozens of men die at his command, die because it was necessary, die because he was a killer, die because he was protecting me, and I hate what I see in those memories, I hate him for being that way, for pulling me down with him, for putting me in that vault with him, for standing there and letting himself die while I lived.

A voice . . . breaking over everything:

Come back.

Back away from this.

It will be the death of everything you love to give in now.

"Goddammit, snap out of it, Elroy!"

The voice breaks over everything, and I realize it's not in my head.

It's not the voice of my masters.

It's not the better angels.

It's the woman.

Bennett.

The storm that surrounded us is gone, and the air is still, the prop wash vanished in the cool Texas breeze. I'm on my knees and my knuckles are shredded and bleeding. The helicopter has stopped rumbling, the blades still and silent. And the woman's voice is ringing over mine as her hand grips my shoulder . . .

. . . and . . .

. . . just a little at first . . .

. . . I back the rage off.

I listen to my own heart, which wanted to explode just a few seconds ago. I use that sound to pull myself to shore, the slime and the fire still clinging to me. It hurts. But I make it back. Just a little at first. Then a little more . . .

I look up and I see Bennett. She is kneeling next to me, terrified and bleeding. There are tears on her face. There are tears on my face, too.

For my father.

Dad . . .

I close my eyes and I see him one last time. I see him spinning with the butt of his gun, to club my lights out. I see the look on his face behind the blow. The look that begs me to forgive him.

The look that redefines everything . . .

I see him when I am five years old, sitting in that courtroom—a terrible place that smells like chalk and looseleaf notebook paper and the lies of men. I see his face when they sentence the redneck trash who killed my mother. The face of defeat.

I failed you, son.

I see him when I am eight years old, my heart much colder now, filled with hard realities that only come when you live on the street and eat garbage—we've lived on the street for six months now, moving from place to place, and now he's telling me he has to go away again, for a long time, that he might even be killed on the inside. I have to be a man now and take care of myself. I see his face when he tells me it's all his fault.

I failed you, son.

I see him when I am twenty-eight years old, and he's telling me he's proud of what I've become, that we are a family at last, but none of it is normal and none of it ever will be, no matter how much denial we choose to live in. I steal things and Dad kills people and we bank millions of dollars, but we don't live like kings because that brings the IRS and the FBI running. We live in tiny one-story houses on the edge of Austin. I live with my wife and he lives alone. But we never really live, do we? We are always working. Always moving. All over the world. No rest for the wicked—not now, not ever. And his face is full of defeat.

I failed you, son . . .

His face never changes through any of these memories. He sees the rage that lives in me and is terrified of it. The rage that must be quelled by a life of always working. The only life we know how to live.

I failed you, son . . .

I pull away from it one last time. I realize I'm not

screaming anymore. Bennett's voice comes again, telling me to just calm down.

It takes a few minutes, but I manage to get my shit together. I get to my knees and look her in the eye. Try to make my voice as strong as possible.

"Sorry about that," I tell her.

"You scared the hell out of me. I thought you'd lost it for sure."

"I . . . I have a lot on my mind."

"Me too."

She moves her shoulder slightly and winces. The field dressing she threw together in the vault is soaked through with blood.

I let out a sharp breath, and almost smell roses again. "How bad is it?"

"I think the bullet scraped the muscle. Missed the brachial and axillary arteries. That's why I haven't bled more."

"We'll get you a doctor."

"How? We're in the middle of nowhere."

"I have it covered. The cavalry is on the way. Try to relax."

As the words leave my mouth, the absurdity of a dog giving a cat advice hits me like a sledge to the face. I expect her to roll her eyes and say something all smartass about the man screaming for his daddy telling the wounded soldier to calm down, but she doesn't say anything. Just shivers there, on her knees, looking real scared.

"I didn't sign up for this," she says. "I was supposed to make a million bucks and retire to goddamn Florida. What the hell am I *doing here*?"

"They were gonna kill us both."

"And whose fault is that, Elroy? I told you to shut it down and run. If you had *listened to me*—"

"If I'd listened to you, we'd be just as dead. They planned on killing us right from the start."

"That don't make any sense!" Her face contorts, the bad shoulder twitching. "*Fuck . . .*"

"Are you okay?"

"No, I ain't okay. Somebody fuckin' *shot me*. And filling my head with bogeymen don't help, either."

"Didn't you hear what that asshole said back there? There weren't enough seats for us on the express, remember?"

"That could have meant anything, Elroy."

"Look, just *think* a minute. We went in there for a suitcase full of hard drives. Whatever we were really stealing, they were lying through their teeth about it. And they didn't need us to recover any encrypted data, either—they just wanted me to bust the lock on it. We were all expendable as soon as that vault door opened."

The pain hits her again, and she hangs her head, sucking back hard air. "Maybe you're right, Elroy. *Maybe*. But you still should have listened to me."

"That guy was going to kill you. He would have put that big knife in your eye and bragged about it over beers."

"So I'm supposed to say thank you? You got me into this goddamn mess, Elroy—*it's your fault!*"

"Then just try to remember, I'm the only guy who can get you out of it."

"Fuck you! Just *fuck you*, Elroy!"

I back off and calm myself another degree. "I'll get you to a doctor. I'll even get you to Florida with some cash in your pocket. But we have to stick together. I'm sorry and it sucks, but we're runners now. And those people who hired us—they're dangerous and well funded. Jayne Jenison will come after us, she'll find us, and she will *kill us*. Do you read me?"

Her face is red and wet, the pain stabbing through her body. She sits there next to me for a few seconds, letting the silence speak volumes.

Then she sighs again. "Who do you think she really is?"

"She's no private citizen, that's for sure. Private citizens don't kill their techies after they do the job. That's more like third-world black ops."

"You think she's CIA or something?"

"Or something."

"Goddammit, Elroy . . ."

"There's only one way to know for sure. I have to find out what they had us going after. Hack the discs. Figure out what she really wanted from Hartman."

"And I get to bleed to death."

"I said I was gonna take care of you. Just try to stay calm."

Now she rolls her eyes. "You should take your own advice."

"Look, I'm sorry about that, but I'm okay now. I'm thinking clearly. You'll have to trust me."

She pauses again.

I read the pain clear and terrible as it slashes across her bloodshot eyes.

"I've heard about people like you," she says. "Ragers. That's what it's called, right? One minute you're okay, the next minute you see red and everything goes to hell."

"What can I tell you? It's gotten me in some pretty hot water."

"Why should I trust someone like that?"

"Because you don't have any choice."

She shakes her head and gets to her feet, muttering something nasty. I watch her head back to the chopper and re-dress her shoulder from the field pack. She's a tough one all right—tougher than I would have thought. For a second I think about offering to help her, and then I think again. Lady hates my guts right now—best to leave her alone.

She's right about it all, of course.

I blew it back there and it cost my father his life. It's the terrible thing that will haunt me now until the end of my days—which might be any minute now. Is she right about my rage? Am I a time bomb waiting to go off?

Not if I keep it under control.

Not if I use it to fuel me and focus me.

The rage came with my ability to see equations and logic—the power to bust any lock with my mind and break any bone with my bare hands. I have to use it to get us out of this. I owe Bennett. I owe my father.

I owe Toni.

If she's still alive.

If Jenison was telling me the truth about her.

It could have been a lie to get me in there—to get

what they wanted from me. They fixed us all really god-damn good, didn't they?

Bennett screams out loud as the new bandage goes on.

I go into the abandoned factory building and sit on the dusty floor. Bennett follows and sits next to me. She starts venting—mumbling nervously, painfully. Like she's talking to herself. She invokes the name of Axl Gange a few times. She sounds like a crazy person, her voice echoing off the walls of the destroyed chamber. This place is full of smashed glass and debris from whatever used to go on in here—which was years and years ago. Nothing left now but ghosts and scraps. Garbage and shreds of plastic. And the nervous rattle of a woman I nearly got killed.

I close my eyes and take myself out of there. Allow my adrenaline to crash and burn, so I can calm down. I realize how tired I am. How much I've been relying on broken sleep. Just four hours yesterday morning.

I try to lower my body rhythms, to find some sort of peace, to allow myself a moment of rest . . . but I keep bouncing back, and my adrenaline jolts me again.

Where is Toni? How can I find her now?

What the hell am I doing?

What really happened back there?

The leads start to become visible just as I hear a car horn and rap music driving velvet pistons into the earth from a subwoofer in the trunk of a muscle car.

We walk outside to see a sexy red Ferrari 458 Spider pull onto the landing strip. It is sleek and full of hard angles, like a sultry anime robot from outer space. A shiny new Pontiac right behind it, the robot's not-quite-as-dazzling trophy wife. Beautiful rides, all this year's models. Everything in the latest style, always with Kim. And always, she's right on time.

She steps out of the Spider in sequins and glitter, fake boobs bobbing in the breeze, big muscles throbbing on her arms and hips like one of those female weightlifters. The tattoo across her exposed belly shouts in fancy wedding invitation script: *The Hammer Will Fall*. A pink cartoon cat winking with evil lust under the letters, like she just swallowed the mouse and knows you know. There's a thin young Puerto Rican boy in a blue halter top on her arm and he has a tattoo just like hers, but the cartoon is a mouse with eyes bugged out, like she knows she's about to be eaten, and the fancy words are in Spanish. Two big black dudes step out of the Pontiac and one of them puts the keys in her hands. She smiles and turns to me.

Her voice is like Pam Grier dropped three octaves:

"Hey, hey, gorgeous boy. Still trying to be black, I see."

She means my ninja clothes. I shrug because it doesn't matter.

"We're all black deep down, you know that, Kimmy."

"And some of us got soul we can't control, baby." She laughs and slides me a tentative hug by leaning in with two arms around my neck, the kind of hug girls always give out when they don't want you to get the wrong idea. "Good to see you, my boy Elroy."

"I didn't think you'd come out personally."

"Let's say I was in the neighborhood. Or maybe I couldn't resist seeing your sexy face."

"Bullshit. You just wanted to look me in the eye when this deal went down."

She winks and purses her lips, bigger than life.

Yeah, it's not a typical morning when a fella who once made you six million bucks in six minutes calls up four years later with a machine like this on the cheap.

She hands me an oversized manila envelope, stuffed. "This is my undying love, hon. Have some."

I weigh the envelope in my hands. No way this is two hundred large.

"Sure it's all here?"

"Of course it ain't, baby. Gotta test drive this sweet ride of yours first. If it's the King of Pop, like you said, I'll send the rest with my man."

"And the doctor?"

"Eight o'clock in the p.m., downtown. The Sheraton. Room number's in the envelope."

I look at my watch. Just past seven thirty in the a.m. That's more than twelve hours until Bennett sees the doc. Half a day for the demons to catch up with us.

"How's your security on the place? I've got really bad people looking for me."

"Of course you do. And look at *me*, baby. I'm still standing after a hundred and fifty fucking years of dealing with really bad people."

"In a few hours, you could be taking a risk by shaking my hand."

"I love it when you try to scare me. But don't worry, it's taken care of. Eight o'clock and we're gold."

"My lady friend needs a doctor now."

"Baby, I've got a *business* to run."

"I've seen how you do business."

"You're my special boy, Elroy. Would I lie to you?"

"Sure you would. But you'd kiss me first."

"Take it or leave it."

I think about it for two seconds, then roll the dice. If we move fast underground and Bennett's gunshot wound isn't as bad as I know it probably is, this can happen. Kim's one of the biggest players in town. If she can't protect us for a few hours in a hotel room, nobody can. And it's a better deal than no deal.

I give her the nod and shove the package under my arm.

She looks at Bennett, her arm all slinged up, dried blood on her face. "What's your story, morning glory?"

She shrugs with her good shoulder. "Cut myself shaving."

"We'll get you fixed up real pretty again."

She laughs. Licks her finger and sizzles the air with it. Starts to make some more silly small talk but knows I'm in a hurry. Hands me the keys to the Pontiac. Kisses me in the air on both sides of my face, like a real diva.

"You smell like a man on fire, baby."

"I am."

"Something else on your mind?"

"Toni. Have you heard anything about her? Anything at all?"

"Not since forever. You chasin' after ghosts now?"

"Always."

"That's why I like you, Elroy. You're such a hopeless romantic. But I ain't heard nothing. I'm sorry."

She says it like she really means it.

I don't know if I believe her.

Don't know if it matters.

"Well," she says. "Gotta fly. You crazy kids stay outta trouble."

"Eight o'clock."

"The doctor will be in."

"Better be."

"Oh, gorgeous, don't you worry."

She waves her hand and gets back in the Spider, yelling at someone on a cell phone. A couple of dinged-up trucks approach us, and some guys get out, start looking over the chopper. Kim leans out the window, tells them to hurry their asses. I don't even want to think about who she plans on selling that thing to.

Me and Bennett get our gear out of the chopper, load it in the trunk of the car. The Gold's Gym bag never leaves my sight. Kim blows me a kiss as I slam the trunk shut.

She mouths the words *Good luck, baby*.

The envelope has the cash for the chopper—fifteen grand down payment—plus the car papers and Google directions to the Sheraton downtown, half visible on a sheet of paper run through a printer with a low inkjet. That's where her doctor will see us. Eight o'clock, off the radar. Mob docs trade lab-grade pharmaceuticals in bulk and emergency-room favors for protection—most of them are degenerate gamblers, underage pussy chasers, you name it. I can imagine what Kim has over her guy. The cash will be delivered, too, for the machine.

Room 1006A, on the tenth floor, her place. Everything first class with Kim, all in the latest style. Once I get Bennett to a doctor, it's out of my hands. She saved my life, I got her out of there—we're even.

I have twenty grand taped to my leg, another fifteen from Kim, plus the car. The rest of my money in twelve hours, if she doesn't screw me. My split should be enough to make a few moves. But right now, we need a stack of pay-as-you-go cell phones and some new clothes, maybe some food. And a quick room where we can hole up and figure out what the hell our assets are. Plus lots of Diet Coke. I need to stay awake.

I'm so tired.

Damn.

We find a half-dead Motel Six just inside the Houston city limits. It's on I-10, next to Bill's Diner and a bunch of other restaurants. A Goodwill right down the road. A Walmart, too. Perfect.

I park the car around the side of the motel building where you can't see us from the freeway—the manager's office is nice and out of view, too—and I check us in. It takes ten seconds.

This room sucks. No Internet connection.

I don't dare use the cell uplink in my rig, either. The people hunting us are watching every satellite in the air right now. Has to be a sneaky back door over a common land wire, and there's no wire here. These are dives, these little thirty-dollar-a-nighters. The bigger places, the chain hotels, they're just as easy to break into, but higher profile. Sneaking in the back of the Sheraton downtown tonight will be risky enough. The World Wide Web can wait.

We're good for a few hours, then we have to run again.

Just enough time to do some shopping.

I visit the Goodwill and the Walmart. I get the burner phones and the clothes and some food. We change into our new threads and Bennett cleans the field dressing again, throws on a fresh bandage. The old one is not as bloody as the first time she changed it out. If there's no internal bleeding, she should be okay, like she said.

But always prepare for the worst.

I've slept just four hours out of almost forty-eight now. I'm exhausted and the demons are screaming at me. But I can't sleep—there's no time for that. I gulp Diet Coke and sit in the center of the room and ride the rush, focusing on the plot. It's garbled in white noise.

I'll think of something.

"Okay," Bennett says a few minutes later, leaning against the moldy headboard as I decompose in a blue long-sleeve sweatshirt that smells like mothballs and old people. "We've got the hard drives, the computer rig, ten of these disposable cells, a quarter pound of C-4, wireless detonators, one shotgun with twenty rounds, a pile of these time-release handcuffs, two Ruger SR9 pistols and a Colt Python I plan on holding on to."

"You won't be able to shoot again with your shoulder all messed up like that, even with your good arm. The recoil from that Python will tear open the clots—and forget about the shotgun."

"I'm pretty sure it's not as bad as it looks. Bullet went right through the meat, straight in and out." She indicates the fresh bandage. Picks at the take-out food on the bed next to her. Hushpuppies and chicken fingers from a grungy little greasy spoon next to the motel called Willie's Waffle House.

"Doesn't matter," I tell her. "You're still not a hundred percent."

"Look, don't tell *me* I don't know the difference between a hole that bleeds a lot and being really hurt."

"Just take it easy."

She looks pissed. Probably knows I'm right about her shoulder. Maybe I'm wrong. Hope I am. She munches on a hushpuppy, and shrugs at me with her mouth full. "What the hell time is it anyway?"

"Just past three P.M. We gotta book again."

"Keep moving, huh?" She laughs bitterly.

She's wearing a grubby old secondhand Hawaiian shirt that makes her look like she's on her way to a shuffleboard tournament on a Carnival Cruise, half a bottle of Motrin twinkling through her nervous system. It's really hard to overdose on Ibuprofen, and if you take enough, it'll stop the pain of a rattlesnake bite.

My sweatshirt has a *ThunderCats* iron-on transfer peeling off it: the logo of a sleek feline silhouette in a circle of crimson, hardly attached to the fabric in streaks of wear and age. They remade that show recently, just like they remake everything. The old version was a favorite of the boys in prison. You'd be amazed how well Saturday-morning cartoons go over with guys who murder little old ladies. Lion-O was a real hero with the hardest convicts. The punks all liked *Transformers*.

I take a peek out the curtains. Car's ready to bolt just outside, in case we need a fast getaway. Every minute we have now is borrowed.

We move to a new location at four in the afternoon and it's the worst one yet, held together with peeling paint and cockroach droppings, but at least nobody knows we're here. No one at all. The manager on the front desk is passed out in his own spit, the light of Britney Spears bathing him from an old-fashioned tube TV set. I pick the lock on Room 667 and check us in. I find a small brown suitcase abandoned in the closet and decide it's a better home for the disc drives than a Gold's Gym bag—pretty clean, too, no vermin at all. I expected to find a rat living in there. I stash the payload in the suitcase. They all fit inside just right. Funny how things work out sometimes.

Wonder of wonders, they have Internet here.

"Okay, we're here until seven thirty," I say to Bennett. "Three hours. Try to get some rest. The doc'll take care of you when we get there."

"Thanks," she says, rolling her eyes across the ceiling. The way doomed people do it.

• • •

I'm on my second six-pack of Diet Coke now.

So goddamn tired.

I unpack part of my rig and check the power so
Half-life in the batteries. Good, I won't have to pu
the electricity in this funky room. I start setting it
Bennett volunteers to help, but I tell her to take it ea
She pulls out her bottle of Motrin, eats a few. Wolfs th
rest of a drive-through burger.

Watches me click the numbers, sitting anxiously at
the edge of the bed.

"I never saw anything like what you did back there,"
she says sullenly. "The way you worked those protocols,
I mean."

"I still blew it."

"Maybe that's right. But I never would have gotten
past those firewalls. It was really ahead of the curve.
Never seen anything like it."

"Neither had I. That scares the hell out of me."

"Selling the getaway helicopter to a gangbanger was
pretty original."

"That wasn't the smartest move I've ever made,
either. It'll be all over the street real soon, if it isn't already. Hartman has his ear to the ground, too. I'll have
to deal with him *and* our employers. But it won't be
your problem."

"Oh really?"

"Really. You can go to Florida and live happily ev
after. We'll be getting a big payday for the machine."

She smiles through her pain, sighing. "Pretty
Slick."

I almost laugh, but don't. It wasn't really funny the
st time.

"So," she says, getting back to being serious. "You
iink you can figure out what's on those discs?"

"I don't have much time, but I can try."

She looks off into space for a moment, then lowers
ier voice almost reverently. "I think I should apologize
to you. I said a few things back there I shouldn't have."

"You said the truth. I should have listened to you in
the vault."

"Yeah. But still . . ."

"Still nothing. You were right and I was wrong."

"I might have been right about the decoy numbers,
but I never woulda figured out what the secondary pulse
inside that lead pipe really was. That was a pretty fast
move on your part."

"If I had figured it sooner, my dad might still be
alive."

"I don't think that's true. You might be a scary guy,
Elroy . . . but you're still the best I've ever seen. And I've
seen a lot."

"You're not so bad yourself. We were a pretty good
team back there."

"Damn right we were."

I sigh, clicking the keys, seeing the numbers.

Feeling the logic.

"Computers and programs were invented by men,
not gods," I tell her. "That's another thing Axl Gange
id to me right off. You can solve any riddle invented
omeone smarter than you. All you gotta do is go to
Start at the beginning. Just don't mess with God."

at's one way of looking at it."

Go to zero. I turn the words over in my mind. They were never truer than they are at this very goddamn moment.

Bennett hangs her head, and whispers. "I'm sorry about your father."

"Please, I have to ask you: Don't talk about him anymore. I can't think about that right now. I have to do everything I can to block it out."

The same way I did when Mom died. The shock first, then the pain and the mourning months later, years later. When it finally catches up to you.

The shock is my ally this time. A way to control the rage while my fingers move across the keys of my rig, searching for an answer. But right now, as my mind flashes over those last moments in the vault, it isn't my father's final words that haunt me—it's the Sarge's. He asked Bennett if she had what it took to look in the face of God. Told us all the seats on the express were taken. Said it was resurrection.

What the hell was that? *What did he mean?*

It hits me hard, as I sit there in the half dark, surrounded by the secrets they had me steal. The answers are here, encoded on these drives.

Bennett's voice drifts over to me a few minutes later as I power up the machine. She's scared and tired, wracked with dull pain. "They're gonna find us, aren't they?"

"Yes. Eventually. It's bigger than what they were telling us. Much bigger. I'm getting that old sinking feeling."

"And they'll kill us when they find us."

"Eventually."

I feel her close to me in the half dark of the room. That sleek blur that was at my elbow during the job, her deep red hair and the galaxy of freckles on her face and shoulders, made blacker by sweat and grime and blood, even after cleaning herself up. She's trained in life-or-death survival tactics, and she's even been in the soup, but not like this. Not fighting against enemies who are completely invisible.

"I ain't gonna die like those others," she says. "I won't let that happen. I won't let them torture me, either."

"Good for you."

"I saw a lotta that where I was, in the war. Men who were just like that asshole back there with the knife. All drunk on macho bullshit. It was hard being a woman in the middle of all that."

"Is that why you got out?"

"Mostly. I didn't wanna see people dying anymore. Kind of a joke, huh? I mean, here we are, right?"

"You did right by me in the vault. When the shooting started, I mean. You killed two men to save my life. I owe you."

"You saved my life, too. You don't owe me nothing."

"Yes, I do."

I stop clicking. I turn and face her.

I take a deep breath.

And.

"I was there when Axl Gange died. I watched it happen. You know that, right?"

"Yes."

"You wanted me to tell you about it before."

"Yes."

"You're his daughter, aren't you?"

"Not exactly. I never knew my real parents."

She lowers her head.

There's a long, long silence before she speaks again.

"Axl raised me from the time I was two years old. His real kids were my brother and sisters."

I think I knew it all along. That's why she came down on my side back there—why she's been on my side since before we even met. She came here because it was the only way to avenge her father.

Her father.

Goddamn.

"I left him when I was teenager," she says slowly. "It was because he said he couldn't teach us anything, Elroy. Said he wouldn't show his children how to be like him. That it would lead to our deaths, and he couldn't be responsible."

"He was trying to protect you."

"I didn't wanna be protected. I wanted to be my father's daughter."

"I envy that. I really do."

"What do you mean?"

"I never had a choice but to be my father's son."

And now he's dead, too.

The silence settles again.

The terrible details of Bennett's life shimmer like a vague mirage in front of me: scumbag parents, shot dead during a robbery or belly up in some back room with needles in their arms, Axl stepping up to claim her, because that's what he did back then. Maybe her folks were friends of his, maybe they were just bad people he knew. I decide not to ask her.

Doesn't matter anyway, I can practically see it all right here.

Frozen in the dark, silent spaces between us.

"I hated Axl for years," she says. "I even changed my last name, it got so bad. Then he was gone and there wasn't any way to make it right. I want to know how my father died, Elroy. Please tell me."

"It's hard, Bennett. Even harder than what we went through in the vault. Those were just guys with guns. David Hartman is a sick, sick man."

"I don't care. Tell me everything."

"If it's what you really want."

Her face is like stone.

Her eyes unblinking.

"Yes. It's what I really want."

So I tell her. The words come easy. The pictures never fade.

Ever.

I tell her about coming back from Dallas, at the end of my apprenticeship, on the day my father got out of prison for the last time. That was after the army, after the dojo, the last six months with Axl and his team a grueling hell of final exams, all high-security gigs I walked through like a champ, with Jett Williams as my right hand. I walked straight from that last job to a meeting at Threadgill's with my father. He said he was proud of me. Six years of busting my ass and my mind, all for this. So I could go free and become a slave again—but this time for a lot of money. My father said he owed me, the same way I just told Bennett I owed her, and I remember his face so clearly. As if this was the only way he could pay me back. By making me a criminal like him. I had no idea how bad things could really get. I hadn't been to war, hadn't been to prison. I hadn't yet stared into the face of real evil.

That only happened when I met David Hartman for the first time.

You can't really understand these things when you experience them. They stealth bomb your eyes and your ears and your soul, leaving hard scars you can't feel right off. You have to look back before any of it means anything. At least that's what it seems like now. All of it dirty, swimming in some terrible backwash, sour and wrong. And why the hell not? Someone else is always crazier than you anyway.

I tell Bennett about that next meeting—the one that happened three days later, after I spent the weekend with Toni. I hadn't seen my wife in six months. She met me at the Driskill Hotel, downtown on Sixth Street. One of the oldest buildings in Austin, more than a hundred years of elegance and history, retrofitted with chrome and steel, like a slice off some ancient future world from a galaxy far, far away. It was almost like our second honeymoon, our next pledge to one another, that we would always come back here, to this special place— not just the hotel, but the place in our hearts where nobody could touch us. I remember the moment when I first saw her again like an outsider, because the promise was broken of course.

You see, Bennett, that's how it is.

These things never really last. Something always comes along and screws it up. And you have to stand away from those tarnished moments years later and figure out what any of it means. It might not even mean anything.

David Hartman met us in the restaurant of the Driskill on Monday.

Toni and I had spent our time together already, in one of the cheap rooms, not the special suite where we were married. That would have been bad luck. You don't ever go home like that. Hartman had no idea about our history anyway. About why that hotel was important to us. Not that it wouldn't have made him laugh out loud, but I never gave him the satisfaction. He just liked doing his dirty business there because it smelled clean. That's what he told us—you gotta smell clean when you roll in the mud.

My father had arranged the meeting, while he was in prison. You go inside to be a higher class of criminal. That's something a lot of people don't understand. I'm not sure I understand it myself. Get busted doing a weed deal in a Denny's parking lot, and they send you to graduate school, where you learn to sell smack in strip clubs and kill people. God bless America, you crummy bastards.

I sat across from Hartman in that dark restaurant, Toni next to me, the air between us filled with weird, drippy laughter, his eyes undressing us both. A lot of fat people have that sticky flesh-wobble in the way they speak, but David was worse than that. It was a deeper affliction, something tied right to his soul, swimming in slime. Scarier still, because I knew how powerful this man was, how much he had already taken, how many shooters he had on the street. I could tell he wasn't exactly a smart man, but he had the showmanship that gets you through the door. Horse sense and spider sense. And he had enough to keep the door open, too. Because he was sharp enough to hire men like Axl.

He asked me politely if he could fuck my wife right there.

She politely said no thanks.

The reply I might have given him was drowned in more of that fleshy laughter. Sludge oozing in the spaces between us. A madman's cancer.

He told us about the power and the glory, about how muscle rules the world. About how men like him pull the strings, and how those strings are connected to the fragile necks of every tough motherfucker inhabiting the world of organized wise guys and all those shady businessmen with soft hands who call themselves career criminals. He laughed at them all. His great flabby body shook and rolled and quaked beneath the skin of a five-thousand-dollar suit jacket. It was less like meeting a man of power and more like experiencing a wave of nausea. Not just because he was disgusting on the surface, but because I knew what he was capable of, even before I saw him do it. The lust for all those things that ordinary men turn away from, boiling in his laughter and burned on his face. He told me later that was what gave him his edge. Thinking outside the box, he called it.

He told me Axl Gange had been his boy for six years.

He said that Axl was an arrogant slob who never learned his place.

And that his final mistake was in training me.

Hartman said he liked my style, said he admired a

man with a full skill set. He wanted to watch me hurt someone. Then he laughed again, and the laugh was horrifying. The shrill sound of it, hitting my skin like creeping bugs. And then he stood up and told me to come with him. Said the lady should stay in the restaurant. This next part wasn't for ladies.

I had no choice but to go with him. It's one of those moments you look back on. And you have no idea whether or not you would do it differently.

It just is.

Toni ordered a drink and waited. Hartman hooted across the restaurant and said we'd only be an hour or so. He didn't laugh so much in the elevator on the way up. The air closed in around me, thick with bad smells and the promise of terrible consequences, and I found myself asking him right out if I should be worried about anything. He said why the hell should I worry? I was Axl's golden boy, after all. Hartman was impressed with me, of course.

The elevator opened on the top floor. The walk to the Renaissance Suite was the longest I've ever taken. He said this was the most expensive room in the place—even more pricey than the penthouses up top. It was the bridal suite, with high ceilings, a glassed-in bathroom finished with marble, and a view of the Sixth-Street party drag from the veranda balcony. All those bars and restaurants and pool houses down there like a string of glowing dream-scenes lashed across the heart of downtown, the shame of Oz—old honky-tonks like Casino El Camino, done up in ribbons of touristy sleaze, and dumps like Joe's Generic, with the bar-code sign out in front of one room dripping with dirty blues and stale beer. All of it below us on the street, where all the action happens on a Saturday night for the young-and-beautiful college set and the old beer-gut burnouts of Austin, if you're not rich like us. That's what Hartman said to me. If you don't know the secrets of being rich, if you don't step up and take what's rightfully yours—and if you don't bloody well protect that right with every last ounce of scrappy shit-kicking fury you possess—then you're just down there in a no-name dive bar with all the rest. You don't get what's behind the fancy door. You burn out and fade away, and nobody knows you ever existed.

And then he opened that fancy door.

This is the part of the memory I always try to block out, and I tell Bennett that. But blocking true horror is impossible, really. It's why men like David do what they do. They want to put scars on you that never go away, and they want to look you right in the eye when they do it. It's what makes them worse than gangsters.

It's what makes them monsters.

So, I reduce it to information. I tell it to her in the most abstract terms I can summon. But the pictures never fade.

Axl. You poor, doomed old man.

What did you do to make Hartman hate you so much?

I've always wondered that—what his crimes really were. It could have been as simple as Hartman knowing it was time to retire the old boy, and I was next up to replace him. It could have been Axl pulling a scam that blew up in his face, though I couldn't imagine him being that careless. And then, in these moments when I ponder the terrible gravity of what went on in that hotel room, I realize somewhere behind it all that none of it really mattered.

Hartman was one of the monsters.

That's it.

They had Axl upside down in a harness made of leather and iron by the time I walked in the room. He was still alive, still conscious. What was left of him anyway. He was naked under the straps, burned and cauterized and raw all over. I thought he looked pretty bad, but it was just a warm-up, really. For the main event. The room had been white a few hours earlier. It was a bridal suite, after all.

A place where young people start their lives anew.

I found out later that they had to remodel when Hartman was done. The stains went too deep. The grunts cut Axl loose and held him facedown on the bed, two guys in black ski masks, anonymous street thugs hired for the job at hand, the usual gorillas.

Axl begged them.

His voice was frail and beaten and childlike.

He said he would do anything to make the pain stop.

And Hartman . . . he leaned in close with a tire iron and said something I'll never forget:

Everyone wants to make the pain stop.

But where's the fun in that?

"It went on for about an hour, just like he said it would. When it was all over, they shot him in the back of the head, execution style. With a silenced pistol that still made a lot of noise. And you know what?"

Bennett shivers in the dark, shaking her head, not wanting to know any more.

I tell her anyway.

"He *shook my hand* when he was done. David did, I mean. Pulled up his pants, wiped blood off his face and shook my goddamn hand."

"And you worked for him after that."

"Yeah. But not because I was afraid. It was because of my dad. Because he said we only knew how to be criminals and I believed him. That was ten years ago."

"Do you still believe that now?"

"I'm not sure."

"My father never woulda said that to me. It's why I left. Why I never saw him again."

I see something that might be a tear glint off her face. She reaches up and rubs her eyes. Her voice, at a whisper again:

"You should have helped him. Wasn't there anything you could have done?"

"It was already too late. I'm . . . *sorry*."

"And here we are."

"Yeah."

"I won't be like that. I ain't gonna let Hartman do those things to me."

"He's looking for us now. So is Jenison. When they find us, it *will* get messy. I don't really know how far Jenison's people are willing to go . . . but Hartman . . ."

My voice fades, as I picture Bennett lying facedown at his mercy.

Gagged and helpless.

Not allowed to die in the last few hours of her life.

Humbled and broken, just the way Axl was.

She steels her face and makes her voice strong:

"We ain't like our fathers. And we ain't like that monster who killed them, neither. We're the good guys, Elroy."

"Maybe."

I don't say another word. Just turn back to the computer.

She stares off into the dark.

Haunted, more than ever.

I port one of the hard drives from the brown suitcase and peel open the wrapper. Let's see what all the fighting and dying has been about.

It's got a code key I get past easy with a lockbreaker, and then I'm inside a bunch of numbers. It's all *rows* of numbers, and it won't make any sense unless the other drives are slaved up. Or unless I can talk to it real sweet. Takes me just a few minutes.

You wanna look in the face of God, little lady?

This is resurrection.

I hear those words, over and over. You can't stare into the face of God and live forever. God punishes those who look. You die and go to hell.

If that's what you believe in.

It's an hour later when I finally manage to copy the information on the drive to my hard disc. It's only about 3GBs when it's uncompressed. Walls of numbers appear on the main screens. Complex datastreams, virtual badassery.

"Some kind of software code," Bennett says, leaning over my shoulder, wincing as her own shoulder stings her. "You put it all together like a puzzle off the disc drives, and then you have . . . whatever it is."

"Yeah. But what the hell *is* it?"

"Could be something stolen from the Justice Department. That would make sense. Missing persons, maybe? Some kinda Big Brother system that keeps tabs on people?"

"No. It's more sophisticated. Way too many nooks and crannies. That's why it took so long to copy."

"Put some more of the pieces together," she says. "If you can assemble just a few datastreams, we might see patterns that'll tip us off."

"Way ahead of you there."

She sees my fingers moving fast and shakes her head. "Of course you are."

"I could get a lot of it sorted through, but I'd need days—maybe weeks—to fit the whole thing together. I might not even be able to run the program independently of whatever system it was designed for. Once the puzzle is assembled, it'll require a specific series of entry codes, which are probably what's stored on the little flash drives. Like a key to get past a final security firewall that probably only goes up once the whole system is activated."

"Clever."

"Good thing we ditched the original case these drives were living in. It might have had a tracker or a destruct code built into the metal casing. Still can't believe it didn't explode when I opened it."

And, suddenly, it hits me:

Whoever designed what was in that case designed that vault, too. *Of course he did.* No doubt in my mind at all. The code I'm clicking through has the same devious rhythms—identical patterns that stab you in the back. I'll have to be careful not to look for too much. It might have a tapeworm I can't see, something that eats everything the more you hack away at it.

State-of-the-art.

Manufactured by Texas Data Concepts.

I work through some more of it.

"Definitely a program, not a database," she says a few minutes later. "Definitely something applicable to the military or the Justice Department."

"What makes you say that?"

She points at the screen. "I'm seeing a lotta code here that gets used in high-security defense applications—things like factories that manufacture tanks and bombs. I've been in a few of those."

"It could be anything."

But it's not anything. It's *something.* And whatever that something really is, it was so valuable to these people that they encased it in a steel bear trap rigged to blow the living holy shit out of anyone who went looking for it.

Don't look, son. It's the face of God.

Bennett sees the furrows on my face, as I start clicking again.

She studies the screen intently.

I get on the Internet and ask some questions, using hacker code that only the best can see through. Nobody steps up at first. I create a brand-new secure chat room fortified with radioactive firewalls and I put out the word. I don't use any of my old aliases, not even the ones I went under when I was hacking from the inside. A few guys step up and I get my questions answered. Mostly technical stuff.

Bennett looks real worried. I know how she feels.

And that's right when my fingers get lucky in a sensitive area.

Click.

Pay dirt.

It's a hairline crack that only decodes part of two words from the entry port to a sub-program that governs most of the system, like the sign on a door telling you what dentist you're getting drilled by today. Just fragments.

Mou ain p iority.

That's all it says.

Bennett sees it clearly, even with the missing letters:

"Mountain priority," she says. "See how the *M* is capitalized? It's part of a proper name."

I know there's more.

I go after it, telling Bennett I'm not sure what I'm looking for, but I have a really bad feeling about this. I click fast and get quick results. More word fragments.

Re on Ele en.

She fills it in again: "Region Eleven. Another proper name."

No.

That can't be it.

I will my fingers to key a word search for something specific, using three mean sets of blackware hunters off my rig—a controlled little bit of virus rot aimed like a smart black scalpel right at the heart of whatever this thing is.

I find three letters, half the word I'm looking for.

yen

I don't need it to tell me the rest. Neither does Bennett.

Cheyenne Mountain priority Region Eleven.

Her face goes white.

"Elroy . . . I think we're in really big trouble."

MEN AND BOYS

I pack up the rig and the brown suitcase and get everything in the trunk of the car. I do it at light speed. Bennett moves fast, too. She knows what we're running from is big enough to come after us, anywhere, everywhere. We're holding on to a time bomb. Something that should have been impossible to get. Something we *never* should have gotten our hands on.

You think you have what it takes, kid?

It's the face of God.

Only the chosen few can look there.

That's why he had to kill us. The rank-and-file computer geeks who knew too much past the pearly gates. And my father, too. I *should* have known. We both should have. Texas Data Concepts. Cheyenne Mountain.

A time bomb.

I tell her the plot: We're going to head for the Sheraton. Have to make our eight-o'clock date. A few hours after that, it'll be midnight, October 24. Exactly one full day since we hit the TCD building. More than enough time for our employers to find us. So I gotta make a call between here and the hotel. One of these disposable Walmart cells has seventy-five minutes free when you buy it. They're only good for twenty minutes or so before we have to ditch them. Pay phones are out of the question, of course. Have to stay as far off the grid as possible. Deal from strength.

The sun goes down all the way as I load the shotgun. I zip it up with the rest of our weapons, in the long sports bag I bought at the same Walmart, where I got the cells. The rest of our new clothes go in there, a bag of Fritos, too. All that's left of our road grub. We get room service now. I need a real meal soon so I can try to get my safe deposit box key back again. That money is my lifeline.

That, and what we're going after now.

Bennett tells me she's scared. She knows what Cheyenne Mountain is. It's in Colorado. Strategic Air Command, Region Eleven.

The people who control the hand of God.

We get in the car and get back on the highway into the downtown area of Houston, where anyone could be watching. The blinking, twinkling skyscrapers loom on the near horizon, just beyond winding neighborhoods of sleaze and commerce. I keep the Gold's Gym bag on my shoulder. I feel the warm fingers of sleep deprivation creeping up the back of my throat and my soul, threatening to knock me right the hell out, but I keep it together. I dial a number on the Walmart phone and hand it to Bennett.

I tell her to order half a California roll.

. . .

One stop along the way. Jenny Rose's Body Shop, in the Heights, just downtown. A ritzy flesh palace with a dress code.

We park across the street.

I grab the small brown suitcase, leave a gun on the seat next to Bennett and tell her not to use it unless she has to.

"If I'm not back here in twenty minutes, tops, come in after me."

"You expecting trouble?"

"Always."

I see a man in a white cowboy hat and black boots on the red velvet rope, using a metal detector on clusters of slick suits as they show up in force. He's got long hair in a ponytail and a moustache that makes him look old and weird.

He sees me and nods.

"I hear you're looking for some legal advice," he says.

We go inside together.

Me and Bennett get to the Sheraton at a little after eight. It's in the heart of the downtown megalopolis cityscape that bursts through concrete in the center of Houston. I slip the valet ten bucks and he lets us into the underground garage, where we park the car.

I grab the sports bag with our guns and travel gear.

The Gold's Gym bag on my shoulder has my rig in it now.

We take the service elevator. You're not supposed to

use this ride, not unless you're on staff and you have the key. I never worry about having a key.

We get to Room 1006A and I knock quietly.

A huge, blobby black man with one gold tooth and a reefer in his mouth cracks open the door and gives me a deadly look. A Glock in his fist. An XXL Dead Kennedys T-shirt hanging off his enormous frame like some odd riddle about inner city badasses.

"What's the password?"

He looks and sounds a little like the Notorious B.I.G. I don't like rap music, but I sure as hell remember Biggie.

I remember him because he's dead.

"Betty Crocker sent me," I tell him.

He kind of laughs, kind of doesn't. Opens the door and steps back, letting us in. Looks like we're invited. The place has low-level track lighting, smells like fresh linen and Lysol. It's a suite with lots of elbow room, a few couches and chairs, flat-screen TV—and a hospital bed inside the main living area, racks of drugs and IV drips and other equipment for patching holes, pill bottles and saline bags locked up in tackle boxes. Kim's private ER. I'm impressed. Most gangbangers have their field hospitals set up in a flophouse or a dirty back room off a strip club somewhere.

The mountain with the gold tooth doesn't say a word. Puffs on his joint. Keeps an eye on us as we enter. I can see the outline of another Glock in his waistband, jutting out between his pants and the gravid flab of his gut. Dangerous guy. A keg waiting to blow. His eyes linger a lot longer on Bennett.

An older white man wearing a black dinner jacket

over a flannel shirt sits up from one of the couches and stubs out a cigarette. He's wearing a fishing hat. "You're Elroy Coffin?"

"Yep. I think my friend here needs to speak with you."

"Come over to the table, we'll have a look at her."

Bennett moves over to the doc, sits on the hospital bed, as the guy starts asking all the usual questions. Where does it hurt? How long ago were you shot? Starts cutting off the field dressing on her shoulder with a pair of scissors from one of the racks. Cracks a joke I can't hear and laughs loudly at it. Nervous. I have one ear on him as I turn to the big black dude.

"Did Kim send the rest of my money?"

"Talk to Randall."

"Who's Randall?"

I hear a toilet flush when I say that. Oh.

A door to the main bedroom suite opens and here comes the brains of the operation. He's a smaller white guy. Looks like Eminem, only tougher. Has the weird sleepy eyes, but there's more danger in his face, and a couple of nasty scars, too.

I remember Eminem because everybody does.

He's wearing a windbreaker buttoned only at the top, like a cholo drug dealer. He sees the *ThunderCats* logo on my chest and makes a jagged grin happen. Typical. Glares at the black guy and tries to look important. "You check Lion-O here out?"

"Shit, I ain't feelin' up no white boy on what I'm gettin' paid."

"I don't mean *that*, dumbshit! I mean, is he cool?"

"He's standin' right there, you tell me."

Eminem looks right in my eyes. "Are you *cool*, Lion-O?"

I wonder what the hell that even means. So I tell him I'm cool. He says that's cool. So everything's cool. I guess. Or something. These guys sure as hell won't win any astrophysics awards this year, but they look really hard. Kim likes them hard.

The doc cracks open one of the tackle boxes and finds some antibiotics, some painkillers. He goes to work on Bennett, making bad jokes I don't hear all the way, cutting off the rest of her bloody Hawaiian shirt, cleaning the wound up, chewing Vicodin like they're Flintstones. That's another thing people like Kim hold over their doctors. Habits.

Eminem goes under a couch and pulls out a fat metal briefcase, tells me to sit down and we'll count the cash together. This could take a while.

"Don't worry," I say. "Just let me look it over quick, I'm in a hurry. I trust Kim."

"Gotta count it. Those are the rules."

Whatever.

I look over at the doc, hunched over his work with sweat beading on his face. Bennett almost smiles at me, half naked, her olive sports bra spackled red. I almost smile back. "How you doing, kiddo?"

"Never better."

Eminem latches open the case, starts counting out stacks of hundred-dollar bills in bundles of twenty thousand each, then handing them to me. I set them on the floor in neat rows at my feet. I don't count any of it. Eminem gives me a dirty look but doesn't say anything.

"Man, that's a lotta squeezin' green," says the fat guy.

"What's a motherfucker gotta do to get in on a score like that around here?"

"Shut your big black ass up," says Eminem casually. He probably shot five dirty white boys for breakfast yesterday. That's how it works. They send the white guys to deal with the white guys, especially Kim. She once told me honky gangbangers were like pastry ninjas in action movies. The kind you eat, one after another, with a machine gun.

She sent the right guys to handle this much money.

One false move and I'm really dead, and right now that makes me really comfortable in this room. Security is covered.

I almost fall asleep, watching him count the money.

Hypnotized by the repetition.

So goddamn tired . . .

Ten minutes later, which seems like ten lifetimes later, he hands me the last wad. Two hundred large, with the fifteen I already had in the bag. Then there's the getaway insurance. Almost twenty on my leg, my walking-around money. I tell him I'll buy the briefcase for a hundred bucks and he throws it in for free. I put half the cash back in the case.

"You guys have Internet in this dungeon?"

He jerks a thumb towards a computer set up in the corner on a table, next to some piled-up stuff that looks like swag: new clothes, a display case of jewelry, a stack of Blu-ray players still sealed in the boxes.

"Be my guest," he says.

I get up and walk over to the hospital bed. The doc whistles while he works. And I was right the first time—Bennett's wound is awful. The bullet took a nasty chunk off her shoulder, the skin all gouged and blue. "You gonna be okay, kiddo?"

"I ain't a kid."

"You're right. What you are is a very rich girl right now." I pat the briefcase and set it next to her on the carpet.

"I like that song," she says, her voice wavering in the fog.

I narrow my eyes at her. "What?"

"*Rich Girl.* By Hall and Oates. I used to really love them."

"More eighties, huh?"

"Actually . . . that's going back to the seventies. A lot of people don't know that about Hall and Oates. I raided my dad's record collection a lot."

"I never knew he liked those guys. He only listened to hair metal when I was working under him."

"People change, I guess."

"Yes they do."

Her dad.

My teacher.

Goddamn.

I squeeze her hand a little, looking at the doc.

"How long will it take to get her fixed up?"

"She's in pretty rough shape," he says, not looking up from his work. "Her wound should have been treated sooner. But she'll stabilize in a few hours. I have to keep her under observation for at least twenty-four. Did Kim tell you how the money works?"

"No, not really. What do I owe you?"

"Five yards for the house call. Five large for the treatment. Drugs are on the house."

I pull out a stack and peel off five bills, then another five grand. He stops working long enough to fan through the green, smiling. Rolls it up and stuffs it in his coat pockets. Slips on a new set of rubber gloves and goes back to work. His face is filled with shame and secrets, all pushed down hard. Guess she could be in worse hands.

"Looks like you're holing up here for a while," I say to her. Then I turn to Eminem. "How secure is this place? You guys got people in the lobby?"

He laughs. "What the fuck do you think?"

"Don't worry," says the fat one. "This motherfucker is locked up tight."

That sounds like grim death coming out of his mouth.

Good.

Bennett starts breathing a few bars of a tune I don't recognize. Something about going too far and it doesn't matter anyway. The words drown in the lull of her own voice, drugged and floating between worlds. I'm reminded of all the lives I could have lived. All the records I could have memorized, like any other kid. Hall and Oates. Madonna and Metallica. I could have had all of that.

But we both chose to be here, she and I.

We both chose to be our fathers.

I pull out the second of my ten Walmart phones and dial Kim's number. Goes right to voice mail. I try a text instead. She pings back immediately. Women.

ARE WE HAPPY, BABY?

I click it quick:

WE'RE HAPPY. AREA SECURE? NEED A PLACE TO WORK.

A few seconds, and:

ME CASA, U CASA. B OUT 2MORROW @ CHECK OUT TIME.

Okay.

Four hours of sleep has officially caught up with me.

I'm going on adrenaline and diet soda.

I ask Doc for a shot of something. Need to be focused, even if I'm ghost tired. He asks if I've ever done speed before, and I tell him not much. A little back in the old days, when I was prepping big projects. My dad was worse. The Doc taps five white pills into the palm of his hand and tells me to be careful with this stuff. I dry-swallow three of them and chase it with a Coke from the wet bar. This place is probably good until morning, but I can't take that chance. Two hours and I run.

Then again, maybe I shouldn't.

Maybe I should just let them come get me. I have what they want, in a safe location. I could make a deal with them.

No. Not yet. Play from strength.

Find Hartman first.

I visit the bathroom, try to get my key back, but nothing happens. While I'm in there, I stash the girl's Colt Python under the sink.

I take the bag of weapons into the next bedroom and shove them under the bed. I throw a few things into the Gold's Gym bag. Things I need to keep safe.

And some insurance.

I walk out of the suite with a Ruger SR9 in my waistband, tell the Zebra Force I'll be back in ten minutes.

I walk down the hallway, every shadow an enemy.

I go back to the parking garage and get in the car, drive it out of there. I smell the city and take it in for the first time since I got here.

Houston is different from other metroplexes in America. No zoning. New York is a grid, Chicago is clusters. Houston is chaos. Gotham City, only smaller. Buildings from the forties squat shoulder-to-shoulder with brand-new high-rises. Aboveground railcars run near the bus station, a block away. They used to call it Space City in the seventies. They don't call it that anymore. It smells like hard concrete and oil floating on top of seawater. Can't keep myself in it for long.

I find a five-story long-term ramp two blocks away. Get a ticket from an automated meter and pick a cherry spot on a floor where all the cars are really expensive. Some inspection tags expired by a few months. Guys on extended business trips. My ride will blend in okay here.

I park the car next to a green Honda. It's a late model with an inspection sticker that went south just a few weeks ago—maybe belongs to a rich kid on a backpacking trip through Europe or something.

I shut off the engine and pop my trunk, unscrew the

recession in the floor where the spare tire goes, stash the Gold's Gym bag in there. Set the spare on top. Slam. Lock it up tight. I drop the keys into a little magnet box I bought at Walmart, stick it under the chassis, near the main transmission shaft.

Now, my insurance policy.

The last thing I do is drop one of my cell phones on the passenger's seat.

Just in case.

Okay.

I walk back to the hotel, looking at everything.

Everything's looking at me.

I really need some sleep.

Up the service elevator again, I run into an old black maid who gets snippy with me. I tell her I'm visiting a friend and want to surprise him. She says that's no excuse and that they have a health code in this place. I don't argue with her. Put up my hands. She gets off on the ninth floor.

"Remember the health code," she says again, and she sounds irritated with old on top now, like a schoolmarm getting her period early. "Next time *use the stairs.*"

"No problem," I say.

"Don't 'no problem' me, mister! It's never a problem to do what's right!"

The elevator door closes on her while she's shouting and I'm still putting up my hands, trying to look innocent.

Damn, that was dumb. Should have kept my mouth shut.

If anyone comes asking, she'll remember every detail of our conversation—ladies like that always do. They have nothing better to fill their lives with.

Real smooth, Elroy.

The Notorious fat guy blows pot smoke in my face again when he opens the door for me. He's still got his Glock in the other fist. Looks at me funny, like I'm an imposter. Backs away slowly and lets me in.

The Internet connection is down. I try wireless, using my rig.

Five networks in range, I piggyback on one of them, using my invisible shield to move fast and silently inside someone else's system. I don't use the cell relay. Only a ghost could catch me. I sneak into ten people's houses across Texas in five minutes. Ask about some things that will get me noticed.

Remo's gone for sure. Murdered. They found his body in a parking lot two nights ago, heart carved out of his chest. It's been on the news.

The Fixer is still maintaining radio silence.

But he hasn't washed up anywhere.

Yet.

No word on the street about the helicopter sale—not from anyone aboveground. I'm not fool enough to contact my lawyer directly. Hell, I don't even know the guy's name. Dad set up everything with these people. It was all double blind, while I was in the joint. I can get to my safe deposit box tomorrow, if the money's still there, if Hartman hasn't gotten to the Fixer yet. But that'll take time and I need tonight for more important moves. The seventy-five grand in the trunk of my car will have to do me, plus my walking-around money. It'll be enough.

Jayne Jenison now.

The lady in black.

There's a lot on her, but I have to look real hard. I find an old e-mail account drifting in the breeze, but she did a Sarah Palin on it a long time ago. Everything important erased. Some clues, though. The names of a few companies, a few senators. Nothing unusual for a private citizen who lobbies against gun control.

But she had me going after Cheyenne Mountain, man. This one's got her finger on the triggers of much bigger guns. What the hell is she up to?

Who is she really working for?

I talk to my wireheads again. I have important questions, and now I've got cash to pay for the answers. The money brings them all running this time.

I get back in my secure chat room with six major players who know their way around government contracting and security. One of them is a guy who used to build guidance systems for nuclear warheads. Another guy had a hand in the 2000 presidential election. I tell them all what I'm looking for. I give them names. They name their prices. I say okay. It has to be cash, night deposits, but they know I'm good for it.

I ask about defense grids. I ask about rich people stockpiling women. I ask about every speck of dangerous military blackware created in the past several years, and the people who are running scared from it. I get names. Big names. Dictators. Guerrilla leaders. Feared terrorists with track records. Half these people are dead already, the other half vanished off the face of the earth.

I think about Jayne Jenison, and how easy it was for her to kill me on paper, just after Hartman took out Toy Jam.

Jesus tap-dancing Christ.

Is Jenison behind all this?

Did *she* kill all these people—and is it real or just on paper? Does she really have a daughter who was kidnapped? And what about Toni?

One of my hackers wants to see some of the code I decrypted.

I send him a sample.

He tells me he can't fucking believe what I'm sitting on.

I tell him yeah, I know.

Two of the guys in the chat room bail—right after using a lot of colorful adjectives to explain that they never wanna hear from me again. The other four triple their fees. I say okay.

Now that we've separated the men from the boys.

B ennett passes out on the hospital bed, zonked.

"She's fixed up okay," the doc says, mixing a drink from the bar, a dry martini. "But she still needs time. I can stay with her until she's okay to move."

"Is that gonna be extra? I want her taken care of, man."

"The five grand covers everything. I'll make sure she's good."

I press some more bills into his hand. "She wants to go to Florida. Can you find her a ride?"

"I'll see what I can do."

"Can't be an airplane. Has to be more off the grid."

"I have a guy I can call." He looks at the cash in his hand. "But it'll take a little more than this probably."

"How much?"

"Another grand should do it."

I give him two. What the hell, right?

"Make sure she gets where she's going. And don't spend all the rest in one place."

"Sure thing."

He finishes stirring the drink and sips at it slowly.

For the next few minutes, the doc nurses his martini, smoking cigarette after cigarette, looking nervous as he flips through channels on the big-screen TV. He ignores the two homies, who throw down some poker in the dining room nook, doing a lot of cussing, playing for real money. Their guns are on the table. I peel an eye at them, from my work at the rig. A couple of hard dudes, no doubt—maybe too hard.

I hope Bennett will be safe with them.

But I can't . . . think about . . .

My eyes close by themselves and I slap myself.

Damn.

So tired.

Whatever the doc gave me, it doesn't seem to be jump-starting my intellect that well. But it's doing an odd rumble in my guts. Maybe it'll at least help get that damn safe deposit key out. Not that I really need it, but it would be a hell of a lot healthier if I didn't have to bust the lock on a safe deposit box in front of God and all his security cameras.

No word back from anyone online. My guys are digging. Nothing on Gmail.

My eyes close again and I slap myself again.

I take the other two pills, chase them with warm sweet caffeine.

I switch off the console and fold it up in my pack, carry it with me into the main bedroom. Gotta do some thinking before I bolt out of here. Have to focus. My next move has to be a location near downtown, where I can get back on the Internet and find David Hartman. It hurts my brain to think about him, or any of my plots. I almost smell the roses, but I fight it off. I'm so goddamn tired. This bedroom has a marble walled shower recessed into a stylish annex all done up in marble and chrome that looks like something off the set of *Clash of the Titans*. The old, good one, I mean. My dad took me to see that when it came out in the early eighties. I was eight years old. All of this other business was ahead of me. All of this—my life, played in target-blips and info-bursts, just before I run again.

I splash my face in the sink. I sit down on the chromed toilet seat. My guts are rolling and rumbling. Nothing comes out. Dammit.

I pull up my pants and move over to the door of the bedroom and close it.

Unzip the long bag and pull out the shotgun—feel the weight, check the chamber, full load. These Mossbergs are monsters. I hold it in my hands for a few minutes, just standing there in the room, feeling anxious, feeling tired. Can't lose it now. Have to think about a few things.

I sit in the center of the room cross-legged and watch the door, the shotgun across my knees. Only one way into this room. If anyone comes through, they get shredded.

I watch the door.

It doesn't open.

I can hear my bodyguards arguing over cards in the next room. The TV tuned to *American Idol*. The doc sucking back martinis in there, earning his dirty money by hanging out with gangsters, or whatever the hell we are.

I breathe slowly, taking myself out of the room.

Trying to see the plot.

Their plot.

Jenison's plot.

Were you ever really within my reach, Toni?

I still have to find you.

And to find you, I have to get Hartman.

And to get Hartman, I have to stay off Jenison's radar.

I have what she wants. Hartman wants it, too. My friends in this town will be my enemies by morning. I have to deal with them all. Gonna be sticky. I start in just a moment. I'm in the future now, with Toni. She sees me and she smiles, though I can't see her face. I realize I'm dreaming as she comes for me and her hands melt in the thick air, turning into long tentacles, with thorns that pierce my flesh, but in a gentle way, a way that hurts as it loves me, a way of love because it's tough . . . because they're not tentacles at all . . . *they're roses creeping on vines . . . slashing as they envelop me . . .*

I'm dreaming and I have to wake up.

I hear the sounds of men arguing and the blare of a TV commercial about maxi pads, just on the other side of all this.

I have to wake up.

I smell the raw vegetation of the vines and the sweet smell of the roses as they invade my heart and my mind, filling me with wet dirt and sick perfume and the reverberating *boom-crack* of the magic bullet that took my one true love away from me.

Have to focus.

I hear something shatter, and there is a scream . . .

Have to . . .

My eyes open and I'm still sitting in the room. TV still blaring outside the door. The shotgun in my lap. My watch says it's nearly one in the morning.

My body just gave up for four hours, shut down without a warning. That never happened to me before, not even in prison. I feel like someone just used my head for a toilet. What the hell did the doc give me?

I get up and wash my face in the sink. Look at myself in the mirror. I need a shave, need a shower. A new set of eyes. Mine have bags that go all the way around them. My head's tingling—what's left of the drugs that didn't work.

I pick up the shotgun and go over to the door, open it carefully until I see movement in there. I go into the room, not aiming the gun at anything. The movement in the room was from the TV. A rerun of *Melrose Place*.

Then the smell hits me.

■ ■ ■

The doc got it the worst.

I only look as long as I have to.

The two homies are next to him on the couch, missing a lot of themselves. Most of it's on the floor.

The smell. It's so bad.

If there were any shots fired in this room, it wasn't enough to bring anyone running, and this was mostly a hack-and-slash job. Real hands-on work. Knives, maybe power tools. God. It took a long time for these guys to die. There's deep red all over the walls.

And . . .

Oh no.

Bennett.

Her face is full of peaceful calm—she never saw it coming. Her throat cut while she slept. She lies on the floor, her long red hair floating in a sea of blood.

The briefcase I gave her is gone.

Goddamn.

Goddamn.

No.

Don't think about her.

Survival, man.

Stay alive.

I check the shotgun in my hands and all the cartridges have been removed. Right from under my nose. While I was dead to the world and everyone else was dead, period. My twenty grand walking-around money is still taped to the inside of my right thigh, the same place it's been since we pulled out of Jenison's compound.

Were they in too big a hurry to strip me down?

Whoever came in here cleaned house and emptied my gun, then left me right where they found me. There's not even a drop of blood on my clothes. It all went down while I sawed logs in the next room. They made sure I wouldn't know a damn thing. What the hell is that?

Am I still dreaming?

The tingle does a spider dance all over me, jacked up by the sudden rush of knowing that it's always darkest . . . right before you're 100 percent screwed.

How long were they watching this place? Do they know about the car in the lot three blocks away?

I realize something else.

They took my rig, too.

Goddammit.

Why am I still alive?

This has to be a dream. I tingle all over. My right arm hurts. I look at it. There's a bloody needle hole that wasn't there before I hit the blackout, set inside a welling purple bruise, like a meteor crater in the flesh of a giant zombie.

Where they shot me full of something?

Why?

To keep me under while they cleaned house? Is that why I feel like so much hell right now?

I sway on my heels.

Tingle.

Shit . . .

I fall right on my ass, try to fight it while I'm on the floor and it sort of works. Look up at the computer in the corner. Look back at Bennett, her face frozen unknowingly in her endless sleep. Then my eyes fall on the TV screen . . .

There's a cable box on a little glass shelf right under the flat-screen that says what today's date is.

October 25.

Just now one in the morning.

Twenty-eight hours since I went to sleep.

DEAD GAME

It all comes crashing at me like a revelation of God in a bucket of ice water.

They came in here *yesterday*.

In a blip that lasted just three seconds on my radar.

But it was really twenty-four hours and some change.

I crashed and burned . . . *and they just left me in that bedroom*. Which means I'm alive because Hartman wants it that way. It has to be Hartman who did this. He's the only one crazy enough. Just like the store in Austin, killing all those people, making a riot happen. A monster in broad daylight. He sent a message again, and it's simplicity itself: I'm goddamn dead already and I might as well cut my own throat.

I have to try something, *anything*.

I have to . . .

The cell in my pocket rings.

The smell of blood crawls up my nose, sharp and wet and stinging, like salt water dripping from a rusty razor. I never got used to that. I always avoided it.

But some things are inevitable.

● ● ●

"Hello, *Mister Coffin.*"

I expected to hear the voice of the man who destroyed my life.

It's not David Hartman.

It's her.

Jenison.

"*Did you sleep well, Mister Coffin?*"

Now that I hear the voice, I can smell her in this room.

She was here and she let me live.

"*Hello? Are you there, Mister Coffin?*"

"Yeah."

"*I asked you a question. Did you sleep well?*"

"Okay, I guess. It's the waking-up part that's been hard. But you know that already."

"*You did seem quite dead to the world last night.*"

"No pun intended?"

"*Obviously.*"

"What the hell do you people want?"

"*Why don't we talk in person?*"

I hear the killer in her voice. That terrible need to be hands-on with her work.

I tell her I'll meet her in the lobby.

And she says:

"*Excellent, Mister Coffin. The drinks are on me.*"

I leave on the *ThunderCats* sweatshirt, throw on the threadbare corduroy jacket from Goodwill, the one from the long zip-up bag that had our guns in it. They took the guns, left the clothes. Left the bag of Fritos, too. Mighty white of them.

I get the Colt Python I stashed under the sink in the bathroom. They couldn't have been in much of a hurry to get done with business. They had all the time in the world. That's why the homies in here got it so bad. And yet they left me twenty grand and a loaded pistol. Maybe they just didn't think about it. Had me cold, after all. Has to be a camera in here, keeping an eye on me. That's how she knew right when to call. How much else do they know? What kind of game is this?

I can't figure it out.

My head is swimming.

My head shouldn't swim.

I just slept for a day and a night.

Focus, dammit.

Focus.

The *ThunderCats* logo burns on my chest, just under the jacket, like a target. I shove the gun in my left front pocket. It's small enough to fit in there. My reflection dances in a wall mirror stained with blood.

I leave Bennett behind me, like everything else.

I took care of her, didn't I?

I did all I could, right?

It's not my fault.

Right?

Right.

Game time.

You bastards.

. . .

I open the door and walk down the hall. Check the time: one forty-five. It smells like a hundred different bad colognes and aftershaves out here, all covered up by that expensive new-carpet scent, and the essence of cleaning fluids. Every ritzy hotel smells the same, even on the penthouse floor. Nobody in the hall. The elevator waits around a corner. The ice machine makes strange clunky sounds in an alcove near the snack vending boxes. Five bucks for fifteen M&M's and a Diet Coke. Someone's always stealing from someone else.

I hear someone cough and there's no one near me.

My heartbeat hammers my chest.

Tingling.

I push the glowing button on the silver plate next to the elevator door that has an arrow pointing towards the lobby. Something goes ding inside the wall. I take two steps back. Another ding. The red arrow above lights up red. The doors roll open.

Something screams at me. A flabby old woman in a tank top laughing at a skinny man in a suit, who just told a joke she likes. I watch them as they stumble drunkenly out of the elevator, around the corner. Their voices, like phantoms, receding away from me. The elevator is empty.

My heart.

Pounding harder now.

Gotta be calm.

Gotta keep it under control.

I step in and hit *L* for Lobby.

I think about Bennett back there. Alex. That calm

look on her face. I wonder what she was dreaming about when they killed her. Was she a child again, listening to her adopted father's records and wondering about the eighties? Or was she strung out in terror beneath the blade of a crazy hatchet man? Choking on her own blood, trying to sing a song for me. Going down slow and awful, just the way she said she wouldn't.

My head is pounding with the thought.

Tingle, tingle, tingle.

Heartbeat, heartbeat, heartbeat.

The car stops on the next floor. I step back from the door, seeing the redness on my face in the mirrored surface of the elevator wall next to me. I look like a tomato. About to blow.

An old lady stands there when the doors open, asks me if this is going up. I aim for the lobby with my finger. She says thanks but no thanks. Tells me God bless you, son. The doors close on her. Maybe she's gone forever, maybe she's not.

Express, straight down. No stops, all the rest of the way to the lobby.

The fresh air-conditioning hits me in the face as the doors open, the coolness like a Taser burst, the tingling in my head flushing across my skin, making my eyes water for a second.

I almost fall on my ass again.

Catch my snap.

I step across the threshold, and feel like I'm walking somewhere doomed, because I am. The floor is marble. Smoked glass and chrome. Lots of people crowded around the front desk. A huge court area with couches and tables for wireless Internet in the center. Two res-

taurants closed down for the night—a Chili's franchise
location and something called Teighlor's Pit. Looks posh,
like an upscale barbecue joint. An open bar area, near the
Wi-Fi lounge. Security cameras in every nook and cranny.
Lots of people. The bar is pretty well traveled this morning. They stop serving booze at two—goddamn Texas
church laws. This place is nice and public.

It won't do me any good.

Not with these monsters.

The tingling in my head begins to transform into a
sparkle.

Something grinding inside me.

My heart is doing ninety in my rib cage.

I start to walk across the marble floor, feeling the
cold through the soles of my cheap Goodwill tennis
shoes. I put my hands in my jacket pockets, hunch over
a little. When you try to look anonymous, you end up
looking suspicious. That's why I never wear sunglasses.

The bar, just thirty feet away now.

I'm looking at every face. Looking for the lady in
black. For anyone who looks like a bad guy. I'm walking
in the crosshairs of a dozen shooters. At least. If they're
smart. If they know me as well as I think they do.

The bar, twenty feet away now.

A guy in a jogging suit gives me a wink. A young lady
in a print dress smiles at me as she passes by. I see that
the bartender is a dirty-blonde in a blue tank top, her
bra straps fighting for space on her shoulders. A piece
of plastic hanging off one of the straps says her name is
CHARLENE. Hair up in a bun. Five barflies with half-dead
soldiers, jabbering at her aimlessly. Six tourists standing
around, waiting for their late-night cocktails.

Ten feet away, the bar.

About fifteen people in the place, total. All of them are dead if I do this wrong.

Five feet. Three feet. I order a gin and tonic.

Pay for it with a twenty I tell Charlene to hang on to. She smiles and it reminds me of something pleasant, something comforting. A woman's smile always does that to me, I guess, even though I'm a walking dead man. My eyes scan the room—the whole lobby beyond the bar area. Low-level lighting in this corner. Careful.

A hand on my shoulder.

I feel it slap there like ice, even through my jacket, and I turn to face a man I've never met before. Mussed-up hair and bad sports jacket, thin face like a rat. He's holding some ice in a glass and has a smoke dangling from his lower lip. Makes a clicking gesture with his thumb and asks me for a light. Slurry voice. I tell him I don't smoke. He says that's okay and staggers past me, clunks his glass on the bar and asks for a refill.

I walk casually, ice tinkling in my hand. Find an empty couch sitting in front of a glass table, facing a plush chair. I don't sit in it. I check every face in the place, twice. Nobody familiar.

I look at my watch. One fifty.

Sink the rest of my drink and go back to the bar.

Charlene asks me if I want another and I tell her no. She gives me another one anyway, says it's on the house. Sets it on a napkin for me.

I take the drink. I notice there's something written on the napkin. Looks like a phone number. I look up and she winks at me. I notice she's very pretty, even with her hair up like that. Her shoulders are creamy, all strapped down. I look at the number again. Then I look back at her.

She tilts her head, like a question. Like, *Do you wanna?* I shake my head slightly, give her a look right back, like, *Maybe next time.*

My heart tingles now, along with the sparks in the back of my eyes.

She looks down at her work behind the bar, rejected.

I want to tell her to run. To get the hell away from here. That something very bad is about to happen. I don't say anything to her. Change my look to urgent instead. Throw my eyes towards the main entrance of the lobby. *Run like hell, lady.* She jacks up her eyebrows, wondering what it means.

It's a few minutes to two.

A piston begins to thrum in my head, jackhammering my heart now. I'm working on adrenaline. *What the hell did they shoot me full of?*

I watch the door of the lobby. I reach into my pocket and run my finger along the smooth cold surface of the gun. Nobody comes. I wander back to the empty couch with the coffee table and sit down.

And I wait, sipping slowly.

Yes, here I am.

Just sitting and sipping slowly.

I try to calm myself.

The tingling is a slow nag in the back of my skull now. *Keep it under control.*

The bartender looks at me, concerned. I nod towards the exit again. And when I do that, I see two men, across the court area, near the front desk. Big guys. They look almost familiar. I would know them if I'd seen them before. They're not walking over here, though—they're headed for the elevator.

Two more men, opposite side of the court area. Also not looking at me. Headed for the valet station near the sliding glass doors to the outside.

The man who asked for a cigarette is staring me down now from his perch at the bar.

Gordian knot.

I remember the phone in my other pocket. The number on the napkin. I look at the bartender and she winks again, not smiling this time. What does her face remind me of?

Oh.

Yeah.

Now, I get it.

I pull out the phone and tap in the number.

Ring.

Ring.

Ring.

Click.

A woman's voice I don't recognize says hello. I say hello back. It's not the bartender. She's still standing there in my line of sight, not talking into a phone at all.

And then the voice says this:

"*Baby, get the hell out of there. They're going to kill you.*"

"Who the hell is this?"

Click.

I try the number again. No answer. The two men who went into the elevator are walking back into the lobby.

Very slowly. The other two men I saw are doing the same thing.

I look for the bartender.

She's gone.

I get up, just as someone comes out of nowhere and sits down in the chair in front of me. She has bright blonde hair and her smile doesn't remind me of anything. She's wearing a black blouse and suit coat.

"Hello," she says.

I stand there.

Jenison's expression still doesn't look like anything, even when she crosses her legs, and yet somehow, I'm trapped by her eyes.

"How are you feeling, Mister Coffin?"

I stand there, looking at her. The men from the elevator are at the bar with the drunk guy now. He doesn't look so drunk anymore. Now two more men in the lobby, with long overcoats on.

Toni . . . was that *you* on the phone?

I didn't recognize you . . . *but* . . .

The phone is still in my hand.

My thumb almost tries the number again.

"Who were you calling?" Jenison shifts a little when she asks me that and I look at the men in the lobby again, then at the guys she has on the bar. I don't say anything.

She has no idea who I was talking to.

"I'm starting to get mildly irritated, Mister Coffin. That makes two questions you haven't answered. Don't mind my security. They're just creating a perimeter. I would expect by now you've surmised that there is no way you're getting out of here."

I sit down. Real slow.

"Why not just grab me? Why all this song and dance?"

"I wanted to illustrate the odds against you, Mister Coffin. Sending a message is important. You've not understood that until this very moment, I think."

"I understood it when those guys shot up the toy store."

"No, you didn't. Or you wouldn't have stolen my helicopter."

"So you thought you'd leave me passed out for twenty-four hours in a room full of blood, just to scare me? I'm not sure I believe that."

"You think housekeeping would have called the police? *Please*, Mister Coffin. My people have been in control of everything inside this building since last night. We've been watching you closely. The pills you took had to run their natural course . . . so we just let you sleep while we talked with your friends."

"Not sure I believe that, either."

"Believe what you want. I thought we could speak like civilized people, in a place of comfort. After all, there's no need for us to get *ugly* with you, Mister Coffin. Torture and murder are such barbaric means of getting what you want in situations like this. We're just going to have a nice, *pleasant* conversation."

I don't like the way she says that.

Like she knows something I don't.

She let me walk right out of that room, where they could have killed me in my sleep, just the way they killed Alex Bennett . . . and now here we are . . . and she wants to buy me a drink? Did I think that was all so absurd just a few seconds ago?

I don't like the way this all seems so pleasant, just like she said.

Pleasant.

That actually sounds kind of . . . okay right about now.

What?

"And please don't think of any grand escape this time, Mister Coffin. All the bases are covered. You can't run from us in this building. If you had tried after we spoke on the phone you would have been brought here in any event."

More thugs in the lobby, behind the first flank. Four now, three on the bar. All exits blocked. All elevators covered.

That seems okay somehow.

As it should be.

This isn't okay at all.

My head goes light for a second when I think that, and I look at the hole in my arm. "What . . . did you shoot me up with?"

"A little cocktail. Not exactly sure what it's called, but it will dull your reflexes . . . and, shall we say, *enhance* your senses? Your long slumber softened your system for it quite nicely. The effect will soon be permanent, I'm afraid, but we *will* have our time together. At least long enough for us to have a conversation without incident. The doctor kindly prepared your prescription before he expired."

They've shot me up with something that will kill me.

I have to make them take it out of me.

I have to . . . *have to* . . .

"I have a gun."

"Our guns are bigger than yours, Mister Coffin."

"Go to hell."

She pauses before saying: "Let me make my position *perfectly* clear. You have items in your possession that belong to me. The helicopter can perish in flames, for all I care. I want what you brought out of that vault. There were traces on your machine in the hotel room, but not everything. Our original contract was for two million. Your account has been adjusted. Now . . ."

She looks right in my eyes.

". . . tell me where the disc drives are located . . ."

Right into my eyes.

". . . and I'll buy you a drink."

"You're going to let me die anyway, why should I talk to you?"

"Because you want to, Mister Coffin. You *want* to."

When she says the word *want* . . . it seems right somehow.

I *want* to tell her what she *wants*.

I want that, don't I?

No.

They've drugged me.

This woman intends to kill me.

"You *always* planned on killing me."

"Not in the beginning, Mister Coffin. We had to re-evaluate things when you became difficult. You've been snooping around the edges just a little too much. You're very smart. My organization has issues with very smart people."

"You use them and then you kill them."

"Only when they become difficult."

"You've been working with Hartman all along. The whole damn thing at that toy store was a setup to scare me straight."

"You're half right. Hartman and I are *former* business associates. Unfortunately, we had a parting of ways not long ago and it became necessary to appropriate what he would not allow me to purchase from him."

"You're planning on stealing nukes. That's why everyone's running scared. That's what this whole thing is about, right?"

"Nukes? You watch too many movies, Mister Coffin. Nuclear weapons are antiquated. They serve only as a deterrent and a smokescreen in this day and age. My organization requires far more . . . shall we say, *practical* means?"

"You're full of shit. I saw what was on the discs."

She makes a dim smile happen.

Shakes her head slightly.

As if to tell me I'm *almost* right. *Almost, but not quite.*

"This whole thing is about *many things*," she says. "You're only one part of it, Mister Coffin. And I never had anything to do with what went on at the toy store. That was all Hartman."

"You would have done it anyway. You killed Alex Bennett without thinking twice."

"Oh, believe me, I *did* think twice about it. Just like I thought twice about cutting you loose from jail, even after reading your psych report. An obsessed man is a dangerous man—but we've had this conversation before, haven't we?"

My head swims now.

I fight the next wave of euphoria, focus on my hatred of this woman . . . but my rage slides away from me . . . like it's oozing with a tide . . .

My rage.

All I have left to fight with.

Going away now.

The drug is taking it from me.

And words come out of my mouth that sound like this:

"You said you *understood* my obsession. I think you're just a maniac. Like Hartman."

"I'm nothing like Hartman. You know me only a little. I find that comparison insulting."

"I don't know you at all."

"Fair enough. But David Hartman is a loose cannon and a rapist of women, with no vision beyond the here and now. A shallow, degenerate monster. If it hadn't been for his disgusting theatrics, it never would have been necessary to force him out of our organization and pull you from prison in the first place."

"So you cooked up a story about a human trafficking ring and dropped the seven of us in a meat grinder. There was never any chance of finding my wife at all, was there?"

"Oh, she's *alive*, Mister Coffin. I can at least promise you that. But even if you were to walk out of here, you'd still never find her. She's gone underground. *Very* much. And I wasn't lying to you about Hartman's operation. He's quite obsessed with beautiful women. That was, ironically, one of the many reasons why we parted ways."

Then who was that on the phone?

Baby, get the hell out of there. They're going to kill you.

I hear the voice in my head, and it's sweet, just like the word *want*.

Little fingers are tickling my belly, making me feel very good.

My rage, all replaced by hearts and flowers and . . .

Oh my God. I have to focus.

She just said something about my wife.

Said she was alive.

"Did Hartman tell you where she was?"

"Like I said, we were business associates until recently. But it's a long story."

"So David grabbed my father for some fun in the dark, and you went against him to bail us both out. Because you knew you needed us."

"I needed *you*, not your father. But it's all in the family, yes?"

"You're full of shit."

She uncrosses her legs, leans forward on her knees. "I have no reason to lie now, Mister Coffin. No reason to mislead you about anything. I used your talents and I ordered your execution, that's all true. You and your father did your best to escape, and you did very well. You can go to your grave knowing that what you did for my people will be very, very important."

Important.

So very happy, that word.

Someone else said that to me. Was it a lifetime ago?

Focus, Goddammit!

I have to keep her talking, find out more.

I want to talk to this woman.

The word *talk* is so very, *very* . . .

"So how did you find me here?"

"That's a trade secret, Mister Coffin. Also, you should be more careful about who you sell an army surplus helicopter to on such short notice. Let's just say a . . . *woman* like Kim Hammer doesn't hold up well under questioning."

Oh Christ. They killed her, too. They killed everyone.

Kill is such a friendly word.

"You underestimated my reach, Mister Coffin. My organization is all over Houston. All over the world, really. You've been dead game ever since you flew off into the sunrise with my package. We've just been waiting to see what your next move would be. You've been somewhat predictable."

My voice is slurring now: "Dead game? Sounds like . . . an action . . . movie."

"I enjoy action movies. Which is your favorite, Mister Coffin?"

"This one."

She doesn't laugh. Still looks like nothing. Says everything monotone. But that's really nice, isn't it? We're just sitting here. Having a nice talk.

Yes.

I'm in my own favorite action movie.

Action and *movie* are such *important* words . . .

"I was always partial to Bruce Willis myself," she says.

"Now who's . . . kidding who?"

"I'm serious, Mister Coffin. I always enjoyed his style of machismo. It came with less branded stoicism than your standard Dirty Harry types. More of a regular guy. You bought into him a little more when he jumped off a burning building with a gun."

This is a nice conversation.

This is getting me nowhere.

I like this conversation.

Snap the hell out of this.

DO IT NOW.

"So we both like action movies," she says. "I think you like *many things*, Mister Coffin. I think you want to *tell me* about what you hid before you came to this place. You want to *tell me* whom you've spoken with. You want to *tell me* where the seventeen disc drives are."

No.

If I tell her, it will be my most terrible mistake.

I've let so many people die, even my father.

If I give up what she wants, millions more could die.

But . . . millions dying wouldn't be so bad, would it?

"Come on, Mister Coffin. Let's not forget why we're here."

Even more of her goons in the lobby. Three flanks of men. Six guys with guns. More on the exits and the elevators.

I only have a choice of how I will go out.

Can't fight them all. They will kill me, regardless.

The drug will kill me, regardless.

"One last question," I say, slurred and beaten. I want to make my voice stronger, but I can't. I can almost *visualize* the words . . . *I can hear them in my head* . . . but they struggle out garbled and awful . . .

"Make it quick," she says. "We have serious drinking to do."

Waves hitting me now.

I hardly find my voice at all now.

But I manage it.

"Did you . . . mean . . . what you said . . . when we first met . . . about family being important . . . do you . . . really . . . have . . . a . . . daughter?"

"That's two last questions, Mister Coffin."

She just sits there, not looking like anything. I stare her down. Keeping my focus on her. Losing it every third second. Keeping focus. Losing it. Keeping. Losing.

"Yes . . . I do have a daughter, Mister Coffin. And she was also taken by David Hartman. That was not a lie. I want you to know that."

She wants me to think that I like that.

That I'm cool with that.

But I say this:

"Go to hell again."

She leans back in her chair.

For a whole minute, she smiles.

"Very well, Mister Coffin. Let's have that drink anyway."

She nods to her goons at the bar. They start towards me. The men in the lobby cover the area. A small platoon, now. She keeps her eyes on me. Knows they're there, doesn't even have to look. All the time in the world to round me up. It all swims behind a wall of happiness, my vision filled with an image of endless evil. I fight it with everything I've got.

I reach into my jacket pocket.

"Tell your . . . gorillas . . . to back off . . . *I've got . . . a gun.*"

"They're not coming to kill you, Mister Coffin. They're coming to bring you a drink. I hope you don't mind whiskey."

"I'm *warning* you . . ."

"You have nothing to threaten me with. Certainly not with the gun in your pocket. Would you like to know how I *know* that, Mister Coffin? Beyond the fact that you hardly even have control of your mind at this moment?"

The men surround us now. Two on either side. Even at my best, I couldn't take all four, not from a sitting position, not with that many guns.

But that's okay, right?

Sure it is.

One of the men hands me a glass full of ice swimming in amber liquid.

"Bottoms up, Mister Coffin. There is nothing to fear anymore. Nothing at all."

Nothing to fear.

Nothing.

Have to try something.

Anything.

I flex my shoulders and realize I don't want to.

All the bases are covered.

I take the drink. I *want* to drink it.

I fight the word "want" so hard . . . like it's steel and flesh pushing against my mind.

"You still haven't answered my question, Mister Coffin."

"Question? You . . . asked me . . . a question?"

"Would you like to know why you have nothing to threaten me with?"

Threat.

Yes.

My hand touches the handle of the gun in my pocket, fingers trembling.

My other hand holds a glass filled with ice.

Both things that I touch are deadly. Both are things I'm fighting with everything I've got.

She knows.

"If I say the words, these men on either side of us will kill you right here in this bar, and they'll do it without even considering the consequences. That is something you will *not* do, Mister Coffin. I know that about you. I know that you've never killed anyone in your life. It reminds me of a story. Something I'd like to share with you. Would you like that?"

Like that.

Yes.

Story . . .

She sees me contort, sees my struggle.

She leans back, and her voice is like deadly silk:

"When I was five years old, my father took me to see a dogfight. He was a hustler, my father. Dirt poor. But he taught me about the way things really are. It prepared me a lot for the legitimate business world. For politics and lobbying. For the organization I've been a part of for decades. Does that surprise you?"

I don't say anything.

The men surrounding us have blast-furnace breath.

I concentrate on that—on the bad.

"My father brought me along on a lot of his scams," she says. "A little girl laughing in your lap always makes the other guy less suspicious. That *shouldn't* surprise you."

Fight them.

"Anyway . . . a small-time bootlegger who also bred fighting dogs had us meet him at a location in El Paso near the border of Mexico one afternoon. We were delivering a bag full of chopped aquarium rocks and baby laxative dressed up as cocaine. He was a crazy man without any juice at all. A thousand dollars in cash was the score. That was a fortune back then. He put it in our hands without even thinking, then handed us tequila and said we had to see his boys fight."

Fight it.

"We crossed the border, hiding in his truck, and walked into a room filled with sweaty, screaming men and the roar of simple creatures transformed into monsters—bottomless inhumanity disguised as grand sport. Like something in a nightmare. Two pit bulls in the center of the room, ripping each other apart until one of them couldn't even crawl anymore. I wondered how they made those dogs hate each other so much. It left me with nightmares for years. Haunted me, really."

She leans forward, with a victorious little grin right in my face.

"They called the loser *dead game*, Mister Coffin. The pit bull that has no idea when to quit, even after he's crawling in his own blood, long after he's lost the fight. That is what *we are* right now. Do you understand? We are, every one of us, fighting a losing battle against evil men who don't care if we live or die. We are focused only on our own *dead game*."

Her victory.

My death.

So close . . .

Her smile goes away as she leans even closer.

My hand is gripping the gun.

My hand is gripping the drink.

"And in your eyes right now I can see it," she says. "I can see the *look* of that very same dog crawling in his own blood. A dog who doesn't even know he's dead already. The question you have to ask yourself now, Mister Coffin, is really very simple: How long do I want to make this last? How long do I want to crawl in my own blood? Ask yourself that."

On her face, finally . . . the look of the devil.

Right on her face.

It's good. It's right. It's complete truth.

"Ask yourself that."

I let go of the gun. Take a sip of the drink. It doesn't taste like anything. The grunts from the bar surround me. I'm okay with this.

Everything's cool.

"Now, Mister Coffin. I think we finally *really* understand each other, yes?"

"Yes."

"Tell me where the disc drives are located. All of them."

I say the words she wants me to say.

It doesn't matter anyway.

My rage is broken.

It's all over.

The world is evil and we cannot be resurrected, not any of us.

Now, I see her face.

My love, my Toni . . .

I tell her what she wants to know.

Jenison smiles. The men from the lobby advance, pulling machine guns from under their jackets. And then a really funny thing happens.

They all start shooting at each other.

THE ENEMY OF MY
ENEMY'S ENEMY

The first shots crack off in the lobby like a string of tiny bombs. I'm shaken momentarily from my trance, the drippy sweet ooze following me, pouring over everything in a neon overdrive, making it all look like a video game. It comes rolling on fast-forward, high-def in 3-D, and I get every detail. Everybody who isn't a shooter throws themselves on the floor. I freeze, like the ice tinkling in my glass, and I catch a glimpse of Jenison still just sitting there in the chair in front of me, crossing her legs again with a bizarre expression that might be the shape of resignation, or might be a crooked grin signifying some sort of victory. The four guys surrounding me go for their guns, spinning on their heels pretty fast for meat puppets, and I can see that it's an ambush from the rear flank of men in the lobby. There were three waves converging on the bar, two men each, and the third wave in back is the one picking the fight, ripping away with a scythe of what might be 35-caliber bullets from compact machine guns—though caliber is hard to get much of a real bead on with all that big-time reverb keening back across the walls and marble floor, blowing my circuits every other microsecond. It all turns into one giant, ear-thrumming megaphone blast of killpower running together over the screaming sounds as I bolt for the nearest cover, which is the couch I was sitting in a few seconds ago. I think I jump right over it. Whoom. My glass hits the floor and explodes there. Crash. The two guys near the back of the lobby take down four men instantly and the big guys over here readjust their target priorities as the bodies hit the marble. Their Glocks and Rugers rip muzzleflashes and create a lot of property damage—it's all mostly panic shots—but a couple of bullets get a little more ambitious and blow holes in one of the shooters with a machine gun. The middle two flanks of men in the lobby are obliterated in the crossfire without a chance, but it doesn't take long before the five or six other guys who were watching the exits get into the act and everything turns into a war zone. I can't even tell who's shooting who by about thirty seconds in—the shit's hitting the fan with such velocity that the whole place is splattered and sloppy in a glorious rush, with stray shells hacking out pieces of the bar and shattering bottles and taking out the smoked glass and chumming the whole front desk into bits of shrapnel. I crouch low and keep my head down in a duck-and-cover, but I'm dead if this shitstorm gets any closer to me and I have to move my ass. You only get so much of a lifeline. I hear large men yell out just as their lungs take massive doses of lead poisoning, and their screams deflate as they fall over and die, like talking dolls cut short in mid-sentence. One of them kisses the glass coffee table just on the

other side of the couch and a crackling shower of diamond dust and glittering crimson blood-beads does this
incredible detonation thing, exploding in the air as the
firefight seems to die off for just a few seconds . . . and
that's when I decide to run like a bastard. I was in a
wide-scale gun battle once like this, with my father, and
he got us through the gauntlet without a nick. I've
played a lot of video games, too. The secret isn't neces-
sarily to stay low—the bullets can get to you wherever
you are—but in a room with this many shooters firing
all crazy at deflective surfaces and advancing on your
position, you don't want to stay still for very long. This
is so easy to put together in my mind. So fast, and yet
with all the time in the world. Vanilla ooze. The zing of
funny little cartoon insects all about me. I'm scrambling
around the couch, skittering like a spider, grabbing Jenison, who still seems like she's just sitting there smiling
with a cocktail in the middle of World War III, and I
throw her in front of me. I find my rage again, like it's a
special power-up on the final level of a first-person
shooter. My whole body becomes a burning, seething
weapon. Let's see if you care about my gun *now*, you
bitch. Bruce Willis cheers me on. A fake crystal chande-
lier I never noticed before disengages from the ceiling
just a few feet away and comes crashing down in a
razor-slashing death-from-above surprise package—it
makes a lot of noise and sends glass everywhere. Jenison
tries to wriggle loose when my mouth yaps open at the
spectacle but I jam a fist into her windpipe—a weak effort, but it has the desired effect. I *think* it does. It's like
pushing my hand into chewy taffy. She struggles to
breathe. I drag her backwards on the floor, hoping she

doesn't get shot because I really think I need this woman alive for some reason, or maybe I just want to kill her later, all by myself. My head is spinning. I really don't know what the hell's going on here. The next wave of shooting busts out now and I see that the rear flank has taken cover by what's left of the front desk. There's blood everywhere, bodies all over the place. It all just happened so fast. Blinked my eyes and there it was. I have no idea which of these shooters are the good guys. Jenison thunks a limp elbow into my midsection and squirms, trying to get free. She's not afraid of me, but I've got a pretty good hammerlock over her throat now, the power of some mad phantom whoopie spiraling in my bloodstream like corpuscles set on fire, injecting pure rocket fuel right into my heart and my hands. One of the last two meaty guys standing—the one who gave me the drink, I think, and wasn't that damn awesome of him?—finally notices his boss being dragged off and spins to do something, and that's the moment when a crisp fan of machine-gun fire stitches through his face like a jagged connect-the-dots tracer burn, blowing his right eye out, turning his personality into a thick pink-and-red *ploosh!* It splashes all over the face of his buddy next to him—a slightly smaller fellow who's already down on one knee with three in the chest. The brainless, eyeless wonder on his right falls like an anvil in a cartoon and they both go down for good—piles of meat wearing cheap clothes. I hear footfalls behind me almost as fast as I react, the fire in my muscles spinning me in a weird sort of slow motion as a new push of euphoria hits me, two shooters coming into my line of sight. I forget about Jenison—what did I even want her for in the first place?—and I try to do something with the gun, but my finger won't pull the trigger. The two shooters covering me have really inefficient weapons: Uzi 9-mils. Gangbanger junk from 1982. I see all the primitive little lever-action cogs on the slick metal of the two machines in their hands as another circuit in my brain flash-fries—and, holy shit, I get a *really detailed memory flash* about how my father said you never wanna go full auto with one of those because you only get about a second and a half of continuous fire and the eighth round or so almost always jams in the breech, causing your average dumbass to reach for the bolt on instinct, and that's when your average dumbass will touch some part of the noninsulated metal and burn the hell out of his hand, causing him to drop his weapon . . . and the memory flash dies down . . . and I'm looking at my death, which comes in the form of really cheeseball weaponry purchased from a clip-out coupon in the back of some jack-off magazine for weekend mercenaries, and these men are going to kill me but that's cool because everything's a video game now and I'll get an extra life and I can hit the reset button and . . . and . . . AND . . . the euphoria wave backs off me, and the world calms down again just for a second. And they're gonna kill me. But that doesn't happen. They don't shoot at all. One of them opens his mouth and words come out that I don't understand. All the sound in the room goes gooey again in the next second, my vision tilting and whirling. The drug was *time release*—I realize that somewhere behind it all, the most logical part of my mind screaming at me in a room full of insane people. It's dragracing my system now, hitting me hard.

They never planned on having me under the knife—wanted me to talk, not bleed. She was going to sit in that chair and we were going to talk about betrayal and best laid plans and Bruce Willis movies until I was hallucinating that she was my best buddy and I'd tell her whatever she wanted to know. Did I tell her anything? What else did we talk about? I feel something writhe loose under my arms as the next wave crashes into me, and it feels terrific, something cold and warm and full of the best parts of being a child, the room all streaking by now, the shots from the guns behind me—all a fun little bit of nothing special, or maybe it *is* special, maybe it's firecrackers on the Fourth of July, maybe it's hands clapping for my latest triumph . . . maybe my brain is melting and that's just fine . . . just fine and dandy . . . and here I go . . . under the *goosh* of it all . . . and I try to stand up . . . and the two shooters with Uzis are running towards me . . . and someone screams . . . I think it might be *me* . . .

. . . and down I go, into a deep, dark hole now.

Something pulling me back as I go . . .

A voice.

A woman's voice.

I'm back up.

Turbines to speed, one-quarter impulse power.

Batman and Mr. Sulu, fighting for control of my self-destructing brain.

I'm running down a stairwell, following a big meaty guy, and our footfalls bounce off the walls like basketballs, slapping against my eardrums. I'm waking up running. That's never happened to me before. The euphoria is still hanging on like the clingy remnants of a really amazing dream. And it sleets back in tiny little slushies as I feel another presence in my system, like a cavalry charge delivering a new attack, backing me up somehow. My logical mind is wondering if the drink they gave me back there was some sort of reagent to take the edge off my hallucinatory state, or maybe I was hit with something during my blackout? My senses quickly drown out Mr. Logical as we get to the bottom of the stairwell, and a door opens and I smell the stuffy subterranean concrete. Seems like a parking structure. Something out of an old dream I had years ago. Someone is shoving me from the back. A screech of tires on smooth concrete. The smell of burning rubber and gasoline.

The hands shove me forward again. That woman's voice again. It's like Tinkerbell back there, telling me to move my ass or Captain Hook will stab his naughty metal pig sticker right up in my bad place. It's almost like being a kid again. I wonder why I never tried recreational drugs before tonight.

I'm suddenly in the backseat of a car that smells old and moldy, and there's a woman on my right side and a very big person on my left. Feels like there's a lot of room back here. Who's driving? Does it matter?

"He's fucked up," the woman's voice says. Someone shines a penlight in my eyes. Then she says something else, something about my pupils being dilated.

The big guy next to me smells very familiar. Why does that comfort me? The car accelerates as the next wave tsunamis over my brain. I feel this one like a wall of water, splashing in my face. Wait. It *is* water.

Someone just threw water on me.

"Stay with us," the woman's voice says.

Why can't I see her?

Why can't I see anything?

The fast neon and glimmering lights of the city hit my face—we're racing up into the street. I'm jerked around as the driver makes some fast moves, getting us into the chaos of downtown. Oh great. Downtown Houston in the middle of the night while I'm overdosing on some lab-grade truthtell. I'm about to really lose my mind, I think.

But the fear buries itself fast, smothered in a wave of security, as a voice comes out of the neon in my eyes:

"Hang in there, kid. You have to detox. Just try to stay awake."

It's really familiar, the man's voice.

The cavalry.

I see his face in the streetlights flashing by above me and he smiles, his bleached blond hair sparkling, like maybe the way an archangel is supposed to look after it saves your ass.

"Franklin," I manage to say. "What the hell took you so long?"

I see him give that old smile of his, and he makes some kind of remark that sounds funny, but I can't tell. I don't hear it all the way because by the time he finishes talking I'm under the wave again and the woman is telling the driver to stand on it. I turn in the direction of her voice and I try real hard to see her face. The neon dreamlight sparkles her up as we come out from under an elevated freeway overpass, and she looks really familiar.

Like another angel.

There's something I have to tell these people, but I can't remember what the hell it is. Something important. About Bruce Willis, I think.

Something about an action movie.

I calm myself as we leave downtown behind and plunge into the heart of . . . somewhere. My eyes are fogged, my face and hair soaked with sweat and water. Doesn't feel like my clothes are wet, which seems odd at first, but I don't pay attention to that for very long. I'm concentrating on storefronts and clubs racing by on either side. A time-lapse blur. The voice of the woman, telling me to stay with her. It seems like a million years later when we pull into a driveway in some neighborhood that feels like it might be in the center of a whale and everything is slow, slow, slow now. Sheets of molasses coming down hard, trying to pin me to the earth as they hustle me out of the car and walk me to the rear of a house that looks huge and old and wooden, but I can't be sure. My feet stick to the ground and I have to pull them up with a lot of effort. Finally, I just stand there in place . . . and someone has to grab me and fly me through the air. Wind in my eyes as that happens. Cool breeze and air-conditioning. A soft bed to land in.

Where the hell am I now?

Someone wearing white looms over me, asking a question in some alien language. I think when I try to open my mouth and answer the question, my lips are stapled together. Something cool jets into my heart. Someone moving over me.

Receding back.

Down and down.

Backwards across the universe.

To the end of everything.

So this is what the edge looks like.

I'm looking right at it.

The woman's voice calls me back. I struggle to find it and I swim like hell. My father is here, too. The Sarge stands right next to him. Tells me not to look.

God is laughing at me.

Don't look.

I feel it for the whole five hours it takes for me to detox. I never pass out or go under. They won't let that happen. Someone is always with me. But none of these people have faces. Sun creeps into the room I'm in, slotted through old-fashioned blinds. I can see trees outside, just a little hint of green, the chirping of birds. Somehow I can feel it when the woman comes in to watch over me. She forces me to drink lots of water. Sometimes she gives me fruit juice. Food is right out of the question. And I can feel Franklin, too. I want to know what's going on, but I can't ever make my mouth work. I hear someone say something about it being too late, that I'm a vegetable now. But that's not true. I made it back from the edge hours ago, days ago, weeks ago. Years ago. I'm smarter than the average bear. I play video games better than anyone else. Really, I do. These people saved me from maniacs. The bad guys are on all sides of us now. They are the enemy of my enemy's enemy. I want to tell them all these things but

I have to undo the staples on my lips first. Have to pry my mouth open. Have to do it soon.

"Who are you?"

Those are the first words I say to anyone. I say them to the woman sitting next to the bed. She was reading to me from a book about sniper guns just now. She is beautiful in the way that plain women are beautiful, in the way hard women are beautiful. She reminds me of my mother.

She smiles when she hears my voice.

"My name's Marcie. You're in our house."

"You're very pretty. Are you his wife?"

"Whose wife?"

"Franklin's."

She makes a funny thing happen with her face. "I'm Bob's business associate. We own this house, along with some others."

"You're all war veterans. He told me about you."

"Did he now?"

"Thank you. For saving my life."

"You don't have to thank us, friend," says another voice from across the room. "You have to *pay* us."

I almost smile, because this time the joke is funny.

Franklin comes through an open door I never noticed and has a seat on the other side of me. He's got his cowboy hat on, a white one, and he's duded-up real fine with a jacket and string tie, silver stars flashing on white collars. He tips his hat and smiles at me. "You remember what we agreed on, right? You're good for it?"

"Yeah."

"I hadda walk right off my shift at Jenny's place to bail your ass out, partner. The lady here thinks we should charge extra."

I almost forgot. Bouncing drunks at the titty bar.

"Wait," I tell him. "This place might not be safe. I can't be sure what I said to those people. I might have told them—"

"You'll be good for a while. Don't worry, I made sure the package is secure. Just like you told me to."

And he showed up just when I said. That was our arrangement. If I don't call in within twenty-four hours, come and get me.

Smart us.

But . . .

"It can't be safe here. She was asking me questions about the stuff. About who I'd talked to. I was completely out of my mind. They'll show up at the club looking for you."

Marcie closes her book and looks at me hard. "What kind of shit did you just involve us in?"

I roll my eyes at her. "The kind of shit that involves a billion people killing each other in a very public place, lady. Or didn't you notice we just walked out of a war zone?"

"It wasn't that bad," she says. "I've seen worse."

"I'm telling you, something big is going on. Did Franklin tell you he was working for them, too, a few days ago?"

She looks at him hard. "Must've slipped his mind."

Franklin almost shrugs his shoulders, but doesn't.

All in a day's work, I guess.

"Do you people have Internet here?"

"Yeah," Franklin says. "What about our money?"

"It's taped to my leg. And I have extra, stashed. If you can help out with some more legal advice."

"Man, we nearly got *killed* back there," he says, like he never signed up in the first place, like I never told him how dangerous it was going to be. "Two guys I know real well bought it in that lobby. People who lived here."

"You didn't have to bring your friends."

"It's a damn good thing I did. Otherwise, we'd all be dead."

"More money for you, then," I tell him, remembering what he said before. About being in the Gulf War. "Feel like making some more?"

He pushes back his hat. Scratches his forehead. The woman shrugs.

"What did you have in mind?" Franklin says.

After I tell him what the plot is, he says he has to run it up the flagpole and see who salutes. I roll up my pants and peel my walking-around money off my leg. On any other day, tearing off all that duct tape might actually hurt.

But today?

Shit.

Franklin hands me a pair of scissors and I open the package. Twenty grand in cash and a photograph from a digital camera, folded in half. The photo Jenison gave me at our third meeting. I look at it a second, then hand it to Franklin, telling him that's my wife and that I have to find her. He considers my words with a half grunt, his eyes narrowing against the fuzz and the grain of the image. Shakes his head, like he's telling me he has no idea who those people are. Doesn't matter. I need these guys for their guns, not their smarts. I hand him fifteen thousand dollars in cash, and top it with another four. I tell him to think of it as a down payment.

He says we'll have to see. Gotta run it up the flag-pole first.

I don't tell him about Jenison. I don't tell him about what Jenison told me. That terrible story about the dog crawling in his own blood. It wasn't just about the dog. She was telling me something else, about all of us.

We are all crawling in our own blood.

We are focused only on our own dead game.

I remember that part really clearly, even though my mind was half gone when she said the words. I also re-member her telling me it's not about nukes. Nukes are impractical. What was she saying? What the hell was she really trying to tell me?

Don't look, son.

It's the face of God.

I don't say any of this to Franklin. This is strictly need-to-know. A serious table with serious stakes. But I have an advantage: one of the players is David Hartman. He knows what's really going down. Why they want to break the mainframe that controls Cheyenne Moun-tain—and why it's not about nukes.

And David Hartman might still have my wife.

That makes this a no-brainer.

Franklin brings me some fresh clothes that look like they'll fit pretty well. Jeans and a black beefy tee, striped flannel workshirt. Typical twentysomething slacker uniform. What to wear when you wanna blend right in on the corner.

He shows me to a bathroom, just around a sharp corner on the second floor of the house—which is huge, built in the fifties, with creaky stairs and floorboards and dirty rugs that smell like marijuana. The wallpaper is peeling off, revealing a skeleton of rotten stucco and wood struts. This place is nestled in a pretty remote location just on the outside of the Bellaire subdivision, past the Galleria. A place for people with sad pasts to hide out from whatever. The bathroom is a tiny thing, but it has a shower. Franklin leaves me to it.

He keeps the stack of nineteen large in his hand the whole time.

When I am alone, I peel off a second skin soaked with blood and sweat and I wash three days' worth of running scum down a tiny drain in a narrow stall with a glass door. The steam smothers me, makes me feel like a ghost. My feet seem like mirages, way down beyond a woozy shimmer. The water is hot. My head begins to pound. I feel Toni, closer than ever in this fog. Screaming my name now. Almost there. *Almost . . .*

I grit my teeth and the rage sparkles somewhere.

Sparkles like the hot water.

It wants to show me her face.

It almost comes . . . *almost* . . . but the wave crashes back.

Not ready yet. My mind is too fried. The buzzing becomes an afterburn as the rush leaves me. I almost sink to my knees. But I hold myself up.

Have to hold myself up, man.

Don't lose it now.

The face of Alex Bennett—Alex *Gange*—fades into view, shimmering in the fog.

I can't look at her, either.

She only smiles at me, but I can't look at her.

I want to tell her I'm sorry, but I can't. I want to tell her this is all my fault, but it isn't. I want to apologize because I failed her . . . because I failed her father . . .

But what could I have done?

Alex . . . Axl . . . *I'm sorry*.

She doesn't hear me because she's dead.

The basement staircase is just past a locked steel door hidden in a hall closet. Down the stairs, in the center of the subterranean chamber, Franklin snaps on a hanging bulb over racks of ordnance. They have everything down here from slingshots to grenade launchers, all in neat rows, the rifles and pistols shiny and polished, the slick surfaces swimming in beads of dull light. A couple of concrete safes, too. That's probably where they keep the C-4. You could start a miniature revolution with this gear. Their intel center is fairly respectable, too. Maps on the walls, a couple of dry erase boards with names and dates on them. A watercooler and a full-sized refrigerator. Modded laptops with satellite interface, a couple of big machines with king-hell memory and maxed-out dual processors. He tells me someone named the Weasel put the rig together and to play nice with it or I'll get my ass kicked. When he says that, my head goes light for a moment, and I picture a couple more cells in my brain flaming out. I sit down in the chair in front of the computer system and rub my temple.

"You better take it easy for a few days," he says. "They had you on some heavy drugs. You almost died."

"I don't have a few days."

"Four grand rents this basement for a while. You should take it easy."

"I have to work. There's not much time."

"Suit yourself. There's a cot in the corner. Marcie will be down to make sure you're treating the place nice. Help yourself to whatever's in the fridge. There's a shitter over there."

He aims a finger toward the far end of the chamber, where I see a dirty toilet under a stem lamp. Old issues of *Hustler* and *Playboy* scattered around like tattered snapshots of dead bodies. Reminds me of T-Jay's old prison cell.

"One of your guys used to live down here?"

He almost nods.

"I'm . . . sorry about that."

"We're all sorry for something."

Profound, man. I think the last time I heard someone say that, it was in an Indiana Jones film. Almost makes me wonder what the hell I'm doing here with these losers.

I should run away from this place. I shouldn't trust anyone. I'm taking my life in my hands by even sitting still for more than a few hours.

So what do I do?

I look right at him and say I'm sorry again.

This time he doesn't reply at all.

• • •

I lie down on the cot for a moment, as Franklin gets a snub-nosed revolver from the rack. Smith and Wesson. Checks the spin chamber, full load. Clicks it home and stuffs it into a shoulder holster.

"Gotta go see a man about a horse," he says. "When I get back, the rest of the guys will be here and we'll see about helping with your problem."

"You can't go back to work at the club. Jenison's people will be looking for you."

"I'm not going back there. I've gotta pick up your package."

"That's risky. We should stay low."

"I don't wanna be involved with this any longer than I have to."

"Maybe we should just leave it hidden for now. These people are like cockroaches. They're everywhere. I'm starting to think they have government guys involved with them. If that's true, they've got eyes in outer space that can watch us wherever we run."

"You know how much money it takes to adjust the lens on one of those satellites?"

"No."

"I'll be okay."

He doesn't tell me the passwords to get into the computer system. I almost wonder why. He turns on one heel and leaves me lying there in the half dark. His boots do a creaky *clop-clop-clop* up the rickety stairs. The steel door slams.

I get up and sit on the concrete floor, trying to focus. Trying to put it together.

There are so many things that don't make sense, and my mind is still too fuzzy. I concentrate hard and try to see past the white noise, to see Toni's face, to find the calm she taught me, to remember what her voice sounded like. All I get back is the old sharp pain and the weird flower smell, made even worse by the hangover. But the drug warp is receding. The shower helped. The new clothes are like a fresh skin. I can feel strong potions guest-starring in my bloodstream, backing the sickness off.

I try to bring the rage again, but it hurts too much.

No hurry. Just think. Think hard.

Focus.

Toni . . . was that really you on the phone in that bar?

Did you leave your number with that bartender, knowing those goons would be there to kill me? And why did Jenison leave herself wide open for an ambush like that? Why didn't they just grab me and start cutting my fingers off in a dark room?

Answer: Jenison knew I wouldn't crack under that kind of questioning. She knew about my training. My ability to guide myself out of anything, just by putting my mind there. They had to trick me into giving it up. They had to destroy what makes me tick.

But there are so many other questions.

Kim Hammer was the first one they hit. She would have told them everything she knew about me. They could have killed her and everyone else working for her easy. That's how they found me—at least that's what Jenison said. I have to look into that. Gotta know for sure if Kim's off the street.

I know I must have talked about Franklin. They

would have known how to contact him. They'll be looking for him now, for all of his buddies.

I have to assume this location is secure for just another twenty-four hours, tops. If these guys don't decide to help me fast enough, I'm stealing a car and going it alone. The big question that hangs over everything is this:

Did I tell them about my backup plan while I was under the serum—about hiding the last piece of the puzzle in that parking garage, along with the rest of my money from Kim Hammer's deal?

Did I really give them what they asked me for?

The system they're hunting won't work unless they have all seventeen discs, like the one I stashed in the Gold's Gym bag. The one currently sitting in the trunk of the car Kim sold me. Maybe it's still there. They might have found the car by now. Jenison's people are smart.

Did I tell her everything?

I concentrate hard to remember if I did. It doesn't seem that way. I guide every last ounce of brainpower I possess into that memory:

Sitting in front of her.

Talking about action movies.

Thinking I was dead game.

I sure as hell told her *something*.

She asked me whom I'd spoken to, and I may well have given her Franklin's name. But I don't think I said a word about my insurance policy. If Franklin was telling the truth, only he knows where the rest of the discs are. I wouldn't have been able to give them the location. I can only hope I'm still operating from strength.

It's all one big mess and I have to move really fast now.

The Weasel's computer isn't encrypted at all. It doesn't even have a password. My new playmates must figure on nobody being able to get past the steel door up the stairwell. Anyone could spy on them through a wire. This is a sloppy system. I check for blackware and virus infection programs. I'll need them if I want to go deep into the underground without leaving a slime trail. They have some stuff, but it's dated. I'm taking a risk. Everything's a risk now.

Screw it all.

The first thing I do is sneak into some houses— a few shooters, well-known guns. Street mechanics who would know about Kim Hammer. Those guys all communicate silently, through private IMs and secure chat rooms. The odd e-mail here and there. Three of them have antiquated computers running software six or seven years old, and they haven't updated their firewalls. Amazing how people give themselves up like that, just like they used to blow their cover on the phone doing drug deals. All their secrets are easy to pry. You just sneak in and grab them.

It doesn't take long to find out Kim is long gone.

I check the cop records from the last few days and it's confirmed. A heavy hit on her own house in the downtown Montrose area. That's the shady side of the inner city, where a lot of petty crime goes down, and a lot of big crime, too. I used to do major deals with heavy players there. This is major, too. Ten shooters found dead at the scene and five of Kim's boy toys. There are even a few pictures. Awful stuff. Heads blown to pieces by hollow-point rounds. Buckshot retirement packages, signed in deep red. It all went down the same night I was holed up with her Zebra Squad at the Sheraton. They made a positive ID on most of the bodies. One of them turns out to be the Puerto Rican boy she had on her arm when we did the deal. They were all being slaughtered while I was counting her money. Goddamn, man.

I remember texting her. Asking her if the area was secure. Whoever texted me back wasn't Kim Hammer. It was Jenison's people, keeping me in their crosshairs for the kill. I was dead game and I didn't even know it.

The funny thing is that there's no body on record with the cops or the Houston coroners—no positive ID that matches up with Kim. She's MIA. Maybe made it out alive, maybe not. If she did survive, she's not surfacing anytime soon. Probably halfway to Havana now on a private jet or a charter flight. All smart gangsters have a getaway plan and backup cash stashed somewhere. I hope she made it.

I dial some numbers through Skype scramblers, talk to a few people directly, using fake names I dig up. None of them tell me anything—not even the things I already know. Ghosts are roaming the streets, and everyone's scared.

It's the city of the living dead, man.

I check in with my hackers, the guys I hired last night from the hotel. There are six e-mails with detailed information, links to high-security databases, passwords and encryption code. And the numbers of bank accounts I'm supposed to wire their money to. Most of what I dig up is background on Jayne Jenison, nothing that helps me now.

I need to know about Cheyenne Mountain. Need to know what could possibly be more final than death-from-above by dirty bombs. Something way off the grid. Yet still controlled by Strategic Air Command, Region Eleven.

Maybe Jenison was lying. Maybe it really *is* about nukes.

But she had no reason to lie.

I was dead game.

Don't look in the face of God, kid.

You don't have what it takes.

. . . Wait a minute, what's this?

A message just popped up from a guy who says he has something he won't share in an e-mail. Has to be more private. I don't know his name, not his real name, but he's heavy in government contracting. His street cred is solid and he has really good references from a man I used to rob banks with. He's attached an article to his message about something called Angel Point—a government project I read about while I was in prison. The Point wasn't a mountain, but really an underground city they were building in Nevada. It made the news in '08. Some sort of government-sponsored land develop-ment scheme, a little like the exurb projects, way out in the desert.

Exurbs. Ready-made cities, created by rich people, for rich people, built outside society. Maybe a model for a new world order.

Angel Point was sort of the same thing, only under-ground.

Subterranean neighborhoods that look like shopping malls.

I get in the secure chat room and type in my guy's code, ask him what's up? He's not there. Damn. I keep the room open while I start making moves on the number I memorized in the bar. It was still in my phone when I woke up almost dead this morning.

I hack my own encrypted database offsite—the cloud where I keep all my special rainy-day blackjack programs—and I pull out some tricky software that allows me to trace the number from the same global positioning satellite this computer is wired up to. It's traced back to an iPhone that's been used a few times in the past twenty-four hours. I get GPS information on every position a call was made from or received at. My two calls to the iPhone were taken in a location just outside the hotel I was in. Then the trail arcs across Houston, ends in the center of a neighborhood with a lot of sleazy business going on. Places I used to know about but never went anywhere near.

There's one address in particular—the iPhone hasn't moved from that spot in eight hours. She ran there and stopped.

I don't recognize the address, but I get a nice picture from orbit.

A big industrial building with razor-wire fences—looks like a manufacturing plant from the outside. I know better. My best guess is they mass-produce drugs there, among other things. Could be Hartman's place. It could be his revolving inventory. His human-trafficking hub. Whoever I was talking to last night, she left her number at the bar, waited outside for the call—then ran like hell, maybe got herself snatched.

Baby, get the hell out of there. They're going to kill you.

That's all she said to me.

Was that all she had time to say?

Was it you, Toni?

Maybe she'd escaped from Hartman and tried to warn me. Or staked out that hotel lobby for days on a hot tip I would be in the building, then got in too deep when the goons descended on the place.

Yeah. It's starting to make sense.

I print a hard copy of the satellite picture. That's the objective now. Get in that building. Offer Franklin's men whatever it takes.

Get in there and find her.

I'm about to call it a day when my secure IM pings.

It's my ghost in the chat room, the guy who sent me the information on Angel Point.

He pops in under the screen name SAVIOR-1. Subtle.

We talk in really elaborate code. He's that afraid of what he has to tell me. I have to use a decrypt program to understand anything he types to me, and even then it's all in broken English, like some foreign guy using one of those over-the-counter Babylon translation programs to talk to you from a coffee shop in Rome.

He tells me the article on Angel Point was just background. Asks me if I've ever heard of the exurbs.

Yes, of course I have.

He says this is bigger than all of that. A massive project with a base of operations built on American soil.

I ask him how he knows about it.

He says there's no way in hell he's telling me who he is or anything else he knows in a chat room. He wants to meet me in person. He names a nice public place in the center of Houston. He'll have to fly in from somewhere to meet me.

I tell him he can drop dead. No way am I exposing myself like that.

He says it's really important. He's afraid for his life. Two of his friends are missing—guys who went looking for answers. He says there's a clock ticking. Says there's not much time. The sky is falling.

David Hartman said that to me.

Said those exact words:

We've covered all the bases and the sky is falling.

I ask him what any of this has to do with Cheyenne Mountain or the code I hacked. I ask him what could be worse than nukes.

He doesn't tell me.

I tell him to drop dead again.

No, he says. *Wait.*

Money time. He names a figure I can't afford, and I tell him so. I tell him he can take or leave my original offer. I have other things to do and I have to use my cash to do them. None of this matters.

He calls me a fool, tells me I have no clue what I'm in the middle of, what I've involved him in. He has a family and they could all be killed because of this.

I tell him tough shit, man. Those are the rules. You go in deep and sometimes you get hurt. I'll honor my original deal with him, not one penny more. Ten grand dropped off in his name at a night deposit box. It's the best I can do.

I'm thinking about that big industrial building.

I'm picturing my wife there.

I'm seeing David Hartman with his filthy, greasy hands all over her. I have to save her. Cheyenne Mountain be damned.

So drop dead, hacker. This is bullshit.

SAVIOR-1 doesn't answer for ten minutes.

Then, the IM pops up with two words.

That's all I get.

Just two words for ten grand.

They're worth every goddamn penny.

Resurrection Express.

GARBAGE MEN

It's the face of God, son. Don't look.

I sit in the basement armory, my fingers moving fast again across the keys of the computer, wondering what the hell I'm doing. I'm checking every available database for information on bomb shelters and defense grids. Big projects built on American soil. Nobody knows jack. At least not anybody who wants to talk. I ask about Jayne Jenison again. Nothing this time. Complete radio silence.

You ain't got the balls.

God is a mean motherfucker and he hates you.

The silence scares the hell out of me. They all wanted to talk the other night—the money brought them running like starving mice to a moldy cheddar lump—and now everyone's scared to death. People don't shut up on secure lines unless the fear of God is in them. I'm starting to think that the less I know about all this crap, the better off I'll be when the chips come down.

But the nagging voice still haunts me—the Sarge's

voice. His eyes, when he tried to cancel Alex Bennett's ticket. The ghost of that sick, mean bastard, filling the silent spaces, spiraling off on weird new trajectories in my head, like the voice of some terrible beast that knows all the secrets about everything . . .

You wanna see the face of God?

He wasn't just being cute.

They've built something big.

It's something called Resurrection Express.

What I'm sitting on might be the key to it. They might not be able to move without it. Turns out I'm using their own nasty plot—whatever the hell it is—as a shield. I can destroy the thing when it can't protect me anymore, smash the discs and toss them in the lake. Let them run their dead game without their little black box. I may be playing with fire . . . but I could be holding all the cards.

If that's true, Hartman knows what it is. Someplace underground. Where my wife went, and all those other girls went, too.

Where something very big is happening.

Which means Jenison could have been lying—Hartman could still be on their side. And their side could be right under our noses.

I do one last check on the GPS position of the iPhone. It's still sitting in the heart of that big industrial building.

Okay, David.

This is it.

This is when I look you in the eye.

If my gamble is right.

* * *

That night, we sit in a room filled with smoke and we do the deal.

The Weasel is actually a pretty thick guy—built like a steamroller and topped by a mane of dirty dreadlocks. He has red slashes for eyes and a nose that looks like it's been crunched back together in the field after being bashed sideways with a rifle. Marcie sits with him on a ratty couch. Every now and then, she reaches over and strokes his shoulder or tries to hold his hand, and he develops a nervous tic and kind of pushes her away. He looks at me with a thin stare the whole time we talk.

"You got two good friends of mine killed," he says. "And now you're sitting in my living room, asking for a favor. I oughta kick your ass outta the world."

I almost smile when he lays that on me. Sounds like a Deep South farmer trying to talk tough. But I know better.

"Shit happens," I tell him.

He doesn't look impressed, either.

One other guy sits at a table near us, weighing bags of reefer from several large bricks. He looks old and badly patched up. A hippie who turned into a soldier who turned into a hippie again. He never tells me what his name is and I never ask. He is slightly more alive than the Weasel when he talks, and has a really odd lower-Bronx accent, so I decide to call him Happy. They make a hell of a sight. Toxic twins, living on bad memories, bad chemistry and scag weed. Happy starts smiling at my bad joke, his voice croaking out a grim little staccato:

"Hey, man . . . good business is where you find it."

Franklin paces the room, which is dim and feature-less and falling apart, just like the rest of the house. His cigarette is burned almost to his knuckles. "This is a high-risk situation we're talking about. How much cash do you have, Elroy?"

"Enough."

"That's not an answer."

"I have close to a quarter million stashed here in town. And a key to a safe deposit box if we go into sud-den death."

"Sudden death." The Weasel snorts. "Really fucking funny, kid."

"It wasn't a joke."

He pulls his arm away from Marcie again. "I'm start-ing to wonder if you even know who the fuck you're *talking to*, kid. You got any idea how much bread a guy like me pulls down just to kill somebody?"

"I'm not paying you to kill anybody."

"You're not paying me to do anything. Not yet."

"Calm down," Franklin says. "The kid's all right. Whatever he's involved in, it's something major, but he damn well has the cash to pay his way. His father was Ringo Coffin."

The color drains from the Weasel's face. "Bullshit."

"As I live and breathe," Franklin says.

"That would make you Elroy Coffin," Happy says, counterbalancing a Ziploc bag full of dope. "One of my old amigos did a job with you. Remember a guy named Bones McCoy?"

I turn my mouth sideways. "Yeah, he was the doctor on *Star Trek*."

The Weasel hisses. "Notice how you're not making any of us laugh, tough guy?"

Happy shakes his head. Smiles a little. I notice that his eyes never leave the bag of dope. I've already clocked these guys for exactly what they are, and this conversation is nailing it to the floor. A semi-connected bunch of semi-professional killers who are really terrible at playing poker, or maybe they just don't care about hiding who they are. I know where I stand at least.

I rub my eyes, still foggy. "Whatever goes down, it has to go down now. There are people looking for me and I'm not even sure this house of yours is safe."

Franklin steps over to the coffee table, where the brown suitcase I gave him two days ago sits. He pats it with one hand. "This package of yours was still right where I left it. That means we're not *that* hot, at least not yet."

"Not until they decide to tighten the dragnet again," I tell him. "They could be just watching us, waiting for the next move."

Happy makes some slurry noise that sounds like this: "Who the fuck are *they*, anyhow?"

"Whoever *they* are," I tell him. "The less any of you know, the better off you'll be. We have to move now. If you guys aren't in, that's fine. I'll take my marbles and get the hell out of here."

Franklin picks it right up. "A quarter million?"

"That's all *my* marbles. You get a hundred grand."

"That's still a lotta dough. How do you figure we work the transaction?"

"We put my suitcase in a safe locker, and you hang on to the key. We do the job quick, then I take you to the money. You give me the key and I hand over the cash. Simple."

"And I promise not to come in your mouth, either," the Weasel says.

"Look, take it or leave it. I'll find help on the street if I have to."

"You don't have to do that," Franklin says, then he turns to the Weasel. "He was good for it last time. This could be one hell of a windfall."

"Yeah and a few more of us could get killed, too." That's Happy, throwing some more weed on the scale.

Franklin lights another smoke and stands up with his shoulders straight. "I say the kid's righteous. I say we kick in."

"I say you're right," Happy says.

The Weasel rolls his eyes at me. "Well, I guess the 'ayes' have it then, don't they?"

Franklin shifts his weight on one foot, giving him a serious look. "That mean you're in? We go all for one or not at all, you know that."

"Yeah, I'm in. It's a lotta money, like you said."

I don't waste any time. "I've pulled specs on the building we have to enter. Electronic security is minimal. We case the perimeter, kill the alarm systems and go in hard. The way I figure it, nobody gets killed. But no promises. We pack major firepower and do what we have to do. They could have a lot of guns inside the building. I'm not exactly sure what we're walking into."

And the more people you have standing in front of you, the less likely you are to get killed.

Franklin looks like he reads my mind when I think that.

Gives me a really suspicious grin.

"Okay," he says. "Looks like you bought us. Tell them the objective."

"We're going after a woman named Toni Coffin. She could be anywhere inside the building. There could be hundreds of women with her. It may all be tied in with an organization or an operation called Resurrection Express. Any of you ever heard of it?"

They all shake their heads.

"Then you know as much as I do," I say slowly, hoping they can't sense the lie. "We go into the building hard and cover the place, room to room, until we find her."

I pull the photo from my shirt pocket and lay it on the coffee table in front of me.

"This is her. The brunette. I know it's not much to go on, but it's the only photo I have."

And I'm not even sure if that's her, not even sure I'll recognize my own wife when I see her. Hell, I'm not even 100 percent sure she's in there—this whole thing is a crap shoot. But some chance is better than no chance at all.

They don't need to know all the little details, do they?

The Weasel looks intrigued. He picks up the picture and stares at it a few seconds. "This your mother or what?"

"My wife."

"I say no problem," Franklin says. "We've got a name, a face and a location. What we need now is a down payment."

"The five grand I gave you is the best I can do for

now. We don't have time for anything else. Get me in and out of there and you're all rich. I'm a man of my word."

Marcie finally pipes up. "I'm worried about this. Too many ifs. What if we get in there and they're waiting for you? What if these people know you're coming?"

I smile, really big.

"That's exactly what I'm hoping for."

I shake hands with Franklin and the Weasel spits on the floor. I open the suitcase and run my fingers along the black plastic casings of the sixteen hard drives. With any luck, the seventeenth drive still waits back at the parking garage, along with the money these guys are about to earn. They don't need to know about that. They don't need to know shit. We move in one hour.

Franklin closes up the suitcase. Spins the combination dials. He tells me we'll leave it in a locker at the UPS center just down the street—airports and bus stations will be too hot. We'll go there together and leave it there together. Then we're official.

They get armed and dangerous. Mostly Uzis, the same guns they were using at the hotel bar. But they also pack hunting weapons—big shotguns, like the Sarge had. And a couple of HKs for extra kick. Franklin packs that huge revolver—the .357 Korth he saved my life with—but his main axe is Heckler and Koch. I tell him that I recently saw one of those blow up in someone's hand and he just grunts and slings an Uzi on his other shoulder. You know, to be on the safe side and all.

Tough guys. Who can figure them?

The Weasel packs the plastic explosives. It's his specialty—high-voltage killpower. There's no going back after you've used it, he says. Just clears the *room*, man. Happy is on the team, too, and for a second I question the wisdom of giving a guy with that many missing brain cells a gun, but Franklin says he's never seen a better shooter under fire. I don't have any choice but to believe him.

They have a black unmarked van, an old model, I figure around 1995 or so. They call it the Ops Wagon. It'll do.

I visit the bathroom a few minutes before we take off and I still don't get my safe deposit box key back. Hurts bad when I try to force a movement. Feels almost like I break something in the strain. I forget about it fast, flush the toilet. Check the battery life on the cell phone in my pocket. Half bars, good enough. I pack a satchel with some important tools, last-minute stuff. Like my last thousand bucks, busted into small bills, courtesy of the Toxic Twins. I still have Alex Bennett's Colt Python, and I stick it in there, too. Like a tribute to the lady.

Bennett.

I'm sorry for what they did to you.

If you're still watching, I'm gonna make them bleed for it.

A whole goddamn lot.

I show the boys the layout one final time. Tell them the plot. It's simplicity itself. We get close and look at the lay of the land—if the coast is clear, we run in like Indians and scare the hell out of the cowboys. The Weasel says it'll be just like old times. I don't ask him what old times he's talking about.

I look at the computer screen and I picture Hartman one last time.

Picture his eyes.

Coming for you, scumbag.

It's half past midnight when we get to the UPS Center. I walk through the place with Franklin. We rent one of the big lockers along the back wall of a maze. Twenty bucks for twenty-four hours. Good deal. The suitcase goes in and I put the key in Franklin's hand.

"Okay," he says. "We're in business now. I turn this bad boy over when you show me a hundred large."

I nod to him, silently.

It's almost one in the morning when we get to Hartman's place.

The neighborhood is a lot of warehouses and squared-off factory buildings sitting on the edge of wilderness. Right at the far edge of town, just past the last subdivision. There's a loft apartment building down the street. Storage units in rows. No bars, no stores. The air stabs my face with cold needles. I finally notice that I'm still hung-over from last night's party. I'm wearing clothes that are already soaked through with sweat. The inside of the Ops Wagon smells like oiled steel and unvarnished macho.

We park a block away from the industrial building with the headlights off. There's a big chain-link fence surrounding the place, topped with razor wire. Won't be a problem. The five of us split into teams. Me, Franklin and Happy bail from the back of the van and circle the compound, headed towards the main power array, which should be just at the rear, near the loading docks. Marcie and the Weasel go the other way, casing the perimeter. We'll meet them inside, just as soon as I cut the juice to the alarm box.

Franklin is right behind me, his feet falling heavy, his equipment rattling on his back. None of these guys have dressed for adventure—not like those soldiers we did the last run with. Civilian clothes all around. We're easy night targets, but the stealth approach is only going to get us so far. It doesn't matter.

We get to the box and I pry it open with a mini-crowbar from my satchel. It's all wires and circuit boards and fuses that look older than Franklin. Wow. This is going to be easier than I thought. With this kind of arcane power setup, it's a sure bet there's not even backup grids inside the place, which means security is a bad knock-knock joke. They won't have laser sensors or motion detectors. Probably not even a video surveillance system, but we can't count on them being that far back in the Dark Ages.

Still, it's easy enough. I kill almost everything, using a pair of needle-nose pliers, and I leave the main power to the building.

Around back, the fence is wide open, waiting for us.

I tell Franklin to lead point inside the loading dock, which is also wide open, with several gray vans waiting in an area lit up by a big hanging fixture, along with a couple of guys who don't look armed. He gets to them in a heartbeat. Takes both of them out with a silenced pistol. Two shots in the backs of their heads. It happens really fast. *Whup. Whup.* So much for going in without casualties. I shake my head and live with it.

Happy has my back as I move in to join Franklin, who is dragging the bodies by their ankles and shoving them under the vans. Blood gushing from their heads. They were both Mexicans wearing cheap clothes, no sidearms. He shot two unarmed men and didn't even flinch. Can't think about that now. I check the inside of the loading docks for security cameras. Nothing at first glance.

A thick beep sounds in the loading area and a door to the inside of the place opens. Another couple of Mexicans walk right into our guns. These guys are armed—9-mils. They surrender immediately when they see Franklin's Uzi in their faces, putting up their hands. I yell at Franklin not to kill them and I can see that he almost squeezes the trigger before he catches my drift. Happy takes their cheesy little gangbanger guns off their hips as Franklin hustles them over against the nearest gray van and I cuff them together at the wrists, using steel bracelets that are very easy to escape from. But they don't know that.

"English," I hiss at the one on the left. "*Comprende?*"

They both nod yes, shaking like hell.

One of them sees his buddy's feet sticking out from under the van, and turns white. "Please . . . don't kill me . . ."

The other one starts crying. "Wife . . . have wife and kids . . ."

His accent is thick and makes him hard to understand, but a man begging for his life tends to sound pretty pathetic no matter what country you were born in. I grab his face and make him look in my eyes. "We won't kill you if you tell us what we want to know. *Comprende?*"

They both nod and use the Spanish word for yes, but it comes out like weird snakes in blasts of bad breath.

"Don't confuse my friend," Franklin says, stabbing one of them in the gut with the barrel of his Uzi. "You're in America now—speak *English.*"

The guy almost says "yes" in Spanish again but catches himself.

I get right in his face. "Is this Resurrection Express?"

His eyes are glazed and terrified.

Franklin stabs him again with the gun. "He asked you a question."

"Don't know nothing," the guy rattles. "Please . . . I just make the pickup . . ."

"What about the layout of the place," Franklin says softly, right in his ear. "What's inside the door? How many men?"

"I just make the pickup . . ."

I crack a smile. "These men will shoot you both in the eyeballs. You are *going to die*, get me?"

"Please . . . please . . ."

"Tell me about Resurrection Express."

He says the word *please* again, and then it all blubbers into some weird mess I can't understand. The other one keeps quiet, shivering. If these guys really are lying about not knowing anything, they both deserve Academy Awards.

I nod to Happy. "Check the van. Let's see what they were picking up."

Franklin pulls them away and readjusts the gun against the back of the chatty one's skull. "Give up the keys, taco head."

"Not locked. Please don't kill me . . ."

Happy hears the good news and quickly throws open the doors. I realize in that moment that we've just made a very stupid mistake—could be anything, anyone, inside there. We're playing this whole thing by ear. Nobody leaps out with guns to cap us off.

Happy takes a look at what's inside and mutters:

"God fucking damn, man."

At first I can't tell what they are, but Happy knows right off. He's seen this sort of thing before. It's easy to tell by the look on his face.

And then the stench hits me and my heart falls to the pavement.

The van is piled with them, all bound with duct tape. They look like bundles of garbage, their arms behind their backs, eyes like shining copper coins, catching the dim light in a strange way that reminds me of that dreamlike moment when you see the second sight of a cat in a dark room. Dead eyes, all of them. Dozens of dead eyes. They're all women, every single one of them. Franklin doesn't flinch when he sees the bodies, but he orders the two Mexicans to their knees.

The chatty one begs us again not to kill him. I still can't understand most of what he says. Please don't kill me, just here to make the pickup, something like that.

I hiss at him to shut his mouth, looking for something familiar in any of those eyes. Anything at all. Toni could be staring sightlessly back at me and I might not ever know it. I want to cry, but I don't let myself. Happy checks the other two vans. They're both the same as this one. Full of dead girls.

Happy says the words "God fucking damn, man" again and I see him cross himself.

I notice for the first time that the second Mexican on his knees—the one who hasn't said a word—has a tool belt around his waist with several rolls of duct tape hanging from it. He sees me notice that and closes his eyes, like he's ready to die.

Garbage men.

That's all these guys are.

I can see these poor ladies in the last tortured moments of their lives, the same way I've seen so many others. I can see them watching helplessly while it happens to a roomful of other victims. Like gerbils tossed in a snake aquarium, scrambling to escape while their sisters are squeezed and eaten, one at a time. Did that happen to you, Toni? Did Hartman make good on his promise?

Every day you're on the street, people will die.

Maybe someone close to you.

Was I too late to save my wife?

I want to kick the shit out of these two assholes, but I settle for something a little more poetic. I grab the duct tape off the one guy's hip and wrap them both up tight, just like the girls in the truck. We cover their mouths, too. The quiet one starts screaming under the gag when he figures out what we are going to do. I find the keys to the van in his pocket. I lock the door on both of them, leaving them with their handiwork.

Through the back door to the loading dock is a small corridor that smells like motor oil and recent construction. Places like this always have the essence of sawdust and industry. No cameras. As low tech as it gets. Franklin gets a text from the Weasel's team that tells us they're inside the gate and nobody's home. He tells them to stand by, stay out of sight. We may need backup in a few minutes.

The door at the end of the corridor is locked, but that doesn't matter. I get through it in ten seconds. It opens into a big dark room, which is split into a maze of dirty curtains hanging from steel frames. You can hear coughing echo off the high ceilings. Low crying. Voices that pray to God, all just out of earshot. We're in the nerve center now.

I slide back one of the curtains and I see three women on ratty cots. They are still alive, but only by default. Franklin covers me as I go past the partition and get near the three. Two of them don't even see me. The other one shrinks away and brings up her arms, palms out, like she's defending herself from something.

"Please don't," she says.

I say my wife's name. She looks at me and says nothing, keeps her hands up. She smells like womanhood defiled, soaked through with opium. I can see the fresh track marks on her arms. I stare at her for almost five minutes before I realize this isn't Toni, and she has no idea what the name means. Her hair is long and black, and it blends in with the darkness in this evil little room. I can hardly see what she used to look like before the drugs and the cruelty claimed her.

We move to the next section.

The same phantoms in there, squirming and muttering, lost in a sea of blackness.

All of them women.

All very beautiful under the muck.

Strong lines and lean bodies, full breasts and lips, drugged-out smiles that give me a rough demo of what their old lives used to be like, how they were admired by men, how they still might be admired by the right set of eyeballs. They were chosen for their beauty, like my Toni was.

But this is a shantytown, the last stop on the train. This is where they go when they're used up, just before they get shipped out the back door and hauled off in an unmarked van. God only knows what happens to them after that.

Happy, stating the very obvious: "This place is fucking evil karma, man."

We move slowly through the maze, checking behind every curtain, saying my wife's name again and again. Nobody speaks back to us. I look at each woman carefully, searching for traces, taking in their scents. Happy keeps telling me to hurry my ass and I keep telling him to shut up. Ten minutes stretches to twenty minutes in the dark. I am lost in a labyrinth of sweaty perfumes and hopelessness. There are no men with guns in here—no men at all. I hope none of these women are Toni. None of them seem to be her. But he wouldn't have her here, not just yet, would he?

Not unless he caught her and—

Something explodes just to my left, and I hear a woman scream. I only have the fleeting impression of Happy stumbling around with his face half blown off before I get punched in the shoulder by a big steel fist. For a second it feels like someone shot me, as I hear staccato pulse-rattles of machine-gun fire break out across the maze. But the stinging pain never hits my nervous system. It was a piece of shrapnel from one of the steel curtain rods. Bounced off my arm.

I dive for the floor and stay down, inside one of the partitions. The two women in here are blondes who look like they used to be strippers. They are screaming their heads off and it sounds like a symphony of panic, mixing with the dull clatter of Franklin's Uzi. He's on his feet just outside the partition, opening up on gunmen I can't see. Happy is lying dead just inches away from me, his abused brain put all the way out of its misery on the floor in a gory splatter. The enemy gunfire is coming from fifty feet ahead of us in this pathetic little tent city—it sounds like heavy-caliber handguns. Maybe Smith and Wesson. Automatics, not revolvers. Enough grim caliber to take off a man's head with one shot. Franklin keeps shooting back at them but I can't see anything in here. I crawl on my arms and elbows towards the sounds of enemy fire. My eyes adjust to the dim light as I get closer, and I see the boots of two men outlined in the muzzleflashes from their guns, just visible below the curtains, and through them, too. Like the urgent, flashing glow from a couple of panicking fireflies.

They never see me coming.

I sweep the right one's leg as I lunge up from behind them. The moist snap of his ankle thumps my ears as he screams and my foot plunges into his midsection, stealing everything he's got in his lungs. His gun hits the floor and the hair trigger fires it one last time, which puts a bullet in his friend's foot. That gives me a head start on him, just as his gun arm swings around, and I catch the wrist fast, blocking the shot while his big toe explodes. My next move is a combination that puts his face in the center of a shitstorm, then cracks both arms behind his back like lobster claws. His buddy is already on the ground, unable to breathe. I drop him there, and he goes down hard, screaming that I broke his arm. This guy's not Mexican. Sounds just like one of Hartman's old-school thugs. It might even be the asshole who shot me in the head three years ago.

Franklin is spinning to cover us with the Uzi when the lights come on.

Five more guys are streaming into the room from several different entrances at the edge of the maze, all with big goddamn automatic weapons. Franklin has his Heckler off his shoulder in a hurry and while they're all telling us to freeze, he's opening up on them full auto with both guns. It lasts for about three seconds and sounds like one long thunderclap in the chamber—and two guys go down fast, the other three jumping behind what looks like a heavy forklift.

Bad cover, dumbasses.

Franklin never flinches. He's like a robot. Spends

another two seconds calmly tossing away the Uzi and reloading the Heckler, then walks straight at the men behind the forklift and opens up. Bullets spang off the metal and smash through the glass. I hear one of the gunmen scream as he gets perforated and the other one stays quiet for about a second before he jumps out and makes a run for a white hallway just beyond one of the open doors. Franklin thumbs his weapon to semi-auto and fires the last two shots through the back of the runner's skull. His head splatters ahead of him in the white corridor and he goes down like a twisted scarecrow. No alarms. No more men.

And that's when I hear her voice.

Calling my name.

Ahead of us.

It's the same voice I heard on the phone.

I run for the open white corridor, pulling the Colt Python from my satchel, and I tell Franklin to get behind me. We step over the brainless body of the scarecrow, our feet sloshing in blood and pink gore. But I'm not thinking about that.

I'm following the voice.

She's just ahead of us . . .

The white corridor opens into another huge chamber full of looming shadows that turn out to be big machines. Construction equipment. Giant steel arms and bulldozers. Oil drums. The place has a high ceiling and hanging latticework, like catwalks. Real dark in here. Smells like dried blood and gasoline. Rows of curtains in this room, too, but not as many—a labyrinthine zigzag of shadows eating shadows. The voice is coming from behind one of these curtains. Just ahead of me. Right behind me. Bouncing off the walls and slapping back in my head like some terrible accusation. Everywhere and nowhere. Echoes and shapes, slithering now, the shapes of more men with guns, black ghosts moving long across the curtains, surrounding us. On all sides.

The voice comes closer.

Calling my name.

Franklin freezes when he sees the guns. Twenty men now, oozing into view among the shadows. Assault shotguns and pistols with laser sights. Little red dots dancing all over us. We walked right into it and I don't care. The gauntlet tightens as we stand in the center of the room, me and Franklin back to back, and I don't care. I hear the sound of a million billion automatic weapons clunking and clacking and clicking *and I just don't care* . . .

The voice calls my name one last time before she's thrown through the curtain directly ahead of us.

The scent of her hits me, just before she lands on the ground like a broken puppet.

The scent of roses and gunmetal.

She looks up at me and her face is beautiful.

So, so beautiful.

It's all that matters in the world.

Her eyes are like something in a dream I forgot about a million years ago.

My God . . . has it been that long?

Her cold stare freezes me right there, even in the center of this deadly noose, now that she's this close to me—

the smell of hard things and soft flowers wafting out of nowhere to sock me right in the face. I stagger back and drop the gun and it clangs on the dusty floor.

And I just don't care.

It doesn't matter.

Nothing matters.

Just this moment.

Just my wife.

An icicle picks itself into the worst spot in my head— the bad spot where everything was lost—and a hard wave of sour heat comes down across my senses, smothering me. I force myself up through it and pull myself toward the memories, the faceless shapes, those awful missing things that have mocked me for so long.

And as she reaches out to touch me, I see devastation in her eyes. I see worlds destroyed. I see her lips shivering and her whole body rumbling with pain.

I see a version of Toni that terrifies me.

"Elroy," she says. "I waited so long . . ."

Her voice, stabbing me worse. Her scent, reminding me of everything I couldn't see in my mind's eye until just this moment . . .

What has he done to you?

I move to embrace her and something in my head blows like a bomb. No, wait . . . that's not my head. It really is an explosion. A gunshot, right near me. It spikes through the chamber hard, receding to leave me frozen there with my arms around her, my ears ringing . . .

Then, silence.

And a thick roll of sadistic laughter, coming right at me. The man who destroyed my life steps out from behind the curtain, his white suit spackled with bright red blotches.

His eyes flare like cruel diamonds.

His smile is disgusting and final.

"Ain't she a sexy thing," he says.

MANIACS LIKE US

Hartman stops laughing and cocks his head skyward, the pistol smoking in his hand. It's aimed into a dark corner of the wide chamber, not at my heart. I look at him over Toni's shoulder, my hands holding on to her. The warning shot still echoes long.

"Sorry to spoil the moment," he says. "Why don't you be a good boy and let go of the merchandise?"

"What have you done to her?"

"I said let go of the lady."

He aims the gun at me now, getting a bead on my next thought.

I'll never let you go, Toni.

Never.

The next shot cracks just past my head. I hear the slug hit the floor behind me, bouncing back into the room. The thunder staggers me on my feet, and I lose my grip on her. In the same second, a pair of rough hands grabs my arms, pulls me back—and then more hands. I can't fight these guys. Too much pain in my head, the crashing of angels and devils on all sides. The smell of roses, contaminated by sweat and grime.

Toni, just out of reach now.

The world tumbling and turning.

She is dressed all in black—silk pants and blouse, buttoned up the front, revealing just enough of her, like she's peeking out at me from beyond my ruined, black dreams, her form delicate and overpowering, her long dark hair almost hiding her face. She bites her bottom lip, then lets it go, her face defaulting into a quivering question without words.

Hartman holsters his gun under his giant suit jacket, rolling towards us.

The room is dark and frozen, the same way it was ten seconds ago, Franklin standing in place, aiming his HK at the ceiling in surrender. Me and Toni, facing each other, shot through with pain. Two dozen men with guns, making sure nobody goes anywhere.

All of us, right up shit creek.

Hartman strikes a pose, the master of the universe.

"She smells sweet, don't she, boy? Like steel roses. She always did, didn't she?"

I take a breath and I am full of her.

My vision almost blurs, and my legs almost go.

He laughs again.

"You're right on time, buddy-boy. I expected you and the old man to come in with a lot of firepower, but it wasn't really necessary. You could have just walked up and knocked."

I hardly find my voice through the buzz, through the scent, through the dark ice that freezes the room. Through Toni.

"We tried that once," I tell him, and the memory stabs me.

"Yeah, those were some good old times, weren't they? How's your head these days?"

I don't answer him.

I want to run at him.

I want to break every bone in his fat body.

I tense up and the goons grab me harder, the muscles in my legs coiling like some mad beast programmed to eat and destroy and be full of violence. And in this moment . . . the rage finds me . . .

. . . first in the pit of my stomach . . .

. . . then drawling up my throat like the smell of blood and seawater . . .

And I make noise like an animal.

"You stay right there, buddy-boy. Don't even think about it. I might just tell those good old boys to wipe what's left of yer high IQ all over the ceiling."

I almost don't hear Hartman's voice, the thunder is so loud in my head now. I feel the shadows on all sides of us tighten, the choking sweat and steel-hard grunge of ten men holding me back. I almost try to break free and spring forward.

But I stop.

I hang on for dear life, in a clutch of stinking muscle.

I look at Toni, who bites her bottom lip again—she looks like a movie star full of self-doubt when she does that. Some impossibly beautiful porcelain doll streaked with one fatal weakness that throws the whole illusion. It makes her human, makes her dangerous and elegant in mysterious imperfection. As the image rolls at me, and the mythology of her is rewritten from one second to the next, I want to reach out and touch her face. And I am stopped cold. So many gorillas on me now. Wholesale slaughter aimed point-blank at my head. More guns behind them. Hopeless.

Two of the men step over and remove Franklin's machine gun from his hand. They pat him down and find the Korth revolver, too. He stands there like a statue and lets them do it. The guy holding me takes my Colt from the dirty floor where I dropped it, and I notice for the first time that he looks like a mule wearing a dirty suit. He smells like his own leavings. They all do. Cheap backup, typical Hartman. But they'll kill me just as well as real professionals.

Toni stares at me with those eyes.

The pain almost recedes as the mythology mutates further.

Hartman does one of his wet snorts, and keeps himself from laughing out loud. "Ain't love grand? I just *knew* this would be a right teary-eyed little reunion."

I look at her hard.

I'm filled with the scent.

She shivers in the real world, wobbling on her feet. I look harder now. I see that her long black hair is sweaty and hanging in her face, makeup clots running down her chin like some kind of goth-harlequin nightmare. She stares at me, a lost ghost.

Shivering. Shaking. Unsure of anything.

I felt the tremors in her body when I touched her. I can still feel them now, like electric shocks in the space between us. She's been drugged. Or worse.

Hartman laughs again, soggy and awful.

"We've had a lot of fun since you went away," he

says. "I guess you know that. She was a wild one, boy. But everyone has their breaking point, don't they?"

She bites her lip again.

She is so beautiful when she does that.

My rage, held barely in check:

"What have you *done* to her?"

"Lots of things."

"*Fuck you.*"

"Don't make me angry, boy. Just don't do it."

The heat shocks through my body again, and this time I try to break free—but they still have me good. I scream Hartman's name. I writhe and I kick and I get smothered under the gorillas again. Dumb laughter and drool in my ears, the thunder of a dozen heartbeats . . . David, you son of a bitch . . . *you son of a bitch* . . .

The big guy doesn't look amused anymore.

He shakes his head as they hold me down.

And he says:

"Okay, fine. Have it your way."

He rolls over to one of the curtains and pulls it back along the steel bar. On the other side of the curtain are racks of equipment. Tools. A butcher's block on a table. On the butcher's block is a meat cleaver. There's blood all over it.

Just to the left of the table is a really big guy.

He's upside down.

Naked.

Strapped helpless into leather and iron.

The Weasel.

Hartman looks at me and burns.

"You're just so goddamn smart, ain't ya?"

• • •

The Weasel gurgles through rivers of blood. He's been worked over pretty bad already, his nose mashed back the other way on his face like a pulverized fruit.

Marcie lies at his feet, facedown.

Out cold or dead, I can't tell.

She's half naked and part of her midsection looks hacked away.

Hartman's face stitches with a hideous crooked spider-grin, scrawled there like bad sidewalk art, his fist grabbing the handle of the big meat blade.

"Looks like you're running with a new posse, huh? Guess that means the old man is out of the game. That's a shame, ain't it? Old Ringo was a hell of a lot better at sneaking up on someone than these two idiots."

He looks right in the Weasel's eyes.

"What's your name, boy?"

The Weasel tries to say something and the sound crashes and burns, a blubbering nonsense full of hatred and agony—but it's a lot louder this time, right in Hartman's face. And then he finally gets the words out: *"Fuck YOU!"*

Hartman grabs the Weasel by his dreadlocks and spits: "You know it's a funny thing, boy. That's *my name*, too."

He holds the meat cleaver up to the guy's face.

I look away. I hear it loud. The Weasel doesn't scream.

But the sounds he *does* make are horrifying.

Like a baby choking back its own birth.

And then Hartman slices him again.

And again.

When I finally look, part of the Weasel's face is gone, peeled away, dripping awful. Franklin's fifty-yard stare never changes. Doesn't even shake his head or flinch once. Can't tell if he's seen worse, but he's cold as ice under fire.

Toni doesn't look, her back to the whole thing. She doesn't even have to close her eyes.

What have you done to her?

Lots of things.

I tense again. Almost try to fight the goons again. Hartman sees me move and wags his eyebrows, tasting the blood on his finger.

"Just stay right there."

"David . . . don't hurt him anymore. He's just hired help."

"Well, then you shouldn't have hired him. You knew I wasn't kidding when I told you people were gonna die. After you hit my vault, it got pretty damn nasty around here. These boys will tell you all about that. My girls will tell you all about it, too."

He turns and hacks off one of the Weasel's ears.

I almost don't look away fast enough.

I hear Hartman's wheezing breath as he does the deed with three long, hard thrusts—this was always a real workout for the fat slob.

The Weasel still doesn't scream.

A couple of the goons giggle like animals.

"You made a real sloppy getaway, kiddo. Hell, it was all over the street about your meeting with Kim Hammer in less than twenty-four hours. Of course, Jenison got to you first, the lousy bitch."

He points at Toni with the cleaver.

Blood drips on the floor.

"I thought I'd send you a familiar voice," he says. "At the hotel, I mean. It was a long shot, but I figured what the hell? You were always so good at following the bread crumbs."

"Like SAVIOR-1? That was you, too, wasn't it?"

"You like that? One of my hackers. But you probably had that figured, didn't you?"

"Actually I didn't. You keep surprising me, David."

"I'd like to take credit for that—but you know I ain't a guy who likes to change his act, not like you. If I need an extra brain, I just *buy* the fucker."

Never underestimate the power of cold cash.

Shit.

"I had to do some real shopping when you went in the can, kiddo. *You're* a tough act to follow. You've been talking to a lot of my ghosts in the last few days. They tell me what to do and I bring the hammer down."

"So this is Resurrection Express?"

He grabs the Weasel by the hair.

Licks a tiny spot of blood off his face, then winks at me.

"No. But you're damn close."

I look away, just as he does something much bigger and a lot wetter to the guy. It's a huge sound of metal on flesh, right in the Weasel's thick side flank. I hear it happen, deep and terrible. And the poor bastard almost gets to scream this time, before the backwash drowns him. Then, silence.

The air freezing again between us.

Hartman rips out the cleaver and giggles.

"Here's where it gets fun, kiddo. See, you can break

a hunk of meat like this one in half so easy. You put another notch in your belt and move on to the next good old boy. But a woman like *yours* . . ."

I look deep in her eyes, trying to find what he took from her. I see tears, finally welling in there. Her whole body quakes, her lips trembling.

". . . now, buddy-boy, *she* was a challenge. That's why I always wanted her. That's why it became my own little *project*. I saw what she did to everyone around her and I knew the old gal was special. A prize."

I see months and months of torture.

Chains in a dark place, hard cocktails mixed in syringes.

Cruel steel and endless dark.

"She *glowed*, the old gal did. She made every man who could come up with spit drool all over themselves. And she could make a man *love her*, too. On the dime, just like that."

I don't want to see it, but I do. She was broken on the rack while I rotted in jail. Forced to stay with him at gunpoint, at knifepoint—at lifepoint. Drugs and madness and endless doubt. Just like the sickness that claimed me. The endless spiral.

The whole world, dropping out from under you.

"There ain't a whole lot of beautiful ladies on this earth who *have* that power, kiddo. Most of them just rely on what they look like. This one was smart. She had the sass and she had the *glow*. You were right as hell to love her like you did. Right as hell to go crazy like you did. So damn crazy and screwed up and shot to hell that you couldn't even remember her *face*. That was a new one on me. Damn strange."

He sees my eyes fill with shock.

Laughs.

"Does it really surprise you that I know about that, buddy? It shouldn't. I got a look at all your reports and medical records after you went in the joint. Had to protect my investment, after all."

"What investment?"

"The *lady*, stupid! I made a promise to her that I wouldn't kill you, so long as she stayed with me. Had to make sure you never croaked. Plus, you're just so damn smart—I knew I might need you one day. Didn't you ever wonder why I never let my boys kill you when you came in my house and raised all that hell?"

"Not really."

"That's why I spared no expense with all those doctors. That's why we fixed it to keep you in that nice deep hole of yours for so long. I was watching you every day when you were in prison. I saw your shrink reports while you were in there, too. That shouldn't surprise you, either."

"It does and it doesn't. Didn't think you would care."

"Now that just *hurts me*. You and I are pals, aren't we? And pals look out for each other, don't they?"

"Go to hell."

He laughs. "I even knew the exact *day* Jayne Jenison bought you out of the joint. Tried to stop it, of course . . . but her people are pretty serious."

"Something like that."

"Didn't matter, though—I always had my trump card handy. The lady. She's such a sexy thing, ain't she?"

Toni stares at me as he laughs again.

Goddamn.

He fixed us all real good.

Took everything from her, and from me, too.

And here we are.

"Jayne told you I was running some kinda white slavery racket, didn't she? Well, I guess maybe that's true . . . but it ain't *exactly* true, either. You might say I've been saving up for a rainy day. You know all about the rainy day, too, don't ya? Those . . . evil sons of bitches. *Jayne . . .*"

Toni, I . . .

Wait.

What did he just say?

Christ . . .

I am filled with pain and the smell of roses. The side of beef is almost dead now, hanging there in pieces. Still trying to tell the world to go fuck itself, still failing like an animal cut loose in the world of men. The smell of blood almost energizes me—cancels out the pain in my head.

I hate that so much.

Hartman nods to the goons holding me, and the knot uncoils, letting me go. One of them shoves me towards the boss like a real tough guy. I want to turn around and rearrange his mule face. I move towards Toni instead.

"Don't touch her," Hartman says sharply, growling a little. "If you touch her again, I'll have these boys shoot you where it really hurts. And you won't die, either. We'll open up that steel can in your head and play some more games. You won't even be able to *smell her* when we're done with you, boy."

I freeze in place.

He really has done his homework—all those reports from the hospital and the joint, all those doctors who could never explain why she was locked away behind a wall of shadows that smelled like roses.

He read all of that.

He knows everything.

Fuck.

Hartman licks his lips. "Remember the other day when you asked me what I wanted? Back when I took a shot at you in the street?"

"You said it was the sixty-four-thousand-dollar question."

"You know what that number *means*? You're too young to remember. I used to watch that old game show when I was knee-high to a grasshopper. Everybody back in the fifties watched those shows, like it was some kind of religion."

"They cancelled it 1958."

His eyes light up, his perfect white teeth gleaming just past fat, wet lips like a rich man's beacon slobbering through slime. "Yeah, they did, didn't they?"

"Changed it to the *128 Thousand Dollar Question* in the seventies."

He still looks really impressed. "I always wondered about that. Why they didn't round it off to a hundred and thirty, I mean. Always seemed like an odd number."

"They doubled it, that's all."

"Yeah, but it's still odd-sounding. I figure someone was doing some heavy negotiating somewhere. That's how these thing tend to work most of the time. One guy comes up with an idea, another guy talks him out of it, and then the whole thing starts over. Until you've got a number that just don't make any sense."

Then he slams the cleaver into a side of beef.

Wham.

"You're just so goddamn smart, boy."

He tosses a piece of the Weasel on the carving block.

Sears me with his next look.

"Come over here, boy," he says, tapping the block with the bloody cleaver. "Come over here and keep me company. I've got a great game we can play right now."

"You haven't changed at all, have you?"

"You *may* be right . . . but, see, there's a big difference between me and Jayne Jenison. People like her aren't maniacs like us. They want to do things that will put me and you outta business forever."

"I'm not like you. I'm not *anything* like you."

"And yet we do keep finding each other, don't we?"

He slams the meat cleaver down, into almost-dead meat. No screams now. Just the terrible sound of destroyed flesh. The gurgle of an animal trying to be a man.

Keep the big guy talking.

Say anything.

"I have what you want, David. What I stole from the vault. I'll give it to you right now, tell you where I hid it."

"I know you will. But that's for later. I need something else first. See, it all comes down to *negotiations*. That's the way it was when I had your old daddy on my ranch. He wanted something and I wanted something. He named a price and I named a price."

Yeah.

Down in a dark room, just like this one.

"I wanted his *hands*. He wanted your *life*. Startin' to get the gist?"

Dad's flesh and bones on the chopping block.

Madness and blood.

"We were just three fingers into the deal when Jayne's people grabbed him. Your daddy welshed. Probably by default, but that can't be helped. A deal's a deal and he broke it. And now *someone's* got to pay. So I'm negotiating with *you*."

Dad's body, hung from a hook and left to bleed, if Jenison hadn't saved his life.

And for what?

"Did they tell you, David? Did she tell you what they were going to do?"

He smiles thinly. Then stops himself from laughing, keeping the gruff chuckle deep in his body. Shakes his head. Waves a finger in front of his smirk.

Wouldn't you like to know?

"Dammit, David, you have to *tell me*. What the hell is Jenison going to *do*? What the hell is Resurrection Express?"

"Calm down, kiddo. We've got all night for that."

"This isn't a goddamn *game show*!"

"Says who?"

He looks at the ceiling again.

I throw a glance after him and I see the cameras, finally. Six of them, bolted to the steel supports and tangled up in a mess of wires and connections, glimmering with red lights, like embers from a dying fire.

He's recording all of this.

Wants it for later.

I feel his breath roll across the room in a long, terrible sigh, and his next words come slow and dark, floating like phantom traces, as he stares away into some remote dark corner: "I know you think I'm pretty sick. I know that's what you've always thought. And who can blame you . . ."

He looks right at me now.

His eyes, terrified.

I've never seen him like this, not ever.

". . . but believe me when I tell you that I'm *nothing* like those assholes who let you out of jail, Elroy. They've been crawling all over the world forever, doing their dirt. Controlling things, while nobody is looking. You *don't* negotiate with people like that. They have priorities that go straight into the Twilight Zone. And there's more of them out there than you can imagine."

He pulls the meat cleaver close to him.

Speaks to someone far away, reflected in the bloody metal.

"When you first came to me, Jayne, didn't you say I was the only man who could help you? And weren't you right on the money, you nasty bitch? Didn't I make you millions? Wasn't it Christmas every day of the week? You always said I was your best asset. You always called me a sick man. But I'm not evil like you, Jayne . . ."

He smiles at some faraway image of her, through blood on stainless steel.

Then winks at her.

". . . and I know *right where you live*, don't I?"

David.

You've gone completely insane.

He looks right at me again, and I see that insanity, more pure than it ever was before, right over the edge, deep into nowhere. Crystalline. Terrifying.

Final as all hell.

"You saw it, too," he says to me, his voice a whisper now. "You saw where she lives. You were right there and you *saw it*. I gave it to you, just like I gave you a reason to exist while you were in jail."

He's not even making any sense.

Babbling.

Toni moves closer to me. She wants to touch my face. I feel so much terror in her now, as Hartman's madness fills the room. He looks at me wetly. His smile shines, like nothing else shines in this room. Shines in deep red.

"Now *get your ass over here*, boy! Do it NOW!"

I don't move.

"We're gonna get there, one way or another. You hear me talking, smart guy? *I said, DO YOU HEAR ME TALKING?*"

"I hear you talking. And you heard *me* the first time . . ."

I look him right in his crazy eyes.

". . . go to hell, David."

He almost screams at me again, chokes it back. Like he's about to cry . . . but instead he laughs. Shifts his gaze on Toni.

Smiles at her.

"I will go to hell, boy. We'll both be there soon . . ."

He snaps his fingers, motions to the goons.

". . . but the lady goes first."

Two of them start dragging Toni toward the table.

• • •

I'm only vaguely aware of the hands on all sides of me again, the floor almost vanishing under my feet as the stink team pulls and pushes and rips at my clothes without mercy. I fight them with everything I have left, but it's a wall of steel, muscle on muscle on muscle. Like being at the bottom of a suicide tackle on the fifty-yard line, just shy of victory. Useless. Trapped.

Toni doesn't scream, doesn't struggle.

Her hand is on the chopping block now.

Held there by animals disguised as men.

Hartman, still smiling at me. "Last chance, kiddo. You can still save her. But only if you walk over here on your own two feet and give it up. Going *once* . . ."

He raises the cleaver five feet over her hand. She looks right in his face and doesn't beg. Doesn't scream. Broken and waiting.

"Going *twice* . . ."

Can't fight them anymore. It's useless. I go limp in the steel arms of stinking thugs . . . and I scream at him. Scream that I'll give him what he wants. I can't even hear the words, they're so loud, and the pounding in my head is so hot and awful. I see myself yelling like I'm in a dream . . .

. . . and Hartman stops his downward stroke.

Stops with the cleaver and looks at me.

The wall of stinking thugs loosens around me one last time.

I stand on my feet, facing Hartman.

"Okay, David. You win."

• • •

I walk over to him. Slow steps. He savors them, cutting the air with the cleaver, back and forth.

"You know that I'm a man of my word, Elroy. You know that if you put your hand right here and let me have what I want, she'll live. I'll even turn her loose. Let you *both* go free. You'll never work again, but you'll be out of here. Or you can stick around and be a part of the family again. I'll even protect your ass from those motherfuckers who are hunting you. We'll be *good friends* again, Elroy . . ."

He taps the chopping block with the cleaver.

"Just put it right here."

I take two quick breaths.

I look at Toni.

She stares back at me, two men holding her. They look like dark ghouls, featureless and black. Nightmares made flesh. Two guns aimed at her head. Two red laser dots bouncing off each other on her forehead. Hartman turns one corner of his mouth up at them.

"A little insurance, kiddo. In case you decide to change your mind. Move your hand one inch and they take off the little lady's head. Got that?"

And I realize I have no choice. None at all.

I put my right hand on the chopping block.

I spread my fingers apart.

Hartman smiles incredulously—like, *you're really gonna do this, huh, buddy*? But he doesn't say a word. I only hear his breath quicken. Another black shape comes over and pulls a small black canister with a stainless steel nozzle attached to it from a shelf near the block. Turns a little knob on the nozzle and lights the end with an Aim-A-Flame. The gas jet ignites and hisses to a bright blue.

"That'll keep you from bleeding out. We're doing this one finger at a time, just like your old daddy."

I nod slowly.

The guy with the torch gets in close to us. He has a face like rocks busted apart. A neutral expression like nothing at all. I wonder if he was the man who cauterized my father's wounds.

Toni is watching me. That's all I really wanted, wasn't it? To know she was still there. To have her back for just one moment . . . even if what we once had is broken beyond repair. To know she still loves me . . . *though love cannot stay* . . .

"That's a good boy," he says. "Feel that adrenaline pumping? It's sweet, ain't it? Just like the lady."

He takes a long breath, leaning closer to her.

"Like steel roses, Elroy. *Steel goddamn roses.*"

I am filled with the smell of her.

It's all I've had for years. It's all I have now.

He licks his fat lips. "Are you ready?"

"Yeah. I'm ready."

He raises the meat cleaver three feet above my hand. I close my eyes and concentrate hard on her. I take myself out of there.

To the place where I won't feel this.

His voice slithers in my ears just before the blade whistles down:

"Oh, and by the way, buddy . . . *that's not your wife.*"

MAYHEM AND DEATH RAY

What happens next is in less than three seconds: My eyes open and I feel my hand jerk out of harm's way on instinct as I see the steel chunk down hard, right into the wooden butcher's block, a micromillimeter from the spot where my index finger was waiting, and it almost seems like the blade sliced into me—I feel it cold and sharp against my skin—but that's just the cool chill of the metal itself, and my eyes are wide open, looking right into Hartman's, and he looks back at me in shock, landscapes of frozen insanity like dull yellow ice across his face, eyes like bloodshot diamonds beaming a mad burn, and I can swear I hear God yell, "FUCK YOU!" in a terrible, dying voice, and somewhere in the corner of my eye, I can see a bright red glimmer on the Weasel's shredded wrist in one split second—a digital watch set to a twenty-minute timer, an old-school dogface trick, the count reading 00:00—and I hear something pulse in the room at the same time, a high mechanical *blipping sound* . . . and I see Toni in the other corner of my eye, standing there unwavering, as if made from invincible steel . . . as the thunder and the fire comes like a giant fist . . . and I realize at the very end of this long, elastic moment that it's not the Almighty saving our asses at all.

That wasn't God yelling, "FUCK YOU!"

It was the Weasel.

With his final breath, tearing through wetness.

And then everything goes straight to hell.

Boom.

The combo feels like a half pound of C-4 rigged to one of the big oil drums and it really rips up the place, sending fire and debris everywhere. The flash registers in my peripheral vision as an enormous white phosphor flash knocking over the giant construction crane and sending men scattering like dogs. A giant steel girder falls from above and smashes the two guys who were going to shoot Toni flatter than pancakes. It's a shriek and a crash and a sharp shock of sulfur and twisted metal up my nose that snaps me wide awake and pings the chaos volume up to eleven. I stand in the center of a meteor storm, watching Hartman scream wordlessly as his entire world blows up. The bloody curtains around us catch fire. Gorillas ignite and shriek as they burn, bipedal torches.

My hand balls back into a fist and flies right for Hartman's face. His shocked expression shatters as his nose explodes. The cleaver falls from his right hand and I grab his middle finger and break it. He chucks hard on his own blood.

This is the moment, David.

This is it . . .

Someone shoots at me and I feel the bullet just above my head, as I swing Hartman by his arms, using his own weight like a battering ram. He crashes into the confused gorilla who's doing the shooting and they tumble together like bad lovers, into the rack of gear. The gorilla's gun clatters along the thundering, quaking floor. The torture harness holding the Weasel's shredded remains tilts and falls on what's left of Marcie. Hartman makes a lot of almost-human noise, gurgling in bloody backwash—just like every one of his victims. The thugs still scattered in the burning room are way past confused now, wondering what the hell comes next.

And that would be the rest of the Weasel's C-4 package.

Franklin makes a dive for the floor, as everybody spins on another giant explosion—the big one. It rips the world in half. Knocks everyone down hard. Oil drums are tossed and tumbled. Toni is the only one standing now.

She stands in the center of the inferno.

It seems impossible, but the scent of her still reaches me through the sharp pings of fire and metal and burning gas in the room—as if she is above it all.

And I love her for it.

That's not your wife.

Panic fire breaks out among a few of the men as they try to gain their feet, but they don't have anyone to shoot at and they end up doing a lot of damage to each other. I can see Franklin somewhere in the chaos, screaming at us to run out the way we came in, hard metal raining down in black chunks, the whole place self-destructing.

I don't follow him.

There's something I have to do first.

Hartman.

You son of a bitch.

Come *here* . . .

Hartman has his hands up as I crawl over to him. A chunk of the ceiling lands one foot from his head, shattering the concrete floor. He doesn't even notice that. He only notices me. And he chokes on his own blood as he tells me to stop. But stopping is not something I feel like doing right now. The world tilts again and trembles as I yank him halfway to his feet and look him right in the eye. I've played this moment a thousand times. It's never as sweet as you think it will be.

But it's enough.

"We're there," he says, and his voice is garbled and drowned. "You and me, buddy . . . *we're finally there* . . ."

In hell, he means.

We're both there at last.

I stand in hell with David Hartman, beating the crap out of him.

There's a myth that the bigger you are, the harder it is to hurt you. It's one of the first things they debunk in the dojo. Fat guys are really simple to mess up. This particular fat guy breaks in every spot I hit him. His jaw, his ribs, his teeth. It all goes real easy for a few seconds, but he surprises me with a block to my fourth blow. Puts all his forward weight into a lunge that throws me off balance. I stumble back and my legs go out from under me. The ground comes up in a violent shudder as another blast kicks off in the room, fire pluming up and vanishing in the concussion of a powerful wave. He stumbles back into the fallen butcher's block. Yanks the cleaver out in a clumsy move and comes at me with it. Screams my name. Screams that I'm a bastard. I don't hear him over the roar of the explosions.

And then a gunshot shatters his right kneecap, dropping him in front of me.

Toni, aiming the pistol with unshaking hands.

My love.

But he said she's not my wife.

You twisted freak—*of course you would say that.*

I see the animal grace of her, the cruel elegance, all flowing from her eyes as she finds the killer instinct, fighting to be herself again. It's everything I remember, and something else on top. An even newer version of her, seething in the dark with the rest of us maniacs. My head pounds in time with the explosions.

That's not your wife.

Hartman goes down in a pulpy sprawl, the meat cleaver hocking into his own shoulder as he falls. His garbled scream thrums hard in the room, which explodes again with thunder and flames. Her next shot goes in his other knee. Bone shards and blood clots detonate ten feet in every direction, and he looks up again, begging her not to kill him. She takes three steps forward. She hovers over him, point-blank. She bites her lower lip, this time with confidence. She is the most beautiful woman I have ever seen when she does that.

And then he looks up at her and I see something I'll never forget.

Fear in his face—absolute, endless fear.

I realize that this was what I was looking at before, when I thought I saw the purest shape of his madness, shimmering in a bloody reflection. He wasn't insane in that moment. He was afraid. Terrified.

Like he is right now, in the final second of his life.

Staring into the eyes of my wife.

And I can almost hear her voice:

We win, after all, David.

And that's that.

His head caves with a wet crack as the last bullet in the gun strikes him right between his eyes, spewing in a chunky-pink fantail of blood. Each one of those chunks is thinking of her. He falls flat on his back, twitching. I almost lick my lips when the life runs out of him. Almost. I don't get off on it, not like he does. I never did. Just needed to watch him die.

I promised you, my love.

I said I would kill him for you.

I stand next to her and we watch him die together.

We follow Franklin out of the place. The back rooms we came through are still not on fire yet and we barely make it as the whole warehouse behind us fills with rolling hell. Franklin stops just long enough to grab a tiny revolver and Glock 30 automatic off the dead scarecrow in the corridor. Behind us, the storm rages on and I hear people screaming. I hate that sound.

A whole goddamn lot.

Toni grabs my hand. "Come on, we've got to move."

She is strong and fast when she does it, pulling me to safety.

She is my one true love.

That's not your wife.

Toni insists on getting as many of the women out as we can.

Franklin screams at us that the place is coming down fast and we don't have time for this, but Toni screams back at him and she's mighty damn convincing.

Her voice, stronger now.

The real her, coming to the surface, as the world explodes.

I look at her and I see so many things.

That's not your wife.

We pull the girls from their burning shantytown and Toni tells them all to run like hell. The fire turns into a thundering beast which eats the entire inside of the building, punching against the walls to be free. The smoke begins to seep through the windows in a ghostly glimmer and I hear glass shatter.

Just outside the fence near a cluster of trees, we hold our position and watch the last few women come streaming out. Most of them are shrieking like little girls. There's some life still left in them as they bolt. I guess that's a good thing. Twenty or thirty of them cower in the glade with us, scared out of their minds.

The rest take off into the darkness, bound for wherever. I hope they have someplace to go.

Toni huddles with the ladies near us.

Tells them all it's going to be okay.

I see the lines in her face illuminated by the pulsing yellow light of the fire, listening to her voice as she speaks to those poor lost girls, and she amazes me. Her face is hard like stone now, the trace of the broken little girl I saw before almost banished. Like someone hit a switch and made her a new woman, just by showing her something really awful—by giving her the chance to blow away the man who broke her, shoot him right between the eyes. She's still holding the gun she killed Hartman with in both hands. The dull metal captures the pulse of the burning building, shimmering. I look at Toni and my heart does strange things.

"He said you're not my wife. What did he mean?"

As my words come at her, I hear something else explode.

Fire lashes violently through the roof, crackling, hissing.

I glance over at the three vans in the loading dock. The Mexicans we duct-taped inside there can't scream for help, but the fire won't get to them. Not just yet anyway. When the cops show in a few minutes, they'll pay for being garbagemen. They'll say it was all someone else's fault. And no one will believe them.

"He was crazy," she says.

Her voice never wavers, not for one moment.

Her voice is deep and strong.

Cruel in her elegance.

Elegant in her regret.

Everything I only saw in faceless silhouette before this moment, brought into terrifying relief.

But . . .

"What happened in there?" I say. "What did he do to you?"

"I have to get my head together," she says. "They had me drugged for a while. I can tell you more when I've had a chance to think."

I put my hands on her shoulder.

She's still caught in some kind of warp—but she's pulling herself up from it like a champ. She's strong, and I can see that strength, emerging a little at a time. Hartman couldn't really break her, could he? He was toying with my mind, wasn't he? Saw my psych reports like Jenison did, and he wanted to hurt me—wanted to make me bleed in my heart. Make me doubt the ground under my feet and the shades of my destroyed life. This is his revenge from beyond the grave, the son of a bitch. That awful, lingering doubt. His last words before the killing stroke.

That's not your wife.

The roses in my head sear me, white-hot.

She bites her bottom lip softly, flames reflected in her eyes.

She tells the girls everything will be just fine.

Franklin leads us away from the place, along the tree line behind the burning warehouse. Toni pulls me by the hand—it's all about us. All about escaping.

I can see the red and blue lights of fire trucks and cop cars just on the other side of the place as we circle

around. It's turning into a circus fast. One of the big red machines cuts off the street where the Ops Wagon is parked. Cops all over it, too.

Franklin curses just under his breath, wordlessly.

"Looks like we're on foot for a few miles," Toni says. "Let's move."

A final explosion blows the roof off the place, just behind us. I hear a stormburst of screaming and the sirens close like crying birds. I can still feel the heat from the fire, three blocks away. It almost matches the pain in my head.

The smell of metal and flowers, filling me as I hold on to her hand.

Toni, so close to me, so close at last.

My mind, hovering in and out of memories.

I know right where you live, you nasty bitch.

Hartman's voice, buzzing in my head.

A terrible buzz.

Damn it all.

This neighborhood sucks.

All industrial flatlands and railroad tracks, clusters of trees, storage facilities. Not one car I can steal. We follow Franklin along the back side of the warehouses, as more cops speed towards the scene of the crime. We keep to the shadows, covered by the night.

Toni pulls me.

She moves with precision grace.

Doesn't say a word.

• • •

We haul ass for miles, until we get to the freeway. We stay hidden in pools of shadow. Nobody sees us. Away in the distance, deep in the heart of a neighborhood made of pipe and steel, I can still see the flames. More cop cars and EMS vehicles blast past us, but we are invisible. Toni says they'll figure out what happened eventually and she's right. The Mexicans will try to finger us. They might even ID Franklin. But even if they don't, the cops will run a make on the Ops Wagon, which means they'll trace the title on the vehicle to the Weasel, which means we can't even go back to Franklin's house. We're lucky if black-and-whites aren't already there by now. We need a safe place. Just for a while.

Until we figure this whole thing out.

Two brightly lit auto dealerships with giant American flags whipping in the wind above them tease us with fine rides full of high-tech alarm and surveillance systems I don't have the tools to break. They're all spanking-new models. Most of them have computerized keyless entry with fail-safes programmed right into hard drives that shut the engine off and call the cops a half mile away if you don't have the right codes. We don't need those hassles, and I don't have a smartphone with satellite uplink, either—usually all you need is a GPS scrambler to pick that kind of lock.

"I've got an idea," Toni says.

We make it to the nearest convenience store and she calls a taxi from a pay phone.

Sometimes the very obvious is the best answer.

The guy who pulls his Yellow Cab into the service-station area of the Lucky Seven Mart is big and black and looks like he could use a few extra bucks. I hand him two hundred in cash and tell him to shut off the meter. I tell him he never saw us. He says we'd be a lot more invisible if there was five hundred in his hand. I give him six. It's a pretty respectable dent in my cash supply, but that situation won't last long.

We settle back for the ride and Toni speaks softly to me, her breath so close and so sweet: "Where are we going?"

"We need a place to hole up," I say. "And I need to ask a few questions."

"What questions?" she says.

"I have to find out what Resurrection Express is. Did Hartman ever tell you?"

She hesitates before answering.

Then:

"He might have said something . . . but I can't really remember . . ."

Franklin snorts. "I just want my money."

"You'll get your money," I say. "But we have to play it safe first."

I look at Toni and my mind races.

Her scent is weaker now, but it still fills me.

That's not your wife.

• • •

The driver drops us in the Montrose area downtown. The busy neon and flashing lights of Westheimer Street tell fancy lies. Traffic is heavy, human and otherwise. We walk into a bar full of loud heavy-metal music blasting from a jukebox, then walk right out the back exit.

Down the block is a smaller, darker place called Blythe Spirits. I knew the owner when I was four years old. That was before my father got him locked up.

We go in through the out door.

It's one thirty by their clock, almost closing time. The joint is quiet this morning, jazz music floating lazily around, a waterfall splashing rocks against the back wall. It's blue and black and almost neon in here. Eleven tables and a center bar made out of decades-old polished oak. We light in a corner and a young waitress chewing gum finds us fast, slaps coasters down on the table that advertise St. Pauli Girl beer.

"What'll it be?"

Her voice sounds like a waitress named Flo. She's got a thin waist, large talents, short black hair and a barbell through her tongue, hard features traced in tacky dark makeup. Stunning, really, if that's your thing. Toni orders us all whiskey shots, beer backs—something nice and forgettable. The waitress doesn't smile at us. There's a tattoo on her belly, visible through a stylish rip in her black fishnet tank top, and it says, in thick red Valentine's Day calligraphy: *Ellie Mayhem*. Underneath the lettering,

a pink cartoon mouse, squealing like she just saw something real bad.

She sees me looking and scowls:

"That's my name, don't wear it out."

She's one of Kim's.

They're all helpless mice under the Hammer's killer kitty.

I almost don't say anything, it comes as such a shock. But I have to think this over. Came here for a reason. I say to her, very slowly:

"Is Mollie Baker here? I need to talk to him."

She stops chewing, leaves her mouth open. "You know Mollie?"

"It's a family matter."

"Yeah, I'll bet it is."

"So is he here or not?"

She looks around. Does some sort of check-in with her personal gods for a moment while she sizes me up. This might have been a giant mistake. The second I think that, she tosses the tired once-over back over her shoulder and starts chewing her gum again, making a real Southern gothic trailer-trash spectacle of herself as she smacks the next bit:

"Mollie hasn't been around in three weeks, honey."

"Do you know what happened to him?"

"No."

"Is there a way to contact him?"

"Someone else has been running the place."

"Who's that?"

"Fella named Ray."

Franklin snorts. "You mean Ray *Carver*?"

"Yeah," she says. "You know him?"

"I used to."

Ellie Mayhem cocks her shoulders and head, looking tired. "Look, honey . . . it's almost closing time and my feet hurt. You can come back tomorrow if you want."

"Okay, thanks."

"No problem."

She drifts away, keeping an eye on me for a few paces, then starts barking orders to the greasy guy behind the bar. Franklin pulls out a cigarette and doesn't light it. You can't smoke indoors anymore because people under twenty don't bother to vote. His question floats across the table like something really obvious:

"What was that all about?"

"The guy who owns this place was a friend of my dad's. They got in some deep shit back in the seventies. Haven't spoken in years."

"So what?"

"So my dad tried to bring Mollie in on the job we did for Jenison. That was before they bought me out of jail. Would have been just about three or four weeks ago."

And now the guy's MIA.

Like everyone else who knows anything.

"The lady could be lying," Toni says, checking out Ellie Mayhem through the corner of one slitted eye. "She isn't exactly Florence Henderson."

"I've got a feeling she isn't lying. She knew that I recognized her."

Toni makes a face that almost looks jealous. "*Recognized* her?"

"The tattoo on her belly. She's part of a crew that helped me out a few days ago. They're all MIA now, too."

She blinks once, then huffs. "That trash could be *anybody.*"

I give Toni a sharp look. "We gotta hang here anyway. Twenty minutes, just to be sure our driver is nice and confused about where we're headed."

She rolls her eyes. "Where *are* we headed?"

"It's a secret."

"Well, aren't you the man with the plan," she says, looking halfway amused. "Maybe we should go see a movie while we're at it."

I smile at her.

Cute, darling—real cute.

In this moment, I can see it in her face: something false, something not right. Like maybe she's trying a little too hard to be in charge of everything. That's exactly like my Toni . . . but somehow not quite.

That's not your wife.

Before I can say anything, Franklin pipes up: "Look, kid, I'm still on the clock." He pulls the locker key from a shirt pocket and holds it up for me. "If you want this bad boy back, we need to get to the *money.*"

"It's safe. We gotta let the heat die down before we move again."

"We can't stay here," Toni says.

"I know where we can go. Try not to worry so much."

She sighs. "Who's worried?"

This time Franklin rolls his eyes.

I turn to him with a serious look. "So . . . what about this Ray Carver guy? How come I've never heard of him?"

"He keeps low," Franklin says. "But he's pretty

dangerous, too. One of those pimp-slash–drug dealer types with his fingers in a lot of pies. I ran shotgun on a pickup for him six months ago."

"If he stays so low, what makes him dangerous?"

"He covers his ass by shooting first. And he enjoys the hell out of it. Nobody works with him much because he's such a goddamn cowboy. They all call him Death Ray."

I chuckle. "Clever of them."

Toni looks at Franklin calmly. "So this guy is running someone's bar now?"

"More likely he's the new owner," Franklin says. "Ray isn't the kind of guy who works for old-timers, and he doesn't like partners."

And if he's such a cowboy, that means Mollie's out of the picture.

Maybe permanently.

The drinks come and Ellie Mayhem smacks gum and calls us honey one more time. She sees me glance at her name again. This time I look up from the tattoo and right into her eyes. Asking. She stops chewing, gives a glance towards a small little cubbyhole near the back, where a tiny hall jerks around a corner. An old white sign with a big red arrow says that's where the bathrooms are. I nod at her. Message received.

She wanders off.

Toni looking jealous again.

I hear Hartman's voice in a distant echo, telling me she's not what she says she is, and I snuff it out quickly.

Franklin belts down half his beer . . . then in a long sigh:

"I had a real goddamn job yesterday."

He shakes his head and stares off into space. Like maybe he's thinking about his friends back at Hartman's. The woman and the Weasel, all hacked to death and burned to hell. Or maybe he's not. Maybe Franklin's got a point about all this.

Toni stares at her drink intently.

It has to be you.

Don't tell me my mind is so messed up that I can't see another woman taking your place. Just don't tell me that.

Because if that's really true . . .

Then I can't trust the ground under my feet.

Everything's suspect.

Everything.

I think about Mollie Baker and my father for a second.

Dad told me it was a bad getaway that ended their friendship, over thirty years ago in 1972. When the cops nail you, it's always because *you* screw up, not because they're great at what they do. Your average officer of the law doesn't care about busting the bad guys unless we hand them our heads on a platter. A lot of them are dumb rednecks, especially in Texas. But God help your ass if those rednecks get their hands on you and nobody is looking—if they get just ten minutes alone in a room without air-conditioning and a hot lamp in your face. My dad told me the whole story one night when he was really drunk. Said it was like being slowly crushed to death. While sick lizards with whiskey breath take their turns spitting in your eye and calling you names.

They worked Dad over a lot longer than five minutes.

It was six days before he gave up Mollie, and his employers.

Suicide for guys like us.

My father was lucky to be alive after they were done with him—even luckier on the inside, where the mob guys he sold up the river made six attempts on his life. One of those vindictive old trolls had to die of a heart attack while Dad was still in prison before the syndicate decided he wasn't worth the effort anymore. A real lucky break. The first job when he came out had to be free, and the one after that. But people forget for the right price. Mollie never forgot, though. He was in jail three years longer. Now he could be dead.

Because my father wanted to do right by him.

Because he went to Mollie first.

Because Dad tried not to involve me.

I sit there and I think about it for a very long time. I think about Jayne Jenison and David Hartman. About how ruthless and smart these people are. About what David said back in that room full of blood and horror. He said he knew where Jenison lived. And he said I saw it, too. Said he gave it to me.

I gave it to you, just like I gave you a reason to exist while you were in jail.

I thought it was just crazy talk.

But now . . .

Now that I really think about it . . .

Jenison's people could be watching this place. Coming here might have been a real bad idea. I decide that it's almost certain they took out Mollie Baker after my dad talked to him. It fits the profile. No loose ends. Everybody pays.

But Ellie Mayhem, she's a loose end, too. A loose end they don't know about. They would have killed her if they had.

And Toni.

It has to be you, baby.

It just has to be.

But it might not be.

I want so badly for it to be.

But it might not be.

My voice is almost a whisper, but she hears it clear as a bell.

"What did Hartman mean? When he said you weren't my wife?"

Her face flushes almost red with anger. "How can you ask me that now? *How dare you ask me that now?*"

"Calm down. It's a simple question."

"This is me, Elroy. This is *Toni*."

"That wasn't what I asked you. I asked you what Hartman *meant* when he said you weren't my wife."

"Hartman was completely crazy. He killed dozens of those girls. Took them in the room and killed them."

The room.

Christ.

I don't even want to know what that means.

And the worst part is . . . I suddenly have no idea if I'm right.

Have no idea if what she's saying is true.

I am filled with her beauty and her scent, all those memories assigned to something that looks exactly like her. But those memories wore faceless masks before tonight. Did Hartman know? Did he know what it would take to push me into some sort of waking dream—a delusion powered by desperate need? My own insanity, used against me.

No, I won't believe that. It's impossible. Hartman couldn't have been that smart.

And I know it's you.

I know it.

"I heard all those other girls screaming," she says. "I thought he was coming to take me in there so many times. I lost myself for days and weeks. They had me on a lot of dope, too. There's so many details I can't remember."

"Funny . . . I've been having the same problem for the last three years."

"I'm telling you, *it's ME!*"

She makes a fist and slams the table, her words cutting across the room.

I sink back into my chair. "Don't make a scene. Just calm down."

Sure enough, Ellie Mayhem comes back over, empty soldiers balanced on her tray, giving me a look that comes from women who get slapped around and don't like to see it happening to someone else. "Everything okay over here?"

"Yes," Toni says, very calm, fixing me with a lethal glare. "I'm okay. Everything's fine. Isn't it?"

Ellie Mayhem gives her a suspicious twitch. "You *sure* about that, honey?"

I hold up a twenty-dollar bill. "She's one hundred percent sure. Can we get some more shooters?"

She nods like she doesn't believe me, like all men are

scum. Snatches the bill and wanders off with one eye on us.

Damn.

I ask Toni a few more questions she doesn't have answers for. She says she doesn't know the details about Hartman's plans for me. She still has fire in her face, frustration and fear. She is so much like the real thing it breaks my heart.

But if there's a chance she isn't . . .

If I really am a crazy man, seduced by the promise . . .

That might at least mean that the *real Toni* is still out there.

Christ, what the hell am I saying?

You're saying you just ain't sure now, buddy.

You're saying you believe me finally—that ain't your goddamn wife.

Shut up, David. Just shut the hell up.

I look at Franklin. "Once I put a hundred large into your hands, you and me are square. But I'll have a little left over. Just how dangerous *is* this scary Death Ray guy?"

"Depends on how you come at him. You'll need backup."

"That's what I had in mind. Say, a five-K bonus?"

"Ten."

"Done."

"Always a pleasure doing business with you." He lets out a tough sigh, then settles back in his seat, rubbing his chin. "I think I might know where to look. I'll make a few calls."

This could be suicide.

But I have to know for sure about Resurrection Express and I have to know about Toni. I have to know if I'm crazy or if she's a liar.

And there's a missing piece, still nagging in my skull somewhere.

Do I really know where Jayne Jenison lives?

Am I searching for a ghost?

For a strange moment I'm reminded of Jimmy Stewart in the movie *Vertigo*. About that kind of obsession. About wanting a woman back so goddamn bad, you *make it happen*, in spite of yourself, in spite of everything. And then it leaves you, because it can't stay. Because it was artificial, something you created yourself. Even if she loved you all along.

Am I Jimmy Stewart?

Toni, is that really you, sitting right there?

Or is the lie true, this one time?

And the evil men who want to put us all out of business . . . what about them?

Resurrection Express.

She doesn't say anything. Her gears are working, too. All of this is triggering something. Memories. Traces. She keeps it to herself and I don't press it.

Not yet.

We get up to leave and I tell them to hang by the back. I get Ellie Mayhem's attention as I move casually toward the bathroom alcove. She follows me over with her tray empty in front of her. I slap a fifty on it. Bitch insurance.

"You never saw us," I tell her, palming another two

hundred in one fist, making sure she can see the crumpled green. "We understand each other?"

"Mollie's dead," she says, not chewing gum. She's real serious now, almost whispering the words. I can see all sorts of cruelty etched on her face, up this close in the new dim spill of light from the bathroom corridor. There's a couple of fresh scars running along the right side of her forehead, just covered by the bad makeup. Blood almost cracking through the base application.

"I know he's dead," I say. "You need to forget you ever saw us. *Understand*?"

She nods, grim. Like, *I can't make any promises.* But she doesn't say that out loud. What she says is this:

"I couldn't help but overhear."

"About what?"

"You're looking for someone. He's real bad. I want to hurt him."

I look at the scars again, and I can see there are bruises on her face, too, hardly covered. The whole scenario comes real clear now:

She's one of Kim's whores. Whoever killed the Hammer slapped this little lady around and told her who the new boss was—left her alive because she was valuable merchandise. That means it wasn't Jenison who did the deed. It was a contract hit. Someone street level, who plays by street rules.

"Death Ray," she says. "I can give him to you."

DREAMS IN THE DOLLHOUSE

Ellie Mayhem gives us a number to call tomorrow. Six P.M. sharp. She says to drop Mollie's name and tell Ray she's working for me now. The guy's real big on keeping what belongs to him, apparently. She won't come in to work tomorrow because she's hitting the road tonight—heading out to Dallas to stay with her mom. Says that Ray will freak out if he thinks one of his ladies has gone AWOL with another player.

It'll totally get his attention, honey.

Just promise you'll hurt him when I'm gone.

Hurt him bad.

She doesn't say anything else and I don't ask any more questions. I can tell she wasn't with Kim when the shit went down, and she probably doesn't even know if her boss is still alive—but she wants Ray's head. I see it burning in her eyes and under her skin, even without the sting of her words. She is red with the lust. For payback.

It's my one link back to Jenison.

Back to Resurrection Express.

I don't ask any more questions.

It's a hell of a thing when the planets line up like this, and you're always really damn amused when it happens to you. But if it hadn't been Miss Mayhem, it would have been Mollie, and if it hadn't been Mollie . . . well, I would have worked something out. Hartman had it right—I've always been real good at following the bread crumbs.

We leave the bar and go house hunting.

There's a neat trick you can still pull these days, when you're on the wrong side of a job gone bad. When motels are too hot and you need a place to hide—yesterday.

It was one of the last things Axl Gange taught me.

Always go in with confidence, but prepare yourself for the worst.

Part of preparing for the worst is the ace I've been holding in my shoe since we went into the vault: three tiny pieces of steel. The most important components of Remo's manual lockpick set. Not enough to open a car with keyless entry and get away clean, but enough to jack something made in the nineties. And you can also usually find a mom-and-pop hardware store or a pawn shop in a neighborhood like this with ancient locks. That's after you pick up your old-school ride to go cruising in, and there's lots of those in the alley behind Blythe Spirits.

We're on the road fast.

It's a 1997 Acura with a huge dent in the passenger's side.

Ten minutes later I'm inside E-Z PAWN, blowing

through their cheap SERIO-SYSTEMS alarm system by entering a row of sixes into the keypad just inside the back entrance. The beeping in the room stops and the police have no idea there's a thief in here. I wipe everything I don't steal with a paper towel, just to be on the safe side.

I grab a duffel bag and stuff it with the tools I need.

Franklin and Toni wait outside with the motor running.

It's almost four in the morning when we cross from the Montrose ghetto into the River Oaks area, where rich people live on the border of everything scummy. That's another weird thing about Houston: it's a giant melting pot of degenerates and oil tycoons, and they all live across the street from each other. You have very interesting neighborhoods where falling-down crack houses face freshly built Victorian-reproduction town homes from less than twenty feet away. Some of those crack houses are ready to be torn down—just so much rotten wood hanging in a frame. The other places cost more than a high-end drug dealer makes in six months. We cruise a main drag just on the River Oaks border and find a street that hovers somewhere in the middle of the spectrum. We look for nice houses without any cars in the driveway—but not too nice. Toni spots a three-story colonial job with elegant French windows and a lawn that looks like it hasn't been mowed in two weeks. The mailbox is stuffed, no newspapers on the front steps. People who don't worry about money don't read newspapers anymore. It's all on the net these days. We pull into the open driveway. There's no fence. A garage in back. Nobody's home.

I get to the power box with my bag of tools and start working the leads and connections. No matter how far in the future we go with our handy-dandy technology, some things never change: you can scope a ghetto-rich family on vacation just by looking at the front lawn, and you can bet anything they haven't spent too much money on a security profile. I cut the balls of the alarm system by rerouting the power to a grounded circuit, and then I reboot the breakers. The older the lock, the easier it is. You just need a screwdriver and a soldering iron.

We're secure inside of fifteen minutes.

I break out gloves from the duffel bag—three sets of blue rubber dishwashing gloves that will keep our fingerprints off the grid when we leave this place and the owners discover they've been burglarized. Axl Gange was a really smart housekeeper.

The keys to the garage are in the kitchen. We get our new car hidden fast.

Inside the house, we've got high-speed Internet, flat-screen TV, hot showers, and even a wine cellar. Not much food in the kitchen, though. Some Popsicles and frozen meat. A few jars of condiments. Cheerios and shredded wheat. I have a feeling these people eat out a lot.

Twelve hours before we make the call.

I tell Franklin to watch the front door. He flips on the big TV and thumbs the remote to a news station. Nothing local at half past four in the morning. Not sure what he expected to find. I tell him to shut it off because the glow from the screen will seep through the drawn blinds. That could give us away while it's still dark out, if one of the neighbors has insomnia. You take your chances on a block like this.

He nods and kills it.

"We should get some sleep," Toni says. "We're blown, all of us."

"I'll be okay," Franklin says.

She sits down in the chair across from him. "What are our assets?"

I smile at her.

Always in charge.

Always my Toni.

Even if she isn't.

Our assets:

Ruger Centerfire pistol, the gun Toni killed Hartman with.

The compact revolver and the dull gray Glock 30 Franklin took off the dead guy.

Not much, man.

The Ruger is a 40S, not an SR9, but they look almost exactly alike, with the same shiny silver slide and black plastic handle, no rounds in the clip. Twelve bullets in the Glock, three in the revolver, which looks like a Charter Arms Bulldog special, snub-nosed with rubber grips, a tiny little thing—the kind of close range weapon you walk up behind someone with. Gangbangers keep them in their cargo pants pockets.

We put our guns on the glass coffee table and I stare at them for a very long moment.

"Okay," I finally say to him. "A baker's dozen bullets to take down a really scary guy. You think you can handle it?"

"One bullet is all it takes," he says.

"There's a lot of heat out there," Toni tells him, like he needs to be reminded. "The cops are going nuts right now. All the shooting that's been going on."

He almost laughs. "You ever been to Houston before, lady?"

She looks insulted. "Of course I have."

"This place has the highest concentration of gangland shootings outside of Los Angeles. The police don't give a shit about who gets killed if they were scum to begin with. It's like trying to call 'time out' on the beaches of Normandy."

"That may be true," I say. "But Kim Hammer was a major player. She would have had contacts inside the Houston Metro divisions. Somebody has to be curious. And that's not even counting what happened at the hotel last night."

Franklin shrugs. "Those people were all scumbags, too."

"Maybe," I say. "But you can't blow up the lobby of the Sheraton and walk away clean. Not for long. That kind of property damage paints a big red bull's-eye on your forehead."

"You think the cops have any idea it was *you and me* in there?"

"Jenison told me her people had the place locked—but she couldn't have covered all the bases. I mean you guys got in, right?"

"That took a lot of doing, man."

"Someone had to see the security recordings. The cameras in those places all stream to offsite locations now."

Unless the cameras were shut down by the bad guys.

That makes a lot of sense—but it also scares the hell out of me.

"Kim wouldn't be the only one with friends in the police department," I say. "Jenison's foot soldiers are everywhere—that's what she told me. They'll be using every dirty trick they know to track us."

Toni leans forward in her chair. "Then what's the plan?"

"That depends," I say.

"On what?"

"On what Death Ray has to tell us."

Franklin makes a resigned sound that could be a laugh. "One thing I've learned in these situations, kid. Never ask too many questions, because everyone's got a different answer."

"And God against all?"

"There ain't no God, just like there ain't no hell."

"Maybe. I still have things to do. You should come with us. I could use your help, even after we're done with the scary guy."

"No thanks, kid. I figure I'll retire after this."

I still can't tell if he feels any remorse at all about his buddies. He's cold and efficient—a man of war. You don't make friends on the front lines, his stare tells me. You run from score to score and live off the profits. Street mercenaries are all the same.

"Your people died," Toni says to him. "Every damn one of them."

"No hard feelings about it. You roll the dice when you're in close combat. If the kid comes across with what he owes me, we're square. I'll help you guys one last time, then we go our separate ways. No more adventures for this old man. I'm gonna get myself out of the world. Drop out of sight for a while."

"That might be a good idea," I say. "But . . ."

My words freeze into silence between us.

He hovers on the edge of an uncertain laugh. "But what?"

I take a deep breath. "What if the world *isn't there anymore* when you decide to come back?"

Toni cocks her head. "What are you talking about?"

"This whole thing . . . everything I'm figuring out about it . . . it's all adding up to something crazy. Hartman knew Jenison's plot. So Hartman was stockpiling women. There's something else, too. Something underground. Groups of people all over the world, holing up in fortresses."

Franklin shrugs again. "People have been doing that for years."

"What if there was a reason for it all along? What if some of those people were *organized*?"

"You sound like a crazy conspiracy guy now," Toni says.

"Something started the rumor," I say.

Franklin settles back in the couch and dismisses the whole idea. "Shit."

I don't let him off that easy. "Whatever's going on, it was enough to scare the hell out of a monster like David Hartman, and that has to be really big. Maybe bigger than all of us."

He tosses his hands up. "So, what, you think it's some kinda nutty doomsday plot?"

He doesn't sound straight-up when he says that.

The nut jobs and the above-ground mainline hot-weather crowd have been crying about the end of the world for years.

But.

"The stuff on those hard drives is really sophisticated," I say. "Texas Data Concepts does government contracting for Strategic Air Command. They could have developed some sort of new defense application. Something state-of-the-art that nobody knows about. If Jenison is really planning on using it for whatever reason . . . then maybe her people have figured out some way to survive what happens next."

Toni loses a breath. "Jesus, Elroy. You're not serious."

"It's serious enough for these jerks to send shooters into public places and kill innocents in broad daylight. Serious enough to keep us all in the dark about what they were really doing."

"Starting a global nuclear war, though?" she says. "That would make the whole planet toxic."

I don't smile. "Yeah."

She starts shaking her head now. "It wouldn't work. Even with a hundred giant bomb shelters. If all your primary and secondary targets were hit on both sides, it would be a soup for decades. All the fallout and everything. It's the kind of cosmic stuff you see in movies."

"These are pretty cosmic people we're talking about."

Franklin laughs. "She's right. It just ain't *possible*. Jenison would inherit a world of shit. Someone inside her organization would wise up sooner or later and go against her. They can't *all* be that crazy."

No, they can't.

Not if it wasn't a nuclear war they were plotting.

Not if they knew exactly what they were doing.

Not if they had their apocalypse mapped out with surgical precision.

"Someone *did* go against her," I say, looking right at Toni. "And I saw it in his *eyes* before he died."

"You mean Hartman," she says.

"He was terrified."

Franklin laughs again. "Yeah, well, everyone's terrified when someone's about to kill them."

I shake my head. "It was something else. *Big* fear."

"How would you know?" he says. "Have you ever killed a man before?"

"No."

"Didn't think so."

I let a sigh roll out. Maybe he's right. Maybe Hartman was just looking death in the eye and being a pussy.

And maybe he wasn't.

"My father was a killer," I say. "It was easy for him."

"It'll be easy for you too," Franklin says. "When the time comes."

"I don't want to kill anyone."

"You won't have any choice."

"I wasn't able to do it before, even when there was someone aiming a gun at my head. Remember back at the toy store? *You* had to take the shot. It saved my life."

"You're welcome, by the way. But that doesn't mean anything. It was just *your life* on the line when that went down. Had nothing to do with making a real choice."

"What are you talking about?"

"Let me put it to you this way: how many decisions have you made that involved someone getting wasted?"

"A lot, I guess."

"Then you're already there. Don't kid yourself." He sighs in that macho Zen way he's got, and leans forward in the comfy chair. "See, there's this big lie in the world that the hardest kill is the *first one*. I've heard some people say it's like falling down a well, like you lose your soul in that moment or something. It's bullshit. Guys like us, we get people snuffed just by making a phone call. Every animal on earth kills because they have to. We're the only species smart enough to call it a sin."

"Doesn't make it right."

"Hell . . . some people just *need* to be killed. You know that."

I almost laugh, but then I don't.

Toni lets out a sigh and stands up. "This is fucking *nuts*. And I'm too tired to think about it anymore."

She starts for the master bedroom, then turns to me.

"Are you coming, Elroy?"

Yes.

Of course I am.

She stands in the center of the room, at the foot of a bed that smells like clean things, decent things. A bed I stole for her, so we could rest and be here. Just for a moment. Before we run again.

My head swims, so close to her.

My pain, so deep and so permanent.

Love cannot stay.

Walled on all sides of us are glass cases filled with Barbie dolls. Hundreds of them. All reshaped and customized in really elaborate handmade outfits and hairstyles. There's Punk Rock Barbie, Soccer Mom Barbie, Army Paratrooper Barbie, Rock Star Barbie . . . and every other walk of life that bridges worlds, all with the same face, all with the same eyes. There's even a series of Homeless Gutter-trash Barbies and Rotting Zombie-Freako Barbies, and they look real happy, too. I can't imagine why.

I close the door, and we're alone together.

"Nice bedroom," she says, not looking at me. Then she sort of laughs. "The little lady must be a collector."

"It's a whole Internet subculture. Customizable dolls like this. I've never seen this many in one place before."

"They're beautiful."

"Kind of creepy if you ask me."

She hangs her head and sighs. "You know, if you wanted to play house with me, we could have just found a cheap motel. This is a little much, don't you think?"

"No. We need a solid position. I need to check some things before we move again, and a motel is way too public now."

"What kind of things?"

"A minute ago, you said something," I say, staring deep into her. "It was something Toni never would have said."

"You still think . . ."

"You dropped the F-bomb. In ten years, I don't think I've ever heard Toni say that. Not even with my father. Not even Hartman."

She moves closer to me.

I take one step back.

"My memories have been ruined for years," I say. "You can't know what a nightmare that's been. The most important thing in your life, taken away and replaced with . . . *nothing*. I came to find my wife in that awful place. I wanted so badly to find her there. All I've had for years to go on was the smell of her. The smell of *you* . . ."

I breathe her in.

It's still Toni, but weaker and weaker all the time. Like the memories that abandoned my mind on the operating table. Like the years that teased me, shadows and whispers.

"And now I can't be sure at all," I say. "I feel like I'm floating in some far-off place, surrounded by strange new faces."

"You're wrong," she says. "Can't you believe your *eyes?*"

"I didn't even know what my wife would look like when I found her."

"I'll prove that I am who I am. Right here, right now."

The smell of her armors my heart—makes me believe again. Does it even matter who she really is? Could she be Toni anyway? A new version of her that came back to rescue me in the burning dark—to rescue me from Hartman?

We all tell ourselves lies. We all sell out every day.

I could stop right here and accept the lie and move on. I could be happy with it. Because even if I saw the real Toni now—even if she's still alive and she still loves me—I would always remember *this version of her*. She would always be here in this room full of dolls, her scent filling my heart and burning my soul. Does that convince me, deep down? Am I Jimmy Stewart, dressing up Kim Novak in fancy clothes?

Am I really that far gone?

I put my hands gently on her shoulders. My breath touches her ear, and she whispers softly that she loves me.

I love you.

She closes her eyes and all the breath leaves her body, resigned.

And she kisses me.

The kiss is good, full of things you remember. Like promises made and secrets kept, anger and fear and desperation colliding somewhere in a dark place you can't find your way out of. I feel the uncertainty in that moment and I want to believe more than ever that she is my wife, the electric bolt of it shocking through my body and leaving me breathless, as we melt into one another. I caress the slope of her neck with one hand. My lips meld with hers. It all comes so easy. Like we've been here so many times. Like we know each other this well, just by sensing. Just by feeling.

I love her because she is my wife.

But she isn't.

Nothing ever felt more right and more confused.

So we go deeper.

Our souls vanish in the hot shimmer, leaving us naked of all our sins, hovering without flesh, without blood, without anything but this endless longing to find each other. To find anything.

Even if it's not real.

It's full of fear, this one moment of love, but it's also beautiful. I think it might be the most beautiful moment I've ever shared with a woman. Because it moves through me so fast and the taste is so sweet that I don't even know it's there when it happens, and the memory fades instantly. Like we made something together, something to survive the ages, and then we shattered it, because it was perfect. Because it couldn't last. Because happiness is not something that stays in this world, even when it does. All that's left is the trace of something vague and promising, like a dream that breaks your heart to wake up from, and then you make yourself forget because it hurts to remember. It's something you have to let go. Something impossible to define. Something that never really existed.

Or maybe it did.

I pull away from her when the kiss is done, unsure of everything.

She bites her lower lip softly.

"Why did we do that, Elroy?"

"I'm not sure."

"It felt good. Didn't it?"

"Yes."

She touches my shoulder, looking up into my eyes. "We're still in a lot of danger. They could grab us any time. The cops. What's left of Hartman's crew."

She stops, then looks away. "I love you, Elroy."

I know it's a lie.

I know it's not really her.

Dominatrix Barbie stares at me lustily, all done up

in leather and lace and diamond studs. I wonder if the diamonds are real. It chills my blood a little.

"I know what you're thinking," she says. "But you're wrong."

She pulls me close to her again. I don't fight it. I feel the sweat on her face, salty like tears. I feel everything and nothing, all at once, deep inside me and coming loose. We stare at each other in the dark. We're still wearing blue rubber gloves, the two of us. I almost laugh at that, it's so goddamn absurd. We stay very close for a long time, standing here at the edge of everything. A million painted eyes stare back at us from the glass cases. We don't say a word to each other. We communicate in soulspeak.

Or at least that's what it seems like.

That's what I tell myself.

But it's not her.

It's not her.

It's not her.

It . . .

I wake up in the middle of a dream.

I know it's a dream because my father is here with us, and I am with Toni, and there are no questions about anything—everything is simple and beautiful and perfect. All the answers are easy. Nobody wants to kill us.

We've come home.

To the house of Jayne Jenison.

And I am clicking the keys on a computer console, speaking words that sound like numbers. And my father looks over my shoulder. And David Hartman looms over his shoulder. And the voice of the Sarge comes loud and clear:

It's the face of God.

You ain't got what it takes.

But I've come home. To Toni and my father and my family that never was. I click the keys. The numbers come at me. It's a wall of rubber that bounces me back.

A wall of numbers that kills my father.

David's voice now . . . so far away . . . fading . . .

This is where that nasty bitch lives, buddy-boy.

I struggle to stay here.

In this house.

The smell of roses pulls me away.

No . . . have to stay . . .

Have to . . .

The dull light hits hard as I peel my eyes open.

Morning now.

I can't remember going to sleep. I was holding Toni in my arms, we were so close, and then I was dreaming. I feel it all dance in front of me in a cold shimmer. Am I dreaming now?

I hear the TV come on in the next room.

Franklin, scoping the news for some word.

I realize I'm lying next to the girl, and she's already awake. We're both still wearing our clothes. Maybe she never went to sleep. Guess that's appropriate. We might be complete strangers.

My head still hurts.

Slashes of overcast morning gloom filter through the drawn curtains, capturing tiny swirls of dust. It's like we're hovering just outside our own light, in some lost place where only our shadows have substance. Hovering just outside the dream.

Just outside the house of Jenison.

What did it mean?

I sit up at the edge of the bed, looking out at all the dolls. Toni's voice is somewhere, speaking to me now. So close to me, and a million miles away.

"You were talking in your sleep," she says. "Something about a wall of numbers. You said Hartman's name a few times. I wanted to wake you up."

"Why didn't you?"

"I was afraid to."

Somehow, that needs no explanation. I rub my eyes, looking at the clock on the bedside table: 8 A.M. Slept for three hours. I want to sleep for three years.

Gotta pull through this, somehow.

I hang my head and let loose a long breath. "Had a dream just now."

"What about?"

"The bad guys were right at my shoulder, telling me things in plain English."

"Do you remember what they were saying?"

"Just things I've already heard. Stuff about the face of God, and seeing Jayne Jenison's house. I was looking at numbers."

"Maybe the numbers mean something."

You know where she lives and breathes, boy.

You saw it.

I see myself in the vault, sweating bullets. When the time locks were kicking my ass. That row of numbers I couldn't ever figure out, always reorganizing and coming back in the original pattern. A ploy to fool hackers like me. Or maybe something else. Something put there by David Hartman. Because only a maniac like him would do that.

Don't look.

The face of God.

Alex Bennett thought it was a decoy code and I didn't believe her. Maybe we were both wrong. And I still have the numbers burned into my memory, the same way all numbers burn forever like snapshots, deep down, so I can leave them there and forget them.

Burned.

The same way God burns you when you dare to look in his face.

"Yes," I say to her. "Hartman put the numbers there. It was his vault and he put the numbers behind all that security. I memorized them. I thought it was something it wasn't. I thought it was the key to open the door."

It was the mistake that got my father killed.

Hartman hid the damn thing in the deadly bear trap, where nobody could get at it—nobody but me.

The Sarge told me not to look.

They both knew it was the end of the world.

And I didn't hear them.

Franklin sits glued to the big TV.

The local news channels are reporting the fire at Hartman's compound, and there's a continuing piece on CNN about the shootout in the lobby of the Sheraton. It spools all day long, but there's no breaking information. They're calling it TERROR IN THE HEART OF

TEXAS, and there's a lot of pundits and reporter-types arguing about the nature of the attack. That's what they're calling it now—an attack. Like what happened at Toy Jam in Austin. Some people are wondering if the two incidents are linked, but the official word is nil. Complete police blackout. There hasn't even been a press conference yet. That probably means I was right about the security cameras—and Jenison's people have to be combing the city for us right now. They'll find us and kill us. They want what I have. And the cops want blood, too.

They're not saying anything.

But someone has to pay.

Anyone.

We move in three hours.

But first . . .

The ghetto richies who live here invested a few grand in a nice civilian computer setup, with a printer and a scanner and everything. Cute. Getting past the Mickey Mouse security on the rig, I discover that they own a local business—a stationery shop in the River Oaks Shopping Center—and wifey has a side hobby selling those customized Barbies on eBay. The hottest one she had was a Britney Spears model, and the damn thing fetched near a thousand bucks from a collector who calls himself ILIKEDOLLSMAN666. This business really is creepy.

I hack the family e-mail account and find their travel plans, airline itinerary, the works. I even know the name of the ritzy kennel where they sent their dog to live for the next three weeks. That takes me ten minutes. Should have taken three. It's always a little harder with gloves on.

Then I get into my offsite location and dig up some zipped blackware I'll need.

An hour later, I'm riding the datastreams.

A ghost among ghosts.

I run a scan of the girl's hand through the Houston Metro police database and come up snake eyes. I'm even not thinking of her as Toni anymore. Starting to doubt everything now. Starting to feel the ground shift again. Hartman's hackers are all long vanished from my chat rooms. Everyone's staying real low. I'm on my own now, back in the city of the living dead. There's no way out but the way down.

I hack into a Global Positioning Satellite owned by Google.

It's real easy.

Then I feed it the numbers I memorized in the vault.

And that's exactly what the numbers are.

GPS coordinates.

It's a complicated road map and this rinky-dink consumer imaging software isn't sophisticated enough to look very close, but I do get a fuzzy picture: sixty or seventy miles of desert in Wyoming. The girl leans over my shoulder and asks me what the hell it is. I tell her:

"It's the house of Jenison. And we have the keys to it."

JUST ONE MORE THING

I shouldn't do this.

I have the discs and I know the general area where something big is located. It might not be Resurrection itself, but it's all I need. I should run screaming from it, hide somewhere safe and wait for the sky to fall. I should use what I have to cut a deal with someone, anyone, for protection. But who do I go to? Who the hell do I trust? Can I even trust myself to see the truth—in anything? It all hovers in front of me. The plot wants to be figured out.

But there's one more thing.

Toni.

I have to know for sure if I'm crazy. I have to know the truth about Resurrection Express. And only one man knows. Maybe.

I shouldn't do this.

But I do it anyway.

I route my voice through a cheesy Skype-friendly microphone I find in a drawer and feed it through a series of filtration programs, making an encrypted digital signal that dials the phone number Ellie Mayhem gave us last night in the bar. It's 6 P.M. sharp, just like she said.

A rough voice answers on the third ring, gravel cut with razor blades:

"Yeah?"

"Ellie Mayhem told me to give you a call."

"Where is that bitch? Who you is?"

Who you is?

He's a real mind, this guy.

A dangerous mind.

"I'm an old friend of Mollie Baker. And Ellie's with me now. I think we should talk."

The razor-blade voice goes silent for a long, long time before it speaks again.

We get to the club at eight fifteen and the sun is long gone.

Texas Hardbodies says the lasso of neon revolving on the roof.

It's one of those all-day-all-night joints that went way south from a strip club or a watering hole a while back—it's a cheap mudslide instead, warped and tacky, full of beer signs and antlers on the walls, all traced in Tex-Mex bric-a-brac and dim Christmas-tree lights. The main room has six poles where the ladies let it all hang out. Most of them are teenagers with skinny legs and fake IDs. I try not to look. Three bars on three walls. Two pool tables. Plenty of private lap-dance booths, and some gated VIP escort rooms. A balcony full of rich depravos swarming like trolls in the dark, with the dull glimmer of lit cigarettes and fat cigars tracing their silhouettes. The gaudy thud-boom-twang of country trance music, which is the worst kind of noise in the world. Sounds like bowling balls pounding out a rhythm alongside a fiddle player having a seizure.

We're early, me and Franklin and the girl.

The girl I thought was my wife.

We move through the room, towards the swinging doors at the rear that have a rolling set of police cherries on either side and a sign across the top that reads WEL-COME TO THE PUSSY MACHINE. There's a booth near the doors, dug deep in a corner. In the booth sit three men. One of them is the man we came to meet.

I can tell it's him just by the way he looks.

He looks just like his voice.

A big guy with extra-wide shoulders, black jacket over a leather vest, his chest naked. Something heavy in a holster, almost visible under his right arm. Bald head and bloodshot eyes, rough dark skin like bad road, split across the chin with a long scar. It looks like recent damage, maybe six months old. Hasn't healed well because he keeps moving. Crazy guys like this have to keep moving or they drown—they're like sharks.

His two homies sag next to him in windbreakers, checking us out as we come over to the table. He opens his mouth and those rusty razor blades spill out:

"You the man?"

"I guess that depends," I tell him. "Are you Death Ray?"

"Only to motherfuckers who ain't got no respect."

I let the pounding backwoods techno-screech of the music take up the slack as I stare him down. I learned this in prison. With danger men, you don't back down. They get the message loud and clear.

Sure enough, he nods.

"Okay, boy. You got my attention. We're in a nice public place. Nobody's gonna fuck with nobody."

"You sure about that?"

"Who's the Mount Everest motherfucker standin' next to you?"

"He's my doctor. Says I've got three weeks to live."

"Nice hair, doc." He does an evil thing with his face, and the scar almost winks at Franklin across his chin. Then he looks at the girl. "And what about this fine bitch here? You bring me a present or what?"

Ray's scar winks at me again as he smiles.

Franklin nods to me.

Stands, with his hand under his jacket, inches from the gun in his waistband.

I sit across from the homies, and I notice one of them has silver-capped teeth—real silver, not a mouthpiece, like the rappers. That's the flunky to Ray's left. The one on the right is wearing sunglasses framed in Day-Glo yellow, like a reject from *I Love the '80s*. They both look ridiculous sitting next to a danger man like Death Ray. Then again, maybe I'm just easily impressed by a voice on the phone.

"I'm nobody's present," the girl says, standing next to me.

Her voice comes during a lull in the music. The song has downshifted to something slow and dirty and R&B, the announcer crowing from his nest that someone named Lady Death is hitting the center stage.

"You my present if I fuckin' *say you is*, bitch!"

Ray stands up like a shot and pushes the table back when he says that. The two homies look like they're going for pistols under their windbreakers.

"Be cool," he tells them. Then he looks right at me. "Where my fine-ass Ellie, motherfucker? Where she *at*?"

"She won't be coming around anymore," I say. "Told me to tell you so."

Ray walks right over to the girl, until just inches separate them. Smiles like a demon. "Then I guess this here bitch really *is* mine, huh?"

The girl looks at me, then gets right in Ray's face:

"You're a disgusting pig."

Franklin moves his hand deeper under his jacket. I shake my head at him but he doesn't back off. I stand up and get right between Ray and the girl.

He looks right at me, and:

"You and Mount Everest get the fuck out. I'll take it from here."

"I don't think so," says Franklin. "Not until my boss says our business is done."

"That's real courageous," Ray says. "But that don't mean nothin' to *me*, man."

He locks his arms across his chest. Stands there like a stone bastard. His voice, crackling now with rage hardly contained:

"Now I gonna tell you motherfuckers the *news*, and that news be this: any deal you thought we was gonna be doin'—that's all off now. This bitch is *mine*. It be last call for dumb white boys. You get to turn your asses around and walk outta here with your heads still on your shoulders. I be a nice guy and let that happen. I be real fuckin' polite about it."

He shifts his weight, passing a serious sideways glance to his crew. Then aims the last bit at me. One crushing syllable at a time:

"But if you ain't happy white boys, that ain't no problem. If you wanna go and look a gift horse up its motherfucking ass, that's no problem either. Because I ain't got *no problem* with makin' your motherfucking asses bleed. Now you can nod once for yes and twice for no . . ."

Spit falls from his mouth. He's snarling.

". . . or you can sit right there and watch yourself die."

Well.

I guess that's that.

Time to do my Colombo.

Turn toward him on one heel, scratching my head.

Looking real innocent.

"Oh . . . just one more thing, Ray."

"Yeah?"

"Kim Hammer."

His eyes get big when the name floats over to him, like he just saw a ghost.

Maybe he did.

"I'd like to know why you killed her," I say. "Was it personal . . . or were you doing a favor for a friend?"

"What the fuck is it to *you*, white boy?"

"It's simple. I think we know the same people."

He forgets about the girl.

He forgets about Ellie Mayhem or the room full of people.

Forgets about everything but the gun under his leather vest.

Franklin draws down on him fast with his Glock 30. The bullet does a merciless midair burn just inches past the girl's face, blowing a huge hole in Ray's chest before he gets the pistol halfway out of the shoulder holster. Everything shatters in a series of shrill thundercracks. The girl lunges forward and lands on Ray, the two homies pulling their iron. Cheap shots go long across the table from pissant little popgun pistols, like annoying insects buzzing around Franklin's head, missing him by miles. The 9-mil discharges hardly make a sound, but the load rips apart one of the nearby beer signs. The big double-bang from Franklin's Glock is still the loudest thing in the room, even over the syrupy R&B music, and lots of people start screaming. Death Ray goes down, bleeding, twitching, and the girl is on top of him. His buddies don't get a second chance at killing Franklin. The big guy pivots like a robot and kills them both instantly—two in each head. *Bang bang* and *bang bang*. He's got one bullet left when the homies twitch hard and decide they're dead. It goes down in less than three seconds. And the whole room is nuts now. People running for the exits. Girls leaping from the stage, half naked and hysterical. Death Ray on the floor and the girl with her hands around his throat, spitting in his face. He hocks back blood and doesn't die. His thugs, sprawled like broken stick figures, oozing brains across the table. How did this happen? It all happened so fast. And it keeps on happening in a series of flash frames, like disco-kinetic thundersplooshes lit up in the spaces between eye-blinks. I jump through the strobe light like a man stumbling in stop-motion, and I crash to my knees and try to force the girl away from Death Ray, but her grip is like steel and she won't let him go, and she's screaming like everyone else in the room—screaming that Ray is a bastard and a son of a bitch and she hates him—and it damn near breaks my heart because it's not really Toni, it was never really Toni, but I don't let it break my heart, because I know, somewhere in my mind, that it's just not this simple, none of this is simple, and she smothers him with her hatred, smashing his head into the floor, forcing his last breath to come to the surface, and she brings him close to her and asks him how it feels—*how does it feel, you son of a bitch BASTARD*—and something cracks inside him and he almost screams, he almost chokes, and he manages the word *motherfucker* right as I finally get her to let go of him, and he hits the floor again, making wet, strangled sounds, and my own voice is hardly audible over the storm of chaos blasting through the room as I spit at him to tell me who wanted Kim Hammer dead, and I expect him to yell Jenison's name . . . I expect him to *choke on Jenison's name . . .*

But he tells me to go fuck myself and dies.

And that's when a roomful of assholes open fire on us.

The chaos speeds through me in a series of rhythmic staccato color bursts, people winding and screaming and scrambling ahead of us and in our wake, as the wreck-ing crew pours into the room, guns first. About four of them, Ray's backup, coming in fast behind a series of jagged lightning bolts—muzzleflashes burning gunpowder, setting the sleazy air on fire. I dive for the floor as patrons scatter. Franklin dives after me, his Glock still in one fist. He doesn't fire at anyone with his last bullet—what's the point? Too many targets. Too much insanity. We retreat through the storm, crawling low. The whole joint sparks in a million points of white-hot ignition, hellfire and the screaming of innocents. I see the vaguest shattershard of the lady who said she was my wife, somewhere behind us, falling on the dance floor, blood splattering in the confused spaces between us. Bodies falling on all sides, like living dead corpses piling up in a horror movie. It all comes in faster than thought—I'm trying to slow it down, but my heart accelerates to attack speed. The lights blind me. More shots. More blood. Complete insanity. I move almost on autopilot as Franklin pulls at me . . . and we're crawling along the floor through the screaming crowd . . . and we get to the back exit fast, as the shots die off . . .

Standing up and coming through the door is like surfacing from a punishing ocean of light and noise.

Everything slows down.

Our car waits in the alley.

The air outside the club is colder than it was before—it hits me like an electric shock, shaking me loose from the mayhem.

It's almost 9 P.M. We just walked out of a war zone again.

We're damn lucky to be alive.

I can still hear shots in there.

And the girl . . .

"We have to go back for her," I find myself muttering, taking a step toward the door. But a hand slaps down on my shoulder, pulling at me.

"She's gone, kid."

That seems like Franklin's voice . . . but it's so far away now . . . behind a wall of city noise, and sirens closing on the block . . . as everything slows again . . .

"Get the fuck in the *car*!"

That's definitely Franklin's voice.

He's yanking me back now, and I'm going along with it.

I hardly hear the doors slam or the engine gun.

A bunch of really scared people watch us peel out of there.

Franklin doesn't say a word as he drives.

His hateful breath comes short and labored, and I know just how he feels.

Cop cars scream by us in the opposite direction as Franklin punches it like a pro, getting us into a side street. No one sees us. We are damn near invisible. As we race between pools of shadow, everything comes in fast and forces itself through a long black tunnel without detail. My voice, Franklin's voice, the world speeding in crazed midtown blurs and streetlamp supernovae.

"We have to go for the money and the discs," I tell him. "All bets are off. There's too much damage on the street now."

"You got that right. There's gonna be roadblocks. They'll be watching the bus terminals and the train stations."

"We have to get to the money and get hidden again. You and me will finally be square, at least."

"That's damn fine by me. I never wanna see you again."

"Yeah, it's been a real pleasure, huh?"

"Fuck you."

I'll use the rest of my cash to buy some time. I'll dig deeper, using what I brought out of the vault. It's the only thing that will shield me, the only way I can figure this thing out. I'll find Jenison somehow, off the radar . . . *somehow* . . .

Goddammit, why did Franklin have to shoot the guy? Death Ray was my one real link back to Jenison. Back to Resurrection Express.

And Toni.

I go a little crazy from split second to split second, thinking about it—and about the moment when the girl fell in the strobe lights. Blasts of crimson detonating in the air between us. Civilian casualties on all sides. I don't get a clear picture of any of it. It replays like bad video, shot through with static. The smell of roses and ammonia should be hammering me now, but it's not. The familiar shriek of the rage should be rezzing like hell in my throat and my heart, but all of my armor is compromised, all of my thoughts suspect. Everything I believed was true five minutes ago, blown away and replaced by the absolutely goddamn inevitable. I've become a hapless bystander in a world made of evil bullshit.

Jimmy Stewart, lost in a maze of blood.

"You shouldn't have left the girl," I say. "She didn't deserve that."

"She was dead, asshole. You wanna go back there and bury her properly, that's fine by me. But you do it later—when we're *square*, understand?"

"You're a real hero, aren't you?"

"I'm the hero who just shot our way out of that mess—so fuck you again. If those cowboys back there were scared enough by your Colombo routine to try and cap us in a public brothel full of eyewitnesses, that should at least tell you *something*."

"Like what?"

"Like we were damn lucky to be alive a long time ago, and right now, we're playing with fire and I want off this crazy train. Do you *understand me*, Elroy Coffin?"

I almost find myself laughing. "You knew I was playing Colombo, huh? Pretty slick, Slick."

"Fuck you."

"But you say 'fuck' too much. That's not so slick."

"Fuck *you*."

He's not laughing at all.

Because he's right. Colombo only got shot at when the bad guys he busted were crazy and desperate. He always played it laid-back and humble, until the very last minute. I always wanted to be just like that guy, but nobody's ever that cool under fire. Especially at the last minute. Especially now. The world spinning in space and traced in neon, screaming at me that I never should have looked for the answers.

Death Ray knew that I knew about Jenison. He figured Ellie Mayhem set him up for the kill. Maybe I was a cop. Maybe . . . *shit, I just don't know.*

I grit my teeth and live with it. I tell the girl I'm sorry. I say it out loud.

"I'm sorry."

Franklin makes a stoic face, stares straight at the oncoming road.

We should have at least pulled your body out of there. Should have let you take your last breath in the street, where the air was clean.

She doesn't say a word back to me. She can't say a word to anyone.

She's dead.

And I never even knew her name.

"I have to crack those discs. There's no other choice now."

Franklin nods, driving hard.

We ditch the car downtown and walk ten blocks, to the long-term garage.

The car is right where I left it, on the fifth floor.

Right next to the green Honda with the expired inspection sticker.

The place smells like secrets encased in concrete.

I find the keys in the magnet box under the chassis. I pop the trunk and unscrew the spare tire. The Gold's Gym bag is still there. I unzip it and Franklin gives a solemn sort of grunt when he sees the green. Sitting on top of the money is one black plastic square that contains a terabyte of very important information. Right where I left it. It might be the key to the end of everything. I hand the Gold's Gym bag to Franklin and slam the trunk closed.

When I'm not looking at him, the son of a bitch shoots me in the back.

UNBREAKABLE

The discharge is so loud and it spreads out so long across the entire floor of the garage that I don't hear it at all. I almost saw this coming. Rule number one in the field is that you never turn your back on anyone when your cards are on the table. I gave him the bag so he would show his hand and he played into it, but I didn't see the revolver—that sneaky little Bulldog with three rounds left in the chamber. Must have had it up his sleeve. So I almost don't turn the right way when the bullet hits me—the way they taught us about rolling with point-blank concussion—and I feel the scraping white-hot sear of the hard lead against my rib cage. It scrapes me just under my skin, blowing out a foot below my armpit as I spin, and the bullet keeps on going, shattering a car window three rows down. I don't have time to concentrate on the pain, or the blood loss. I'm using my momentum as I spin in the next microsecond, whipping my arm around to catch his wrist and shove the gun three feet to the right so that his next shot blasts off past my shoulder and punches a hole in a Corvette right behind me. I manage to twist his arm, but he's not soft or afraid like Hartman—his muscles are honed and programmed, and he's a cold machine. The tendons gnash under my grip like iron coils. I get to an important nerve and he drops the gun, but he comes back at me with a really fast left hook and I have to let go of him to duck it. His arms are big and he's got his whole weight behind the blow. If one of those touches me, I go down fast. You know those movies where guys beat up on each other for twenty minutes while the music blares nice and heroic and you hear all those meaty slapping noises? Those are sound effects. It's all bullshit. Your average fistfight is over in less than sixty seconds.

Then again, me and Franklin aren't average guys. He's trained, like I am. But he's big, and big guys tend to overachieve.

His first move is proof of that.

He comes in with a big dumb lunge, which allows me to sidestep him and kick the revolver away. He gets to the other gun in his waistband when I do that but I bend fast in a spinning kick that chops it from his hand before he can fire that last nasty bullet. The metal clanks on the cement. He spits the word "fuck"—it's been his favorite thing to say lately—and falls back into an attack crouch. I circle the gun and kick it under a nearby car. A stinging, unforgiving pain jabs me in my side, and I realize with some faint left-over amazement that he actually shot me, that I didn't duck the first bullet all the way. I feel warmth running down my leg in a slow rolling cascade, like heat waves leaving my body. He sets the Gold's Gym bag on the hood of the car and doesn't smile at me.

"You're hurt bad. You should just give up. It'll be less painful that way."

I'm overwhelmed with absurdity in this moment.

Picturing the face of David Hartman.

And I say:

"Where's the fun in that?"

Franklin starts to circle me seriously, not saying another word.

I see the black glimmer of betrayal in his eyes, all the masks off now.

He was working with Jenison all along—that's why he killed Death Ray instead of going for the good wound, that's why he's stuck to me like glue, this whole goddamn time. That was why Jenison questioned me in the hotel lobby and set herself up for their ambush—when Franklin jumped in there and pretended to save me. It was all a carefully scripted song and dance, all designed to make me believe he was the good guy. Jenison sacrificed her own men to make the illusion complete. And Franklin *didn't* care about his buddies getting carved up or burning up at Hartman's place. He just wanted to get paid at both ends. Handed over the discs to Jenison the second I handed them over to him. Was waiting for me to lead him right to the missing piece.

With the money as his nice little cherry on top.

I think for a second about the clever way Franklin showed me the suitcase back at his house, about how he let me open it and inspect the disc drives, how we dropped them in a safe place together. They were dummies. Decoys. I should have checked them on the computer. What the hell was I thinking?

You were obsessed, I hear Jenison say.

They left my walking-around money taped to my leg when they busted into the hotel room—they could have done anything to me while I was sleeping, but they gave me money and they left me a gun, too. So I would think I had a fighting chance. So I could use the cash to buy Franklin and his men. They were three steps ahead the whole time. Why didn't I see it?

You were obsessed, I hear Jenison say again.

An obsessed man is a dangerous man.

An obsessed man is in a hurry to his own funeral.

An obsessed man can still kick your fucking ass.

He comes at me again, this time using a *giman* attack maneuver—I can tell he's going to fake me out and try for my wound, to end this fast. I don't let it happen. I've been trained to see the definitions of his movements in Japanese. I block his right arm and lower my shoulder into him hard, coming up with a crossed knuckleball into his nose. That knocks him back and he sees stars for a moment, but I didn't break anything. Just a love tap, so you know who you're messing with. He might have figured I was schooled hard, but I can see by the shocked look on his face that my ability to ignore pain has come as one hell of a surprise. They teach you that in the marines, too. It doesn't work if all you're going on is dull machismo and no meditation technique. I'm concentrating hard on nothing but defeating this man. There is no hole in my side. There is no stinging in my muscles or throbbing in my fist. There is only the enemy and the destruction of that enemy.

Destroy him.

Destroy him now.

He comes at me again and I sidestep and stab fast with a sweep to his legs. He spins and catches my knee in midair and I almost feel something go *snap*, but I sway like a reed in the wind, rolling over sideways and kicking him with my other foot. This time I find pay dirt. His nose breaks and he lets go of me. I press it and jam both palms into his midsection, trying to send him into the car behind us. He knows about pushing-hands, I can see by the silly look he gives me when I hit him, and there's nothing he can do about it as he flies backwards . . . but he bounces off the car and burns through my next block with a fist that feels like a metal battering ram when it gets to my head. I turn my face so he doesn't peg my nose, but the blow still dazzles me and I waddle backwards a few paces. He stabs again and I grab his wrist again. His own inertia carries him face-first into a windshield and his head splits safety glass into a jagged shape that looks like thick plastic wrap imploding around him. The whole thing goes *poosh!* I can hear him almost yell out in pain.

But he's back at me like a rubber bullet, really pissed off now. Blood trickles down his face. I duck three more swings. His style is not elegant. He knows the moves, but he's not put together like I am, not built for speed and accuracy. I jab the nerve center just below the carotid artery in his lower arm and it paralyzes that whole side of his body for just a few seconds, long enough for me to hammer his face again. He spins, sensing my moves now, and I just graze him. I don't realize I've left my wounded side open until he hammers me there and I feel a rib crack in the middle of a white-hot explosion.

Got me good. Goddammit. Stupid.

He hits me again, but I manage to roll with it. The pain is still almost unbearable. I almost drop, but I can't drop. He's coming right at me again, like a tank. Have to break his arm fast, level the playing field. It's like trying to beat up a concrete wall. He sees it coming and he's armored with thick cords of muscle and callused scar tissue. My blows bounce off him. My next trick is another combination grab-and-thrust, but he slips my grip easy and comes back at me hard. I duck the first swing, but he anticipates my move. The next one gets me three feet down, a horizontal chop right in my throat. *Dammit*. Should have . . . seen that one . . . *coming* . . .

Wham.

Right in my midsection.

That might be the ball game.

I drop to one knee, clutching my side. I can see the girl—she said she was my wife—in my mind, standing there for just a split second. Watching us kill each other. With no look on her face at all.

Snap out of it, you dumb weak shit—*this guy is gonna kill you.*

Blood gushes down my side now, the bullet scrape giving me hell.

I have no air.

I can't let him win.

The gun—the revolver with one bullet left.

Just out of reach.

I jump for it and he jumps after me. Lands like a boulder. I feel something in my spine give a fraction of an inch. He picks me up off my feet, raises me into the air above his head like a TV wrestler. The air up here is crushing and stale. And I'm headed back for solid ground in way too big a hurry now. The pavement comes up like a wall against my back and I lie there, looking up at him as he comes down fast again, like a giant about to squash an ant. He doesn't see my foot until it stabs him right between his legs. Everything I've got goes into the kick. He feels it hard and screams out loud. Doubles over, choking. I struggle to my feet . . . and it takes all the mind over muscle I possess. The pain stabs me, my bones grinding and shrieking now. I have just a few seconds before the burst of adrenaline that comes with a blow to the lower regions armors him again. He grits his teeth and staggers back and I unleash everything I have left on him. Double combinations to his deltoids. Hard balled fists against his kidneys. Another shot to his groin. He acts like it really hurts and I think I almost have him . . . until I feel the tearing sensation in my guts . . . and he smiles, halfway doubled over, sneering:

"Getting a little tired, kid?"

His fist hits me while he's still talking.

My nose holds, I don't lose any teeth. I hear one of his fingers, the little one, break against my cheekbone. But it's like I'm inside a church bell, the entire world vibrating and quaking and shaking every thought I have into a jumbled mess . . . and I can't see anything anymore. I feel my legs go next. He has me on the ground now. I feel his blood dripping in my face. Unbreakable. The son of a bitch is goddamn unbreakable. And he's about to break me in half. Has both of my legs in a scissor hold, folding me like a green twig, my back flat on the ground. This is a death grip. I'm going to die. He's going to kill me. Whatever it was that gave in my spine is going again. It's a terrible sound, rumbling and popping in my throat. I try to move my legs but they won't listen now. I look around for the gun—there, just a few feet from me. My hands make a reach, but it might as well be a million miles away.

He sees me go for it and almost smiles.

Lets go of me.

My whole body collapses on the concrete.

Franklin sees that I can't move, spits blood onto the ground next to me, then walks over to the gun. Very slowly, he does it.

Knows he has all the time in the world.

I try to get up, to face it on my feet, but I can't. I'm lying here in a pool of my own blood, shot and bleeding and broken right in half.

I've failed you, Toni.

I've failed us both.

And now I'm going to die here.

He stands over me with the pistol. His voice is brittle and coarse:

"Here comes the big surprise, kid."

He lowers the gun.

"I'm not gonna kill you."

He tells me I fought him good. No one ever messed him up like I did, not even back in the war. He says we were pretty evenly matched, that it was just chance that put me on my back and left him still on his feet. I'll live through it, if I'm lucky. I can't hear his exact words—it's all muddied and garbled and blown back to me in bizarre waves—but I can tell that's basically what he's saying.

I can't move.

At all.

"I'm gonna take your car, kid. Hope you don't mind. And I'll be sure to give your regards to Jenison's people. They won't be looking for you anymore, now that we have this."

His voice is clearer now—I focus on it to stay alive. He pats the Gold's Gym bag, tosses it into the driver's seat.

Leaves me here.

"There's no hard feelings. I think you're okay. I would have shot you dead if you hadn't been so scrappy. Kinda makes me feel like we ain't so different. I had you pegged for something else altogether. I'd get to a hospital soon, if I were you. You're bleeding pretty bad now."

You son of a bitch. You don't believe in anything. You didn't even care about your so-called friends getting hacked to death.

The Weasel was more a man than you'll ever be.

He pauses in the open door of the car and cocks his head back at me, like an afterthought. "You're a tough kid. But not tough enough."

I tell him to go to hell, but the sound chokes in my throat.

He understands.

"Sticks and stones," he says, chuckling. "So long."

He slams the door and starts the car. Pulls out of the parking space and leaves me there. One of the tires rolls through a pool of my blood, painting a jagged crimson tendril on the concrete.

• • •

The car is long gone when I reach into my pocket for my cell phone. I almost expect it not to be there, but it still is. The same phone I called the girl on, back in the hotel bar. I dial a number and don't expect anyone to answer. But the right person does.

Franklin.

"Kid? Is that you?"

"Yeah," I tell him, finding my voice through sheets of pain and blood bubbling in my mouth. "There's something you should know. You were right, after all. This is the easiest thing I've ever done."

The sound of my voice over the cell phone activates the two circuits in the remote detonator I made from Alex Bennett's leftover gear.

I hear the car explode from two blocks away.

Unbreakable.

That's the word that comes back time and again, echoing across the wavering, fleshy chambers of my mind as I swim in a dream, the faces shimmering all around in an infinite darkness—everyone who ever mocked me, cursed me, tried to kill me. Only a few ever loved me. They aren't here. Just the bad guys. Somewhere out there in the real world, I am bleeding and broken. I can see that, too. I'm not all the way under, not yet.

Unbreakable.

I can feel that I'm willing my upper body to drag me towards the girl, who said her name was Toni, who is another face that mocks me, another question I have no answer for. I'm fighting back the maelstrom of voices and memories, resisting the temptation to give in completely, because I know if I do, I'm dead. I have to save myself. They can't break me like this. I have only a few moments to act.

Where are you, my love?

Tell me what to do.

Like you always did.

Make these screaming faces go away. Make them stop laughing at me. I have things to do. I am crawling on my elbows now. I can feel it way back there. I can feel the tears pooling in my eyes from the strain on my upper body. I can feel my teeth clenching together, my legs dangling uselessly behind me. The sound of Franklin's words, the finality of his voice . . . just before I killed him.

You're a tough kid. But not tough enough.

The sound of sirens, somewhere in the distance— the terrible soundtrack of my life these days. How long has it been since he left me here? Can I see the girl in front of me? Toni's weird doppelganger, crying in a misty half darkness, desperate to be saved, like I am.

She said her name was Toni. I want to believe her. I have to. She proved it, didn't she? With a kiss in a room full of dolls . . .

So why does this all feel so wrong . . .

I'm a killer now. Like my father.

Murdered someone with my own hands . . .

The nightmare shifts gears and the punishment comes now, sparks of memories spritzing on and off like the channels on an old color TV set with the sound turned way up—so that the voices and the muzzle-flashes and the music top out the speaker system and overload the amplifiers—static blowing past me, empty stations hovering in the blank canyons of absolutely nowhere. Pieces of my life, shattered and flickering in a horrible slipstream, slashing me, mocking me . . .

You're a killer now, son. Welcome to the monster club.

I see the first job I ever did, the one that didn't go so well. Two cops on the street when we walked out. My father, his finger fast on the trigger. The sneering smiles of a million angry gods right in my face as the gun blows my mind . . .

Unbreakable.

I see the first time I was in jail, surrounded by the smell of sweat and stale cigarette smoke and plots that go nowhere because you're a loser. The face of the man who called himself Shanker, the first guy who ever tried to kick my ass, and his blood still salty and desperate in my mouth . . .

Unbreakable.

I see David Hartman, sitting behind his desk, telling me about the power and the glory, all those god-awful life-worn clichés dangling in front of me like a joke told to an eight-year-old who doesn't understand anything . . . and his cruel stare . . . his hand on the meat cleaver . . . telling me he has the last laugh after all . . .

. . . and I fight him.

I fight his image back.

Because I beat this asshole. I won already.

I'm not a killer, not the way they are.

I am better than monsters like this.

Unbreakable.

• • •

Toni . . . it's Toni now. I see her face, for real, just a glimpse—and she looks like the girl who tried to fool me—but then it's gone. And then it's back. And then it's gone again. Urgent flashes in the dark. Telling me I have to get up. I can't stay here. It's time to run like hell. I mutter something to the ghost in my head, telling her my legs are gone now. They got me good. *You can only dance the edge for so long . . . and love does not stay . . .*

Get up, she tells me.

Don't pussy out.

She touches my face and her fingers are cold. They smear something on my cheek, and it's warm. Streaks of blood. It's just a dream.

It's the girl now, right in front of me.

The girl who looks like Toni.

Or maybe she looks like Toni.

The fingers form into a hard slap across my face now. I can hear her voice, telling me to get up. It wasn't Toni, it was just some girl. The voices that mock me . . . they recede back ever so slightly . . . and the parking garage smears into view for just a moment. I realize I've been crawling towards a hallucination this whole time. I'm up for air and I have this one chance. I open my mouth and words come out. I control them in quick bursts, through the shoots of pain in my side.

I speak into the cell phone and call for help.

My fingers have dialed 911 and I'm telling them to come get me.

They'll find me.

They'll arrest me.

But they'll save my life.

The girl nods yes.

She looks so much like Toni when she nods like that.

Get up, she tells me.

Don't pussy out.

Get up now.

GET UP AND RUN!

And as her voice rips through my head, the pain in my body explodes like magma, the images shattering like fragile faces blown to hell . . . and it's the worst pain I've ever felt . . . the final pain . . . *the pain of losing everything in one moment of absolute failure and weakness . . . and I'm screaming . . . SCREAMING . . .*

The rage thunders back, crashing upward from my destroyed bones, blasting through my eyes, setting the metal in my skull on fire . . .

. . . and there they all are . . .

. . . my father . . .

. . . my teachers . . .

. . . *Toni.*

It's you.

Not some phantom, not a woman that tells lies.

It's really you.

I've waited so long for this moment.

This moment happened so long ago.

It's our wedding, solidifying all around me in beautiful detail, the white-on-white of the room that surrounds us, all full of silks and curtains and fluttering lace, rose petals at our feet, her sharp scent swirling like invisible tongues of sweet dragon breath, her face smiling with all the promises we made before this, and the promises we make now. She stares at me with eyes that can see across time, see into the future. The image of her face is so clear now, and I keep expecting to lose it, keep expecting her eyes to turn black or fill with blood, while the pain in my head punishes me and the voices slither back to mock me . . . but this is the moment . . . *the real moment* . . . brought back to me because I'm almost dead in the real world . . .

Yes.

Almost dead.

I can almost feel my body back there.

Almost feel the blood running from me, my bones shattered and useless.

But I don't care.

Because she moves towards me in the white room, her black hair stunning and shimmering against the backdrop of heaven, the sleek lines of her soft chin and high cheekbones tracing perfection. Her skin creamy white, flawless. Black lipstick in the soft, sweet shape of a heart as she speaks her vows to me, telling me that it was destiny, that it was fate, that she will never leave me in a million years, even if she does. She tells me we are bonded by so much more than flesh and blood. So much more than the idle promises human beings make when they think they can. In this room, there is no one else, just the two of us. And I hold her in my arms and I feel the perfection of her flesh, the swell of her breasts, the slope of her waist and the canyons of her back, my hands running deep there. And I see the years that will come after our wedding superimposed on the flutter-ing silk walls, like movies: all the hard times and the good times and the jobs we do together, every moment brought back in one single burst, like a doctor administering a shot of something heavy. Someone tells me it's okay as I lie there and watch it all. Someone says I'm going to be all right, and I believe him, because I can die now, watching the memories, the images of Toni, fully formed and smiling at me, exploding in layer upon layer. I'm on a stretcher, and I can tell we're moving fast, inside a moving vehicle. But the memories jet over me faster, still superimposed over my sight, and Toni says she loves me again. A siren overhead, screaming back into the street behind us. I can't move and I don't feel anything. Toni smiles and her smile is more beautiful than anything. I expected to be handcuffed but I'm not. There's no cop in here, nobody to tell me I'm in deep shit or asking me questions I don't have to answer because I have the right to remain silent. The room we were married in hovers just out of sight now, years down the line. David Hartman is in the room now, killing Axl, and he has no idea that we gave our vows there, and I never tell him, because that would give him everything. I beat you in the end, David. I avenged everyone you ever murdered in that white room. And I got her back. She's mine again. As I lie here, unable to move. As the EMS guy hovers over me with the defib paddles, telling me it's all okay.

"Nobody dies in my fucking ambulance," he says.

Something punches into me like a fist, and I go back to the white room again.

THE TWO TONIS

One more time, back from the dead.

They're rolling me down a long back tunnel.

Jumbled voices.

People crying.

The smell of sterile things, like scalpels and rubbing alcohol.

I feel the grinding vibration of wheels just under my body.

I decide it's a comfort.

Even though I'm 100 percent screwed.

The next few moments may happen over a few hours, a few days, a few weeks, a few years. It's a mosaic scattered in front of me. Shattered bits of images, people. No memories. No emotions. No Toni. Just the here and now, whatever it is, wherever it is. The beeping of a life-support monitor. The clinking of metal instruments. The cursing of professionals. The scent of blood, crawling up my nose like salt water dripping from a rusty razor. Something I never got used to.

Things that are inevitable.

Back.

For keeps now.

I peel my eyes open and there's another white room all around me. I know this can't be heaven, because I'm pretty sure that heaven doesn't exist. I know this isn't the bridal suite of the Driskill Hotel, because that all happened a million years ago. My arms move on their own, and I feel my face, making sure I'm still all there. I feel no pain, but I see tubes and wires attached to me. An IV feeding my bloodstream saline and a drug pump doing something sleepy to my mind. There's a blue-and-white smock covering my chest, a sheet and a thin blanket over me. I'm in a bed with steel rails along either side. My wrists aren't handcuffed to anything. I decide I'm not dreaming.

My legs.

I can't feel my legs.

An old nurse sits near me in a chair, next to the life-support devices. She looks up from her newspaper, her expression neutral.

"Hello there," she says to me.

I'm surprised to find that making my own voice happen is easy, though it sounds like a gravel road. "Where am I?"

"Ben Taub Trauma Center. You're okay. You had to have emergency surgery."

Ben Taub. This place is notorious. A charity drop. A drug lord sent his posse to shoot the place up a few years back. Said it was revenge for something bad.

"I can't remember . . . how I got here."

"You've been here three days." That's all she says. She gets up and folds her paper under her arm. Turns sharply and leaves me in the room. Thanks a lot, lady.

I sit and I try to organize my thoughts.

Three days.

Does Jenison know I'm here?

Does anyone know I'm here?

They have me on a morphine drip, or maybe something stronger. I can tell that because my thoughts are damn hard to organize. The room is small, private. The door is wide open and the hall outside is dark. They have the lights on in here to wake me up. I wonder if they figured on me ever waking up at all.

My legs.

I can't feel them, not at all down there.

I look to see if they're still attached, and they are.

But I can't feel them.

I can't move them.

Ben Taub is part of the Hermann Healthcare Center, near the Fourth Ward barrio just past the Montrose area, just a few miles from where the bad business went down. I can hardly remember getting here.

I just remember being in the bridal suite again.

I remember Toni's face now.

Clear in my head, like the smell of roses on our wedding day.

Like the scents she mixed herself—the scents that fooled me later.

And, yeah, I see that other version of her, too . . . still vaguely assigned to my memories. That girl who tried to be Toni. She remains in my head as a sort of reminder. She snipes at me and laughs that I was ever such an idiot.

The two Tonis are a lot alike, actually.

They both have long black hair.

They both smell like roses.

They are both strong, powerful.

But the real Toni is taller, blacker. Like a sleek bird traced in neon, her face angled upward, elegantly like an empress or a rock star, her skin so white you can see through the empty space and into your own soul. Her body is slim and corded, wide shoulders cascading into a creamy canyon, flowing into her hips and legs like a liquid metal goddess in perpetual motion, a statue carved in flowing milk and muscle, like rivers leading downward and downward, the sleek curves of her waist and the soft innocence of her navel so white and so washed in sin and wisdom . . .

Before I can think about it anymore, I hear the sharp clock of expensive shoes in the hallway outside, and they enter the room, attached to a guy in a black suit and a thin white coat. I always wonder why they make doctors wear those. I think it's to sell the lie that they know what the hell they're doing half the time.

"Hi guy," he says, a little too cheerfully. He's not an old man, but not quite young anymore. He could be anybody.

Have to play this careful.

"Hello," I say to him, sounding as confused as I can. It isn't hard.

"How are we feeling?"

Terrible. I have no idea how *you're* feeling.

I don't say that out loud. Instead, I open my mouth and words come out that sound like this:

"Where am I?"

"Hermann Hospital. You had emergency surgery two days ago." Then he gives me the edge I need: "Do you remember anything? Can you tell me your name?"

"I . . . don't know. You have my ID, don't you?"

"There was nothing in your pockets. You were admitted as a John Doe. We found the cell phone you called the ambulance with. You were still holding it when the EMS techs got to you."

"Ambulance?"

"You had a close call, guy. They had to zap you on the way here."

"What happened to me?"

"Looks like you were mugged. Beaten and shot. My guess is that they left you for dead."

"I can't remember anything."

"Can you remember your name?"

"No."

I let the lie drift across in a pathetic croak. Looks like he buys it. I can tell from the dull snort and shake of his head. Like this happens all the time.

"Doesn't surprise me," he says. "You were in a coma for several hours before you stabilized. Had a pretty severe head concussion. Someone hit you real hard, maybe with a pipe. You have a small plate in your head, also. Looks like it could be the result of a gunshot wound. Do you remember how you got that?"

"No."

He lets that go. Then summons his courage, looking at the floor.

"I . . . have to *tell you* something. It's bad news."

Yeah. I know.

His next words still hit me like a tidal wave.

"You've lost the use of your legs. You're paralyzed from the waist down."

The wave drowns me.

"The damage appears to be the result of something cumulative. Stress factors over a long period of time. When you got banged up, it was sort of the last straw. So to speak. You're a damn lucky man."

Yeah. I know.

He gets a little closer to me and I smell his cheap cologne.

Disgusting.

"During surgery, you flatlined, and there were other complications. You almost didn't make it."

I know that, too.

I got Toni back when that happened.

I had to die for her.

I always knew it would be that way.

And now I'm half a man because of it.

Half a man.

"You've been healing very well," he says. "The wound in your side is doing fine. It didn't hurt you that bad. You'll be out of ICU tomorrow, and we'll move you next door to the Hermann Medical Center. We have an excellent physical rehabilitation program there. I'm . . . sorry."

Yeah. I can see how sorry you are.

"A staff member will be in here tomorrow morning to discuss insurance with you. Do you have any questions?"

I shake my head at him.

He snorts and shakes his head again.

"The law requires me to inform you that the police have been notified about your shooting. We'll also have to inform them about your previous injuries. They may want to ask you some questions, they may not. Most times in situations like this, an investigation doesn't actually happen, unless the family requests it."

"I understand."

"Someone will be in to check on you soon."

He turns and leaves without another word.

I'm just some broke welfare street scum to him.

I feel a wave of hatred rising in me, and I crush it fast. I have to think about getting out of this place. Can't think about the finality of what's happened to me. It'll kill the only thing I've got left to fight with—and that's my mind.

I'm swimming in the wave, trying to focus.

I traded my manhood for my memories.

I'll never walk again.

DAMAGE CONTROL

I calm myself, breathing hard, closing my eyes, trying to take myself out of the room. Trying to see the leads.

Voices laugh at me.

I try for a long time to see the leads. All I can find is the end of everything.

Have to focus. Take myself out. Guide myself through.

I'll never walk again.

Finally . . . my heartbeat slows.

I find calm in the storm.

Damage control, just for a few minutes.

I'm thinking carefully now.

If the cops decide to question me, they might run my prints, too. Right now I'm a John Doe. Right now, Elroy Coffin is officially dead, as far as the books are concerned. Jenison had me killed in the Toy Jam massacre, but a lot of people know different on the street. If the cops run my prints through the system and find out that they match up with a dead man . . . well, this could get really complicated. They'll start asking a lot more questions. They might connect the dots to everything. The fire at Hartman's place. The shootout at the strip club and the car bomb that killed Franklin. It's only a matter of time before somebody, anybody, shows up looking for me.

Maybe days. Maybe hours.

I've been here half a week already, though. That might mean something. Might mean Jenison and her people don't know where I am, have no idea where to look. Or maybe they just don't care about me anymore. Maybe I'm no use to them. I blew up the key to their kingdom, after all—blew it up with Franklin. What could they want from me now?

Being dead on the books buys me some time with the cops.

Time I don't have.

The amnesia bit will only shield me for so long. They'll want to know how I can pay my way. I don't have any ID. I could be anyone. And my old scars, from three years ago. That'll bring the cops faster, too. Maybe.

I try to move my legs—I try damn hard.

And I can't.

The damage is permanent this time.

Can't think about it.

I have no legs but I must run.

It takes a few minutes to calm myself again.

Must not let this break me.

The mind is the most powerful weapon.
Focus.

What happens next?

They'll move me to the Hermann Medical Center next door in the morning. They'll give me access to a telephone, because they want my money. I have to figure on being interviewed by the cops sooner than later.

The Hermann Medical Center is where they took Gabby Giffords last year, when she was shot in the face. On any other day, the irony might be amusing. Today . . . it's just another joke I'm not laughing at.

Poor Gabby.

I take myself off the morphine drip, or whatever it is. Disconnect the tube at the heparin lock and inch it out of the apparatus taped to my arm. I do it carefully, tracing each movement, because I'll have to stick it back eventually.

I let the drug dribble onto the floor.

I wait for a few minutes to see how bad the pain is.

It's not too bad. My head clears some.

The hole in my side is sutured and bandaged up. Small wound, like he said, well on the road to healed. My training saved me from it being any worse and the patch-up job was good. There was no bullet to dig out. Might have shocked my lung because it hurts to breathe a little. I would have been able to walk away from there if Franklin hadn't crushed me in half.

I'll never walk again because of that son of a bitch.

For the first time in my life, I'm completely helpless.

• • •

The pain creeps up on me—something sharp and scraping in my left side. A throbbing in my head. I put the needle back in the lock, inch it slowly into place. The relief goes down smooth. I can't rely on it for long. I have to get my head on straight. I have to get out of here. I think about it so hard that I feel my mind give . . . and I cross the terminator into night, swimming in darkness now.

Looking for a way out.

Looking and falling.

Down and down.

In this dream, Toni speaks to me. She is no longer a wraith without form, hovering in a black space where my destroyed memories once churned and boiled. No, these are new memories, filled with the new image of her. The sleek, perfect version of her I was robbed of so long ago. It's really her speaking to me. She's come back to stay. I am in a room filled with copper wire and glimmering circuitry, the guts of a computer system are laid bare before my eyes, entangling my arms, keeping me still, my legs vanishing forever into a void that yawns below. Toni is telling me secrets, about what's really going on behind the scenes . . . but her voice is low . . . and soon it fades away . . .

. . . and I see my father on the butcher's block. His hands tied down and guns held to his head. He is not afraid. He speaks to me like *my father*, like a man with wisdom, not like a killer who is drunk and doomed.

Son. I will resurrect you. Follow me.

Hartman hovers above us somewhere. I can hear the shrill, cold slice of the blade through the air. The salty taste of blood in my mouth. My father's hand is on the chopping block. His gun hand. The hand with only three fingers left.

Follow me. Follow my words.

The blade, closer now in the dark. Secrets that must be told. I know the answers now. Know all the answers. But it's fading away, even as I see it all come clear . . .

Come back, son.

Stay with me.

Stay . . .

It's fading . . .

Fading.

Gone now.

Gone.

They move me to the floor below ICU in the morning. Roll me down a hall, into an elevator, down another hall, into the dark again. I'm almost not there for any of it, they have me so doped up. A couple of shots of something, on top of the drip.

Probably Dilaudid.

Hydromorphone, they also call it.

The last time I was shot, they pumped me full of it. It's the stuff Matt Dillon and his junkie posse were after in that movie *Drugstore Cowboy*. Synthetic heroin, like Vicodin is synthetic codeine. All the fun and half the addiction, if you're lucky. I can't get addicted to this stuff. I just can't.

My head gets clear, but I can't tell how long it takes. I

end up in a room that looks exactly like the one I was in before. Someone tells me I'm in a different building now. I'm asleep when they tell me that.

My father whispers to me and I can't hear what he says.

Something that teases me.

Son, follow my voice.

Follow what I've said to you.

Follow me.

Toni winks her glittering green eye in the dark and says it's all gonna be okay.

Somehow, I believe her.

Follow me, she says. *If you can't follow Ringo . . . follow me.*

Sure enough, the accounts rep is a hard old lady and she's right in my face with questions about how I'm gonna pay for my visit to Hermann Hospital. They haven't even assigned me a social worker. I give her the same dog and pony show I gave the doc. He never comes in to talk to me again.

The rep leaves in a huff. She can tell I'm lying about not knowing who I am. It's going to be a problem.

I add it to the list.

I watch the door, all night.

No drug drip anymore. I pulled it again and the pain is dull—not bad, but it doesn't tickle, either. Have to stay alert. Someone will come through that door sooner or later. I have to get out of here.

I go under for just a few minutes and Toni is there again.

There's not much time, baby. The wolves are closing in.

Follow me.

I almost hear the rest, almost bring it back to the waking world . . . but it escapes me again.

A peppy young guy in hospital blues comes into my room at seven in the morning and says his name is Richard and he'll be caring for me. He has dark eyes and brown hair. Well built and beefy in the face. Says he's a fourth-year medical student but not to worry, I'm in good hands. He tells me about how I've been pissing for the last couple of weeks, as if I hadn't noticed. There's a tube hooked up to my bladder—direct plumbing, he calls it, then he apologizes for his bad joke. I reach down and feel my upper legs, inspect the tube snaking out of my lower regions, attached by an IV needle and taped there, running to a plastic bag, half full of dark yellow liquid, polluted and milky, all full of dope. You could sell my piss on the street and it would fetch top dollar.

He changes out the bag, talking about how lucky I am.

All of this happens in a sort of waking dream.

I can't tell if it's the morphine or not.

Have to get my head clear.

Richard pulls back the sheet and gently grabs hold of my legs, bends them slightly at the knee for me. I don't trust his hands when he does that. I notice that his hospital blues match my thin smock and drawstring pants, and for some reason that makes me feel vulnerable. He calls me "buddy" a lot.

Just like David Hartman used to.

He looks at my arm and asks why I pulled my dope drip out. He can tell just by glancing. I say I was delirious, I'm not sure what I was thinking. He looks at me right in my eyes and says nothing.

Right in my eyes.

I don't like that.

He tells me he can get me on a remote-controlled delivery system for the drip if I want it, one of those hand triggers that administers a dosage from a pump that sits alongside you in the room. I don't want it. He says it might be just as well. Those things can be dangerous. I tell him I just don't want to be on dope.

He says good for you, buddy.

He puts back the sheet, makes some more happy noise at me. Points at a wheelchair near my bed, says I'll be doing back flips on it in no time. Leaves me some food on a rollaway table which arcs over my bed on a long arm. I watch him very carefully as he leaves.

Then I look at the wheelchair.

Very carefully.

That night, I use the stainless-steel bars on either side of my bed to lever myself up, squeezing hard and steady with just my upper-arm strength. Without the morphine drip, it's agonizing, and I can feel the strain tearing against the wound in my side. I try again and again, getting just a little farther each time. I'm careful not to push it too far. I'm testing my body, seeing what my limits are. Nothing gives anywhere inside me.

The last time I was shot it was much worse. I couldn't move for a week. They gave me a morphine trigger that time and I used it a lot. Plenty of synthetic heroin. Tried to escape the hospital as soon as I could. That was when I figured out how to remove a heparin lock without tearing open my vein—the older the lock, the easier it is. They had me handcuffed to the bed back then, but the cuffs were no problem. It was the law that did me in. They didn't have any guards on the door, but I got nailed coming out of the service entrance into the parking lot. Two plainclothes, drawing down and telling me to freeze, like all cops do.

This place will have its own police division—guys with badges and revolvers. No detectives, just standard flatfoots. My edge is that they have no idea who I am, that I am not under arrest for anything. And cops in medical centers like this one are always busy on the cancer floor, separating families who are fighting over the off switch on life-support systems. They don't have time for nobodies like me. Not yet anyway. But I have to assume the worst.

I have to assume they've zeroed me.

I start to panic, then I get a grip. I keep my fear handy, but I'm in control. Nobody's come for me yet—nobody that I know about.

But I have to assume the worst, at all times.

I manage to haul my entire body a few feet above my bed, isolating my upper arm muscles to do the job, not using my abs at all. I practice the exercise for two hours.

The wheelchair is just five feet away.

Soon.

• • •

The dream is more vivid now, not surreal. I sit with Toni in an open forest glade, at a picnic table, surrounded by children, by family. This is the life my father never gave me. She smiles and her voice is clear.

Baby, I told you the secret. Right in the beginning.

I knew you would look into the face of God.

And I told you not to.

That's not what you said.

That's what the Sarge said.

Before he tried to kill me.

I ask her what's really going on—I ask her about the end of the world.

Toni smiles at me and tells me there's nothing we can do. Something about the dominoes already falling. Her voice fades away to nothing as the dream ends.

Fades away to nothing.

The next morning, Richard comes in again, all full of pep.

He hasn't been in since yesterday.

"Hey, buddy," he says.

It still sounds wrong, even though my head is much clearer.

He changes my bladder bag again, asks me how I'm feeling again, flexes my legs again. Looks at the morphine tube, not hooked up.

"You still doing okay without the drip?"

"It's better than lung cancer. Can I try the wheelchair today?"

"Not yet. Maybe tomorrow, buddy. Can I get anything else for you?"

"Yeah. Could you tell me what your last name is?"

"Sergio."

"You're Italian?"

"Half."

"Do you see a lot of patients like me?"

"More than you can imagine, buddy. But you're one of the lucky ones. I once saw a guy shot in his spine—he already had one leg missing. An old hippie guy, a drug dealer who got shot during a buy in a parking lot. He had diabetes and a prosthetic leg. He lost the other one during his recovery, developed permanent brain damage. Spent his last three years as a vegetable."

"Bad news."

"They'll start you on physical therapy in two more days."

"I'd like to try the wheelchair *now*."

He laughs. "You in a hurry to get somewhere?"

"I'd just like to try it."

"We'll see. Maybe in the morning."

He walks out of the room after fiddling with my IV machines. Gives me a smile that chills my blood.

I try to will myself to sleep again.

So I can hear Toni's voice.

So I can figure this whole thing out.

It doesn't work.

Later that day, a nurse comes in to see me. She's young and happy, always smiling. Says her name is Shelly, and she'll be taking care of me during my physical therapy. I ask her what happened to Richard.

She makes a strange face when I say that.

Doesn't answer me.

"A man has been here twice in the last two days," I say to her very carefully, evenly, sober as hell. "He says his name is Richard Sergio. Says he's a fourth-year medical student."

"I think you must've been dreaming, honey. There's no Richard Sergio on this ward, but there *has* been some staff floating for the last week."

"What's that mean? Floating?"

She sighs. "It's a dirty little secret in the medical world. I guess I'm not supposed to tell you, but that's how it works in big places like this. We get overloaded and the beds get full, so they have to pull staff and interns off other wards, people who aren't trained properly. They come in to fill the gaps."

"They don't know how to treat trauma patients?"

"Depends. Everyone has to come from nursing school to get a license, you know, but you specialize depending on where you get hired."

"So this Richard guy, he could be from another ward?"

"I think you just need to rest."

Her voice cuts me hard, her all-purpose smile dismissing the whole thing. I shut up and don't say anything else. I have to try for the wheelchair tonight.

They've zeroed me.

Run like hell, baby.
You have no legs but you can still run.
Get the hell out of that place.

• • •

The nurse comes back an hour later, at three thirty. I hear her in the hall with some other men while I'm doing my exercises, and I lower myself back into the bed just as she enters the room, still smiling. She notices the redness in my face. The pain I'm hiding.

"Hello. How are you feeling?"

"Fine."

"You have some color, that's good. Do you think you can handle a visitor or two this afternoon?"

"Who are they?"

"The police. They want to interview you, just for a few minutes."

"I don't know . . . I . . ."

"I can tell them to come back later."

"No. It's okay."

I need to look these men in their eyes.

Have to see who I'm dealing with.

Baby, be careful. Really damn careful about this.

The nurse nods to me and goes back out into the hall. I hear hard shoes strike the floor as the two guys come into my room. Both plainclothes guys. Detectives. One of them is wearing a black bomber jacket over a flannel shirt and has dark skin. The other one has a suit on, looks real young, pale. Maybe a rookie, maybe not. Never can tell about these guys. They both wear their badges on plastic laminates around their necks.

"Hello," the dark one says. "My name is Roger Morales, this is my partner, Jeff Ferrier. We're both with Houston PD. Hear you've had some problems."

Careful.

"I don't remember anything."

"That's what they told us. We're just following up on a lead. Need to ask you a few questions, see if it jogs anything. You up for it?"

"Don't see why not. But . . ."

"Yeah?"

They know something.

"I mean . . . I don't know what help I can be. I don't even know what happened to me."

"Maybe you can remember a face."

He holds up a photograph.

It's a Polaroid of a girl with black hair and wild eyes.

A very familiar girl.

I almost say something on instinct, but I hear Toni's voice again and find myself sticking to the lie.

"I . . . I've never seen her."

"Her name is Heather Stone. She was reported missing six months ago, and we picked her up during the aftermath of something that went down last week."

"What kind of something?"

"A shootout in a strip bar. She'd been shot in the arm, but she was okay to talk to us. She had a real crazy story to tell."

Yeah.

I bet she did.

As I look at the photo, I realize it's definitely her. She looks a lot like my wife, black hair and green eyes . . . but there are imperfections in the design. Things a smart guy could spot. Things I never could have seen a week ago, not right off. And now that my memories have come back, now that I can see Toni's true face in the endless white of our wedding day . . . I could curse myself for ever buying it.

It wasn't your fault.

Did someone make her look like you, Toni?

Was Hartman setting me up?

Don't say a word, baby. They know what's going down. They're playing games with you.

"The lady gave us a description of two men who were protecting her," Morales says flatly. "I don't know whether to believe her story. You sure you don't remember anything?"

He gives me a long, hard look.

Then he does something with his eyes.

Something that almost looks like a wink.

What . . . ?

He sees my face ask the question and he looks back over his shoulder, at his partner, who quietly nods. Did I just give them something?

"The doctors won't let us have any details about your condition," Morales says. "You have to legally consent to release the information. But since you're a John Doe, that also raises a lot of issues and opens some gray areas, too. Wanna tell me about it?"

Don't give them anything. Tell them what they already know.

"My legs are out of commission. I was shot in the side."

"Will you be up to speaking with Miss Stone, maybe in the morning? It might jog something."

I nod slowly. Something going down here.

He gives me the almost-wink again.

"One more thing," he says. "She gave us a name. *Elroy Coffin*. Ring any bells?"

"No."

He knows you're lying, baby. He's checked you out. Knows you're supposed to be dead. Knows something.

But he doesn't say anything.

Turns and leaves me there, surrounded by the fear of the doomed.

The nurse checks on me every hour after that, says I'm doing great, asks me if I still insist on no pain meds. I tell her it's fine. A food service guy in a pale gray uniform brings me food and I eat it. Goes down easy, but tastes like shit. Dry meat and canned veggies. I've watched the nurse when she works the levers that control the bars on either side of my bed, and figured out how to lower them and use the rollaway table as a method to lever myself off, so I can inch my way over to the wheelchair. It's my only way out, and I have to do it now, tonight. While the ward is almost empty, during the morning hours.

The plot is simple.

I'll get out of here through the back entrance and steal a car in the visitors lot. It'll be harder with no legs, but I'll have wheels to get there. It'll be cold, wearing nothing but a smock and thin blue pants, but I'll have to tough it out. It'll take me at least twenty minutes to get in the chair. Gotta do it careful, so that I don't come un-plugged from my life blipper. Once I disconnect, I have to move quick. They won't stop me, because they *can't* stop me, not legally. Unless the cops who questioned me have people in the building now, unless I'm actually under suspicion for something. I have to take that chance. The noose is closing. I can feel it all around me.

I can hear Toni telling me to calm down, telling me not to panic.

I watch the clock on the wall and wait for one in the morning. They never check on me between one and five.

That's my window. I count the minutes.

I leave my food on the rollaway table and tell the nurse to keep it there when she comes in for her last visit. She goes along nicely. Leaves my door open.

The lights go dark in the hall, and I reach down and work the lever on the bar to my right. The bar goes down with a dull metal thump. Now, the rollaway. I set the dinner dishes on the bed next to me and pull myself across the table, using only my arms. A sharp pain stitches my side, but I can't think about that now. Gotta use the bar on my right to push myself off the bed, roll myself over to the chair. It's just five feet away. I push hard and it works. I roll away. Something snaps in the table. I feel the wheels give, and my center of gravity goes all whacked. The floor comes up hard as I crash there. I go down on my back, not feeling the impact.

Goddammit.

Stupid.

The pain stitches me again. I look down to see if there's any new blood oozing through the bandages and there's nothing. Doesn't feel like I reopened the wound. The fall might not have cost me anything . . . but I can feel the deadweight of my legs for the first time and it's terrifying. Have to move fast. The chair is three feet away from me, waiting to get me out of here. I get over on my arms and elbows, start pulling my way forward. And that's right when the voice comes.

"Hey, buddy."

I look up to see him, standing there in the open doorway.

Richard, the happy intern—or whatever his name really is.

"Getting ready to go somewhere?"

I don't answer him. I freeze there on the floor.

I see that he has some sort of bag with him. He smiles, closing the door, crouching low, looking right in my eyes.

Pulls a gun from the bag and aims it at my head.

"You know, I was really hoping it would come to this, buddy."

"They sent you to kill me."

He laughs, still using his phony bedside manner. "You're very perceptive. And clever, too. For a while, we thought you really *did* have amnesia. But your charts tell a different story. And you gave yourself away today, asking about the wheelchair."

You gave yourself away, too, asshole. Your fake smile. Going through the motions. The stories about the other patients you'd seen in here, those were nice touches—but I still had you pegged.

I just glare at him.

"Someone wants to say hello," he says.

He goes into the bag over his shoulder and pulls out an iPad. Sets it up on the floor, clicking the screen on. A face I wasn't expecting suddenly stares right into me. Or maybe I was expecting it.

Her smile is deadly and final.

Her voice is focused like a laser beam.

"*Hello,*" she says.

"**I** *can't see you, Mister Coffin, but you can see me.*"

Jenison's voice crackles clearly through the tiny speakers, stabbing my heart without pity, like the cold, evil stare of the killer hovering above me, his gun fixed on the space between my eyes.

She's got me.

Finally.

"*I'm afraid I've had to record this message to you in advance. Technical reasons. I'm sorry I could not be there in person to see your final moments. I would have liked to. Rest assured, I will see those moments soon. You are about to go down in history.*"

I want to tell her to go to hell, but she can't hear me. She's long gone by now, in a place where I'll never find her. A place where cell signals and Wi-Fi bottom out in oblivion. Underground.

"*I understand you've lost the use of your legs. Quite an unfortunate and ironic turn of luck for a man on the run, wouldn't you say? But even when a man has no knees to fall on, he can still beg for his life. You should know that begging is useless now. And so is bartering. You no longer have anything in your possession that I want.*"

Richard Sergio opens the bag and pulls out a shiny surgical instrument. It's like nothing I've seen before. Like a redesigned hacksaw with sharp teeth, and lots of little barbs and extensions—something designed by a lunatic, meant for serious flesh damage.

"*I have ordered this man to kill you. Very painfully. You've been a difficult man, and what happens in this room will be recorded as an example to the other members of my organization. Your death will live on for years, in fact. You have to keep the fear of God in your own people, Mister Coffin. Otherwise, there's no chance for resurrection. Either figuratively or literally.*"

Richard Sergio sets the instrument on the floor. Pulls out another one. And another. And another. Arranges his toys in a row. They gleam with piercing evil.

He keeps the gun on me the whole time with one hand.

"*But I wanted you to know that I am also grateful to you, Mister Coffin. It may seem strange, but I feel I actually owe you one last insight before you die. This chess game we've been playing has very high stakes, and I respect the moves you have made. Believe me, I do. In another life, or perhaps with more time to convince you of the truths my organization stands for, I might have welcomed a man like you. It's a shame, really. The new future requires creative thinkers. Devious and inventive minds. But it also requires the fear of God.*"

The steel glints and blinds me. Richard Sergio strokes one of the scalpels. Pulls his finger back, streaked with blood. Holds it up for me to see. His sick smile, full of contempt and crazy resolve.

"*That's what makes the youth of this world so easy to recruit, Mister Coffin. People are willing to believe in a fresh perspective when they are facing a world filled with fear and panic . . . and the fresher the perspective, the more achievable it all seems. Our own leaders prove that every single day. They've been proving it for centuries, since this country was built on the bones of slaughtered natives and*" *slaves. And the bogeymen of the world . . . they're only there because we've allowed them to become demons. They are the cover stories and public explanations for why we destroy civilizations. If you had any respect for history, you would see that."*

She pauses. Then almost laughs.

Richard Sergio smiles at me. Rows of shiny steel death, laid at my feet. The gun, still aimed right between my eyes.

"It might surprise you to know that I am only one member of a larger contingent. A sort of think tank, if you will. We've structured something very complex with many layers, and you've only just scratched the surface. And as you've come to know, our foot soldiers are ruthless and dedicated."

Jenison looks me right in the eye from miles away.

No doubt about it now. They've retreated to their fortress and they've hit the button. They figured out some way to do it without the disc drive. And I'm going to become the last martyred saint for Resurrection. Nailed to a cross, broadcast over a wire.

To scare the next generation of assholes.

"I want you to know that I truly believe in everything I'm telling you, Mister Coffin. We're not a movie cliché or a conspiracy theory come to life. We're not a group of government charlatans sitting in an office somewhere, plotting to dismantle the sleeping middle class by promising them a better world through welfare. We don't need to do anything at all on that front—most people are dead already. They live in fear, brainwashed by TV commercials, their lives out of control. I do not pity them, nor do I pity the disenfranchised youth of the world, who are hardly aware that there was ever a past to inform the future. We are men and

women of action, with respect for history. We have been for almost half a century now. We've recruited only those who feel as we do. We've told people the truth and they believed that truth. And the truth is this . . ."

Her eyes, staring right into me.

She is the devil and I am in her hell.

She is the unmaker of everything.

"You, Mister Coffin, are the defender of a lost world. You are fighting a losing battle. You are crawling in your own blood. You want to survive right now because that is your instinct. But you are not ready to accept that the world must be cleansed. You are not even ready to be sacrificed in the name of a greater good. I would call you an infidel, but that would make me sound like a common terrorist. And what we are doing isn't about terror. It's about resurrection."

She almost laughs again, but this time it's grim.

Like she knows the truth and it makes her sad.

"What you are, really, in the end, is an animal. Like all the other dogs I've seen. All the dead game in the world. Those who see as I do—the executive members of Resurrection—know that it's just a matter of clearing away the bodies. Then the entire world will be reborn. And several hundred years from now, the children of our children's children will see you die. They will know you were the last man who stood against us. They will be afraid of the world that existed then. The world you were terrified to let go of. And it will be good, Mister Coffin . . . because by then the world will be very different. There will be no war, no starvation, no selfish agendas created by men hungry for power and money. There will be only the image of you to remind our future children. Remind them never to go back to the way things were before."

She smiles one last time.

"I thank you, Mister Coffin. Really, I do. From the bottom of my heart. And to prove my gratitude . . . I'm going to give you what you've been searching for. What we agreed upon when I first hired you. That's only fair, after all, isn't it?"

What?

What the hell is she . . .

Before the thought can solidify, she moves away from the screen and the angle expands to show the room she stands in. It's a giant chamber, full of half-defined machinery that stretches back in shadowy layers, a never-ending maze that envelops rows and rows of . . . what are they?

Look like upright glass canisters.

Hundreds of them, filed away in the darkness, brought to me on shaky video. Each glass coffin is filled with some sort of thick green liquid. Floating in the fluid are human bodies. All of them are women. All of them naked and sleeping, breathing through tiny respirators attached to tubes, surrounded by their own oxygen bubbles.

It's some sort of human storage facility.

The camera focuses on one of the tubes . . .

. . . *and* . . .

Toni.

I see her floating just on the other side of the glass, hovering like a naked angel in an underwater sea-storm of bubbles, her eyes closed in some sort of coma.

It's you.

Just as clear and beautiful as you were on our wedding day. The lines and canyons of your body, crystal clear like in my dreams, my memories. I smell the roses when I see her.

I smell her.

She is helpless.

"I know this must come as a shock to you, Mister Coffin. But you have my word that she is very much alive. She's breathing a half-oxygen, half-fluid mixture called hydrogenated fluorocarbon emulsion. In a state of perfect hibernation."

The camera goes in close, and I see that her nose is taking in the green liquid, while her mouth pushes out bubbles through the breathing apparatus.

This can't be real.

It just can't be happening.

"I'm afraid this is why we were never able to reunite you with your wife, Mister Coffin. I suppose it would have been much easier to make a trade with you for the disc drives . . . but, then again, now that we no longer require the drives, it's become a moot point."

The camera zooms back out and Jenison leans into the frame again.

She doesn't smile.

"This is the way to immortality, Mister Coffin. Your wife was chosen to be reborn with us into the new age of man. She will live long after you are dead. And soon she will watch you die. I will make her watch. Like I will make all the others watch."

Her face fills the screen now.

Her madness boring a hole in my heart.

Her eyes, blacker than anything.

"She will live, Mister Coffin. But you will not."

And the image winks off.

LIVING THROUGH

"**I**'m going to do a Superman on you. Know what that means?"

I know. But I don't say a word.

"That means you lose everything, buddy. Meat on bones and nothing else. You'll need a respirator to breathe, like Christopher Reeve. Superman. Remember what happened to him? Sure you do. I bet he was the first thing you thought of when you found out you couldn't walk. It usually is, with most paralytics. *Statistically*, I mean. They did a survey on it a few years back. Isn't that funny?"

I can't think of anything funny about any of this.

"This will be worse," he says. "That I can guarantee. I won't kill you quickly. You'll be in a lot of pain. You'll want to die. But I won't let you die."

Where's the fun in that?

David Hartman's face, superimposed over his in a bizarre Jungian flash.

The terrible, knowing grin of every monster in the world.

Madness.

He opens the bag and pulls out another piece of equipment. It unsnaps into three long metal legs and he sets it up on the floor. A tiny nugget of Flip technology tops the tripod, blipping with a deep red light, on and off, signaling the start of high-def video.

"Showtime," he says.

Then he reaches for his instruments. Selects one that looks like a clawed hammer first. Turns and smashes the iPad with it. Smiles his sickness again, holding up the clawed end of the hammer so I can see it.

"We cover our tracks, buddy. No one will ever know we were here."

He sets down the hammer and picks up a tool that looks like a hacksaw mutated into a pair of scissors. Terrible and shiny. I roll onto my back, try to pull myself against the wall. My arms are straining to pull my upper body. The pain in my side is getting worse. I have to let him get in close. Try to take him out. I find my center, concentrating all my energy into my arms.

He puts the gun back in the bag.

Brings out a syringe.

"Don't even think about fighting me. What's in my left hand will kill your motor reflexes. What's in my right will remove your foot, then some other things. We'll get you back in your bed for that. We have at least a few hours together."

No. I can't let this happen.

The needle in his left hand hovers above my bare foot. I can't reach far enough over to stop him. He knows better than to let me get my paws on him.

The needle goes in. His thumb rests on the plunger.

"Beg for your life. I want to hear it. *Beg me not to do this.*"

Go to hell, asshole.

He sees my face, the words almost leaving my mouth. Shakes his head.

"You *will* beg," he says. "I'll make you do it, buddy."

He twists the needle in my toe.

"You won't feel anything while I work, but you won't be able to move, either. The pain will come slowly. You'll warm up real nice. It's going to get really messy, buddy."

Whatever turns you on, asshole.

His face contorts when I think that, and I see the madman there now, clear as day, glaring in my eyes like a black-light beacon from hell. A crazy man with a head full of sadism and cruelty. I want to ask him what his real name is for some reason, but I know he doesn't have one. He's just another shadow in a dark room, sent to kill people like me.

All in the name of Superman.

He twists the needle again, sinking it lower into my flesh.

"I'm going to enjoy watching you break. The smart ones always are the best. The ones who think they can will away the pain. Think they can go to their special place and block it all out. But don't you kid yourself, buddy . . ."

Deeper now.

Almost to the bone.

I can't feel a thing.

". . . things like this have to be *lived through*."

He licks his lips.

Toni . . . I'm going to die. But you are with me. We are together in this final time.

I am ready to be nothing but meat on bones for you.

Do it now, you sick freak.

Something smashes through his forehead and keeps on going, shattering the window near my bed, like a low thrumming bumblebee. He falls over with his thumb still on the plunger, his muscles twitching across my dead legs. The surgical tool falls from his grip and clatters on the floor, spinning there.

Standing in the doorway to my room is a very beautiful woman.

It's the girl who lied to me.

The almost-perfect version of Toni.

The girl who said she was my wife.

Smoke rises from the business end of her silenced pistol.

"Come on, Elroy," she says. "Let's get you the hell out of here."

S he rolls me out into the hallway and there's two hard-looking guys wearing long overcoats waiting for us. One of them has a face like a sausage pizza, the other one is the olive-skinned cop from before—the one who said his name was Morales. They both have shotguns in their arms and pistols with silencers in shoulder holsters. The wall behind the nurses' station is splashed in arterial red, and there's a dead police officer on the floor near the elevator, his memories of the last few minutes floating in a pool that reflects the dim phosphorescence. They used those quiet handguns on their approach, so they could sneak up on Richard the Happy Intern. Damn clever of them.

"Who the hell are you guys?"

"Heather Stone," the girl says. "Nice to meet you."

She doesn't offer her hand. She doesn't smell like Toni anymore—but she still resembles her, just a little. Her face, like an imperfect copy of perfect art.

This is insane, surreal.

"We're friendlies," Morales says. "We gotta move fast. This place crawls."

He's not a cop. Some sort of mercenary, maybe a spook. Only guys with military training say things like *this place crawls.*

Heather Stone motions to Pizzaface, who takes over pushing my wheelchair, back down the hall, towards the elevator at the opposite end, away from the massacre. Morales covers us from behind. There's no one else in the ward. No more blood on the walls. It's just us. My head is light and swimming. Tingling all over my body. Soft needles jabbing the muscles in my upper thighs. I feel the floor rumbling under my feet as they motorvate me. Heather Stone leads point with her big pistol. I can see now that it's a .357 Desert Eagle slide—the Mark XIX, military-grade monster. Those things cost more on the consumer market than a 60-inch flat-screen. She's wearing a white doctor's coat over military black, the heavy gun weighed effortlessly in a practiced grip.

She is something very different from what I thought she was.

She's one of these guys, always has been.

A spook.

Just as I think that, her gun does its low bark again.

I don't even see the cop as he steps out of the elevator. A blast of blood and the mark goes down fast. Heather Stone is a stone-cold statue when she does it. Hardly even breaks stride. We're past the carnage and inside the elevator in nothing flat.

The car fills with electronic bells as we head down. Heather reloads her weapon, unscrews the silencer. Her boys check their shotguns. I can tell now that she's in charge of these men. She has a Bluetooth clipped to her ear and starts speaking very calmly into it.

"I need an all clear in the main lobby. Give me a picture."

Someone's voice says important things I can't hear. Heather pulls something that looks like an oversized iPhone out of her pocket and studies it. I can see graphics pay out, infrared, scrolls of data in the form of electronic silhouettes.

"Okay," she says calmly to her men. "We've got five in the stairwell, on the way up. Two more in the car just behind us. Three left in the lobby, no civilians. Plug up."

The two grunts stand in front of me, pulling out tiny little yellow beads and stuffing their ears with them. They do it very smoothly, professionally. One of them tosses a gas mask in my lap and tells me to hold my breath and my ears. Morales is screwing a shiny steel attachment onto the end of his shotgun.

The elevator car clunks to a stop just as Morales hits the switch that keeps the doors closed. Heather aims her monster gun and pulls the trigger. She's staring at the screen in her hand, which shows her the targets standing on the other side of six-inch steel.

Boom.

The muzzleflashes are two feet long.

She's switched to a much higher grade of ammunition since that last clip went in her gun. The three shots are like thick laser beams, punching neat little holes in the door, knocking down two of the men in the lobby on her infrared screen. The sound almost makes me deaf, even with my fingers in my ears. She hits the switch that opens the door as Pizzaface fires the tear-gas grenade, spewing a long thin contrail of hissing white smoke that bounces off a marble wall and begins to fill the room.

I get the gas mask on my face as Heather steps into the lobby, firing again at the cop on the floor. Another two-foot white flash kicks its high-velocity load right in the guy's face. The cop doesn't even get one shot off before his head turns into superheated jelly, and then the jelly is consumed by the rolling, stinging mist. The load keeps on shredding the lobby after it's done with the cop, finally exploding somewhere in the next hall, twenty feet away. Two other cops are dead on the ground, gaping holes where their badges used to be. Gigantic chunks of the room carved out in the bargain.

Heather moves like a robot, her men right behind her.

Morales grabs my chair and rolls me out alongside Heather and Pizzaface, who spin quickly and step in front of me as the second elevator dings and the doors open. I don't even notice the three of them are wearing gas masks until they fill the elevator car with thunder, annihilating everything inside there. It's like a series of bombs going off and I can't even see who they are shooting at, arms and legs and faces consumed in a quick-time maelstrom of bright strobing and dark red splashes, like the flickering fangs of some greedy invisible monster devouring it all to hell. Whoever was in there had no idea what hit them.

The thunder recedes as the smoke thickens and Heather gets a beep on her hand screen. She motions to Pizzaface:

"Stairwell! Now!"

Morales hustles me into the covered concrete cul-de-sac, which is just outside the main ER entrance doors. Heather right behind us. Back in the lobby, I hear the shotgun roar again and the sounds of more cops screaming as they blast apart. It doesn't take long to chop them all to ribbons. I steel myself and let it all happen—like some kind of nightmare where you just sit there and watch the world explode on all sides of you. I've never seen guys who move this fast, and I've certainly never had a seat this comfortable in the middle of a firefight.

I find myself laughing at it.

Right out loud.

An EMS vehicle shrieks to a halt, tires peeling up smoke just outside the door as I come rolling up to the curb, pushed along by sure hands. The doors are already open and two guys whose faces I can't see behind black masks are leaping out to grab me and my wheelchair . . . and it's all a quick blur as they get me inside, chair and all. Heather is right behind us, leaping in. An unmarked car that looks fast and sleek, like a photon torpedo, pulls up behind us and I see Morales and Pizzaface calmly getting in the passenger's side, pulling off their gas masks. I leave mine on, for no reason that matters.

The ambulance doors slam, and we blow out of there, with the photon torpedo right behind us.

Heather checks her screen, smiles quickly. "We're almost clear," she says into her Bluetooth. "Take the alternate route and stand on it. This area is hot."

The siren on the hood of the ambulance comes on at full blast. Subterfuge. They had this whole run plotted out to the last shell casing.

And Heather?

Is anything about her real—anything at all?

The muscle car runs blocker for us the whole time we're on the road, lagging just a quarter mile behind. My new friends all keep their guns up and ready. Heather watches her hand screen. We show up there as a glowing green target blip. The traffic parts on all sides of us and we punch through red lights all the way. No cops on our tail. Nothing looking for us in the air, either, not yet.

But that won't last long.

I think I can hear sirens somewhere out there—just below the obnoxious scream of the ambulance.

She holds my chair steady as we shift sharply to the right and I feel the open road tilt under our tires. For the first time, I notice that there's a small spot of blood seeping from under her white coat sleeve. Where they shot her at the club. She doesn't flinch at all, if she even feels it.

I look up at her and laugh, pulling off the gas mask. "So . . . do I get kissed on the second date, too?"

"Is that a joke?"

"Maybe. Depends who the hell you really are."

"He told you, we're friendlies. You can relax."

"Thanks."

Her stone expression almost goes soft for just a second. "I'm sorry, Elroy. I can explain everything."

"I'm sure you can."

"I was working under deep cover where you found me."

"Dirty tricks for Uncle Sam, huh? Figures."

"Don't get all self-righteous with me, Elroy. We all do what we have to do."

"Yeah, and you do it *so well*, don't you?"

That stings her. Just a little. I'm almost surprised.

"I just saved your ass," she says. "You should be a little more polite."

"So they put you on the street to get Hartman?"

"Something like that."

"And you look like my wife *because* . . . ?"

"Just shut up a minute. There's no time for that now. I have a *question*, Elroy. It's really important."

I nod to her because I know what the question is.

But then she doesn't get to ask it.

The first RPG hits like a lightning bolt.

I see it outside through the tiny window of the ambulance, screaming from the sky in a swooping whiplash crackle, then someone screams—I think it's Heather—and I see the photon torpedo following us turn into a flash of flame and debris, and the world shudders and my heart stops for three whole seconds, and the ambulance skews across the median, out of control, and

I'm upside down, right side up, and everything is suddenly spinning and tumbling, my head smashing against something hard and metal, and Heather screams again, and the world spins again and something slams into us like the hand of Murphy, and he's really pissed off tonight . . . and as I go under . . . I hear the pavement scraping under us and the sound of roaring shotguns . . .

Sirens.

Angry voices.

Explosions.

I come to for just one second, and see that I'm outside now, on the blacktop. Faceless shapes standing silhouetted against the flames.

Muzzleflashes on all sides of us.

Blood in my face.

Street war, I think. *I'm in the middle of a goddamn street war . . .*

I go under again as the gauntlet closes around us.

I hear the shooting, even in the dream.

I hear them all killing each other, my own heartbeat pounding through it.

Then the deep-bass chug of a helicopter, cancelling out everything.

Someone screaming right in my ear to wake the fuck up.

I go down deeper when I hear the voice.

Down and down.

• • •

Floating now.

It's peaceful.

I made it out of there and now I'm floating.

I see the face of the girl.

Heather's face.

Toni's funhouse-mirror image, distorted and not quite perfect, but perfect enough to fool a man with demons. Enough to fool a man obsessed.

I have to find her.

I want to know why she looks like my one true love.

She was going to tell me.

I was so close to the truth.

I'm flying now.

The helicopters blare at me.

I wake up on a stretcher, an oxygen mask over my face.

We're moving fast, across a flat concrete surface, and I can tell we're outside, the sun shining on my face, and Heather is still alive, yelling at the people pushing my stretcher, but I can't hear her . . . because all around me, metal beasts drown her out, shredding the air and shaking the earth.

Apache AH attack choppers.

A sea of state-of-the-art bang bang.

This is not a dream.

It's real.

You see these machines in movies sometimes. Super fast, super sleek, all armed to the teeth. Sidewinder missiles, 70-millimeter rockets, 20-millimeter cannons. They usually carry something called Hellfire anti-tank bombs, too. Two of those bad boys have enough sheer heart attack in them to erase a bad Middle Eastern neighborhood without breaking a sweat.

Looks like World Wars III and IV are about to go down.

I only see the armada for a few seconds.

They push me away from the chugging beasts, towards a central complex that reminds me of prison. It's a five-story concrete monolith with no windows and a flat roof that has a landing pad. A gunship up there, gassed and ready, spinning its giant blades and rotors—like the king of the monsters. We move into the complex through a thick steel door, opened by a thick steel jarhead.

Heather leads us down a security corridor. Five doors with ancient locks, opened by sentry statues who know we're coming. No laser sensors or motion detectors, just marines in every corner, every six feet. The sounds of heavy combat boots in front of me and behind me. The hall smells like cigarettes and sweat and stale aftershave. Everything is old and rusted, typical military operation. Uncle Sam spends money on guns, not barracks. I've heard tell that some of these places are little more than tent cities in the desert. Almost makes me laugh, the irony is so overwhelming. I can't laugh because it hurts too much. The wound in my side, the throbbing in my head.

I try to think of Toni, but she taunts me, just out of reach.

Have to focus on the moment.

I notice for the first time that I'm still in my blue hospital smock, the urine tube no longer attached to my lower region. I am half naked in this place of corroded steel, even more helpless than I was in prison.

Great.

We stop at a door guarded by two guys in desert brown battle-dress uniforms. They salute Heather and open up. It isn't even locked, but that doesn't matter. Only the Terminator could get through the manpower in this building. I counted fifty grunts on the way up the hall, all armed to the teeth, all on combat-ready alert and itching for an excuse to kill someone. I get all the details in stark relief. Wide awake now.

My legs twitch on their own as they move me through the door.

THE MAN WHO SOLD
THE WORLD

My legs.

They're moving.

No, this is really not a dream.

I'm sitting upright now in the stretcher, cool air tingling the bare skin of my back and legs, electricity seething through my bloodstream, surrounded in a wide metal chamber by more hard-carved men with guns, my shocked breath forced out in quick, bad spasms. I recognize Morales from the hospital—I could never forget that guy's face, stone cold and dark. He's wearing a military uniform now, sidearms bristling on his hips. The other men are backlit shapes against a wall-sized flat-screen monitor, which flashes a video strobe across the room.

"Take it easy," Heather says, calmly.

I look at her, getting my breath back.

"My *legs* . . ."

It's all I can force out.

"Your legs are fine," she says. "That bullshit about you being paralyzed, it's not true. They had you on some kind of spinal block drug while you were in there.

You're having hell coming down off it, but you aren't paralyzed."

I feel the tingle in my legs again.

"How do you *know* that?"

"I saw your charts, the real ones."

"What are—"

"No time. Save it."

She motions to a big man in a high-ranking military uniform, who stands in front of a desk. He's even scarier than Morales. His face is stitched with age and scars. Looks like he could kick Arnold Schwarzenegger's ass. The huge screen behind the desk is filled with a computerized topographical map of the southwestern United States. A workstation there, where a tech manages computer interface, backlit like a faceless sentinel staring into a world of artificial dreamlight. A timer at the top of the screen reads three hours and counting backwards—in hours, in minutes, in seconds.

It's scary, but I'm not sure why.

"Good work, soldiers," the scarred man says to Heather and Morales. They half salute him in return, nodding their heads. His voice sounds like rough wood. Then he looks right at me. "Elroy Coffin."

I nod, like he was asking me a question, but he wasn't. He takes two steps toward me, motions to the wall of monitors.

And says:

"Welcome to the end of the world, Elroy."

He explains that his men were watching the hospital for days after I went in. They had people in the building, but those people had orders not to move on me until the bad guys did.

It was a whole new scam. Of course.

Surround me with lies about how I'll never walk again. Get me so far down in the zero that I have no choice but to believe it. How many of those doctors were actors? How much of it was really bullshit? Some of them had to be on the level—like the nurse, who had no idea who Richard Sergio was. But they had her number. Fooled us all. They knew torturing me with drugs wouldn't work—they had to be more original. And these guys were keeping watch the whole time. Disguised as cops, waiting to see what Jenison's people would do to me, how far they would go. Bastards, all of them.

I flex my legs.

Tingling there.

Just fine, after all.

Holy shit.

The scarred man sees the weight of his words slam into me as he explains the situation, sees my face contort and reshape itself in disgust, my shock at still being whole like a gut punch from hell. He steps closer and says:

"We're the good guys. Believe me."

I manage to find my voice again, and it's rough. "How do I know that? How do I trust anything now?"

"You saw our fleet on the front lawn, didn't you?"

"Yeah, I guess I did."

"That's half the air force and all the marines we could find. They're standing by to attack a fortified position. My men have been given *carte blanche* to deal with our current situation."

"Okay . . . so who the hell *are* you?"

My voice seems to sting him slightly. He narrows his eyes.

"That's strictly need-to-know, Mister Coffin."

Ah, so now it's *Mister Coffin* again.

Jerks.

I give him the evil eye. "Then let's say I need to know."

"Let's say you need to shut your mouth and count your blessings."

"Colonel, we don't have time for this macho crap," Heather says. "He's in really rough shape and has no idea what's going on. We're lucky he's even still alive. You can at least tell him your *name*."

The scarred man snorts. "It's a security risk. We still don't have all the facts about this man."

She's not impressed. "The *facts* are we're running out of time, Colonel. Now do you want to fill him in or should I?"

The big man keeps his big game on his face, nods slightly, like he's humoring her. She has to have a high rank in this room—a lieutenant maybe? Only people with thick stripes get away with mouthing off like that to a colonel. And she was definitely in charge back at the hospital.

She steps closer and lays it down calmly.

"The men in this room and myself are all part of a special team. It's kind of a mixed litter. Special Forces, Delta, Navy SEALs, Army Rangers—all members of the United States Special Operation Command, the best of the best."

"You're the best of the best? I don't doubt it."

She looks at me and her face is cold. I can almost hear her speak the words: *I did what I had to do. You don't have to like it.*

Then she says, out loud:

"We don't have time for this."

She motions to the big screen behind her.

02:56:00

"*That's* how much time we have," she says. "Do you understand what's happening?"

"Not everything . . . but I can make an educated guess."

"Don't ask questions and don't make guesses," the colonel says. "We don't have time for that, either. We're in the middle of a war and I need your help, son."

"I'll do what I can, but—"

"I said keep your questions to yourself."

"Okay."

"Now, first . . . how are you feeling? You're not gonna pass out on us again, are you?"

"I'm groggy. Took a pretty hard hit back there."

The colonel laughs. "No shit, son. Right in the noodle. Those were maximal bad guys we pulled you away from last night. A major firefight. Almost didn't get you out."

Last night?

He sees the question stab my face.

"You're in Wyoming now. The Francis E. Warren Air Force Base. My men brought you here by chopper."

"Wyoming . . ."

The words float off into space, consumed by his.

"Normally my bedside manner would be a little

more sensitive, but we can't stand on ceremony. Do you know what Resurrection is?"

I shake my head slightly. I don't know, not really. I've only been making educated guesses. He takes a step forward and pulls a great gulp of air before he lays it on me.

And everything changes.

Forever.

"Resurrection is a code name for an operation that's been floating under the radar of the U.S. government for over forty years. They're like ghosts. Have people everywhere. From street guys like you to places as high as Capitol Hill."

He lets the weight of his words roll across me.

Then keeps on hammering.

"Part of the objective of this operation was to subvert the tactical defense system grids currently in place across America—it's all under the umbrella of something we call the Black Box. You know what that means, son?"

"I know a little. I know it's not about nukes, whatever they had planned."

"Correct. It's about something a lot cleaner, but also a lot worse. Have you ever heard of the W79 Initiative?"

"No."

The colonel waves a hand at Morales, who steps forward:

"The W79 tactical warhead is a state-of-the-art neutron flux bomb. It creates a high-yield radiation emission in the upper atmosphere of a target area which then spreads out like a cancer on the ground."

"Destroys people and leaves structures intact," I say.

"Mostly," Morales says. "You can level half a city with a W79 variant if it's delivered in the right way. The flux wave acts like an EMP—it's capable of knocking out power sources for miles. The radiation kills every living thing—it can go through lead shielding six feet thick. But the kicker is that the fallout doesn't last as long. *Days* instead of years."

I rub my eyes and shake my head. "Neutron bombs were discontinued in the eighties."

"You only know that because you heard it on the news," the colonel says. "These bombs are clean, and clean bombs are silent bombs. Silent, as in you never hear about them. They've been in the silos for years."

Morales pipes up again. "In 2004, the president announced he was discontinuing the initiative, but it was just spin control. What they were really doing was replacing the existing warheads with fresh stock."

I heave a disgusted sigh into the floor, shaking my head. I've always lived with the opinion that Old Georgie-boy screwed up more history than any free world leader on the books.

And now his legacy is complete.

"The tritium in your average old-school neutron bomb has a half-life of just ten years," Morales says. "When they re-upped, the engineers didn't leave anything to chance. These new babies are solid state. The most dangerous weaponry on the planet."

The colonel turns to me. "The grid that controls the

initiative is a secondary protocol that floats just under the main set of numbers in Region Eleven. Designed to take out the enemy in the event of an anticipated first strike from the other side."

"And nobody in the real world knows the difference," I say.

"Correct," the colonel says. "The W79 Initiative is actually a Special Ops contingency *against* nuclear apocalypse."

Morales almost laughs. "You cut off the balls of the guy aiming his nukes at you before they have any idea you've hit them."

"And those Resurrection guys got control of it," I say.

The colonel nods.

"They developed the prototype system to trick the computers at Cheyenne Mountain right under our noses," Morales says. "And we had no idea they'd done it. But about two months ago . . . David Hartman blew the whistle."

Just like I figured.

Hartman knew Texas Data Concepts had been conned into developing the program that would kill us all, and so he used his leverage with the company to seal the thing in a vault so dangerous that it would blow everything back to hell if anyone messed with it. Then he probably used what he had against Jenison and her people. To get whatever he wanted from them, which could have been anything. Girls, power. Or maybe—

"Hartman was no hero," the colonel says. "He was helping to *fund* those maniacs for years. But I don't think the old boy figured on them actually *using* the system. There'd been talk in the CIA rumor mill of something like it, a virus in the works that could remove executive decisions from strategic defense."

Heather tilts her head, her eyes sort of rolling. "They actually called it the detribalization of civilian government."

The colonel rubs his chin, grumbling. "The idea of something that final was just too crazy for most of us to believe. I didn't believe it myself. Until Hartman started communicating with us. Started feeding us important bits of information. Enough to keep us interested, anyway."

"You were talking *directly* to him?"

"We'd infiltrated his organization several times, using deep-cover operatives, but he always managed to sniff us out. Lieutenant Stone was still in his custody when he finally started talking. We learned a lot about Resurrection. Almost everything except for the location of the main bunker. He said we had to make a deal for that."

"The city underground," I whisper.

"Correct."

"That's where they plan to survive the whole thing."

"Correct. It's a fortified complex a mile beneath the surface. There's others like it all over the world. They've been building these shelters for years and years, but this one complex is the mother of them all. It's armored and way off the grid. It could theoretically survive *anything*."

"Hartman was on the Express until Jenison forced him out," I say. "My guess is that he was greasing you guys to sell off its location, not to mention the software. He would have scalped it to the highest bidder."

The colonel nods. "That's about the size of it. They've

got thousands of people down there. They've been disappearing them for years. Water-powered hydro-electric generators, independent agriculture, environmental control. We think they may even have some sort of advanced cryogenics system. Some way to keep a select number of live bodies fresh in stasis for decades."

I see my wife floating there, breathing green liquid, surrounded by her own life essence.

Just beyond my reach now.

The prize that drives me mad.

The colonel senses my gears working, and he almost says something, but I stop him fast: "That's science fiction. You can't expect me to believe that they've put a whole army on ice."

He almost laughs.

"I think you *do* believe it, son. You may be a smart one, but I ain't no fool when it comes to liars."

"You think I'm lying? You think I'm one of *them*?"

"Anything's possible."

He sizes me up again, takes a deep breath.

Takes one step closer.

"Let me tell you a little bit about who you're talking to, friend. I'm what you call a lifer. Not a veteran. Not a twenty-year man. I've been in it since *day one*. Which means I've seen action all over the world, from way down in the mud to back here in the war room—and everywhere you go, there's always some guy who thinks he can get away with something. Some of them are *professional* liars. You buy their bullshit because it's their job. It works on most everybody. But it never works on me. See, son, I've been around since God created the earth . . . and that also means I've got a lot of kids."

He gets closer to me.

Puts his hands in the air, fingers up—all ten of them.

"That's how many *girls* I'm a father to. And they're all grown up, every single damn one of them. Women are the best liars. They train you to spot the bullshit and terminate it with extreme prejudice. It takes years to learn how a woman thinks, and you have to start from the moment they're born. You have to do it over and over, year after year, decade after decade . . . until finally you can smell lies like gasoline in the air."

He snaps one of his hands into a taloned pointer and jabs my chest.

"That's how I know you were lying just then. I think you know something you ain't telling us. So if you're as smart as I think you are, you'll come clean right now. Or it might just get a little bit unpleasant in here."

"I've heard that from a lot of people lately."

"It ain't how many times you hear it in a day, son . . . it's who says it at the *end* of the day. Think about it."

He gets even closer now. His next words burning right in my face.

"Think about it *really hard*."

Shit.

Are these people really on the level?

Is this some other elaborate mind trip?

And does it even matter?

"I saw the bunker," I tell him. "Part of it, anyway. Jenison recorded a message for me. The guy smashed the iPad when it was over . . . but she was standing in the sleep chamber, whatever you call it. I saw it in the video. It was all women in the tubes. And my wife was there with them."

"You saw the cryo-freeze?"

"It wasn't like that. Something more advanced. Fluid breathing systems."

"Why was your wife there?"

"Hartman must have sold her to them. Or maybe she just got too close."

"God knows how many they have down there. All ready to repopulate the earth after they blow it to hell."

A wave of unreality crashes over me. "It's completely insane. Even with all the bombs we have, it couldn't possibly wipe out everyone on the planet."

The colonel grins big, without humor. "We have enough W70 MOD3 warheads on this side of the line to level the planet *several hundred times over.* In a best-case scenario, we're talking about eighty-five percent of the world's population dead by exposure to high-level radiation emission within forty-eight hours of the first bomb burst."

"We're not just aiming our missiles at Russia or the Middle East anymore," Heather chimes in. "There's a big ugly world out there."

"They're maniacs," I whisper. "This whole wiping-the-slate thing they have in mind . . . starting over with the chosen few or whatever . . . it would *never work.*"

"Well, they sure as hell think it can," Morales says. "The idea is that with eighty-five percent dead on arrival, the remaining fifteen percent will starve in the wreckage and destroy themselves within five years. By then, the radiation would be long gone, and you'd have accept-able damage losses in the big cities. Full-out nukes would make that theoretically impossible."

I picture it:

Half-wasted buildings and abandoned superhighways, littered with bodies.

Fields filled with human wreckage, vaporized and rotted.

A sea of bones and concrete.

And then they put their machine to work, claiming what's left. Their network of shelters, all full of soldiers and scientists and young bodies on ice, ready to have babies.

All opened wide, like the gates of Eden.

"They lit the fuse last night," Heather says. "We're not sure how. They were keeping you alive in the hospital because they thought they might need you, but they ordered your death as soon as they activated the system."

"They must've recovered the missing disc from the fire. After I blew it up."

Or maybe Franklin survived with the package.

After all, I never really saw him die with my own eyes—he might have had time to jump while I was rubbing it in his face on the phone.

Maybe I didn't kill him at all.

"Exactly *how it happened* doesn't matter now," the colonel says. "The tactical grid that guides our W79 missiles has been completely rerouted. New coordinates. Our own soil is target zero. Then everyone else. Their people acted fast when the orders came down. It's been a bloodbath."

"A *real* bloodbath," Heather says, pointing at the monitors. "We've had to shoot it out with a few of them."

"Panic in the year zero," I whisper.

"More like a very well-planned military coup," the colonel says. "The president hasn't even had time to organize a press conference, but they're going live soon with an official denial. That won't matter, either. Fifty-three of our silos in the northwestern United States are computer controlled. Our submarines act on encrypted code numbers. They've already received their orders and gone into communications blackout. Which means they won't back off unless they get the official recall sequence."

My next words come nearly paralyzed now:

"They'll see our missiles coming, won't they? The bad guys, I mean. They'll panic and cut loose on us with everything they've got."

Horror, is what this is.

Sheer final horror.

"The new W79s are stealth bombs," the colonel says. "They might see us, they might not. But there's no doubt that the cow patties are about to hit the fan, one way or another. Resurrection has covered all the bases. Their computer is still running the game. We have to stop these psychos and we only have three hours left to do it. It's brushing off every attack our hackers throw at it. The people who designed the application knew exactly what they were doing, and it's gonna kill us all. You have to *help me*."

Yes.

That's why they brought me here.

The question Heather almost got to ask me, before they started shooting.

The colonel almost has a trace of fear in his voice now:

"*You* were the hacker who went deep into the system guarding that vault. You were the only one who made it out alive. Lieutenant Stone says you brought back the coordinates to the main bunker."

"Yes. I memorized them."

"She was able to tell us that the target is somewhere in northeast Wyoming. Says she saw it on a GPS. That's why we've set up shop on this base. But we don't have the exact location. And we don't have time to finish combing the state. It's almost all over."

"Fancy, that."

"No jokes, son. My men have to go in and talk directly to their machine, and the recall numbers will only work for another three hours. It's a last-ditch failsafe window they put in, just in case. When the window closes, the damage is permanent."

Christ.

They have it all there, at ground zero.

They built an invisible fortress, and created some sort of supercomputer to wipe out the whole world, right in the center of it. They had every smart guy they could find building it for them. Hartman had the keys to it—along with a road map guarded by the most treacherous digital security system ever built. It was his golden ticket. And I've been carrying the ticket in my head ever since.

You didn't put the map there because you were crazy, David.

You put it there for insurance.

It would have made you untouchable.

You could have been the man who sold the world.

• • •

"So your plot is to attack the fortress with everything you've got? How do you plan on keeping that quiet?"

The colonel cracks a dismissing grin when I say that.

"We don't. We're not exactly worried about *quiet* right now . . . but if we do somehow manage to make it out of this alive, let's just say we've got people standing by to deal with any media leaks."

"Very serious people," Morales says.

"Even with a press blackout, an attack this big would be on YouTube within hours," I say.

"Don't make me laugh," the colonel says. "You think some yokel with a phone camera out in the middle of nowhere is gonna compromise national security?"

"It's happened before," I say.

"And we dealt with it then, too," Morales says.

Yeah, I bet you did. Just like those cops who kick in the doors of suspected protestors. The secret police who keep a lid on everything. Just like the public, who always buy it anyway.

Doesn't matter now.

What matters now is my wife.

She's down there with them.

Jenison grabbed her and put her there.

That's where she is.

"Send me in with your boys," I tell them. "I can break their computer in half."

"We have our own people for that," Heather says. "Just give us the numbers. There's no time."

"No. It has to be me."

The colonel gets huge eyes, looking right at me. But he keeps his voice steady, scary. "Have you *lost your mind*, son? We're talking about the end of the goddamn world. You helped them make it happen."

"And you slaughtered your way to me so I could bail you out, so you have just as much blood on your hands as I do. I go in with you . . . or no deal."

"This isn't a *deal*. This is goddamn *war*. Give us the location or I'll have my men hold you down and make you give it to us."

Morales passes a concerned look to Heather.

She almost blinks.

"That kind of persuasion doesn't work on me," I say, looking right at her. "You'd know that if you really did your homework. It'll take a long time to break me, and you don't have that time. None of us do."

"I'm not kidding. I'll do what I have to."

"So will I."

"You *ain't* going in with my boys. As far as any of us know, you could still be one of Jenison's."

I look at Heather. "Do you believe that? After everything we went through—*do you really believe that?*"

I almost see a trace of that frightened liar from the dollhouse appear in her steel expression. But it's gone quickly.

"It doesn't matter what I believe," she says.

"She's damn right about that," the colonel huffs out. "Now . . . I'm gonna tell you one more thing about my daughters. They're very precious to me. My family is precious to me. That's why I'm a soldier. I'm here to protect them. And right now you're standing in the way of that. Are you starting to get the picture?"

"Yeah, maybe I am. But can I ask you something?"

"No. This is not a conversation. This is *you* telling *me* what I want to know."

I ignore him. Straighten my spine and lean forward, the cords in my neck snapping back, the muscles in my legs tightening, the sickness in my guts and my heart a dull ache that drives me forward.

I look right in his eyes.

"I just want to know one thing, Colonel . . . do you or your daughters know what it's like to eat garbage on the street?"

"I'm not listening to—"

"Shut up. You have to listen. You have no choice—and you know it. You wouldn't have brought me all the way out here and put me in this room if you did have a choice. I might have died on this slab and we'd all be screwed. *So listen to me.*"

His face freezes.

Gotcha.

We size each other up. I see him like I see a prize opponent in a fistfight. Circle him, using my mind. He knew it would be this way. He *has* done his homework on me.

I see it right on his face.

I let loose with everything I have left.

It all comes down to this.

"You see, Colonel . . . I'm a guy who ate garbage when he was a kid. And people like me go along with the program because we think it's all in the name of something bigger, something better. That's all bullshit, isn't it? Just some lie told to us by a politician. By people like you. Soldiers who get away with wading through bodies. When it comes down to it, all this is *really* about . . . is dead game."

The colonel makes a confused face.

He's listening to me because he has no choice.

"That's what Jenison said we all are. That's why we're doing this, all of us. That's why they want to blow up the world, that's why you want to save it. We're the dogs who are ripped apart and don't even know we're dead. My *wife* is down in that bunker with those psychopaths. And I'm the only one who knows where it is. So I'm going down there with you . . ."

I flex my legs and . . .

. . . I stand up.

For the first time in forever.

For the first time in my life.

". . . or you can sit right there and watch yourself die."

My words hit him in his face like the hardest punch I've ever thrown.

Then he grabs me by the throat.

I face it standing up, but my legs are the first thing to go, vanishing into a bottomless nothing. His boys are all over me at once. I fight them, but my legs are weak, my arms like licorice. The half-healed wound in my side stings like razors between my ribs. They rip away what's left of the blue hospital gown and pin me down on the gurney. The fight goes out of me fast.

I don't flinch at all.

I don't beg.

I don't scream.

• • •

Heather—or Lieutenant Stone, or whatever her name is—she doesn't look happy about any of this. She takes a few steps forward as Morales manhandles me from the back, cutting off the circulation to my upper arms, freezing me there.

I am naked and crucified.

The colonel looms over me, flicking open a nasty serrated jackknife. "A man with nothing to lose is a dangerous man, ain't he?"

"You're real brave," I hack at him.

"You think you could kick my ass in a straight fight? That, I'd love to see."

"I bet you would."

He moves the blade down my chest, not quite touching the skin.

"You're no better than Jenison," I tell him. "You *get off on it*, don't you?"

"This is war. We do what we have to do."

"You said that already."

"I don't think you were listening very well."

The blade, almost to my waist now.

His face, stone hard.

"You can save your speeches and your indignation for someone who hasn't been on the front lines. I've seen my commanders blow away whole *countries*. Shitholes you've never even heard of. I didn't like it, but those were my orders."

He shifts his weight forward, gets right in my face.

The blade held right over my manhood.

"See, that's where you're *wrong* about people like

me," he says. "We're different than politicians. We do believe in something. Discipline. Honor and duty. The survival of the human race."

"Doesn't make you any better than a maniac."

"You may be right . . . but I act on orders because without a chain of command, it all falls to shit, son. We're down there in the jungle with anarchy. Down there with Resurrection Express. And right now my orders are to go in there and kick *their* asses. By any means necessary."

He takes a breath, then begins to lower the knife.

"Now . . . you've got balls. But you ain't gonna have 'em for long. You feel that? That's just the first taste. We'll go all the way if we have to."

I laugh softly.

As I feel the cold steel.

He sounds like Jenison did, back in the hospital. They all sound the same when they make excuses for their side. I feel his breath sour in my face.

"I can see that you're laughing, and that's fine. But I'm making you an offer and you damn well better take it."

I hork up a ball of spit, and I blow it right in his eye.

"Knock yourself out, asshole."

He doesn't smile at all.

"So be it, son."

The blade comes in cruel, and I hear a terrible wet crunch before the pain shocks up my stomach. In the same moment, Heather jumps forward and screams:

"Tell them, Elroy! *Tell them!*"

The pain rumbles in my lower regions like a meteor now, making bile sting up in the back of my throat, my guts on fire, the cold steel like a laser down there.

And then he stabs me again.

Heather shouting:

"Elroy, you have to tell them! They're gonna *kill you*!"

"Fine," I manage to croak out, rising just above the sheets of blinding agony. "Let them kill me . . . and then you'll all die . . . *you can all go to hell . . .*"

She comes closer, stopping the colonel's next thrust with her hands on his shoulder. He doesn't look at her, but she looks right into me.

And I see tears in her eyes.

"You're right, Elroy—about all of it! We're bad people. But we can't punish the world just because we blew it. We have a duty!"

I hear Toni's voice when she says that.

We must live and our children must live after us.

"Save your breath, Lieutenant," the colonel says. "I think the old boy's mind is made up."

She turns on him with fire. "And do you *like* that? Is this our *job*?"

He fumes at her one second, almost says something and stops.

And she spits in his face: "Your daughters would be ashamed of you now, Gerald. Every goddamned one of them."

He pushes her away, lowers the knife on me again.

Heather looks back in my eyes, tears wet on her face now.

She's crying because we're monsters.

And we've failed our children.

Failed everyone.

The colonel rears back for the thrust that will sever my manhood from my body. His face is full of grim years. Secrets he brought back from the lands of the living dead. I see it all in this moment: life as a father, his wife who was once beautiful, then a mother, then a corpse, leaving him with only this—hard steel and iron resolve to protect the lives they made. The voices of his little girls, grown to become women, who taught him every secret about how the human mind works.

I look him in the eyes and I see it all.

As he backs away from me.

The knife clatters on the floor.

"Goddamn," he says.

And that's all.

The knife doesn't have much blood on it.

As I look down to see the blade, I notice that he stabbed me shallow in the thigh. Not a big wound at all, mostly pantomime—a dirty-pool military trick. He was punching me in the balls at the same time to make the big-time agony blast happen. Painful, but still a bluff.

Goddamn, indeed.

"Guess you're one of the good guys after all," I tell him.

"Something like that, son."

His voice is beaten as he hangs his head and shoulders. I see a tired old man standing in front of me now. A father scared to death. A human being who went down in the dark and became bad, just like Heather said.

We came here because we had no choice.

The men look at each other, astonished, the room locked in a timeless, horrifying freeze.

Nobody has any idea what happens next.

Heather reaches over and grabs a clipboard from the desk. On the clipboard is a sheet of clean white paper. She hands it to me, along with a ballpoint pen.

"There's no time left. *Please*, Elroy."

I write down the numbers.

Then hand it over.

She passes the sheet of paper to the tech sitting at the wall-sized monitor. He enters the coordinates and the screen fills with a satellite image—the same satellite image I saw before, only much cleaner. The best money can buy.

The numbers pin the exact location.

"Resurrection Express," I tell him, as the eye in the sky zooms in for a closer view of the mountains.

It's in the middle of nowhere, miles from civilization. They must have bought the land and cleared it good—it's nothing but desert and ghost towns in every direction.

And right in the middle . . .

Target Zero.

The colonel looks up at the screen and makes a fist.

"Congratulations. You just saved the world."

He looks at Morales. "Lock this boy up. I don't want him leaving the base."

Then he looks at me.

"I'm sorry, Mister Coffin. Just try to remember . . . we *are* the good guys."

I don't say a word as they drag me out of there, but I glance back once, and see the tears still fresh on Heather's face.

22

THE DARK

Basement level, more corroded steel and concrete. The dogfaces drag me buck naked down a straight corridor off a clunky old elevator and toss me in a solitary cell, then throw some clothes on the floor, all lashed together in a bundle with a thick webbed belt. It's freezing down here, which seems odd to me for some reason, and one of the grunts tells me to cover myself before I catch cold, with a crooked cartoon grin pasted on his smug face. His voice comes from the Deep South—maybe Louisiana. That's where a lot of marines breed. He says he'll be right outside with his buddy if I get lonely, and I'm reminded of prison again. That place was no different. A hell-hive crawling with big dumb bastards mumbling in countrified streetspeak, surrounded by mold and corrosion and the smell of piss. I slump in the center of the floor, my legs still tingling, arms still made of licorice.

A key tumbles in the lock.

I know exactly what the gears and metal rods look

like as they move from place to place inside that big steel door.

I could open it using a wire coat hanger and some spit.

Or a ballpoint pen.

I get the fatigues on quickly and I'm shocked to find that they fit pretty well. They must have sized me up while I was under. Thirty-two regular always works. I click the belt into place, holding up desert brown pants, just below a black sleeveless shirt that feels like it's never been worn. No shoes, though. Damn.

I'm reminded of my wife again.

She always shopped for my clothes, and they were always black and white and ordinary. You had to blend right in, she always said. Had to be a ghost in the machine and on the street. She once bought me a boring suit that cost over two grand—told me it was like a shield that made me invisible. Nobody ever tried to kick my ass while I was wearing it, but I'm not sure that means anything.

I'll need boots when I make my run.

I'll think of that later.

First things first.

I look at the pen in my hand, and I'm amazed again that they never took it from me when they hauled my ass out of the war room. I palmed it when I handed back the clipboard and everyone was a little distracted by the big screen after that. I knew they would throw me in a dungeon like this. I knew everything about that old fossil the second I saw him. These guys are soldiers, and soldiers all fall back into thick patterns of two-dimensional thinking. Guns and knives and sharp sticks—straight solutions to complicated equations. And they don't look at the details. They never consider that a bobby pin could bring their whole kingdom crashing down around their ears. And it always does, eventually.

I sit for a few minutes in the center of the room.

Calm myself.

Channel the blood into my arms.

Find my center.

See the leads, running end to end.

Yes.

Time to move.

Fast.

I start working on the lock. This will take three minutes. I can see the two guards through a tiny peephole on the door, sealed off on the other side with metal grating. I can smell their cigarette smoke, hear them laughing.

They have no idea who I am.

I try not to think about what comes next, as I slide the long plastic stem of the pen through the tiny opening near the main lock box. I try not to think about how I plan to get past the two grunts and make my way to the airfield—get aboard one of the choppers somehow. I leave it all to Zen, living from one moment to the next, as I feel the metal rod inside the door give just a bit and work it again, slightly to the left, so that it clicks softly, dribbling saliva down the center of the plastic pen casing to grease the way. I think only about how easy this is, how it all comes back on reflex, without even trying. How I've broken hundreds of locks on cell doors, just like this one.

In two more minutes, the lock will go.

In two more minutes, I will think about my run to the surface.

In two more minutes, I will be closer to you, my love.

I will come for you.

I will make it happen.

Click.

The grunt doesn't hear the lock going or sense it when the doorjamb loosens, just at his back. But he hears it when I say something intelligent through the small grated window:

"Hey, asshole."

I see a sliver of him as he turns, and he makes some redneck noise I can't quite make out—something about my mother. These guys are all the same—throw out a cheap shot and they come right at you, fangs first.

I see his fangs through the grate as they tell me to go fuck myself.

Then I shove the door open right in his face.

It happens really slow, stretched out across five seconds. Something screeches like a prehistoric bird— metal hinges scraping and grinding as I crack the good soldier's nose back into his sinus cavity with a thick wet sound. He's stumbling back on the other side of the door as I force it the rest of the way open, and I hear him bounce off the opposite corridor wall and go down in a heap, still blasting off in stanzas of redneck gibberish, all watered down by bloody backwash. As the door flies open, I sense the other grunt just over my shoulder—he spins with his rifle, gets the bad end right in my face, but when his finger hits the trigger nothing happens because the safety is still on. I see him squeeze again and he says the word "shit" out loud and I grab the barrel hard with both hands, using his own muscle burst when he tries to fight me, turning it back on himself—classic forced-fulcrum technique. It shifts the butt of the gun into reverse, stuns him right in his mouth. He gags on his exploding teeth and falls backwards as I land on him, jabbing again with my bare hands. This time I hit him in the throat—a two-handed straight chop that puts his next breath on hold and almost knocks him out. I pick up the gun and use it to score the final home run. His head knocks back with a weird empty coconut noise against the concrete floor and he goes to sleep fast. I wasn't able to put much muscle behind the blow, but I'm doing okay for disco.

On the other side of the open steel door, the good soldier is wallowing in his own blood, trying to call me a motherfucker with his face oozing between his fingers.

I hear his gun clack loudly in the closed space.

He stumbles around the door as I bring his buddy's rifle up, squeezing the trigger, and the shot hacks into the good soldier's upper arm, the recoil almost knocking me down, the big boom almost making me deaf. I wasn't pay-ing attention before, but it turns out this is an AK-47, top of the line. Never fired one of these in my life. Watching my father all those years, I thought it might be easy, but it kicks bad against my weakened muscles. And the bullet bounces off the concrete walls when it's done chewing through the good soldier's arm, zinging like a microscopic meteorite, finally striking home somewhere down the hall . . .

. . . as I re-aim at the good soldier's head.

I tell him to drop his weapon.

I don't hear my own voice when I say that.

It's all on slo-mo with the sound way down.

He can hardly see me through his rearranged face, spitting blood like an animal.

He uses what's left of his destroyed arm to raise the gun.

No choice now—I aim right between his eyes this time.

I will not miss.

I can do it.

My finger squeezes hard, and the shot blows through the hall.

"Stop!"

The voice breaks through the slurred moment, and my eyes squint in the dark of the corridor to find the source. A woman's voice. It's frozen my target where he slumps also, because he can see her face. I can't because she's behind me.

I realize that the good soldier ducked my second bullet.

I would have killed him, but he saved himself.

"Drop your weapon now!"

I put up my hands as I turn to face the voice. The whole corridor behind me is filled with guns, all aimed at my vital organs. Heather stands in front of her men, black and green in a military assault uniform.

"Put it down," she says, and only then do I realize I'm still holding the machine gun in one hand.

I set it down slowly. Out of the corner of my eye, I see the good soldier lose it and come charging at me, but I sidestep him quickly and stick my foot out, sending him to the floor. He crash-lands on his buddy and stays there.

The ten guns in the corridor don't flinch. She came down here with plenty of insurance.

"Back in your cell," she says slowly.

She closes the door behind us and tells her men to watch the corridor.

No escape now.

It's just the two of us, face to face in the dark room.

She has a black satchel in one hand, a big gun in the other. It's too dark to tell what kind of weapon it is— but the rough shape is something that looks mighty goddamn state-of-the-art. Something Alex Bennett would have known about.

"That was stupid," she says. "You could have gotten yourself killed."

"We all gotta go sometime."

"What were you going to do when you got out of here? They would have taken you down before you got to the first floor."

"Your two guys outside didn't agree with you."

"You were going to kill him. That's what this has all come down to? You have to get what you want, no matter who pays the price?"

"You're a fine one to talk. You lied to me from the start."

"I did what I had to. You were getting close to Jenison. You had the discs."

"Why didn't you just tell me who you were?"

"Would you really have handed over what we wanted? Or would you have used it to get your wife back? I *had* to be her, Elroy. I didn't have any choice."

"You were gonna let Hartman chop my fingers off."

"Yes I was. And you *still* would have had the discs."

"And you'd still be a stone-cold monster."

"This is the *end of the world*, Elroy!"

Her rage calms, and the silence settles between us for just a moment.

Silence consumed by the dark.

"I was right down there with you," she finally says: "I volunteered for this operation because I knew the only way to stop those people was to think like them. I understood what was at stake and I *signed up for it*. That's how wars are won in the end, Elroy. With sacrifice. Just like the colonel said."

"So they made you look like Toni, right? They cut your face and told you how to walk the walk—to trick Hartman into giving up Resurrection. And when that didn't work you just thumbed a ride with me."

"They didn't make me look like her. *You* made me look like her."

"What?"

"You don't really think there's any kind of surgery that could make me look just like another woman, do you?"

"You *do* look like her. Not exactly . . . but enough."

"That's still in your mind, Elroy. Everything you see here is one hundred percent me."

"That's . . . *impossible* . . ."

"Hartman knew how screwed up you were. He knew the only thing you had left was the memory of her *scent*. And I knew you might see what he wanted you to see . . . with the right hair . . . and the right *perfume* . . ."

Roses and gunmetal.

The photo from the bar, still fuzzy in my mind.

Was it really just me all along?

Christ . . .

She pauses, then stiffens. "I was actually pretty amazed when you looked right at me and saw her."

"I . . . I wasn't sure what I was seeing."

I was overdosed on faceless memories, my mind overworked, my brain shot to hell.

Holy shit.

"You lied right to my face," I say. "You let me believe it, just like he did."

"I did what I had to. In the beginning I wasn't even sure what side you were on. I'm . . . I'm *sorry*, Elroy."

"That's what you came down here to say? That you're sorry? That's bullshit, too."

"It's not bullshit. I'm . . ."

Her voice trails off, her steel vanishing.

And she's the broken spirit I saved, just for a moment.

"He knew who I was from the start," she says.

"What?"

Her lips tremble, like she's going to break down and cry all of a sudden. But she pushes through it—does what she has to do, says what she has to say.

Is any of it real?

"Hartman knew who I was working for," she says, and her voice is weaker now. "He tortured me for weeks. Maybe it was months, I can't remember. Made me tell him things. Kept me hovering between the real world and *his world*. Said they sent me in for nothing—that he was talking to the colonel all along. How do you think that made me feel?"

"Kind of like I feel right now, lady."

She shivers again, gritting her teeth. "I was *right there with you*. It was my hand on the chopping block first. Before that, it was endless. Drugs and more drugs and pain on top of pain. They said they kept me around just to make them laugh. They held me down in the dark and spit in my face. I watched them torture your father."

"You're lying. That can't be true."

"Believe what you want, it doesn't matter now. But I might have died if you hadn't come along. I was about to give up."

"We all give up."

"I never knew it could happen to *me*. I've had years of training in the field. I've run dozens of operations where it all went by the numbers. I forgot that one slipup can cost you everything. I underestimated Hartman. Thought he was typical street scum. I thought my act had him fooled. Met him in his own nightclub and it went like clockwork. He let me think that for a long time. I thought I was getting close to finding out about Resurrection. Then he had his men tie me down and . . . and . . ."

She winces, then goes away to the darkness, just for a moment.

Hates what she sees there.

Steels herself one more time.

". . . and when they were done . . . he shot me up with dope and told me I had to be Toni. Said it would be my punishment, and yours, too."

"So I would give up my fingers."

"Yes."

Welcome to my nightmare.

A sick game, all twisted up and dumbed down in the most inhuman gutter.

"All I could see were crazy faces, mocking me," she says. "I didn't know *what was real* for a long time. My mind washed away and came back so many times. If I could describe what that felt like to you . . . if I could make you *understand* . . ."

"Look, just save it. I don't need any of that from you."

She hardens again, just enough. "You have plenty of sins to answer for yourself, Elroy Coffin. As soon as you knew I wasn't her, you charged off and left me to die."

"Yeah, I guess I did, huh?"

"So what's your excuse for being a monster?"

My stomach drops when she says that.

I look deep into her—almost see her soul there. Or is it just another disguise? I remember the moment when I kissed her. That one long moment, so pure and so terrible . . . when I knew it wasn't her, finally. There's still traces of Toni in her face, but the mask is off now. Off for good.

I move closer to her.

She is not Toni . . . but I want her to be. I want to touch her again.

Just to make sure.

She sees the conflict steaming from me. She steps forward and puts her hand to my face. Her body jingles with gear and crackles with heavy olive leather. She is a stone killer in a black disguise, the last reincarnation of my one true love.

Or maybe she isn't.

I don't care.

I just want this last moment with her. And I can sense she wants it, too. She moves so close to me now, her breath hot and desperate. She stops herself. Her lips, just shy of mine. Then she bites her bottom lip slowly, softly. Beautiful and shivering, like a movie star unsure of every word she speaks. That's not like anything my wife would have done.

She's not Toni at all.

She backs away from me, tosses the black satchel on the floor, and she whispers:

"Saddle up, soldier. You're coming with me."

THE LAST PERFECT DAY

There's three ways you come at a job like this.

Three modes of attack.

This is the cowboy method.

With every goddamn cowboy they could find thrown in the mix.

I march with the other grunts to the gunship on the roof of the complex, hiding in plain sight, and I flex my legs, over and over despite the lingering pain, moving up and down in a steady rhythm as I watch the base scramble all around below me. Hundreds of men, running for their rides. The Apache helicopters, gassed and ready, powering up, their rotors and blades starting to hack away at the air, coming to life like thunder rolling across concrete. This is the biggest moment I've ever witnessed with my own eyes. The sound of it is surreal and horrifying. Incredible.

The sun holds itself at high noon, bathing the mountains that surround us in clear, stark light. The sky, blue and spotless. Not one cloud up there.

This might be the last perfect day I ever see.

She sees it, too, standing with me.

The woman who wasn't my wife.

Morales stands near us, at the front flanks of the team, nodding at her. Though my UV-glassed helmet hides my face, he knows I'm with them. He knew it all along. Not like the colonel. We're standing at the edge of everything, he and I. Me and Heather. All of us here to see the end of the world.

That's what everybody really wants in the end, deep inside themselves. To be there when the shit goes down. To know that we are the heroes of our own lives, that it all means something in the end, that we are righteous in the face of so many mistakes and sins.

Everyone wants to be resurrected.

A lot of us die very disappointed.

RESURRECTION

01:36:00

Just under an hour and a half on the clock as we cut through the sky, the world falling away from us in a roar. Outside, hovering in the air all around us, a dozen flying machines armed with the best air-assault technology money can buy, tested in the field and ready for serious action. As I remove my helmet, Morales steps over and offers his hand, telling me his name is really Master Sergeant Geronimo Burke, Special Forces, U.S. Army. He takes a seat across from me and Heather, and they run down a checklist with the men, calling off maneuver points and weapons check. I remember some of this procedure from when I was in the army, but we never rode in a chopper. There are seven men in this compartment with us who are the core strike team, two others who are wireheads from the air force. They're all Special Operation Command badasses, the best of the best, just like Heather said. Burke is second in command. He will order the dogfaces into action when we go to ground.

Me, I'm a civilian, but Heather hooked me up with the same computer rig as the air force wireheads, which I'm carrying in the black satchel across my back. A handgun in a holster at my hip, 45-caliber Desert Eagle. Lots of stopping power. I'm wearing the same colors they are, too. The colors of our most recent wars. The colonel has no idea I'm here and he'll be breathing fire when he finds out. Not to mention what I did to his boys back there in the cellblock—marines don't like it when their foot soldiers are bloodied and broken by an unarmed civilian. If we make it back alive from this, they'll probably only kill me once, along with my new best friends. They're all doing loud clanky things with giant weapons—the kind you only get when you're government sponsored. XM8 lightweight assault rifles. My father told me about them. They fire a hundred rounds every three seconds on auto, if you're stupid enough to go full auto in a fire-fight. *A little dab'll do ya,* as they say. These models look sleek and extra dangerous—they're prototypes, modified with grenade launchers and laser sights. Three of the men wear complicated nightvision rigs on their heads, wired to tracking systemetry. Satellite relays. Burke tells me the gunships will run point to get us past the first entry area, which is a big steel slab dug into the side of a mountain six miles away from the airspace we're in now and getting closer. Past the first entry area, a giant platform elevator drops us a mile down, below everything they've got, in the lowest level of the complex. We won't see most of what they've built. Just the technology they put together to keep it running—and wipe out everything else, to make it one of the last cities on earth. We've used our satellites and infrared scanners to look

right to the heart of the matter, now that I've told them
exactly where it is. I shake Burke's hand when he offers
it again and he says there's no hard feelings. I ask him if
he would have tortured me and he says he would have,
without hesitation. But we're all on the same side now,
even if it ain't official. Heather tells me to stay low on
the approach, stay in the rear. My chances will be better that way. She tells me I'm here because she owes me
one—because the whole world owes me one. She says
she doesn't think I'll last long, but if I do, she hopes I
find what I'm looking for. I ask her again how the hell
they plan to spin all this to the media and she says their
people are already working on it. The president has been
advised of everything. His staff is on the case—and everyone else's staff, too. This is a phantom war that will never
be witnessed, not by anybody. I don't know if I believe
they can pull that off. Not with this many choppers, even
this far from civilization. I ask her how many guns we'll
be facing on the inside. She says she has no idea, but
they've prepped for the worst. Right when she says that,
the explosions start happening.

01:25:00

Something takes the sky and shakes it hard, and I
see fire billowing just feet away from the outside of the
chopper. Everybody braces themselves. The straps holding me to my seat bite hard, keeping me there. The men
hold their guns close to them and their faces betray nothing. Stone cold under fire. My stomach dips and glides as
we do some fast moves in the air. I see the giant flying
machines on all sides of us hold steady as streaks of jagged incendiary light blow across their noses, illuminating

their steel skins for just moments in the shimmering sun, creating blinding flashes. I hear slashing, ripping sounds coming at us and just missing. Another explosion, very near us. A rocket blowing up in the sky. Bombs bursting in air. I almost start to hum the national anthem. The pilot's voice crackles over my headset, telling us it's real hairy ahead and to hold on. We dive for the earth, dipping from side to side in a tilt-o-whirl boogie. Heather yells at the pilot to let us know how many guns he sees on infrared and the pilot yells back that it may be twenty. Fifty cals, dug in the mountain. Maybe some heat seekers. The gunships cut ahead of us and open up. The sound of their Hellfire missiles spewing from the cannons is low and thumping—exhilarating, Burke says to me. No other sound in the world like that. The sound of asskicking and name taking. The sound of America, he says. I realize finally that this guy is not Hispanic, but an Indian—the native American kind—and the irony almost kills me.

01:19:00

Outside, the war is on. Our gunships are taking no shit. The air is on fire against the sun of high noon and the endless blue sky. Even though we're in the middle of nowhere, somebody has to be hearing all this. Somebody has to be a witness. It's just too goddamn amazing. The enemy's defenses are weak and we're punching through them fast. They never expected every badass in the world to come at them, pissed off like this. The pilots all report in as they destroy the cannons set into the mountain with Sidewinders. The explosions are like low, dull godfarts down below, away from us but getting closer. The sky is clear for a few seconds before a heat-seeker stings past our window and blows just behind us. One of the choppers takes a hit and goes down, the pilot yelling *mayday*, *mayday*, *mayday*. Another chopper near us explodes and Heather shakes her head. That could have been us, she screams into her headset. She wants that ordnance *sterilized* and do it now, you dumb motherfuckers. They cut loose with the whole goddamn salad bar, dropping everything on the ground below. I can feel it all in the air, as the missiles tear loose and scream for glory, their marks carefully chosen by the most sophisticated targeting systems in the world. The whole earth shakes. Hail Mary blastwaves. Flaming flotsam and jetsam everywhere, on all sides of us. We sail through it, grinding and shaking, holding steady.

01:12:00

Nothing coming at us now. We've lost three gunships—one in the rear, two more at the front ranks. Acceptable losses, they'll call it. We come in low behind the six choppers that remain, toward the mountain opening. A cavern directly ahead of us, hacked out deep in the rock. Men on the ground, about sixty soldiers, all in fortified positions, firing at us with antiquated M16s and mounted 50-caliber machine guns. Old school, but heavy-duty enough to seal the deal. The front flank of our squadron takes heavy damage and they go down in flames before the second flank rips the enemy to shreds. Big bombs, real smart. I hear them suck the air out of the world, just outside, and Lucifer's hammer slams into the earth, kicking up hell and a half. As the explosions rock us hard and flaming demons make their epic grab for all they can eat, we circle up from the mountain behind the rear guard and come back for another strafing approach. The cave is on fire now, and nobody's shooting at us anymore. They make sure. The big hammer comes down again for the kill. Outside, the day goes supernova.

01:06:00

Two of the gunships left hover over the burning mountain as we follow the rear guard and land, just inside the cavern. Three choppers ahead of us. Heather nods to Burke, and he tells his men it's time to saddle up. They all yell the word "sir" and unsnap the harnesses holding them to their chairs. Sharp metal sounds. XM8s, locked and loaded. Heather looks at me and says to stay low again. My pistol is in my hand. The other two wireheads are carrying big guns, like their buddies. I'm reminded of Alex Bennett when I look at them. Men trained for war, and trained to bust computer systems, too. I wonder what my old freckle-faced hacker pal would say if she'd lived to see this moment? Somewhere inside my head, I'm saluting her, in my own way—not like a soldier, but like the civilians she was sworn to obey and protect. Maybe this is for her, this thing I am doing now. Maybe it isn't. Gunfire clatters from outside, as if in response.

00:59:00

I follow Burke and his men as they stream out into the cavern, and the other men do the same. Heather is a streak of black among them, moving fast and ruthless like a jungle animal. There are dead bodies all over the place, men blasted apart and screaming because they're on fire. Some of them aim their weapons and shoot at

us. The massive caliber discharges resound in the huge
cave like fireworks with muscle. Two of our guys go
down. Another one of us explodes on his feet, hit with
the mounted 50-cal. Burke's boys open up and it turns
into a firefight. I throw myself on the ground, keeping
low, just like she said, as the bullets chew up the air.
The flames illuminate the half darkness in crazy, dreamlike bursts, and inside them I see shapes running and
diving for cover, explosions of meat and blood. A mad
dance with death. I see the kid on the mounted 50-cal
whipping the giant weapon around on its swivel, trying
to re-aim from his position in the dark alcove, but they
turn him into dog food fast. His whole body detonates,
pieces of him raining down on the thick business end of
his gun, fried instantly by the superheat. Now our boys
are ripping the hell out of the cavern, firing at anything
that looks like an enemy, cleaning house. They're using
state-of-the-art Shock 223 subsonic tracer ammunition,
deep protocol stuff that cuts through solid rock, so
there's no bullet ricochets. It all bores deep into the
mountain and never comes back.

00:56:00

It's over in less than two minutes. Four of us are
dead. Twelve men left. No wounded. I crouch low with
the other two wireheads and one of them says he's seen
worse. I can tell he's not kidding. Burke orders his A-Team
deeper into the cavern and orders us after them. Heather
leads the second charge, and I'm right behind her with
the air force hackers. Everyone's on nightvision once we
get past the flames. I slip my own goggles on, at the rear
of everything, looking back at the carnage we just waded

through. Somehow, it doesn't seem all that amazing now. I've been in heavier places, just like they have. This is just a slaughter, outlined in dull green light. It's not even Tech Noir nightvision—old school. I think of Alex Bennett again and I laugh.

00:52:00

The cavern opens into an area paneled by thick steel on all sides. Red emergency lights bathe the room. Six young men with Heckler and Koch machine guns surrender to us, standing in the center of a slab twenty feet wide. The entrance to Resurrection. Its protectors give it up without a fight. Burke tells them all to let go of their weapons and drop to their knees. Hecklers hit the steel slab, clanging like metal deadweight. Two of Burke's men move forward and cover them. Heather strides forward with her gun up and yells at the first prisoner to activate the platform, which will lower us down, and the kid says he can't do it—has to be done from inside. She nods to Burke, and he pulls out a shiny silver handgun. Shoots the kid in the head without hesitation. Then Heather asks the next guy in line the same question. Same answer. Boom. She's not fucking around. Burke follows her silent order like an iron man. This is a war, and in a war people get killed. People sacrifice. It's the same on both sides. I turn myself off to it. Concentrate on what we have to do here. It's the only way my soul will survive, if my bones make it out.

00:45:00

Everything is on fast-forward, without detail, without even voices. It's always this way on a job. I get my head in the game as the two wireheads pull their rigs and start working on something. They've plotted ahead and they're sneaky about it. I figure they're using a remote-sensor recognizer to talk to the computer on the other side of the steel platform. But I've seen lifts like this before, and you can always trick them from the out- side. They're stupid machines. I scan the area and see the panel just off to the right of the platform and I tell the two wireheads to help me get it open. They both ignore me, but one of the grunts gives me a hand. The panel is held down with thick steel rivets. Heather tells the next man in the line of prisoners to activate the lift. He spits in Heather's face, calls her a cunt. Boom. Burke has three flavors of brains all over his nice uniform now. The grunt tells me to back away from the panel and cover my face. Uses his big gun to perforate the edges of the plate. We work together and pry it the rest of the way open with our hands.

00:40:00

The last guard standing begs for his life like a child. He screams that he can't activate the lift and why won't we believe him. Heather tells him it doesn't matter. No more prisoners tonight. Burke pulls the trigger. Tells the kid he's sorry after he falls down dead. Tells his men to haul the stiffs off the platform. Heather asks the wire- heads how they're doing. One of them says he's almost got it. I get it first. A single circuit, just inside the power box, wired up in a super-primitive tangle. I tweak it and the platform begins to lower into the mountain, slowly. It'll keep going until it can't go anymore, right to the ground floor. The wireheads look at me funny from their consoles and I shrug at them. We jump down six feet onto the platform, joining the others as it rumbles on its way, and as I land there, Burke pats my shoulder and says the word *outstanding*. Heather just gives me a dim smile. One of the wireheads asks me how the hell I knew about the circuit. I say the name Axl Gange. Nobody else on this lift knows what that name means. Only him and his buddy. He nods at me and I nod back. The ghost of Alex Bennett is smiling again, and I salute her again.

00:35:00

Ten minutes before we're almost to the ground floor. We've lost a lot of precious time. The levels of exposed steel and carved stone inch by us. Burke and his men reload their weapons. He tells them to form a circle on the platform, and tells us wireheads to get in the center of the circle, with Lieutenant Stone. We'll be dropping into an open steel room annexed to a security corridor. Through the corridor is Ops Central. We have no idea what's waiting for us in that room. The platform is covered in blood already. I have a feeling there's going to be a lot more in a minute.

00:34:00

We lower slowly into the room. Nothing waits for us. Nothing at all. It's a small landing, walled on all sides by metal. A big steel door with an entry panel controlled by a keypad and a retina-identification system. Those are easy. You just eyeball your way in. I'm on it before the other guys are. I pull my rig and a few tools and I start working. First the interface—then the guts. We use power screwdrivers to crack open the panel. Takes ten seconds—just like wahooing an ATM back in the day. Burke tells half his men to cover the lift opening, the other half to cover the door. Heather pulls out her hand screen and yells into her headset for a picture, but all I hear crackling back is static. We're down too deep for all that. We have to rely on ourselves and the technology we brought in here. The two wireheads get on both sides of me, and we work together. They say words I've heard a million times. They know who trained me. They know I can break this console faster than they can. We solder the wires and splice their screen to ours and my legs feel strange under me as I stand here and use the laptop to breeze right through a wall of numbers. If I'd never walked again, I still would have been able to do this. I fool the machine fast. I make it look right in my eye and it sees something else. I do that in less than a minute. The door clunks inside and rolls open quickly.

00:31:00

The tunnel beyond the door is filled with armed men. I see them just as they open fire on us, and something slashes me in three places, one of the wireheads blasting apart like a meat-filled puppet. The clatter of heavy ordnance fills the room. My eardrums almost go. I pull the other wirehead with me as I hit the ground. Burke's men charge the line, blowing everything in the tunnel straight to hell. Somewhere in there, I see Heather running with them, raw and sleek and brave, doomed to die like all soldiers are. Our side takes heavy hits, two more men going down, shredded by machine-gun fire. But we have the superior position, hammering the Resurrection fighters back into a tight space. Alarms go off everywhere. Bullets zing all over the place. I don't get shot again, but I can tell I'm bleeding. The wound in my side stitches me with agony, reopening in a sickening hot ooze down my waist as I crawl after Burke's team. I don't see Heather now. I don't see Burke. I feel wet things popping inside me as I get to my feet and stumble, then run, my legs reminding me I was paralyzed less than twenty-four hours ago. The wirehead stumbles after me. The corridor fills with shrieking strobeflashes and heavy explosions. Grenades blow hard. Men become boys in the last seconds of their lives. Part of the ceiling collapses, just missing us. Steel and concrete and mountain rubble. I run into the storm.

00:29:00

Minutes left. Are we too late already? The tunnel ahead of us opens into a room filled with smoke and dim light and the sounds of men fighting. Screaming. Shooting. Exploding. I can't tell who's firing at whom now. I can't even see the room. Just the smoke. We walk over dozens of dead bodies, staying low, dragging our rigs with us. The shooting dies down. I hear Burke scream as loud as he can—long and shrill and wordlessly—and then I hear the sound of his handgun. It's the last shot fired. I move into the room, through the haze.

00:28:00

We walk in with our guns up. Not low anymore—it doesn't matter. Burke stands in the center of a huge chamber carved in rock and steel, flashing with screens. He's been shot in the neck, gushing. Dead soldiers everywhere, good guys and bad guys floating in lakes of blood.

Sparks flying from a few of the walls. A couple of men who look like wireheads slumped over in their chairs. Someone puts a hand on my shoulder and it's Heather. There's blood all over her face. It's the end of the line, she says, and everybody's dead. Everybody but us. They've all killed each other. Burke motions to a center screen, tells us that's the main console. They've smashed the interface. Smoke rises from the destroyed computer panels. Hopeless. His voice is a croak. The wirehead next to me says we can still get in through there, pulling his gear off his back. When he does that, he winces, and I see blood gushing from his stomach. He says he needs my help. Can't do it alone. Gonna bleed to death soon.

00:27:00

Heather gets in front of me and says to use the recall code. Call the submarines back. Stop those maniacs. I can't hear her voice when she says that—the pounding of my own heartbeat mutes her. But I can see her lips moving, and I can tell what she's saying: that we're all doomed. I ask Burke where the rest of our men are—our backup squad from the surface—and he chokes out that he doesn't know. He gags on Heather's name. He falls to one knee, then all the way over, going stiff at my feet. I close my eyes for just one second, call out my wife's name twice. Nothing comes back but an echo off steel and rock. Did she buy it in here? Is she splattered among all these bodies, facedown in her own guts?

00:26:00

Heather grabs me and tells me to forget about her— I'm all she has left, all anybody has left. I spit words at her that sound like to hell with you and to hell with the world. I only want to find my wife, my love, my best girl, whom this was all about from day one—and I force myself not to think about the bombs in the silos, the submarines in the sea. I force myself not to see the task set before me. I force myself to look right through the false image of Toni, wringing me in her grip like a living doll, slapping my face and telling me we're all going to die— every single one of us. We've done this before, she and I, and was any of it funny the first time? I see Alex Bennett, crying somewhere in the dark. Saying she's afraid of what will come if I don't act now. She screams at me the way Heather screams at me. I only want to see my wife.

00:25:00

The room spins on all sides as Heather lets me go and starts yelling at the other wirehead, who cries because he's been shot, holding his guts in with one hand. I realize as the gunsmoke clears that this place is even bigger than I thought it was at first. It opens into a wider chamber, which looks like it could be several miles long. Rows of those large glass tubes filling the chamber, way back there, machines humming in a glimmering half darkness. Nobody else around. Abandoned. Some of the cylinders are empty, some of them still have people in them, floating in green liquid, breathing in forced sleep. I notice some of them are men, but most of them are women. I want to charge into the maze. I want to find my wife. I start for the darkness. Toni, you're in there. I saw you there. To hell with all these people and all this noise. I want to breathe my last breath into your mouth. I want to clock the last second left to humanity in your arms. I am running toward you. Something stops me from doing it, though. A loud blast that echoes off the walls and zings into nowhere. Freezes me to the spot. I turn and Heather says that was a warning shot and that I'm not going anywhere.

00:24:00

Her face is stern and ugly, full of war paint and hard resolve and something desperate—something that will end my life in one second for the good of our children. She says I'm not going after Toni. She says she will shoot me in my legs and drag me to the console if she has to, and I believe her. They can't do it alone, she says. I can't hear her voice. She is like all the others—deadly silhouettes playing grim games in the fast-forwarded slipstream of my final job, and I only read their lips as it blazes over me and through me. I only read their minds and thoughts and hearts because it's all so slurred and crazy, this far down. I tell her to go to hell and I start to run again. She fires another warning shot and I almost fall down. She says that's the last time she's telling me. Get over here now. Forget about her, Elroy. You came down here to find your wife, but there's no one here—they're all gone. The rest are dead, we're all that's left. We have to do this or the whole world dies. I am surrounded on all sides by a chamber that seems to go on forever, standing in an ops room walled with smashed computer terminals, shattered flat-screens. It's half-dark and flickering with dying starlight, flushed with sparks and flames—like the bridge of some alien starship blown halfway to hell. She is like a shape of the grim reaper, outlined here at the bottom of the world and the edge of the universe.

00:23:00

And here at the edge, it all comes clear what I must do, to keep the world alive a few more minutes—so I can really find her. I put up my hands and move toward Heather. She keeps her gun on me, tells me to hurry the fuck up, and I feel the heat of years at my back, the ruins of my life, the flames that will consume humanity. I see Toni somewhere in the dark, way back there and crying because I came all this distance, and I'm stopping now, to save a planet crawling with murderers and maniacs who hated us so much when we were kids. It all swirls and crashes in my heart and in my mind as I force myself to move my hands.

00:22:00

I tell Heather to stay the hell out of my way while I'm working. I move forward and I yell at the half-dead soldier to help me with the interface, and he gurgles a dull *yessir* and I tell him not to call me sir and it all lurches forward again without detail, without sound, without anything but what I have to do. Toni, please forgive me. I feel your presence somewhere even nearer and I cannot look for you, not just yet. But I will find you. I will resurrect you. I push past Heather and get to work.

00:21:00

We pry open what's left of the main screen, start rewiring things, working around massive damage. It takes a few minutes—time we don't have. I pull away a dead body at the workstation and sit in his chair. I realize that the half-dead soldier next to me is the only other man besides Heather who made it this far. I ask him his name. He wipes sweat and blood out of his eyes and says Mitchell Gant, Airman First Class. He's fast with his tools. We get our screens wired in a few more minutes, but the minutes fly by like seconds. My console beeps and flashes all clear. Mitchell doubles over, coughing up blood.

00:17:00

I port the recall numbers into my rig. I look at them and memorize them. My fingers click the keys. It's the only sound in the room. The ghosts of dead women snipe at me as I work. Swirls of familiar scents, accusing voices, a kaleidoscope of desperation and despair, spiraling in a room full of broken Barbie dolls. I force it out of my mind, but those weird images stay just at the edge of everything, like a cruel backdrop, soaked in perfumes. In front of me, my screens pay out walls and canyons of dazzling information, and I see the complexity of the program they designed for the first time. I've only seen pieces of it before. Now I see it full-on running, talking to the world, sending its complicated signals, still holding at fail-safe for the recall order, still holding up its deflector screen, which keeps out all enemies. I'd never be able to fool anything this sophisticated without an edge. But I have that edge—the numbers. I looked into the face of God and I saw where this place was. I lost everything I ever loved to be in this chair. I crush those thoughts and get in there. I enter the numbers. It doesn't like them. Have to go in a different way.

00:15:00

Down to the wire again. Last time, it would only cost my life. This time, it's everybody's life. I find a hairline crack in the armor and slide in slow. Have to be careful. Have to find the right place to enter the numbers. I stack seven different infiltrator programs, military-grade blackware designed just like their gunships—mean and sleek and state-of-the-art. They run their jive, and the jive works. My fingers move quick. I burn through five minutes like they're not even there. It's coming, coming faster now. Come on, baby, *talk to me* . . .

00:10:00

More minutes fly by like seconds. The system is starting to like me. It was cursing at me before, but I'm sweet talking it now and it's coming around. I find the port at last. I look at Mitchell and tell him we're almost in. He's on his back now, staring straight up at the ceiling. Not a word left in him, his guts leaking through stiff fingers. Burke, gone, too. Facedown in his own blood, where he fell. Me and Heather are the last people drawing breath in this room. I want to tell them thanks for this, for keeping me alive, for standing with me . . . I want to see Toni's face again and kiss her one last time . . . but I can't do that now. I see the clock ticking on the screen. Less than ten minutes now. My fingers move so fast you can't see them.

00:07:00

I see the wall right ahead and I break it. Heather shrieks like a schoolgirl when that happens. She starts crying because we're so close now. A screen flashes at me and asks if I want to abort Resurrection Express. I tell it shit yes I do. It asks for the recall code. The numbers I just memorized. This will stop the signals feeding to our silos, and tell the computers the game is off. The submarines standing by for authentication orders will receive encoded messages not to launch. If this machine listens. If the recall code actually works. The numbers go in quick. It's as easy as breathing, even though breathing is hard now, the pain in my side creeping up into my lungs, making my breath boil. It rolls out painfully and drifts away from me, sweat dripping down my face. I'm about to type in the last number. My finger is almost on the button as something hits Heather hard in her stomach, and she flies back in a spray of blood, hitting the floor next to her dead soldiers. I almost wonder what's happening for a split second before the next bullet chunks into my guts and kicks me from the console, shattering a screen . . . and I land on one knee . . .

00:05:00

. . . and the sting of the wound slashes me, gouging deep into my stomach, oozing slowly inside . . . but it's nothing to me . . .

. . . *not compared to* . . .

Her.

She doesn't smell like perfume or roses.

She doesn't smell like *anything*.

Her mysteries and magic and pheromones washed away—like my home, which was so far down in the dark until this very moment.

The hard, beautiful sight of her flooding back on me like a fast tide, overwhelming my senses all at once . . .

00:04:00

Toni.

Your face hovering above me, your *real* face.

The silken trace of your nose, the long black glass of your hair, eyes green and beaming.

I love you so much.

I've searched the whole world over to find you.

I suffered in the dark, I gave up everything—or would have—just to claw my way to this moment.

You are beautiful like no other woman is beautiful.

You are everything.

"Hello, darling," she whispers.

And her voice is as clear as crystal.

My love, forever.

She stands above me, her white gown glowing in the dark.

Beautiful.

And her voice is real.

Not some hallucination, sniping at me from the brink of death. Not a lie oozing through my damaged mind, like the slow blood dripping from the wound in my guts. *Real.* My logical mind swims just outside of this, screaming at me to get up. I struggle with my legs.

She shoots me again.

00:03:00

My right knee explodes as the bullet tears in.

I go down.

"I'm so sorry, Elroy. I can't let you do it."

I realize it was her final bullet that took down Burke. I realize she was waiting, just in the shadows, to see if we could break this machine. I realize that she is going to kill me. I realize . . . *somehow* . . . in a place of utter hopelessness and despair . . . that it makes sense. I ask her if she became Jenison's woman, if she was always Jenison's woman, and she nods her head slowly.

"She's my mother."

00:02:00

And it all comes clear.

The photo in the nightclub.

Jenison telling me about her daughter.

Her daughter.

My wife.

Everything I ever was, I did it for her.

Everything we ever did, we did it together.

And she always belonged to Jenison.

Belonged to Resurrection.

"You were my life project," she says. "My assignment. My love. You don't understand how many of us there are, how deep it all goes. The power people like us represent. When you knew the truth, you came to destroy it."

"I came . . . for *you*."

"I know you did . . . but this . . . all of it, all around us . . . is what we were *destined for*. Since we were children. We were trained to guard the new future. To watch over all these people."

I see the chamber behind her again, as she motions to it, her hand steady and unshaking. The stasis tubes. Thousands of men and women, waiting there, floating in their artificial wombs. Waiting for everything to be destroyed. So that they can make it all better again a million years from now.

My whole life was about building this.

"I was the first to volunteer. The first to go into wet sleep. And I was the first to come back when your attack began. My mother brought hundreds of us up from the tubes. There wasn't time for more. She wanted me to run with her, but I wouldn't go. She abandoned Resurrection, but I stayed. Because I knew you would come. And I knew if you saw my face you would finally understand."

She looks back at the endless chamber.

All filled with dreamers.

"Elroy . . . they must be *protected*. They must *live*, and their children must live after them. Otherwise, we are not immortal creatures. Do you remember when I said that to you, all those years ago?"

Yes.

And I loved her for speaking to me that way.

Loved her for making me into what they wanted me to be.

For running where they wanted me to run.

Where she ran, always.

My whole life.

A project.

And I never even knew it—never knew I was destroying the world, never knew I was looking right into my wife's face when I was looking at Jenison, even in that bottomless moment in the hotel lobby when my mind was almost gone.

"This is *crazy*," I tell her, hardly finding my voice. "Please tell me you're lying. *Please tell me it's not true* . . ."

"I can't tell you that," she says to me, and her voice is cruel and strained, like some distant accusation that never quite reaches my ears. Insane and lost.

Just like me.

"Toni. Please. I love you."

"I know," she says to me, as she raises the gun again, right between my eyes this time. "I love you, too."

00:01:00

The gun shakes in her grip.

Her mouth trembles, like an angel at the gates of Resurrection. Like an ordinary woman, my woman, staring into the eyes of her entire life. A life spent reporting to a mother I never knew. A life spent seducing and deceiving people, like David Hartman. A life filled with secrets.

Not a life at all.

A lie.

A cruel, endless lie.

00:00:30

She smiles at me sadly. And I can see that she is crying at the end of her lie. At the end of everything.

And she says:

"Oh, *my love* . . ."

00:00:20

The gunshot booms. I spin. Something hits me in the head—right where the bullet came years ago—and the sound of metal-on-metal gongs me into a place between worlds, crashing in my skull. I fall on the floor. Almost fall into oblivion. Struggle to see her through the ripples of pain and the burning of steel in my head.

I see her re-aim.

She aims carefully.

But the next bullet doesn't go between my eyes—it doesn't even come from her gun.

00:00:10

I see a beautiful red flower bloom in slow motion across her breast.

She teeters on her feet.

And Heather shoots her again, stumbling up on one knee.

I see the two of them face each other.

Both of them bleeding on their feet.

My one true love, times two.

00:00:05

My wife falls first, the gun still in her hand. Heather screams at me, but her voice is way down low. I have to type in the last number.

I have to do this or the whole world dies.

00:00:04

My fingers hover over the keyboard. A few seconds is an eternity to a guy like me. Heather careens and falls, choking on blood.

The numbers are gone now. They left me. *I can't find them*.

I reach up and touch my head.

The dent in the plate, where her bullet came and went.

00:00:03

All over now. All of it gone. I look back into the dark canyons and I see nothing. My wife gave me everything, and now there's . . .

Nothing . . .

00:00:02

My fingers fall.
I fall with them.
Like I'm in a dream.
The tears streaming down my face.

00:00:01

I lie on the floor, next to you, my love.
This is our last moment.
We are resurrected.
Now.

00:00:00

AFTER THE APOCALYPSE

I'm sitting in the comfy chair, thinking about what almost happened.

Thinking about a lot of things.

How my wife came out of the dark to call my whole life a lie, and how another version of her stood up to save me from it. How we almost went down to Armageddon, the three of us. How I crawled to the surface again.

I try not to look back.

It wasn't easy at first, but it got easier.

It's been a long time now.

I could have died down there, and I was real lucky again. At first, I didn't want to be. I woke up in the VA hospital and the colonel was there. He said I was a son of a bitch and that I should be arrested. Then he shook my hand and said I'd done my country a great service— that they could never truly repay me. He never even mentioned his boys in the cellblock—those guys I beat up trying to escape.

And I looked the colonel in the eye and told him I had no idea what he was talking about.

He told me the recall code had gone out with just a few seconds left on the clock. The men in our submarines never acted. Two of the W79s were damn near cut loose from one of the computerized silos in Kentucky, where a power surge prevented the numbers from getting through. A strike team stopped the missile launch manually, but the warhead still detonated because someone didn't cut the right wire. There's a crater nearly a mile wide in the middle of Lewisburg right where that happened.

A nuclear accident, they called it on TV.

Acceptable losses, the colonel called it to my face.

I thought maybe it was a miracle at first. That I had failed us in that final moment, and that something else had saved us—maybe Heather, before she went down. Then I remembered my fingers falling on the keyboard, just before I joined her, thinking I was dead. I remembered what my sensei once said about *muscle memory*. My fingers figuring out what they had to do, even though my mind was shot.

Not a miracle at all.

Goddamn.

The colonel said I could have anything I wanted as a reward—like I was the winner on a game show or something. And I told him I didn't *want* to be a hero, didn't want anyone to *know* what I had done. All I wanted was to have my wife back again. For real, this time. The way *we were*, before all this insanity. Before we both went crazy, and fell before separate gods. I wanted the lie back. I wanted my love back.

I wanted to know I'd never been a part of any of this.

I said all that to him, and he had no idea what to say to me. No idea how to repay me for what I'd done. So I cried some more. Cried myself to sleep again and hoped I'd never wake up.

But I always wake up.

Always the last man out.

It was supposed to be this way, I guess.

The bullet to my head was like a hit from a cannon. It kept me dizzy for weeks. It also took forever for my lungs to be rid of the fluid I was breathing when they pulled me out. My leg was the worst, though—held together with steel pins and braces for nearly three months. I almost lost it twice. I got real tired of doctors explaining how lucky I was. My brain was still there, most of it anyway. That was the miraculous thing, they said. I almost wish she'd taken it all, or at least the memories.

Funny thing is, I still can't remember the numbers. She took the numbers and left me the memories. The lie of my entire life.

The apocalypse was *mine*, not the world's.

Burke was right about the serious people they had on their damage-control teams. There were major media leaks about the battle—on cable and on the Internet—just like I thought there would be. And just like Burke said, they were pinched up tight within hours. The cover story about the so-called accident in Kentucky was used to spin it all. It became one of the biggest news stories of the last two centuries, in fact.

The kicker: nobody knew what it was really all about. Not even a little bit.

That wasn't the hard part, they said.

The hard part was tracking down the bad guys in the aftermath. They told me that the key figures behind Resurrection were never apprehended. My wife was telling the truth, at least about that. She'd stayed behind with only a skeleton crew when they all ran. Jenison knew her people would lose, standing toe-to-toe with the entire United States military, even if we failed to abort the countdown . . . which also meant she was nothing but a coward in the end.

Someone who ran away from her own new world.

But Toni was also right about it being bigger than I could imagine.

These people had built a machine more immortal than anything they could have buried down in that hole. A machine grinding away just beneath our own reality, recruiting the young, making them work for the common good, even if they had no idea what the common good was. It took them decades to build their garden of Eden, and we were stealing the cash they needed to do it that whole time—me and my father.

My entire life I was asleep.

And I did it all for her.

While the world on the surface of civilian humanity mourned the dead people of Kentucky and righteous indignation broke out in the Senate about newer and more effective safety measures within the Nuclear Regulatory Commission, the colonel's extraction teams found miles of sealed tunnels leading everywhere under the primary Resurrection bunker, a million places to run, all carved out of that mountain over a period of twenty years, by people who knew they would need methods of retreat eventually. They left behind more than two thousand men and women who'd been kidnapped from society, sealed inside miniature subterranean neighborhoods that looked like shopping malls. A few of them were true believers. Most of them weren't. Some had tried to escape and failed, policed by the same young soldiers who died to defend the underground metroplex. I thought that was really funny. Kind of a last laugh on Jenison's new world order—the children she'd hoped would father the next generation, who would all be scared into obedient submission by the image of my own crucifixion, burned forever on video.

None of them bought it. They were all just slaves.

Captured animals on an ark going nowhere.

I still wonder what might have been, had the bombs actually gone off. What that new world would have looked like. And what the next rebellion against Jenison's insanity would have brought.

The more things change . . .

They found the wet sleep level, too, where I was, with the computers. Another fifteen hundred people there, preserved in dreaming liquid stasis. They might have remained there for decades, had they been allowed to. But they never found the guys who ran for the tunnels, not right then. All they found of the enemy were bodies. The official head count from our assault on the bunker was a hundred and seventeen. That's how many men stayed behind to defend the end of the world. All of them teenagers. All of them soldiers. Every one of them dead because they believed in a lie their elders told them. Their elders who all ran.

Except my wife.

I like to think now that she stayed behind when her mother brought her up from wet sleep because she wanted to be with me in those final moments, not because she wanted to see me die. I like to think that it was seeing me that made her do what she did, in the end. Made her not pull the trigger to finish me off in that long moment, before she was blown away by her doppelganger.

She could have shot me dead.

I like to think she loved me, and because of that love, she didn't kill me.

I like to think that.

And then the truth floods in, and those thoughts turn to madness.

And the madness turns to roses.

The smell of her, lingering like a punishing fog, deep in my mind.

The colonel's name turned out to be Gerald Maxwell. A high-up member of the Special Forces brass who served for half a decade as an advisor to the CIA, during their investigation of Resurrection. He led the hunt for the men and women who escaped the bunker that day for almost six months. They still have military teams combing the world, searching for the other fortresses made by Resurrection. A lot of the smaller ones were found and blown back into the stone age—just like Maxwell said. No mercy was shown to the survivors, what few there were. Most of those guys were pawns.

A lot more are still out there.

Private depravos with cash to burn, still waiting for the sky to fall.

A few of the key conspirators were eventually found

and arrested, living under assumed names, some of them in other countries. A few more stayed in the game, moving fast and cutting new deals with the underworld. None of it ended up on YouTube. None of it ever broke the surface of the real world as even a whisper. They did it all behind the scenes, beyond locked doors—and they cut off every loose end that could have led to the truth. I knew that meant they might come for me one day.

But the colonel just shook my hand and said I was a hero. Said I could have my life, once I left the hospital. *Never say a word, kid. We're counting on you.*

Yeah, right.

I knew when I walked free, there would still be eyes on me. It was gonna take every skill set I had to make those eyes blind—to really slip through the cracks and go unnoticed in the wake of so much cloak and dagger. I would work it out. But I'd always be looking over my shoulder, even in my most private moments.

Then again, maybe I would need those guys one day.

I told the colonel that if they ever found Jayne Tenison, I wanted in on it. That I wanted to look her in the eye. Just something I had to do. He understood what I meant. I never heard from him again. I left them and never looked back, never asked for anything. That was the smart thing to do.

It's been a year since the day of Resurrection.

A year is a very long time.

I've been very busy.

"People are strong," said the woman who saved my life. "Stronger than we ever think. We're both living proof."

She said that to me on the day I first saw her again, in the hospital. That was six weeks into my recovery, when I couldn't get out of bed for any reason, my leg trussed up in traction. She walked through the door on crutches and I smiled at her, wondering if I was seeing a ghost. And that was the first thing she said—that people were strong and we were living proof. I don't think I'll ever forget that.

"I thought you died," I said to her, still smiling.

Heather looked so powerful then.

Like something that could only exist in a dream.

"We should have died, both of us," she said, and her voice was steady and wise. "But apparently I never knew how to give up the ghost. That's what the doctor said anyway. I thought it was pretty funny, actually."

"Wanna see something funnier?"

"Why not?"

I reached over to the rollaway table next to the bed and pulled a tiny metal artifact from where it had been sitting for days. Held it up for her to see.

"Know what this is?"

She shrugged. "Looks like a key."

"It's worth almost half a million dollars. I swallowed it a while back. They found the damn thing in my guts when they operated on me to get the bullet out. Said it saved my life. Blocked a major artery."

"I'll be damned."

"I would have bled to death right alongside you, Heather. How did *you* make it?"

"I just held on. It was important to come back from there."

I looked at her face carefully when she said that, and I thought I saw my wife there, for just a moment. I wondered if it really was her, then I crushed the thought.

She saw the thought and she smiled sadly.

"I'm sorry about your wife. I'm sorry I had to . . ."

"Yeah, I know. You did what you had to do."

"And your father . . ."

"He did what he had to do, too."

"You've lost a lot."

"Maybe not. Maybe it was just a way of going back to zero. Whoever gets a second chance at anything? A *real* second chance, I mean."

"Do you think he would have wanted it that way?"

"He only ever wanted us to live happily ever after. I guess that's what this is, in some way. I spent a lot of years waiting for him to be my father while he decomposed in a jail cell. All that time, learning to be what Toni wanted me to be. What *they* wanted me to be. I was never my own man, not really. Always living for some other person's guilt, some other person's ideals."

"Some other person's plan."

"Yeah. It's pretty strange to think about."

"So you try not to?"

"No . . . I think about it a lot. But it doesn't hurt so much now. I'm back to zero, after all. People are strong. Like you said."

"Where will you go when you get out of here?"

"The money first. I'll need it to start over. I could give you some of it. I owe you a couple, after all."

"I don't need money. But I wouldn't mind starting over."

She looked at me with longing eyes when she said that. Asking me. She bit her lower lip softly, shivering at the edge of everything.

Not like my wife at all.

That's what I told myself.

Toni was dead and Heather had killed her.

I guess some part of me should have been really mad about that, but I couldn't make any part of myself regret Toni's death. Somehow I couldn't bring myself to mourn her. And not because it was her or me down there—not because Toni would have killed my ass deader than hell to protect Jenison's new world.

All of those feelings were replaced by something else.

And I wasn't quite sure what it was at the time.

None of it was Heather's fault, not really.

Then again, maybe it was a big lie I told myself back then, just to get through it all. Maybe someday I would hate Heather for what she had done—what she had to do. Was it a miracle that either of us made it back at all? I decided right then that it probably wasn't. And maybe we weren't even lucky. Maybe we should have followed those other parts of ourselves into oblivion. Maybe those parts of us were truly lost forever.

Maybe.

We talked for hours that day, about everything. About new life and new paths. About the things we hoped to avenge in our futures. We made plans and cast them away, laughing. I was speaking to the strongest woman I had ever met. For real this time.

I didn't see her again until the day I left the hospital, a month later.

She was scheduled to be released three weeks after me.

We both stood at the front entrance, she on her crutches, me in my walking shoes, leaning on my cane.

And this is what she said to me: "We all go down in the dark, Elroy. Only a few of us make it back. I'd like to know I wasn't alone."

You aren't alone, Heather.

You'll never be alone.

We kissed each other then, and the kiss was good. Full of things you remember. Like love and the promise of love. The end of old lives and the beginning of new ones. Something that could stay, after all. I realized in that moment that I'd never kissed any other woman besides my wife. And that I didn't even *know* this woman standing in front of me. Or maybe I did. Maybe it didn't matter. Maybe I'd be back for her.

Maybe.

She bit her lower lip softly, like only Heather would do it, the ghost of my wife looming bitterly over our shoulders.

The ghost of my father smiling like the sun.

I turned and left her there, walking away from it with my bum leg cocked and crooked, the stick clicking on the ground, thinking about the future.

And what I would do when I got there.

I'm sitting in the comfy chair, as Jenison enters my living room.

Three days ago, it was the one-year anniversary of my wife's death.

I haven't thought about her in a long time, but today's the day.

As usual, the lady in black hasn't left anything to chance. She has twenty men with her, armed with shotguns. Guess she caught onto me when I was doing my snoop job at Cryton Electronics, the new front company she established six months ago to shield her movements. She's into all kinds of dirty business now, above and below the radar. She's more hands-on than ever. But she doesn't call herself Jayne Jenison anymore, and she's more careful about who she recruits. She started up with it again, late last year. Has a hundred wireheads working for her now. Double-blind thieves and criminals, all networked together, like it always was. A machine that can never really die. The CIA knows all about it. The colonel and his people are still playing chess with them. Ghosts sniping at ghosts. I've been following them all for months—me and my new partner. It's been an interesting year. Very, very interesting.

Jenison's had my house staked out for weeks, but she's just now making her move. She walks over to the chair and I hear her calm voice:

"Hello, Mister Coffin."

She says something else that I don't quite understand. It doesn't come through. Something about her daughter. Something about revenge. I think I know what she means. I smile as she turns the chair around. And sees that I'm not in it.

Instead there's an iPad on the seat.

I speak to her from a mile away:

"Dead game, lady."

I see Jenison's face drain white on my screen, and she almost swears out loud.

I look over at Heather, who is smiling wickedly at me.

And I put my finger on the detonator switch.

ACKNOWLEDGMENTS

The locations, technologies, organizations, and protocols described herein are partially fictitious, altered as needed for dramatic license, because this is a novel. And like many novels, this one faced a long, long road in order to find its way into your hands. The key figures in this are the people to whom I've dedicated the book. What follows now is a short list of shout-outs to a few additional select folks, who either helped in some way with my career or the inspiration/creation/publication of *Resurrection Express*. I would also like to thank you, dear reader, for buying the book and (hopefully) telling a friend. If you were moved in any way by our humble endeavor, I am moved also. Please feel free to stick around for the sequel. You can visit me for all the updates on this and other matters at: stephenromanoshockfestival.com. There's some fun stuff over there.

My thanks to:

Scott Hiles, Tom Piccirilli, Wiley Hudgins, Billy Spence, David J. Schow (still yodeling down the big porcelain megaphone), Andrew Vachss, Joe R. Lansdale, William Kotzwinkle, Chuck Palahniuk, Don Coscarelli, David Hartman (the real one), Stephanie Crawford (a superior creature), Shawn Lewis (a depraved creature),

Patrick Melton and Marcus Dunstan, Leif Jonker, Briana, Jennii and Matt at Rough Ride Creations (who make my website look good), Grindhouse Releasing, Ellen Leach, Richard Pine and the crack squad of bad-asses at Inkwell Management.

Extra special thanks to:

Jennifer Bergstrom and Louise Burke at Gallery Books/Simon & Schuster, who believed in a guy named Elroy.

To my mother:
I love you and I live on.

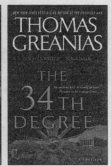

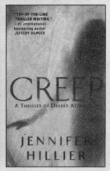